SLICE

the Angels' Cut

Mac Logan

ISBN: 978-1-910166-21-5

Angels Cut is available in eBook and Audio Book formats.

AUTHOR'S NOTE

During the maturation of Scotch whisky about 2% is lost from the cask through evaporation. The UK Revenue and Customs accept the vanished quantity as part of the production process and duty is not claimed. This is known as 'The Angels' Share'.

The Angels'Share series takes the idea, twisting it into a dark criminal conspiracy of self-serving officials, business people, bankers and organized crime. Money 'evaporates' from procurement contracts, drugs and human trafficking.

SERIES

SLICE *(the Angels' Cut)* is the first book in *The Angels' Share* series. The second book, ***DICE*** *(Dark Art)*, is available. The third book in the franchise, ***PRICE*** *(the Devil's Due),* will be released soon.

CRUNCH shares backstories for *The Angels' Share* series. *The First Battle* and *Tripper* introduce some of the characters. It contains extracts from all the thrillers and is free from logan.co.uk.

These edge-of-the-seat thrillers confront crime, corruption and the abuse of power as Sam and Eilidh Duncan, with Tonka, face determined, vicious enemies.

SLICE -The Angels' Cut was originally released as "The Angels' Share". An unabridged audio version (9.5 hours), recorded by a respected British actor, James Warrior, is available.

SLICE

the Angels' Cut

ARMAGH

Spring 1995

1

O'REILLY TRADED tough-guy nods with his driver and stepped into a bright Armagh Saturday morning. He slammed the door shut with a backwards thrust, eyes scanning the street from behind dark glasses.

A message arrived in his pager. The condemned man was enjoying his last meal. Good for him. *Won't meet his maker on an empty stomach.* He smiled.

* * *

The sun gave pleasant warmth in the bustling town and the shade offered refreshing coolness. Choirs of birds sang from fresh green trees. Car tyres rumbled like distant thunder.

The target finished a satisfying Ulster Fry at Flannery's café, exchanged cheery banter with a rosy-cheeked waitress, paid and left.

Unaware of his stalker, he strolled down the road past busy shops.

Bakers, butchers, newsagents, baby-wear, fashions, pubs, coffee shops, the place bustled. People walked, talked and stood, passing the time of day. A child squealed with energetic happiness. A dog barked. The watcher communicated.

* * *

Steeped in 'the Cause' from early childhood, O'Reilly didn't question the rationale for murder. Today would be his fifth street killing. He trailed his man with caution, studying shop windows, reading postcard advertisements, blending in. Cloud shadows dashed up the road.

His quarry crossed the thoroughfare, the photo a good likeness. An enticing scent of coffee and baking bread wafted from a nearby tearoom. Inside convivial people sat round busy tables, the air buzzing with conversation.

In a brown-stone Post Office the target bought a birthday card, watched all the while by the killer.

* * *

Back on the pavement a frisson of uneasiness seeped into the mark's stomach. Battle-hardened experience taught him to trust his intuition. He cast a professional eye over the bustling people. Nothing.

A bird flew into a window. *Bang.* He flinched, gathered pace abruptly, and veered across the road into a public toilet.

* * *

Nearby, the executioner waited, patient and ready. He couldn't kill the soldier in the pisser, not with publicity one of the goals. Tension-fuelled humour rippled in his gut.

* * *

In a lavatory stall, air cut by a sharp scent of bleach, the target pulled out a Browning Hi Power. Next, he jacked a round into the chamber and eased the safety-catch off.

He stepped from the cubicle, ready. Empty space. He made a quizzical face at the mirror, holstered his automatic and headed for the door. The urinals hissed, chasing him away. No evidence, no clues, only inkling. Probably nothing, but he trusted his inner voice.

* * *

Across the way, the assassin appeared to scratch his back, touching the grip of a concealed pistol. He didn't care about the impact of his action on bystanders. Nightmares and trauma lay beyond his concern and taking someone out in public made for an exciting mission.

He visualized the kill: up behind the victim, barrel close to the bump at the base of the skull, the shot, the drop of the body, the coup de grâce … and a swift exit.

Imagining the escape, and excited camaraderie with the driver, gave the killer a fantastic rush. Tension became tense elation as the final trigger-pull neared. Another notch on the gun.

He looked forward to the pub in a few hours. A quiet meeting of recognition with the commander. Glowing eyes and handshakes. The powerful affirmation, adulation and whispered congratulations. Knowing glances and nods.

He dissociated murder from the rest of his life, without doubt a loving family man.

2

THE TARGET reappeared, walking among the shoppers. His wide-shouldered, lean frame, casual dress – jeans, a country shirt, tweed jacket and Chelsea boots – blended in. Easy movement suggested strength and lithe athleticism. Curling dark-brown hair blew about, ruffled by fingers of breeze. The sun brightened the world for a few seconds, only to hide once more behind surging clouds.

* * *

O'Reilly left a shop window and followed walking briskly behind his quarry. Twenty metres, fifteen, ten ... The adrenalin flowed, yet his breathing stayed measured and movements precise. A car door slammed. Bus brakes squealed and hissed. Neither diverted his focus as he closed behind his victim.

He raised his pistol. The sun came out. His toe stubbed on an uneven pavement slab deflecting his aim and affecting his balance. Worse, his silhouette betrayed him as it strode abreast of the mark.

At an instinctive, professional level the prey understood the silhouette's hand movement. The target faced the inevitable. Honed instincts and training meant reaction, no thought required. He wheeled clockwise, flowing into a balanced crouch. His forearms crossed, left hand dragging the jacket away from his body, right drawing the gun. Pure reflex.

The assassin grunted, recovering from the stumble. The brief disruption of his killing move meant nothing, but for his shadow walking beside an alert, responsive victim.

* * *

The target completed his turn, gun raised, and, less than a yard away, fired twice into his attacker's chest. He flinched at a near-simultaneous report from the falling assassin's weapon as the round passed his shoulder, on a downwards trajectory.

The bullet punched into the thigh of a nearby shopper. Her leg jerked away from the strike like a slapped face. Twisting from the impact, she let out a sharp scream and collapsed, like a rag doll, on to her shopping bags. Her chin crunched on the slabbed surface. Blood sprayed from her injury.

The would-be killer crumpled backwards in a slow motion of shock, and flopped on concrete hardness. The back of his head cracked like a pool ball as it hit a paving slab. The woman moaned, a deep guttural sound.

Silence reigned as a collective in-breath froze the world. Screams exploded from a multitude of lungs in wordless howls of terror. People recoiled and rushed from the event in a human starburst of panic, faces distorted by fear.

3

THE HARDENED STREET WARRIOR of moments ago gurgled and mouthed words in splutters of gore. He tried to lift his gun. The target stood on his wrist, disarmed him and tucked the weapon into his left armpit. Nearby, the wounded woman, white with shock, made a final breathless moan and lost consciousness.

Vigilant next to the assassin, the survivor completed a three-sixty observation, high and low. He saw the get-away car drive off: a dark-blue Ford Escort.

He gazed into his prospective killer's eyes and shook his head. The man spoke. His intended victim, crouched and watchful, listened to a liquid voice, wet with blood.

'Did it for the Cause … you Brit bastard … nearly had you.' Thick tones of Belfast. The target continued his surveillance, watchful and cool. In the distance, sirens wailed and came closer.

He turned to the people tending the woman. 'How is she?'

A man kneeling beside her spoke, his pale calm masking distress. 'She needs an ambulance and fast. It's an arterial wound. I've slowed the bleedin'. She's well gone with shock.'

Someone approached. The *Brit bastard's* Browning came up.

* * *

A hard-faced citizen stopped, open hands out from his sides like 'The Angel of the North'. His RUC warrant card in plain sight, identified him as Peter J. Molloy.

'I'll cover you.'

'Thanks.'

'You're a lucky man. I spotted the move. Too far away. Couldn't do a thing. I thought you were dead. You're quick.'

The target took a deep breath, now shaking slightly with reaction. He studied the fading man. 'He wants to talk.'

'Got you.' Molloy pulled out his sidearm and kept watch, his eyes dancing through their own observation routine.

* * *

To the right, a military vehicle drew to an abrupt, controlled halt. Young paratroopers jumped out, weapons ready, movements brisk. They covered the survivor who, with great care, raised his hands to shoulder height, pistol hanging from a finger. O'Reilly's gun remained under his arm. Molloy mirrored his manoeuvre.

One soldier dashed over to tend to the downed civilian, first-aid kit in hand. His mates covered him. With the possibility of a sniper ever-present, the paramedic risked his life. Police cars, security vehicles and ambulance sirens squalled ever closer, echoing like seagulls near a cliff.

A young trooper came over, quick and watchful.

The target said, 'I'm military.' The soldier took his automatic and requested identification. He dragged his ID from a zipped inside pocket with exaggerated slowness. At his feet the wounded man groaned. Sam pointed at O'Reilly's handgun in his armpit. 'This weapon is evidence and needs to be bagged. I touched it when I disarmed him.'

'Thank you, sir.' The solider returned his Browning before taking Molloy's pistol, examining his ID and returning both.

'Good shooting.' He smiled. 'I'll get a bag.'

He returned to his comrades and spoke. They glanced over and nodded acknowledgement, still vigilant, always alert.

Other vehicles arrived. Nearby, two squads of troopers followed a coordinated pattern of intricate moves, devised by military choreographers. They progressed along the street with sharp focus. Weapons pointed, tracked, covered, as the unit performed an active surveillance quickstep.

The soldier returned and collected O'Reilly's weapon. He handled the pistol with a gloved hand, put it in the bag with great care and went back to the vehicle.

* * *

Sam Duncan knelt and watched an ice-cold assassin metamorphose into terrified young man, the aggressive alter-ego now gone for ever. O'Reilly held out a wavering hand to his killer. The victor held the bloody fingers and watched a dying man's face crumple as tears welled.

'My lads. My wee boys … aw *Christ*, I love …' He inhaled a weak, jerking breath. 'I love …' he retched and shuddered. 'Tell 'em an' their mother I loved 'em …'

Duncan nodded his assent to a frothing rasp. 'I'll do that.'

With a faint 'ta,' the hitman's eyes stilled and lost focus. His mouth stayed open - white uneven teeth spattered with bloody stains. Splashes of blood clustered and congealed round his nose and down his cheeks. Blood and urine oozed towards the gutter. The stench of voided bowels seeped into the sunny air.

* * *

Sam watched the young priest rush over, wide-eyed. He fell to his knees by the gurgling man, and launched into the last rites. O'Reilly didn't acknowledge his spiritual helper, shaking and twitching, heels drumming a final jig to a soundless tune as his soul departed.

The pastor bellowed at the killer kneeling beside him. 'You killed him! You shot him!'

Duncan contemplated him, nothing to say. He rose to move away.

The priest jumped up and lunged. 'Look at me!' He grabbed the woollen lapels of Sam's jacket.

With a metallic rustle, attentive assault rifles pointed in the general direction of an enraged cleric. 'You bloody murderer!' The words spat out in a spray of angry spittle.

He broke the cleric's grip with expert, almost gentle, ease. 'Calm down, Father,' Sam said. The pastor still glared at him. 'It's awful,' the clear Scottish brogue almost a whisper. 'I'm sad. His kids'll miss him.' Sam's face twitched with emotion. The priest's demeanour softened.

A police car arrived. A brief conversation between officers and soldiers ended when a trooper pointed at Sam. A gigantic uniformed RUC sergeant came over, both reassuring and fearsome. He said there'd be a forensic analysis of O'Reilly's bagged weapon and he expected it to be untraceable. 'But,' he shrugged, 'you never know. The good news is there's one more of those murderous fuckers off the street. Well done you.'

Sam Duncan half-smiled and nodded, not a time for moralizing. He gazed at the priest: black coat, black suit, black shirt and white dog collar, skinny as a rag doll, and vibrating with nervous energy. His weapon still hung from his hand. He sighed and holstered it.

A closing siren bawled out the arrival of an ambulance for the injured woman.

O'Reilly's body stiffened, ignored for the moment.

* * *

'Did you hear what the sergeant said, Father?'

'Yes. He took a pistol for forensic analysis.'

'Right, Father. The gun that shot the shopper. He missed me and hit her.' The priest assumed a sadder, circumspect posture. 'You'd rather have given me the last rites, wouldn't you?' He managed to swallow intemperate words. 'What would you say to him if it was me lying there?'

The pastor glanced down, unsure. His posture became conciliatory. 'Sorry. My name's Haughey, Brendan Haughey. You?'

'Sam Duncan.'

'Sam, we've both seen a horror today.' He gestured at O'Reilly's corpse, 'I've buried a few of these.' His eyes closed. He sighed and shook his head, 'I've never heard the shots before, nor the screaming of terrified people, nor shriven a man dying from gunfire. Poor woman. Imagine: one moment shopping, the next near death. As God's my judge, I'm shocked.' A pale face regarded Duncan, 'It's the situation, not you. I apologize for what I said.' His soft Southern Irish voice a faint whisper.

* * *

The crime-scene officers asked Sam and Father Haughey to move away and started their routine forensic work: photography, measurement and the erection of a tent to preserve evidence. The body remained for examination and later removal. By the end of the afternoon the street would be pristine.

Molloy, Sam's erstwhile guardian, nodded and moved away.

* * *

'Come on, Father … Brendan. Best get cleaned up.' The cleric gawked at his hands, aware of the congealing and dried blood on them for the first time. He turned ashen, his mouth opened and he bent forward, tendrils of saliva emerged in liquid strands over his lips.

Sam leapt to the side as the padre vomited and, once empty, retched several times with a hollow echo. Sam walked over to two paratroopers standing alert-eyed nearby. 'Are you hanging around for a bit?'

'Yes, sir, covering the Fuzz as they tidy up and talk to the locals.'

Sam inclined his head towards the priest. 'I'm going to buy his holiness a drink and settle him down. He needs to clean up. Please don't leave without giving me a shout.'

'No problem, sir.'

'Thanks.'

4

'ANYTHING LEFT?' Sam said.

'Don't think so.' Fr Haughey swallowed with a slight shudder.

'Come on. Let's nip into the pub.' Sam took the priest's elbow and led him to a bar not twenty paces away. Following the toilet-block aroma they found the gents at the back. A thin slice of cracked medicated soap foamed up as the priest scrubbed his hands. He finished by rinsing his face in icy water. There were rough paper towels to dry with.

Clean-up completed they returned to the bar walking past old wood and etched glass, bright displays of shelved glasses and gantried bottles. A single shiny brass tap offered a dribble of cold water.

'Whiskey, Father?'

'Most welcome.'

'Two large Blackbush, please.'

'You do the shootin'?' the landlord said, a ruddy-faced man with a white shirt, grey pullover and dark trousers straining to contain a significant belly. A foxtail of greying red hair balanced in a precarious crescent on his bald head.

'Aye.'

'Nice one. Another terrorist animal gone. A good day's work.' His tone offered respect to Sam. He turned and glared at the priest, and continued with a snarl. 'You don't belong here.'

'He does today.' Sam spoke at first in quiet anger and, emotions catching up with him, erupted with rage. 'Get the whiskies up *NOW. NOW!* Or I'm going to come round there *AND SERVE MY BLOODY SELF!*'

'I don't have to serve anyone I don't want to.' The objection ended as Sam grabbed the barman's sweater dragged him halfway over the bar, feet off the floor. A lemonade bottle wobbled and fell, to smash foaming on the stone flags, jagged shards protruding like sharks teeth. Sam's and the landlord's faces grimaced less than six inches apart.

'Hold on there, easy, EASY.' The bartender held up shaking hands in placation, 'I didn't say I *wouldn't* serve him.' His face reddened to match his hair, now dislodged and slipping forwards into a parody of a smile a couple of inches above his eyebrows.

The door burst open. A para stepped in while another faced outwards scanning the street. 'Trouble, sir?'

'Trouble, barman?' Sam released the publican.

'No trouble.' He pulled his clothes straight. 'Two large coming up.' He managed a twitching rictus of a grin and lifted two glasses with trembling hands. 'These'll be on the house, gentlemen.' He spoke to the wall with a nervous tremor as he poured the whiskey. 'On the house.'

'Thanks.' Sam turned to the soldiers. 'No trouble.' The paratrooper gave the barman a hard stare and left.

Sam took the drinks to the table. 'Let's drink these quickly. There may be some nutters about,' he nodded towards the bar and rolled his eyes, 'if our friend here is anything to go by. Cheers.' He drank about half the glass. 'What are you doing in the area?'

'I have friends nearby. A Protestant minister, would you believe. I was up the street and heard the shots.'

Sam replayed the shooting in his mind. 'I promised to tell his kids and wife he loved them, Father. Will you help me?'

'Yes, of course.'

'You asked me a question: how do I feel? Whatever it is, I don't feel guilt. He came for me and lost. Far as I'm concerned, it's good to be alive. Idiots like mine-host bother me.' He bobbed his head sideways towards the bar. 'It's people like him, and their stupid, blind prejudices, who're responsible for a lot of this horror. I've seen much more of it than I care to remember.'

Five minutes later, they left the pub, exchanged contact information, shook hands and moved on.

5

BEN CHARLTON, the CO, glared. 'What nonsense is this, Sam?'

'Promise to a dead man, sir.'

'Preposterous.'

'It'll close it for me, sir.' His head shook gently. He sighed. They made strong eye contact.

'I can't approve it.' The silence deepened. A big sigh. 'I see no ships.'

'Thank y—'

'For what? Major, this conversation never happened.' Sam nodded and walked out.

* * *

'Mrs O'Reilly?' They stood on the doorstep.

‘Father Haughey.’ The woman’s voice quiet and withdrawn, yet rich in the tones and inflections of Belfast. She looked beyond him, reddened eyes gazing at her husband’s killer. She swallowed. ‘You’d best come in.’

‘Thank you,’ Sam said.

They passed a small statue of the Madonna, heart glowing with hands open to embrace humanity. The first door on the left was the lounge. An older woman sat, stiff, in an upright beige armchair. Opposite her, three young boys squirmed, restless, squeezed into a two-seater settee.

‘Can I offer you some tea?’ The priest shook his head.

‘No thank you, Mrs O’Reilly.’ Sam stood with respect as she sat on an upright chair beside her sons. The boys gazed at the floor. ‘I’ll stand if you don’t mind. Forgive me for this intrusion into your grief.’

‘You promised him.’ Her eyes flitted between him and the Father. The mother’s face set in stone.

A swift nod of the head. ‘I did.’

‘He spoke to you?’

‘Yes.’ Sam nodded again. He saw the blood, heard the racking coughs of the dying man and, nearby, the stark shock of a woman sprawled on her shopping. ‘His last thoughts were for you and the boys.’

The widow started to sob, joined by the two youngest sons who rushed to her and hugged hard. The eldest boy glared at him. Her own mother stared, both angry and bemused. The silence settled like a blanket of icy dew on a misty morning.

‘I think, Major, you might want to keep your promise, and we can be on our way.’ Three of the five people studied him.

‘Right, Father.’ He caught their eyes, each in turn. ‘He wanted me to tell you he loved you and how much he’d miss you.’

While Mrs O’Reilly groaned and sobbed her eldest boy spoke out. ‘Why did you kill him, why?’

'Self-defence.'

'You murdered him. Just another Fenian to you.'

'Padraig!' his mother hissed. Sam stood for a moment.

'Uncle Charlie told me.' The nine-year-old's voice quivered as he gave Sam an icy stare. 'You'll pay.'

'I'm sorry your dad is dead. I didn't even know he was there until he tried to kill me.'

'He did it for the Cause.'

'The Cause?' Sam's eyes connected with a bright stare and generations of propaganda. 'I won't argue with you, Padraig.' He halted for a moment and stroked his upper lip. 'He came to kill me. I should be dead.'

'You murdered him.'

'No, I defended myself.' The priest made to speak. Sam raised a hand. 'There's only one difference today: it's you and your family weeping, instead of mine. But I am sad.'

The boy broke eye contact, sobbed and went to his mother wiping his eyes on his sleeve.

'We're done here.' Father Haughey nodded towards the exit.

'I'm truly sorry. Mrs O'Reilly.' A bob to the widow. 'Ma'am.' A bob to her mother. He followed the priest. On the way to the door Sam released a long, slow sigh.

The door opened and they faced three men in black balaclavas, two of whom held weapons.

6

'DIDN'T THINK ye'd come down here and walk away, now, did ye?' Cocky bastard.

The priest stayed in front of Sam. 'He did the honourable thing, lads.'

'You won't be harmed, Father. Please stand aside.'

'I won't. You can't murder him in front of the family.'

'We'll take him away.'

'And you'll murder him. He'll be as dead as Orin O'Reilly.'

'This is war, not murder, Father. Now stand aside.'

'No. I can't. I promised him safe passage.'

'More fool you, if you don't mind me sayin', Father.'

The speaker gestured to one of his men. 'Take the Father away.'

* * *

Sam raised his hands. 'I'm covered, boys.'

'No, you *were* covered, sunshine. They're gone. Other pressing work, you understand.'

'No. Pay attention. I'm covered. And we don't want more blood on the streets, do we?' One of the men in a balaclava chopped the man below the ear with his pistol. He dropped like a sack of potatoes. 'He'll live. Now the question is, do you want to?'

'How?'

'No idea. Drop your weapon,' Sam said. The IRA warrior tensed. 'Drop the gun, or else—' Sam shrugged. The man started to raise his pistol. The fighter, who had clobbered his mate, moved with fluid speed. He gripped the gunman's wrist, levering and twisting with economy, power and precision. The popping of tendons and bone echoed, audible on the street. The would-be killer shrieked and continued moaning with a cable tie tight above his elbows. Next, they secured the unconscious man.

'Will you arrest them?' The priest said.

'No. There's been enough trouble already.'

‘I’ll attend to them,’ the priest said.

‘You do that. I’ve got to go.’ Sam turned and gazed straight into Padraig O’Reilly’s scowling young face. Angry eyes, hard as stone, held his for a moment. He walked away. His colleague in the balaclava went with him. A grey Ford Sierra pulled up. Sam entered the front, and his minder, the rear. They left at a gentle pace and rounded the corner.

* * *

After half a mile, the balaclava came off.

Sam half-turned. ‘Nice one, Tonka.’

‘Told you I’d have you covered.’ The West Midland accent as always: calm, quiet and unhurried. No smile, all business.

‘And me thinking it’d be more of a wham-bam.’

‘If your poncey English pal here had listened to me there’d have been a couple less of these fuckin’ bastards in the wild.’ Fuss Cathel shared a broad Glasgow reaction.

‘Thanks for driving, Fuss,’ Sam said. Fuss grunted and glowered his attention at the road.

Tonka tapped his shoulder. ‘Someone pulled the cover team.’

‘Who?’

‘Dunno. Usual incompetence. Some idiot brass hat somewhere.’

‘You including me?’ Sam chuckled.

‘The fuckin’ cap fits.’ Fuss couldn’t keep the smile out of his voice. ‘You fuckin’ Ruperts are a’ the same. Goin’ to visit a grievin’ terrorist family … What’re you like?’

‘Safe with Tonks here and you at the wheel, sweet-cheeks.’

‘Fuck off!’

7

'I THOUGHT we'd seen the last of each other, Mr Molloy,' Sam said, their meeting room well inside the barracks.

'Some routine questions to assist with our enquiries into the O'Reilly killing.' Peter Molloy shared a weary face.

'I think you saw more of it than me,' Sam said.

'Pete.'

Sam smiled, 'Pete.' Molloy stayed serious.

'You know Sean James and Brendan Docherty?'

'Of course. I've been working with them.'

'On corruption and bank robberies.'

'You're well informed, Pete.'

'This is our wash-up. You're out of here, I need information.' Pete's eyes probed. 'Is there any reason you can think of why O'Reilly would be tasked to kill you?'

'We're getting warm with our investigation. Some patterns and timeline stuff, you know.' Sam said. 'Sean and Bren can update you.'

'Of course they can, but what do you think?'

'I would say we'll know much more in the next couple of weeks. I'm sad I won't be here.'

'We have to stay,' Molloy said.

'Given a choice, I'd stay and bottom the investigation. Those two are great investigators. They've taught me lots. We had an encouraging debrief this morning. There's no foreknowledge of O'Reilly, although he seems to have been something of a killer.'

'Yes, always suspected, never indicted.'

'You sound cynical, Pete.'

Molloy shared a lopsided smile. ‘Corruption and criminality lubricate forgetfulness.’

‘Sorry I can’t help more.’ Sam’s soft Scottish brogue fitted well with his next words. ‘Fancy a dram?’

Molloy sighed and stretched. ‘Why not.’

Sam pulled a bottle of Talisker out of his pack. Picking up two plastic cups from a tray and poured two fingers from the Isle of Skye’s finest into each. ‘Wrap your laughing gear round that.’ Molloy smiled and saluted with his flimsy container.

They sipped for a moment in silence. ‘I’ve an uncomfortable feeling about this, Sam. You should be dead.’

‘Glad I’m alive.’

‘I don’t mean that. What if O’Reilly dropped a ball and it’s still bouncing?’ He held Sam’s eyes. ‘What happens next?’

‘I’m out of here in a little over an hour, reassigned for my own safety.’

‘Safety?’

‘You know … place where they only want to kill me, but without the extreme personal prejudice.’

‘You know where?’

‘A week off and then they’ll tell me.’ Two weeks later Sam Duncan arrived in Bosnia.

SLICE

the Angels' Cut

1

'I FEEL LIKE a spy, Eilidh, it's so exciting.'

'And your information is ever so important.' Eilidh's eyes searched Sophie's across the table.

A lens peered into the café, three blocks from Oxford Circus tube station. Across the road a car streamed high-resolution video.

'I've got some good news and I've got some fantastic news.'

'Good news?' Eilidh said.

'Managed to finish the worked-through examples of our audit process.'

'Thanks so much … and, the fantastic news?'

'Guess who's been promoted?'

'Am I speaking to her?' Eilidh said.

'You are, tug your forelock. I'm leaping two grades at a single bound.'

'Nice one. Same place?'

'No, the Foreign Office, all this excitement, and now postings to strange and exotic lands.'

'What fun.'

'Yes. Sad thing is, our meetings will end. I won't be here anymore. Different job and all that.'

'I'll miss you,' Eilidh nodded, 'onwards and upwards. What can I say? All the best, you deserve it.'

'We're not done quite yet, Eilidh, have a look at this.' Sophie tugged a large manilla envelope from her bag. 'I'll walk you through it.' Eilidh moved round and sat beside her. 'We'll start with the summary, and then I'll cover the detail.'

The information flow began. Sophie gave a precise, up to date analysis of fraud across a range of complex government contracts.

* * *

The watcher made a call. 'On them.'

'And?'

'Documents under discussion.'

'And?'

'Can't get audio, sitch happened too fast.'

'And?'

'Do you want me to take any action?'

'Meaning?'

'Murder, robbery, assault.' *Bloody idiot.* 'What do you think?'

'I need to refer. Leave her for now. Follow her. See if she off-loads the stuff and where.'

'And?'

'Shut up and follow instructions. Watch. Don't be seen. No physical stuff. *Capisce*?' The connection ended. *Bastard.*

* * *

Eilidh's informants held jigsaw pieces for a massive, complex puzzle. Nearly 30 people provided evidence, names, times and dates. They connected threads, highlighted cosy supplier relationships and spanned several major ministries and departments. Brave individuals. 'You've been such a help,' Eilidh said.

Sophie smiled, 'this last chunk of information, means you're up to speed on all my current cases.' She passed over five or six sheets of A4 paper. 'These cross-reference everything. They link to a complete background and structure for each of the contracts. There's a full electronic copy in the pen drive.'

'Excellent work, Sophie.'

'After the interview for the Foreign Office—in all honesty, I didn't think I did so terribly well—I attended a meeting with two of our senior managers. They told me, in confidence, that some top people took notice of my work. They say it's more helpful than I'll ever know.'

'Fantastic, I couldn't be more pleased for you.' Eilidh said.

'They say they're looking for people like me in senior positions.'

'And now, a promoted post.'

'My training starts a week on Monday, and I'll be abroad within the next few weeks.' Sophie said. 'They want me in the new Outreach team in AFTA. Means lots of great food I suppose.'

'Exotic.'

'The EU is actively in there already.'

'You're going to be ever so busy.' Eilidh said.

'My new boss says we're AFTA a horse that's bolting.' Sophie laughed.

'Talk about cheesy.'

'Yes, but it's promotion and a chance to use my skills.' Sophie said.

'Exciting isn't it? … So, why are you completing this task for me? Why not just say goodbye, everything's fine, problem solved?'

Sophie's eyes brightened. 'Duty? The crookedness runs deep, and this is my contribution. If they're trustworthy, I've nothing to fear. If they aren't …' she shrugged and sucked her lower lip.

Eilidh raised an eyebrow. 'Something else?'

Sophie struggled to find words. 'If anything happens to me, make a noise.'

'You don't trust them …'

'Don't know. No action yet, nothing's being done. It's a huge amount of money. Got to go.' Sophie sprang to her feet. They hugged.

'Did you hear that?' Eilidh whispered in her ear.

'What?'

'Sophie's thunder rumbling in the distance.'

'Ha …' Sophie grabbed her pack and left. She turned with a smile, waved, crossed the road and hailed a taxi.

Eilidh put the dossier in her bag and paid at the counter. She followed Sophie's route across the road, and, turning right, headed for the Tube. The camera transmitted it all.

2

THEY WERE EXCELLENT surveillance photos, clear, crisp images. A striking young woman crossing a road. Bouncy stride. Cowboy boots, jeans, loose-fitting sweater, good figure, with wind-blown strands of blond hair caressing high cheekbones. A close-up in a café, even features and a straight nose, sea-blue eyes locked in conversation, generous mouth half open in speech, her coffee cup held in two hands below a dimpled chin. A beauty.

'We want her scared, very scared.'

'Damaged? Marked?'

'Do as we've discussed! Take her out of circulation and frighten her off.'

'Always good to do business with you.' A hard, battered face twisted into the distant relative of a smile.

An envelope containing the photos and a small dossier changed hands.

3

IN THE PORT of Hull, a forty-ton truck from Rotterdam came out of the ship, a snake's head from under a stone. Brakes hissing, it inched out behind other vehicles. Ramps clanged. Customs officers in yellow vests swarmed around.

The control room reeked of stale coffee and sandwich fillings. A bank of video screens displayed the action on the ground. Electronic systems read each vehicle's registration and monitored the journey through Customs. The boss, a UKBA Entry Clearance Manager, rose and put on his bright waistcoat. 'I'll take Lane One for a while.' The hydraulic arm clicked and the door wheezed shut. A minute later he appeared on the monitors.

People started talking as kids do when a teacher steps out of class. 'Says he's keeping his hand in, never used to be this interested.'

The first truck was not selected for a thorough check and took less than half an hour to pass through, with paperwork completed and the driver told to have a nice day. In barely an hour he would be cruising on the M62, listening to his favourite music, unaware of the 200 kilos of pure heroin on board, street value £10 million. The next vehicle in line received a thorough inspection.

Before returning to Control the boss shredded and flushed away a note with the registration number and ID. He preened in the mirror, making happy eye contact with himself, already enjoying the holiday he'd earned.

Later, in London, a satisfied administrator recorded the transaction on a bland-looking spreadsheet. The next day, a bank in the Middle East credited an anonymous corporate account with half a million pounds sterling. The third payment in a month from this route, now one of four, delighted all the partners, especially as the drugs revenue was still less than the other exceptional and expanding income streams. A business to kill for.

4

AT SANDSIDE, Scarborough, Eilidh Duncan gazed out of a tearoom, engrossed in the view over the harbour to a turbulent grey-green North Sea. Her contact, an HMRC Senior Preventive Officer from Hull, was ten minutes late for their meeting … as usual.

Whipped by a gusty wind, halyards clink-clanked against the masts in the marina. The rage of seagulls echoed from the shop fronts. Cloud shadows raced cars along the road. Eilidh watched her contact, a brisk walker, slalom between the bike stands, pavement tables and in through the doorway.

A tiny brass bell jingling at the top of the door confirmed his arrival. Pausing at the counter, surrounded by cakes and the sweet scent of baking, he spotted her, nodded and headed over. His movements were a little quicker than usual, edgy.

She shook hands with him, smiling. 'Hi, John, tea?'

'I could kill for something stronger.'

'Coffee?'

'Not funny, Eilidh, I'm shitting bricks here. My family could be in danger.'

She poured a steaming cup and placed it beside a white milk jug and a steel bowl stuffed with sugar packets and sweeteners. He sat down, sighed and snuggled his bottom into the seat cushion.

'I don't know who I can trust. It's *bloody* stressful. You can sit there and nod and be sympathetic —'

'—I am,' she said.

'Fine, excellent even, but it doesn't ease the *bloody* pressure.'

'You followed through on that suspect consignment?' Eilidh said.

'Yeah, I spoke to a senior contact in the Drugs Squad and they're already talking witness protection. It's scary, fuckin' scary.'

'Made the papers too.'

'Yes. 200 kilos of coke were recovered. The police want another stop in a couple of months.'

'Why's that?' Eilidh said.

'Confidence. One bust is convincing. Another's lightning striking twice in the same place. Still, it loosens up the budget. They're building a case and want evidence. The vehicles I finger are under surveillance. For now, they're being tracked for patterns and destinations in the distribution network. They tie back to a senior officer.'

'Progress?'

He shook his head. 'Maybe, but don't forget the downside. The police are telling me to be cautious and keep a low profile. The amount of money involved makes life, my kids' lives, cheap.'

'It must be incredibly wearing,' Eilidh said. He sighed and nodded. They both looked out the window for a moment. 'So much money to be made. High risk for you, high rewards for the bad guys.'

'Right. Volume and reliability are important. You get more for more. If they're doing regular business, landed and past Customs, that load was worth megabucks to the shipper.'

'Big money.'

'Huge.' He leaned forward on his elbows. She looked into troubled eyes. 'This must be our final meeting for now. I'll keep uploading data to the Internet. I may have to stop altogether.'

'Of course, I understand.' A gentle squeeze on his arm soothed him. 'You've been such a help.'

He nodded his thanks. 'One thing, Eilidh, my police contact wants other potential links. He's aware we've been talking but not who you are. He asked me to say the police will cooperate at an appropriate time. Can you name another port where this may be happening?'

'You understand I won't reveal sources.'

'Yes, of course. Keeps me safe.'

She broke eye contact and, head down, considered for a moment. 'Immingham.' She looked up and shared a thoughtful smile. 'I'd best get back to London.'

They shook hands.

'Take care.' Eilidh said and wondered how communicative he'd continue to be.

'You too.'

He didn't have to justify his fear. Considering the stakes, terror might have been more realistic.

5

THE OFFICE BLOCK had a void in the centre, like a doughnut. Eilidh hated the dilapidated meeting room where she and her editor Jamie Carron worked at a battered cup-ringed table. The second hand clunked round a still smoke-stained clock face on a faded wall. Stale air offered little in the way of refreshment or stimulation, yet they were buzzing.

'Good stuff, Eilidh. It works, loads of detail, credible sources and strong evidence.'

She blushed, wanted to shriek 'YES!' and cavort around the room, but somehow managed to appear cool.

'Thanks,' she said.

Dressed always in black, Jamie only varied his tie colour, today bright orange. Greying gelled hair stood to attention above a long pale face. His sharp brown eyes took hold of Eilidh's. He gestured at the flip-chart sheets, smothered in writing and arrows.

'We're going to rattle some top-level cages.'

'That bother you?' Eilidh said.

'Mmm, cautious about twisting expensive knickers. We can expect injunctions, smears and threats.'

'Publish and be damned!'

'Prudent would be a better word. Publish and be prudent. The tale's a no-brainer for the front page.' He wiggled his eyebrows like Groucho Marx and smiled. A burst of laughter, then serious again. 'Let's take care. You've done a professional job. The challenge from here is keeping things low-profile until the presses roll.'

'I can't wait,' Eilidh said.

'Over the next couple of weeks, the internal team will top and tail the story. Legal will go through it.'

'Do you expect problems?'

'Nope. The facts stack up. We'll need to create a drip feed strategy for release,' Jamie said. 'More of an editorial thing. Leave it to me.'

Jamie's confidence wrapped her in a warm blanket of regard. Their merciless, objective review had taken all morning. Then, as devil's advocates, they revisited their work and again tore away at its structure and credibility. The facts and interpretation were solid.

They went on to discuss the pressures on Eilidh's sources. One of the Customs informants had decided to lie low for a while. Civil servants were putting jigsaws together in six major ministries and the evidence of procurement abuses was scandalous. People became scared as they realized the extent of the corruption. One person withdrew, citing promotion as an excuse.

'This is a criminal conspiracy on the grand scale,' Eilidh said.

'And they expect to get away with it. Your research gets behind the fog, fudge and spin, to name a law firm.' They both smiled. 'The establishment lot won't risk a cover-up with the expenses scandal so recent and the financial meltdown still with us.'

* * *

They paused for a moment and gazed through dirt-streaked glass into the central courtyard, a grubby area where people sucked furtive smokes and left fast food wrappers in overflowing bins. The view was ugly, reminiscent of the indistinct and shabby world the investigation was uncovering.

'Is the information secure?' Jamie said.

'Everything's backed-up on disk and the Internet. There are hard copies under lock and key. You have the only detailed summary.

'Excellent. The summary is more than enough for my purposes.'

'We're there?'

'Yup. I'll run it past the numpties.'

'I hope they like it,' Eilidh said.

'Editors love good stories. I'll be in touch in the next few days.'

The meeting ended.

Drained by the task they shook hands and separated at the door. The feeling of accomplishment lightened their step as they walked off in different directions.

* * *

From a window, Jamie watched Eilidh walk across the street and into the Tube. The thoughtful frown on his face might have concerned her. He bit his lower lip and turned away with a shrug. This story was going to change their lives, one way or another.

'SOMETHIN'S FUCKIN' wrong.' Fuss's voice grated from the radio.

'What's up?' Adrenalin poured into Sam's system and his stomach churned.

'The look of that …'

A culvert bomb blew the back off the Land Rover. In an instant, Sam rode in an explosion-propelled roller-coaster. G-forces pushed and pulled. Face pressed against the windscreen he watched the world rotate a few times, then grass and foliage hurtled towards him.

The roof shuddered as the disintegrating vehicle shot across a field upside down. Sam lay crumpled like a twisted foetus watching the show through bullet-proof glass, caught in the destructive grip of the explosion, an onlooker inside the event.

With a groaning crunch, the vehicle stopped. Stark silence settled as tinkles and bangs subsided. In the background rifle shots cracked.

A bawling sound started. Sam tried to sit up. He couldn't. At first, he thought it was a siren … That's quick … but it wasn't. The top half of Tam the driver lay on Sam, his lower body blown away. Tam howled, an awful strident bellow reaching its crescendo in a glass-sharp shriek.

* * *

Tam's noise died with him. Looking down past Tam's bulging eyes, Sam realized that the blood and entrails oozing over his legs weren't his own. He gasped in horror as the squaddie's face slid up against his, nose pressing against his mouth. He struggled. At least his brain sent some messages, but little happened. He started to shout, pushing weakly at the horror on top of him. A hand gripped him. Tam? He jumped and gasped. Not Tam!

'*Sam. Sam.*' A gentle, feminine voice and a tender stroking touch. A change of awareness and his eyes opened. He lay in bed sweating, disorientated. 'Rough one?'

A pause. 'Karen?' The familiar room echoed his shaky sigh. 'Thank God for that, for you.'

Karen leaned across and held him. 'It's been a while.'

'Years.'

'Tam?'

'Tam. Just like before. Must be a one-off.'

'What do you think triggered it?'

'No idea, PTSD is a strange beast. I can't think of anything.'

'I hope so, darling. It's awful to watch.' She gave her husband a gentle nurturing kiss. He kissed her back, a question. A tongue caressed his lips and eased into his mouth.

They made love with urgency, driving the dark away with their passion. The warmth of release and a deep sense of closeness broke the demon's spell.

Afterwards, Sam lay in the dark, uneasy. Next thing it was morning.

7

FRESH FROM the shower, Eilidh pulled on some jeans, chose a top and did a shimmy for the mirror. The tensions of the day were gone.

'You're looking gorgeous tonight, Toots.' Shirl, her flatmate leaned in the doorway.

Eilidh grinned. 'He's a dish.'

'Then why aren't you flaunting what you've got?' Shirl pouted and wiggled her hips.

'Not my style.'

'Me, I'd have my boobs hanging out one end and my derrière out the other,' Shirl said.

'And you'd be shagging before midnight.'

'Been known, but not as often as reported,' big sigh, 'sadly.'

'I don't want to shag everything that moves,' Eilidh said.

'Me neither, only breathing males.' They enjoyed a mutual snigger.

'He's gorgeous. Dark eyes, curly hair and fit.'

'So, where are you off to?' Shirl said.

'Somewhere near Tottenham Court Road. Neon something. Anyway, we're meeting in a pub first.'

'It's time you went out socially.'

'You're right. It's been a while. All work, no play and all that,' Eilidh said.

'Change your day job.'

'Can't. Love the life. Need to get my first big story into print and earn the large pay cheque. Waitressing helps ends meet, and the tips are a bonus.'

'Mexican food'll make you fat. Just as well you're smelling of perfume instead of onions tonight.'

'You're jealous,' Eilidh said.

'Too right. You're off partying and I'm staying in reading boring old medical texts. I'm green.'

'I'm off.'

'Make sure to file your report with me in the morning,' Shirl said.

'You betcha.'

8

EILIDH MET CARLO in a pub five minutes' walk from Tottenham Court Road Underground. Smiles, small talk and a

Cuba Libre got things off to a good start. Carlo warmed her with constant attention and enjoyable flattery.

Forty-five minutes later they sat in the nightclub. The lighting was dim, intimate. The fabric on the seats stroked like velvet and gave her goosebumps. Carlo excused himself and headed for the gents. Enjoying the moment, Eilidh watched him go. He was physically attractive, moved with grace and had a cool line in chat. Could a girl say no to him? Tingling, she wondered what the night might hold.

The air pulsated with loud music, penetrating vibrations and rhythmical lighting effects. They danced, drank and schmoozed. It was after midnight when she became unwell.

Carlo's voice distorted and sounded far away. 'Hey pretty girl, you okay?'

'No, I'm woozy.'

'Poverina, let's get some fresh air.' His face distorted and changed shape.

She lurched from the table, stumbled and fell against him, every step becoming less coordinated as they staggered into a corridor. The words 'Fire Exit' were bright, convoluted, changing size and focus. Concrete steps wobbled upwards, she gripped a railing and pulled herself forward. The touch was solid, the view multi-coloured and changeable. She vomited down her front.

Carlo looked at her, face distorted with disgust. 'Dirty girl.' He turned and spoke to someone. Something metal slammed, hard.

9

THE FIRE EXIT burst open with a bang. The mechanism rattled and groaned as its securing rod grated on rough concrete. To Eilidh's eyes, an uneven, dirty surface rippled like stirred porridge. Behind her, she could still hear the whump-a-whump of a bass line and squeals of laughter from the club.

'Wha's happnin' t' meh?'

'You've come over all woozy. Look at you, covered in sick, you're disgusting.'

'Harn't drunk mush.' The ground distorted like jelly as she slumped towards it. Her hair started to drag on the soggy surface.

'Some friends'll take you home, *filthy bitch.*' The beginnings of fear sent a spark of tension to her stomach. Carlo let her drop. Damp soaked through her jeans and the sleeve of her blouse as she flopped on the squashy ground. Her face slapped into something wet, clammy and soft. The horror of the sensation sharpened her awareness for a few moments.

'Give me a hand here.' Indignant familiarity suffused Carlo's voice. Two men stepped out of a van parked in a shadowy area. Paralysed and watching two strange contorting men lumber towards her added to the sense of nightmare.

The van men wore overalls and boots, one tall, one short, both chubby. The larger man gave Carlo an envelope and received Eilidh's handbag. Neither spoke. The big man put her bag in the van and returned.

* * *

The men grabbed an arm each and dragged her upright, nipping the skin enough to make her groan. They lugged her to the van, one knee and her toes scraping the ground. Vision fading she was thrust towards a sliding-door in its side. Rough hands pushed her into the vehicle. Her head thumped against some metal on the way in. She felt a tickling trickle of blood in her hair. The door closed with a clang and she sensed the weight of the two men getting in the front. Both doors slammed shut.

'Nice tits,' were the last words she heard as everything faded.

* * *

In moments, the van was gone. The lane returned to silence. Brackish water filled a tyre pattern impressed on soggy newspaper. Damp earth and grit held the scrape marks of shoes and some indentations from a hip and knees. Stuck on a muddy lump, strands of golden hair fluttered in a dank breeze.

* * *

Later that night, confident of his growing credibility in the right places, 'Carlo' was filled with self-admiration. Man, he was 'moving up the ladder' as he told a friend over lines of coke and more than a few shots of vodka. Eilidh belonged to the past, she'd never cross his mind again.

10

STRONG VEINED HANDS moved the head and body inexorably towards the water. The hands of a trained killer, hard and calloused, with some scars. Sam Duncan's left arm cradled the baby. Her tiny form tucked along his forearm and into the crook of his elbow.

He wore a serene expression when he baptized the infant, dipping his right hand in the font and marking the sign of the cross on the little forehead. Sam gazed calmly, with an element of search and challenge, at the child's family gathered in Sunday best for the baptism.

His blue eyes were clear and warm beneath grey-streaked chestnut brows. Jeannie, his eldest daughter wanted his eyebrows trimmed because bushy wasn't cool. Alice, his youngest, naturally disagreed.

Sam glanced at his wife Karen. Some less than holy thoughts crossed his mind as he admired the gentle swell of her breasts against a prim blouse.

He beamed at the congregation, his broad, open face supported by a strong jaw and high, intelligent forehead. A faded scar on his left cheek and a certain unevenness of nose suggested past adventures. His step was light as he passed the baby back to her happy mother.

A man waited for him at the church door as he left.

* * *

Back home after the service and baptism party, Sam and Karen relaxed on the kitchen couch over a cup of tea.

'So, Johnny asked you to be Minister again?' Karen said.

'Yeah, his needle's a bit stuck.'

'Bless him.'

'I just did,' Sam said.

Karen cackled. 'You're not going to change, are you?'

'No, I'm not cut out for parish ministry, but I'm happy to do the odd service and support friends.'

'You're quite sexy in your robes.'

'So you tell me. Sexier out of them if I remember right.'

'Men fancy nuns, why can't women fancy vicars?'

'Ministers.'

'Don't go all Scottish on me.'

They bantered on, snuggling up to each other.

* * *

The phone rang. Karen answered.

'Abby.' Karen handed him the phone.

'Hiya, Mum.'

'Oh, Sammy … Oh God, son …'

'It's not Uncle Willie?'

'No, son, he's on the mend. It's Eilidh.' A strangled breath. 'She's missing.'

'Say again?' Sam said.

'Eilidh's disappeared.'

'Disappeared?'

'She promised to call me about her visit next week.'

'That doesn't mean she's missing.'

'She hasn't been at work since Thursday. Hasn't called in sick, hasn't been at her flat, hasn't been in touch with me … and she promised.' A resonant sob. 'It's not like her. Why didn't she stay in that newspaper job in Edinburgh, where her friends are? No, no, she had to aim for the top.'

'Calm down, Mum.'

'Oh, Sammy, I'm so worried.' Abby started to splutter. Moments later, she was silent … expectant.

'I'll call Cal, he's got good contacts.' Silence. 'You want me in London, don't you?' Silence. 'I'll come and see you. Should be there for eight o'clock.' God! She could be difficult.

A touch more demanding quietness. 'Thanks, Sam. I'll have some food for you.'

'We can decide what to do when I'm there.'

'Thanks, darling. Something's wrong …' her voice rose, 'I just know …' When Abby knew, she knew, and she wouldn't budge.

'Right, Mum. I'll be there soon. Have you called Hec?'

Her tone changed. 'Hec's been away in the fleshpots of Spain.' Hector, Sam's older brother, owned a medium-sized construction business and was, commercially at least, as tough as concrete blocks. Twice married and childless he found a single lifestyle suited him. 'I called him. He told me to stop being silly. Wait till I get my hands on him.' At last, ta touch of lightness entered her voice. 'He's coming home.' *Good lad.*

'See you shortly, Mum. Don't worry.' Abby hung up with a sob. 'Shit!' Karen enquired with her eyes. 'Did you get most of that?' She nodded. 'Mum's convinced Eilidh's gone missing.'

'What are you going to do?' Karen said.

'Go and see Mum. Give her a good listen, get her story, and calm her down.'

'She wants you in London?'

'Yes, and I'll go. The diary's clear. With any luck, things'll be okay when she's had time to calm down. Hec's on his way back and that'll help her settle.'

Sam reviewed the business schedule for the week and e-mailed his team. They'd handle everything. He took a few minutes to relax before the journey, imagining a bright protective glow surrounding his little sister.

Given a crystal ball, he'd have sought stronger protection … and for more people.

11

EILIDH FLOATED in a vague place, drifting in and out of awareness. Sometimes voices whispered near her, accompanied by the sharp jag of needles. A woman helped with the toilet. It wasn't nice. The world was in dim sepia. Now and then people spoke in quiet and impersonal tones in what sounded like a corridor.

At times, she drowned in a churning mental soup, a minestrone of documents and meetings, mixed with vivid episodes from her own life. Her mother's bawling hysteria when a bomb blast caught Sam in in Northern Ireland merged into her first experience of love. The births of Jeannie and Alice became Cal clowning and then Hector held her six-year-old hand in a queue for fish and chips—she could smell the vinegar.

Next Jamie was pressuring her for the story and pushing for deadlines, and his tie kept changing colour. The investigation tumbled round in her mind like clothing in a drier. Muddled fragments of investigative interviews played and replayed in random disorder.

For all the confusion, she couldn't shake off a cold sense of extreme danger and dread.

12

THIRTY MINUTES after leaving home, Sam drove through Hawick in the Scottish Borders. The big blue Citroen C5 ate the miles with ease.

At 19.00 the massive towers and cables of the Forth Road Bridge floated in a surreal golden cloud of dissolving sea fog. An hour later, he arrived at an old stone-built property, thirty yards from the beach, in Elie. His parents had moved there twenty-seven years before as they followed their retirement dream. Dad died a year after the move when Eilidh was ten months old.

The door opened before he could ring the bell. His mother grasped him in a bear-hug wrestlers spend years aspiring to achieve. She led him to the kitchen where seated at her solid pine table, she poured him a steaming cup of tea. In moments he was tucking into toast and a brace of St Monans kippers.

'Oh, Sam.' He took her hand and absorbed the familiar view of the dresser with the willow pattern plates. The pan tile floor provided a soft echo to their conversation.

'Hard day, Mum?'

Teary-eyed, her face twitched with emotion. 'A bit stressed.'

'Tell me all about it.' Her fears flooded out in a confused babble. 'Slow down, I can't make sense while you're blowing bubbles out of your nose and speaking at two thousand words a minute.'

'I'm a silly old hysteric, aren't I.' Her embarrassed smile and a deep breath were followed by a rapid sharing of her concerns. Eilidh living in London. Not calling as promised. Met a gorgeous guy. On a date but never came back … the Neon something or other, and no answer from her mobile. Gone missing. Of course, she understood how, nowadays, people have a fling, but no call? A day, maybe two at most …

Sam listened without interruption until his mother was repeating herself for the third time. 'Okay, okay, I've heard enough. I'll ring Cal and go to London in the morning. I'll speak to Shirl and chase up leads.' Abby beamed at him.

After twenty minutes of chat, they said goodbye with a hug. Seven hours of driving to provide an hour of comfort and worth every minute.

On the road home, mind ticking over, he experienced a faint tingle of foreboding.

13

WELL AFTER MIDNIGHT Sam entered the house and called a gentle 'hello' up the stairs. Barney, the family dog, rushed from the kitchen whimpering with excitement, tail whipping backwards and forwards, cracking against the furniture. Sam squatted, gave him a hug and a scratch behind the ears to happy groans of pleasure. 'Now, off you go to bed,' He watched the cross Collie-Labrador trot through the kitchen door and heard the contented thump of Barney's body on his bed.

Entering the lounge, he switched on and dimmed the lights. The rugged ramparts of the Castle Mount, lit by a harvest moon, were framed by the window opposite the door. The movement of the carriage clock on the mantelpiece whirled in golden silence. As he walked past the hearth on the thick green carpet the softness soothed him. Tension fell away as he eased into his armchair. Kicking off his shoes, he relaxed into supportive cushions and continued to think about Eilidh.

Karen came in moments later. Perching beside her man she wrapped her arms around him, laying her chin on the top of his head. Sam loved being hugged by his statuesque honey-blonde wife and, slipping his hand under her sweater, enjoyed stroking the smooth skin of her lower back. The reward was to be squeezed a little harder, sufficient to tell him he was precious. They luxuriated in the warmth of connection, snuggling together.

'Man on a mission.' He gazed up into her tawny green-flecked eyes.

'Tell me … I've checked the times and booked a London flight.'

'Still sceptical?' He loved the way the tip of her nose moved gently up and down when she spoke and how her generous mouth shaped words, flashing even teeth in the process.

'Not anymore. I have to find her. Make sure she's okay.'

'What about Cal?'

He made a face. 'I called him. Got up his nose a bit. He wants time to look into things. I didn't give it to him. He's annoyed, called me Mr Pushy.'

'Mmm, you can be pushy, Samuel. The pair of you can kiss and make up tomorrow.' She giggled.

Sam sighed. 'Like it or not, I'm committed and I'm going to get things moving.'

'There you go, Pushy Boy.' Karen kissed his forehead.

'I'm for bed and an early start. If you fancy a spot of pushy you'd best be close behind.'

She lifted his head and kissed him full on the lips. 'You'll have to take "yes" for an answer, Mr Pushy.'

They left the lounge hand-in-hand.

An undertone of excitement, perhaps the risk, floated in the air. Sam looked forward to the trip, fool's errand or not, nothing like a spot of action.

14

THEY MET, three days after Eilidh disappeared, in an elegant UK government building at 09.30, just off Cockspur Street in London. Corinthian columns and marble floors gave way to a drab interior. Four directors sat around an undistinguished table in an anonymous, secure meeting room. There were no windows, only Magnolia walls framed by white woodwork. Refreshments were available from a catering trolley. Biscuit wrappers rustled and cups clinked as people settled down.

The working name 'Bizz' seemed sexy, even powerful, which they all were in their chosen careers. Power didn't guarantee freedom from hassle or difficult decisions. An aggravating investigative journalist was the main item on the agenda, a new challenge. Eilidh Duncan was the first person brought into line by the evolving criminal operation.

The Chair, a large Afro-Caribbean woman and top civil servant, Maybelle Jones, started off. 'Okay. Let's get started.' Conversations stopped. 'Our tabloid crusader should be less of an irritant now.'

'I still have reservations about what we've done,' Gemma Smythsone said.

'She's persistent, she's been talking to people and rocking the boat. I don't like it. We don't like it. We're getting ripples at the top and must avoid serious waves further down. We had to do something.' Maybelle didn't appreciate being challenged.

An upper-crust baritone entered the discussion. Devlin Forsyth said. 'Quite right, Maybelle. We've got to protect a good set-up. The cell system works. Recruitment is steady. Revenue is growing. Our partners love us. The money's offshore. It's a cracking deal.'

Gemma said, 'I accept the need to protect our position. We were a bit hasty and should have taken more time to decide on our action regarding the Duncan woman.' Lovely as an early spring morning, and just as cool, her beautifully modulated English accent emphasized 'protect'.

Devlin made intimate eye contact with her, raising a brow. 'Perhaps we were somewhat over-eager in our action, but what's done is done.'

'Actually, what we're doing is risk-management.' A broad Geordie accent joined the conversation. 'We needed to decide about kill or cure, and I'm not sure I'd have chosen cure. We haven't been ruthless enough.' Jim Thomas, a senior MI5 asset, was blunt as usual. 'Risk is risk. Our operation is being disrupted. We've neutralized one source, with kindness and promotion as it happens, but neutralized it just the same. There are other sources and we don't know who they are. The Duncan girl must be sorted out. The question for me is have we done enough? In my world, we'd have eliminated the problem.'

'We made a decision, we agreed our plan of action, and she's being dealt with. Let's end it there,' Maybelle said. People nodded.

Jim Thomas turned to Devlin. 'How'd things go?'

'She was taken early on Friday morning. One of our customers has specialist skills in the kidnap department. The frighteners are being applied and she'll be out of circulation for a few days.'

'Sadly, necessity dictated.' Gemma looked sad but wasn't. 'What happens next?'

'No idea. Left it to our contractor … need-to-know. The bottom line is she's been taken, she's being warned off and the arrangements are unknown to us. She'll be released in due course, suitably chastised.'

'Makes sense.'

Maybelle Jones concluded things. 'Good. Action taken and disappearance to the extent we've approved. Let's get on with our day jobs.'

* * *

After the meeting, Devlin Forsyth and Jim spoke briefly.

'Well done, that man. Your contact seems to have sorted our dilemma.' Jim patted his shoulder.

'Thanks. Your surveillance photos and information were a real help.'

'No problem. Catch you later.'

15

A DISCORDANT blare of traffic noise greeted Sam as he walked from Victoria Station. Humidity and exhaust fumes were a cloying counterpoint to the clean breeze of the Border country.

In the taxi rank, a horn tooted. Cal, a greying, large, somewhat battered version of Muhammad Ali, stood beside his car, hand raised. He wore a smart pair of slacks, white shirt and a comfortable looking Harris-tweed jacket. Sam crossed to him.

'Calvin.'

'Sam.' They hugged. 'How you doin', you pushy Scots git?'

'I'd rather be pushy than ugly.'

'Let's get a coffee,' Cal said, 'you're looking fit.' He started the engine.

'Aye, still training.'

'Moving well for an old un.'

'Gotta keep the edge, sunshine.'

'What for? General health or World War Three?'

'Both. What's with you?' Sam said.

'You were a bit OTT last night.'

‘More than you know,’ Sam half-smiled.

‘I’ll always help you. No need to throw your weight about.’

‘Sorry, chum. The Eilidh thing’s bugging me. I didn’t mean to get up your nose. Let me say it again, I-am-sorry.’

‘Right. And I-am-glad-to-see-you.’ The bright, craggy smile could have lit a bonfire.

* * *

The journey was manic for a while. Cal concentrated while rushing drivers hurtled into half-spaces accompanied by the angry blast of horns. Once things calmed down the conversation resumed.

‘What do you think about the Eilidh situation?’ Sam said.

‘Maybe she’s met someone, you know, swept off her feet and a temporary lapse of daughterly duty. That sort of thing … happens all the time.’

‘You might be right, but in her case more of a reason to call Mum with a juicy titbit. Our girl almost always calls Mum. But she didn’t.’

16

CAL PARKED the car. The tiled front of Romero’s café gleamed blue and yellow, the name picked out in a mosaic. Inside, bright pastel colours with fishing nets and tanks of tropical fish provided a London-Mediterranean atmosphere. Cal and Sam ordered, chose a table in the rear, and got on with business.

‘Any luck with the phone numbers?’ Sam said.

'Pay as you go, switched off, no lead. How'd you get the landline number again?'

'Abby used 1471.'

'Right. We think Eilidh phoned home from someone's house. It has no apparent connection to her disappearance. I'd exclude it for now.'

'Okay, you're the cop.'

'So why don't you leave this to the professionals?' Cal said.

'Your needle's stuck, Calvin. Mum called the locals about a missing person … all listening and no action. Before you say anything, I know there are rules and timeframes for escalation. Mum thinks your colleagues can't act fast enough or be interested enough or take things seriously enough. And here I am.'

'Abby leans on you and now you're leaning on me,' Cal said.

'Right. Mum's not alone. Shirl Johnstone, Eilidh's flatmate, is worried too. That's Johnstone, with an "e."'

'Bit of a character by all accounts. Eilidh's fond of her.'

'Yeah, somewhat laddish. She seems to be either hung-over or working on the next one. Typical medic by the sound of things. They've been sharing for a while. They're on their second flat together,' Sam said.

'What about the boyfriend?'

'You grilling me, Inspector?'

'Answer the question before I charge you … for the coffee.' Big smile.

'Hardly a boyfriend yet. Eilidh started to date someone recently, a beautiful boy I hear, Mediterranean type, "Carlo". They've dated once or twice. Last time at a nightclub somewhere near Euston … you know, I told you.'

'Then she was gone?' Cal said.

'Yup, Eilidh went out to meet him. Never came back.'

'So, Abby and Shirl think there's something wrong.'

'Right,' Sam said.

'Anyone else?'

'Eilidh's been moonlighting in a small restaurant called the High Sierra, a Mexican place about five minutes from Oxford Circus. The manager's worried. She's missed her Friday shift. He went through the standard clichés, you know: not like her, lovely girl, good with customers, hope everything's okay.'

'Hmm, three people saying something's not quite right,' Cal said.

'Four if you count me. I've heard enough to make me wonder.'

'Might be significant, might not.' The cheeky grin made Sam smile.

'You're an old sceptic, Cal. Okay. So she's disappeared in the last few days. Remember the police liaison bit I did?'

'Unforgettable, Duncan the Detector as I recall.' A frosty look. 'Sorry, Sam. I know it's serious.'

'I worked on investigations for nearly two years with the RUC, and a few other places besides. The guys were good investigators and always said, the warmer the trail the faster the find. That's why I'm here. The trail is getting colder. It's well past the bloody Golden Hour.'

'Ouch!' Cal said.

They sipped their coffees in silence for a moment.

With him on the road to recovery, after the first Gulf War, Abby had volunteered to look after Cal while his parents were in the West Indies. He liked her dry sense of humour and the disarming twinkle in her eye. Religious yet not overbearing, Abby was a handsome woman who loved him as one of her own.

'So Abby's worried,' Cal said.

'I'll say.' The tension eased.

'I owe Abby.' The sigh was deep and concerned. 'Your little sister's family to me. God, Sam, we meet up quite often. She's gorgeous and fun. Makes me smile.'

'We all know how she feels about Uncle Cal … More coffee?' Sam said. Before he could leave the table, his mobile rang.

17

HE CHECKED the display, 'Hello, Mum … I'll write that down. Give me a sec.'

He pulled out a pen and wrote on a napkin plucked from the chromed container on the table.

'Yep … yep … got that … Ward 37, South Block, St Mary's. Right. Right. Knickers, nightie, toothbrush, toiletries, flowers, fruit … okay. Hmm, okay … okay. Ma, let me get going. The sooner I get there, the sooner I'll be able to update you. Don't worry, I'm here. Everything should be fine. Just before you go, how is she? … unclear … I'll find out more and get back to you.'

He turned to Cal. 'You'll have heard most of that, chum. She's found. St Mary's Hospital. Paddington isn't it? I've got the number. Shopping to do as well. How are you fixed for time?'

'Took the afternoon off,' Cal said. 'One of my guys was to contact Abby if anything concrete came up. I'm all yours for the rest of the day. I'll get an update.' He keyed his mobile, no answer. He left a message.

Anticipation vied with tension. With Eilidh found and in good hands. 'I brought my dog collar, just in case it was needed to open doors,' Sam said.

'Change in the car.'

'Yup. I know Mum has said buy loads of stuff, Cal, but screw that. Let's get to the hospital.'

'Okay,' Cal said.

'We can shop later.'

'Right.'

'Mum seemed vague about how Eilidh is …' Sam said.

'My guys wouldn't tell her any bad or unhappy news, that's our job. I hope there isn't any.'

'Let's get there.'

'Oooh, you're so masterful, bwana.'

'Right, so get that size twelve on the gas.'

18

CAL'S PHONE RANG near the hospital entrance. They stopped and he stepped away for privacy. He returned grim-faced.

'Bad news,' Cal gazed downwards for a moment. He took a deep breath and locked eyes with Sam as he spoke. 'Eilidh's been in the wars. They found her below a bridge near Waterloo around four this morning. It's believed she lay injured for a couple of days beforehand.' He struggled to keep his police face on. 'Cracked ribs, a fractured skull, broken cheek, three lost teeth, two fingernails torn off, a broken arm and multiple injuries.' Sam stood immobile, expressionless. 'Also raped … they think by more than one assailant. They identified her by her plastic, a Bank of Scotland credit card.'

Sam, white-faced in an instant, said nothing, shook his head, puffed out his cheeks and exhaled a shaky breath. His nod invited Cal to continue.

'Worse than bad, mate. Her head injury is critical. She's in Intensive Care, already had one emergency operation to stabilize her. They daren't do any more work at the moment, she needs healing time.' Sam remained silent. Cal took a deep breath, eyes glistening, mouth twitching and then setting into a firm line as he regained his composure.

They went to Ward 37 in silence. People squeaked past on the shiny floors. There was a pervasive smell of disinfectant. The approach to the reception area was, somehow, impersonal. Sam leaned on the counter and waited for the Charge Nurse to finish a task. Her hazel eyes, when she looked up, were gentle and tired looking.

'Hello, I'm looking for Eilidh Duncan,' Sam said.

'It's early for a pastoral visit, chaplain.'

'I'm sorry, Sister …'

She cut him off. 'She doesn't need a man of the cloth, poor darling. She needs her Ma.'

'I'm not her Ma, I'm her big brother.' He was pale. 'Take me to her.'

The nurse blushed. 'I do apologize, sir, please follow me.' She led him to the Intensive Care Unit. Nearby, in the waiting area, Cal found a chair.

In the ICU, Eilidh lay unconscious. 'She's gravely ill. Did the police brief you?'

'Yes.'

'The crisis is ahead. You need to prepare for the worst.'

'I'll sit with her for a moment if you don't mind.'

'No, not at all.'

Sam sat and stroked the back of Eilidh's hand with his thumb. Her head was swathed in bandages. She'd lost weight. He could see a taped broken nose, stitched split lips and a partially visible, swollen black left eye. He watched IV teardrops fall in measured sympathy. The monitoring equipment made reassuring sounds of continuing life.

When she woke up, someone she knew and loved would be right there. Sam thanked God as an icy cold anger started to grow. Eilidh groaned and gripped his hand. Her visible eye jerked wide, its brown iris surrounded by a red-streaked white, bulging with distress and fear. She sucked a jagged breath. Sam jolted upright. Whoever's hand he was holding, it wasn't Eilidh's.

19

LESS THAN six miles away a woman in a corridor pulled on a white balaclava. She filled a syringe with some fluid from a small vaccine bottle and opened the door into Eilidh's cell. Her movements were observed on the video monitors in an office.

Eilidh's left arm was handcuffed to the bed. The woman showed her the syringe, enjoying the pleas from her charge. Eilidh struggled and the woman delivered a slap to the face that made her eyes water. The needle was jabbed into her left forearm, among a cluster of bruises from previous shots.

'Silly girl. This wouldn't be happening if you'd kept your nose out of matters that don't concern you.'

The same bloody words every time. I've got the bloody message. Eilidh struggled to stay conscious but the drugs took hold and, in seconds, she slipped back into limbo.

Once more in the corridor, the woman pulled off the balaclava and looked up at the camera. Every bit as ugly as her treatment of Eilidh, she smiled.

The planned nightmare continued.

20

'IT'S ALRIGHT, you're safe in hospital.' The injured woman made mewling sounds because of the pipe down her throat. 'You've been through a lot.'

The nurse came back. 'Hmm … joined the Wide-Awake-Club, have we?' The girl in the bed cried, tears soaked her bandages adding a tinge of blood on the left side. Her nose started to drip blood. Sam continued stroking her hand.

'I know you can't speak at the moment. Can you understand what I'm saying? Just nod or signal.' The girl nodded weakly. 'It'll be okay.' His smile gained a grimace in response.

'Okay, Vicar. Time for you to go while we sort this young lady out.' The nurse wasn't asking his opinion. He was stiff from two hours in the chair. The girl clung to his hand, pulling at him as he stood. Her eyebrows formed a question.

'I have to leave. I'll be thinking of you.' He stopped on his way to the door, returned to the bedside and leaned down. 'Whatever happens, get well. We'll look after you.' He squeezed her hand gently.

Sam left the room stretching the stiffness out of his muscles and joints. The girl's eyes followed him. He waved from the door wondering if she was bright-eyed with hope, medication or a bit of both.

At ward reception he spoke to the nurse. 'The girl through there isn't Eilidh Duncan. She's not my sister.'

'That's who the forms say she is.'

'That is not Eilidh Duncan.'

The charge nurse rocked back in her chair. Cal jerked upright, took out his mobile phone and made a call, murmuring in the background.

21

Shaken, Sam stepped out and called Abby.

'Hi, Mum.' His hissing in-breath spoke first. 'The woman here isn't Eilidh.'

After a pause and a deep breath. 'Not Eilidh?'

'No. She's not Eilidh.'

'You'll find her won't you?'

'I'll do everything I can.'

'Good enough for me.'

The conversation was stiff, formal and devoid of the emotion churning in each of them. They dared not acknowledge the unstated reality glowing icy cold in the dark of their fears.

'Hector'll be here in about thirty minutes and he's going to stay.'

'Fantastic.'

'Bye, dear.' Her voice broke and she couldn't hold back a low sob as she hung up. After a long deep breath Sam exhaled with a slight whistle. Cal eyed his friend with stalwart sympathy.

Eyes closed for a moment, Sam rubbed his forehead and dragged his fingers through his hair, face set, stony. Moisture leaked from the corner of his right eye, blotted in an instant by a drying finger. He blew his nose. Back to business.

* * *

'What d'you want to do?' Cal said.

'Hang around and see if anything emerges when she's more alert.'

'I'm with you.' Cal said. They took a seat near the door and spent forty-five minutes catching up.

Alarms sounded, a 'crash' team appeared and rushed into the ICU. Sam and Cal heard a flurry of action as the squad worked. Next, the medics emerged pushing their patient down the corridor with urgency.

The charge nurse came over. 'Mr Duncan, I'm afraid we have a brain haemorrhage on our hands and the young woman needs emergency surgery. Good luck with finding your sister.' Sam and Cal watched her walk away.

'How are you?' Cal said.

'Not happy, I'm hurting, scared and bloody angry. I better give Karen a ring.'

* * *

They went outside where Sam found a quiet spot of pavement to make his call. 'Hi, love, the lassie we found isn't Eilidh.' He explained the situation finishing up with, 'She's been beaten within an inch of her life and raped.'

'How are you?'

'Worried. Girls okay?'

'They're fine.

'Good, give them my love.'

'… and you're hurting.' Karen said.

'Mmm, yup, can't talk at the moment.'

Men! 'When will you be back?'

'Tomorrow or day after.' He paused for around thirty seconds. Karen could tell he was thinking. 'The lassie came around for a couple of minutes, frightened and battered. In one way I'm so glad it wasn't Eilidh, but where is Eilidh?'

'Have you a trail to follow?'

'Yes, we're investigating.'

'How's Cal?'

'Fine. Same as ever. A bit shocked like me.'

'Give him my best. I'll call you in the morning for a proper chat.'

'Right. Cal sends his love. Take care. Love to the girls.'

'Bye, tough guy, love you.'

Cal and Sam left the hospital and, talking as they drove, planned their next steps.

22

TOMMY BAIN worked in import and export: importing toys, fancy goods and people. He exported young women and boys, amongst other things. Money rolled in.

The operation used road, rail and air freight services, with a little help from 'sympathetic' officials. He shipped out of London, the East Midlands, Glasgow and Manchester. If necessary, he stored merchandise. The 'goods' were well-fed, drugged enough to keep them compliant and provided with reasonable accommodation and a good line in TV.

A systematic person, Tommy used people he could trust, and would kill to protect his investment. He didn't respect or even like other humans.

* * *

The phone rang. 'Job done. We got the girl's stuff back.' Jackie Steele sounded pleased.

'Good.'

'You wanted action, Tom. The situation is cleared up. Taff and Gorki are feeling bloody stupid.'

'Yeah, I'll be having a serious chat with them. They'll not be driving a van for me again. Imagine, screwing a junkie whore in the van before they disposed of evidence. It's no surprise she nicked some stuff. I'm speechless.'

'Any roads, the Young Bloods delivered. Piece of cake.'

'And that's another thing. Don't use fuckin' riff-raff like them for me ever again. Nazi bovver-boys aren't exactly low-key. On top of that, they've no brains. Three schoolboys could've done the job.'

'Whatever you say, Tom. Where do you want the goods delivered?'

'I don't. Burn 'em. And Jackie, mate, make sure they're destroyed. No money-making on the side, got that?'

'Clear as a bell, Tom.' Tommy rolled his eyes and shook his head as he hung up.

* * *

On the up-side, Tommy thought, at least he'd got a result for Mr Forsyth who arranged the 'oversight' service for his shipments, at a price. They'd needed a favour and he'd provided one. The taking of Eilidh Duncan had been professional: £9,000 profit after expenses, plus the £5,000 for preparation. The glow of satisfaction warmed him. What a sweet deal.

Time to relax now the mistake had been sorted. It had been a straightforward contract. 'Do the job, no questions'. He couldn't understand why they hadn't disposed of the girl. Soft amateurs. They'd soon learn. The only pain in the process was the van men dropping the ball. Mistakes could cost lives.

Tommy checked his merchandise. The screen showed Eilidh in her cell. Pity he couldn't sell her on, she was valuable goods.A one-off commission, she would be shipped out soon and stored by people in the North. The contractors could be trusted to release her as agreed, physically unharmed, mentally, a different story. Still business was business.

23

BY 21.00 the streets had quietened down. They'd been in the hospital for nearly four hours. Incredible.

'Take me where they found her, Cal.'

'Okay.'

A light drizzle fell as they arrived near some old brick arches below a railway junction. Wet walls reflected misty street lights. Scattered cardboard boxes provided accommodation. Empty bottles, bereft of solace, lay scattered amongst the organic and inorganic trash. The odour of damp clothes and unwashed humanity was interwoven with spicy food and stale alcohol. The miasma added a unique edge to the dank, motionless air.

'Must've been around here somewhere,' Cal said.

'Someone must've seen something.'

'They won't give us the time of day.'

'We'll see.'

'Sam, these people live in a crazy, unhappy world with no reason to love folk like us.'

'Understood. Let's wander about and get a sense of the place.'

'Fair enough.'

A gentle bass voice with a plummy accent resonated from one of the arches.

'Don't worry, Archie, I'll find out if Wizz is at any of the hostels farther down the river. He's well able to look after himself. If he's had a bad high he might've been lifted. I'll check with the police if needs must.' The talker came nearer and the shape of a man started to separate itself from the gloom. He walked with a brisk, straight-backed stride.

Not too many people wore a dark overcoat with velvet lapels down here. The material strained over a portly stomach. Rheumy red eyes peered from a pale, pasty face surrounded by meaty jowls. The man slowed as he noticed Cal and Sam standing nearby. He gave them the once over.

'Good evening, gentlemen.'

He strode up to Sam who could now see his red-veined face, and a nose like a large slightly squashed strawberry.

'A young woman was attacked here recently and badly injured.'

'A Scots vicar, no less. Attacked you say? That'd be Jenny. Pretty young thing, hammering herself with drugs, drink and paying customers. Sad little soul. What news?'

Cal took over the conversation, 'In an operating theatre, fighting for her life.'

'Pity. She's not a bad lass, you understand, bit of prostitution, spot of thieving, but then you've got to get by. Left home in a hurry perhaps three years back, Somerset, I think, so she's been in the area for some time. Are you police, sir?' He ignored Sam and stared directly at Cal.

'Yes.' Cal showed his warrant card. 'We're making enquiries about her and the events leading up to her injury.'

'I'll ask around.' The man opened his coat to reveal a rough tweed jacket and a light waistcoat. A gold chain hung across a protruding belly. He pulled out a pocket watch.

'Meet me at eleven tomorrow.'

Sam said. 'Tomorrow at eleven, Mr—?'

'Parker, Stanley Parker. Meet me here.' Walking away he caught Sam's eye, winked and gave a furtive smile. He marched to the corner and, turning right, vanished.

'What now?'

'Some food, then a spot of nightclubbing. I've got a picture to show someone.'

24

WITH A CURRY tucked away, they found the nightclub.

'Sure you want to go in dressed as a vicar?' Cal said.

'Too late to go back and change, I'm sure they've seen stranger sights. Maybe some tarts are looking for a vicar.'

'Har, har, har.'

The Neon Orchid sign flashed above the door, flashing out like forked lightning. The bouncers ambled about with a hint of menace, thick-necked and solid, guarding the entry to a dimly lit passage with stairs going downwards at the end. A Neon Orchid logo was printed on the top half of a prominent anti-drug poster, the bottom half used the strap-line 'Just say NO!' Beneath the slogan there were stylised symbols with the ubiquitous red circle and diagonal line superimposed on them. The muffled thud of music gained and lost volume as some yet-to-be-seen door opened and shut.

‘Evening, gents,’ one of the bouncers, a massive barrel-shaped man with a shaven head, did his best to look friendly. ‘I’m not sure this will be your scene.’

‘You’re probably right,’ Sam said. ‘But I’d like to experience it. How much to get in?’

‘Nothing for you, Vicar, or your mate. Reckon you’ll last ten minutes max.’

‘Thanks.’ Sam nodded and stepped through, Cal close behind. The disco sound was almost liquid in its loudness.

The bouncer picked up a phone on the wall as they entered the club. ‘Colm, you’ve got a vicar and the fuzz coming down … nah, we were all respectful and polite. Never gave ’em no lip. The cop is black. They don’t look like trouble.’

A big man with wide shoulders and a welcoming grin awaited them at the bottom of the stairs where the venue seemed to widen out. The bar on the left was buzzing with customers and waitresses collecting orders. Nearby, some seats and tables were filled with schmoozing people. Through an archway, the dance floor heaved with rhythmic bodies lit by a stark, colourful light show, all surrounded by more seats and tables.

‘Gentlemen, welcome to the Neon Orchid. How can I help you?’ His voice carried over the music with an accent as Irish as a shamrock. He gestured for Sam and Cal to follow him through a nearly invisible door to the right. This led into a brightly lit room with a desk and some cushioned chairs which had seen plenty of use.

‘Is this official?’

‘Not at the moment,’ Cal said.

‘I’m Sam Duncan.’ He offered his hand.

‘Colm O’Casey.’ O’Casey was a solid customer with a round face, raven-black hair, a pale complexion and an almost gentle set to his features. His luminous golden eyes stared directly into Sam's.

'What do you do, Colm?'

'Co-own and manage this place.'

'I'm looking for my sister.' Colm studied Sam. 'My much younger sister. A twenty-seven-year-old accident thinly disguised as a blessing. She came here, we believe, four nights ago. She disappeared. We don't know if there's a connection. Will you help me?'

'Why the police involvement?'

'Inspector Martin is my friend. He's helping me.'

'Are you a vicar, seriously?'

'Yes. Think of me as a businessman who dabbles in religion.'

'Okay, I'll assist, but one-to-one. No offence … eh …'

'Inspector Martin,' Cal said. 'Give me a coffee and I'll wait outside. Here's my card.'

O'Casey nodded his thanks and pressed a button on the desk. The door opened and the bouncer who'd spoken to them when they arrived came in. 'Arnold, please take Mr Martin for a cup of coffee.' The big man courteously waved Cal in front of him. Sam and O'Casey got down to business.

25

SAM HANDED O'Casey a photograph.

'She's beautiful. Same forehead.' He considered for a moment. 'Right, I believe you. I will help but don't get your hopes up. Can I keep the picture?'

'Sure.'

'I'll ask around. Who knows, maybe you'll be lucky. The odds must be long.'

Sam said, 'Thank you. Have you got a piece of paper?' O'Casey yanked a sheet from a printer. Sam folded the paper and wrote on it. 'This is my mobile. Please call me if you get anything.'

'Will do. Were you ever in action?'

'What makes you ask? I was a soldier, not a Padre. Why do you ask?'

'Just wondered.'

'Okay, are we done for now?'

'Yes.'

'Follow me,' O'Casey led Sam to the table where Cal nursed his coffee. They shook hands. 'I'll be in touch.' At around 01.00 Sam and Cal headed for the car.

* * *

'What now?' Cal sounded tired.

'Give me a moment.' Sam pressed some keys on his mobile. 'Reverend Duncan phoning to enquire about …' He made a few 'uh huuh' noises and finished by thanking the person he spoke to.

'She's back in intensive care now: not stable, no visitors, sounds critical. I need a sleep. I'll go to the hospital first thing.' Sam yawned. 'Okay, Cal, what's on your mind?'

Cal looked serious.

'This isn't my patch and we don't want to rock the boat. Especially not with Macho Mike in charge over here.'

'Macho Mike?'

'Yeah, Mike Swindon. Puts the hard in hard man. An excellent investigator who's aggressive and gets results. Yanks would call him “lean ’n’ mean”. I’d add balding, broken-nosed, ugly, backed by an in-your-face, no-shit, no-fools attitude. For some mysterious reason, his people love him.’

‘Hmmm. We’ll need to win him to the cause. I’ll walk back to the digs and find my own way to the hospital.’

‘Right oh. See you tomorrow.’

* * *

Sam knew the hotel from his old life. The night porter welcomed him and they enjoyed ten minutes of chit-chat while Sam downed a whisky and water.

In his room, he thought of the injured girl and his wee sister. He disliked being on a battlefield without knowing where and who the foe was. Mulling things over, Sam fell asleep.

Trapped behind glass Eilidh, was beyond reach in Sam’s dream. She’d hold out her hand and his fingers would bump against icy cold crystal as he tried to grasp her. The desperation and fear in her voice echoed and re-echoed.

The scene and sounds kept repeating until his alarm went off stopping the treadmill. Twenty minutes of meditation eased things, a good way to start the day.

He couldn’t shake the feeling he was being watched.

26

BACK IN THE HOSPITAL by 07:00, Sam and chatted with a charge nurse.

‘Does she have anyone?’

‘No. Nobody’s come near, except you.’

‘Prognosis?’

‘Critical. She hasn’t been helped by her poor physical condition and, as well as the brain injury, fractures and lacerations. The beating caused internal bleeding. She’s very poorly.’

‘Okay to sit with her?’

‘Why not?’ The nurse took him to the bedside.

Sam looked around. More than once he’d been plugged into similar systems. This young woman lay at death’s door with no one there for her, alone in the medical machine. He sat down and gently took her hand.

At times like this compassion and true sympathy welled up in him. He imagined her life before the assault, noticing the tracks of intravenous drug use on her arms and the broken-nailed, dirty-fingered hand he held.

Her chalk-white face lacked expression with shut eyes and a slack jaw. Only the battering and contusions added colour. With a tube still taped to the side of her mouth and her head swathed in bandages, Sam couldn’t detect any improvement.

What benefit would survival bestow on her? Might she recover only to return whence she came, perhaps to an untimely death? Would she still sell herself for money to buy drugs or food? Was a return home a possibility? Had she a home to return to? Who cared enough to spend the time to help her help herself? He dozed.

Around 07.30 the girl’s hand twitched and her eyelids fluttered. The rhythmic tone of the monitor altered. The alarm blared. A crash team burst in, blocking the exit with action and equipment.

Sam retreated to the wall and admired the teamwork as the display continued flatlining.

She was declared clinically dead at 08.13.

No one noticed Sam and, when the door became free, he walked out. Someone was waiting for him.

27

THE FEMALE attendant shook Eilidh awake and, when she moaned, slapped her face forward and back with enough sting to make her aware.

'Wakey wakey.'

Eilidh couldn't raise a protective hand, dressed in ill-fitting, overalls, a belt around her waist had handcuffs attached. Her guard blindfolded her with a stretchy black cloth that came down over her nose.

'Moving day, you little bitch.' The voice was harsh.

'Moving where?'

'To the country, will you miss me?'

'What's to miss?'

Eilidh couldn't see the slap coming. She smelled the rancid warmth of her captor's breath as the woman leaned close to her face. 'You're lucky you have friends in high places or I'd have had you.' Next, a sticky tongue licked her neck. She shuddered. Then the sharp jab of a needle.

The buzz and limp feeling started. The mantra began:

'Silly girl. This wouldn't be happening if you'd kept your nose out of matters that don't concern you.'

The woman pulled up her own balaclava, squeezed Eilidh's lips into a pout, kissed her wetly and sniggered. Eilidh spat in her face and scowled. 'Fuck off.'

She tensed for a blow that never came as an electronic voice said, 'Back off, you stupid cow.'

Unseen by Eilidh, her captor raised her hands and backed away. 'You'll miss me where you're going.'

There was a flash of distress on Eilidh's face. Drugged unconsciousness overtook her torment as she sailed away on a nightmare sea.

The dark lens on the wall saw everything. Behind it, the observer guessed her future. It wasn't good.

28

SAM HEADED BACK towards reception. A balding, broken-nosed, somewhat ugly man leaned against the corridor wall, arms crossed. Dressed smartly in a blazer, slacks, shiny black brogues and a red and blue striped silk tie, he was tall and fit looking, maybe forty years of age. He moved to stand in front of Sam, dark reptilian eyes staring from a belligerent scowl. His lips compressed almost to invisibility just before he spoke.

'So you're the holy man who persuaded a certain black man of my acquaintance to get off his bloody patch!' The voice rasped in a sharp London accent, overflowing with restrained and angry energy.

'And you'll be Macho Mike.' Sam offered his hand. It was ignored.

'It's people like you who're more trouble than you're worth, screwing around in things which are none of your business. In the bloody way, all the bleedin' time.'

'Have you thought about Clorets?'

'What?'

'The breath freshener.'

'Hnn …?'

'Your breath smells worse than my dog's and, if you must stand so close, something minty would do a lot for your PR.' Somewhere out of sight a suppressed snicker snorted out.

'*You're on my patch.*' Mike squeaked with indignation.

'And you are badly out of line.' Sam's voice resounded with military formality and bearing. 'Are you trying to start a battle or communicate with me?'

Silence. The policeman took a step backwards. Intimidation usually worked just fine. Sam said, 'A number of points, Inspector. One, the black man of my acquaintance is an Inspector and colleague of yours whom I know and respect. Two, I hope racist tendencies didn't drive your disparaging remark about the hue of Cal's skin, given recent events in the Met.' Mike Swindon made to speak but Sam held up his hand in a forceful stop gesture. 'Three, I'm not bleeding, at least not last time I checked.'

The Inspector tried to speak again, only to be stopped once more. 'Now, there's a choice here. Start again or escalate to a final conclusion. What would you like to do?'

Swindon gazed at the man in front of him. His eyes were hard, calm and perhaps a little angry. The 'Vicar' stood full square in his space and challenged him: not scared, not going to back down, ready for him. 'Start again,' Swindon said, quiet, stalled for now, but not forgetting.

SAM AND MIKE entered the waiting area.

'Ahh, you two have met.' Cal said. Both nodded. Cal noted the paleness in Mike's face and wished he could have watched the exchange, although hearing it was pretty good. He wanted to laugh and chewed the inside of his mouth like a schoolboy.

They went to the hospital's police office. Two constables picked up cups of tea and left the room. The three men sat down around a worn table, scarred with the hieroglyphics of use and vandalism. Mike became business-like.

'Cal tells me you are down here looking for a missing relative.'

'Yes. My sister.'

'You aren't using normal channels.'

'No. Not now. Normal channels aren't working.'

'We haven't the time to be working on every little problem that arises. Why don't you go home and lean on someone else?'

'Cal is willing to help and I'm here. A girl thought to be my sister is lying close by, dead. She died a few minutes ago — I was there. Now, Inspector Swindon, why did someone think she was my sister?'

'A credit card belonging to Eilidh Duncan was found on her person.'

'And that led to me being asked to come to this hospital. You can imagine my relief it's not Eilidh, but also my consternation, growing concern, and frustration with petty games some people are playing.'

'Okay, so what we've got here is a mystery and one we'll try to solve. But, I want you out, you've got nothing to contribute and you'll probably slow us down.'

'Right. I'm willing to stand back, stay out of your way and, shortly, I'll leave town. There must be results, Inspector, and I will be back.'

'I don't take orders from you.' Mike's voice was surly, almost childish.

'No. Just do what you said. Solve the bloody mystery.' Sam turned and walked out with a brisk step before anything more could be said.

30

MIKE TURNED to Cal. 'He's not your common or garden vicar.'

'No, he isn't.'

'Who is he, this fucking holy man pal of yours?'

'A man I owe my life to and a bloody good friend,' Cal said.

'An ex-squaddie like you?'

'Something like that.'

'Army goon?' Mike said.

'If you say so.'

'A fuckin' padre too. He's probably gay!' Locked in bully mode Mike had neither the will nor inclination to stop his tirade. 'Likes playing the hymns, does he?' Mike said, nodding conspiratorially to an uncomfortable young police officer who now stood by the door, waiting to speak. 'Tell your gay priest friend that he better keep his fuckin' nose out of my patch until —'

Cal's punch added a further split to Mike's upper lip below his left nostril and he swayed as the lights went partially out. The constable moved towards Cal who quickly stepped back and put his hands up, stunned by what he'd done. Eyes still wide, now filling with anger, Mike sat down, slightly dazed.

'You're in the shit, Calvin.'

Cal shook his head. 'You're a sorry, sick bully.'

Mike rubbed his injured face and looked at the blood on his fingers. A spotless white handkerchief appeared in his hand.

'You two leave and close the door.' Sam's bearing made leaving obligatory. Cal and the PC left.

'I've had enough of you to last me a while, Mike.'

Macho Mike's eyes bulged as he started to rage. 'Who the fuck do you think you are? Just who?'

'I'm an ex-soldier, husband, father, brother and son. And you're trying my patience.' Sam's voice never raised above conversational. 'Now, we need a meeting of minds here …'

31

OUTSIDE THE DOOR, Cal apologized to the young policemen with minimum explanation. They both heard Macho Mike's initial roar of enquiry. Cal told the junior officer to tell the truth and he'd better wait until Inspector Swindon gave him further instructions.

After ten long minutes of silence the door opened. Sam came out, Mike invited the constable in. The door closed. Two minutes later the constable exited, nodded to Sam with respect, possible reverence, and left. Mike asked Cal and Sam to go in.

'I wish to apologize for provoking you.' Mike spoke with subdued regard. Sam turned to Cal.

'Accepted. I shouldn't have struck you.' Cal knew Sam didn't appreciate lengthy explanations at apology sessions.

'South Division will proceed with the investigation. You will be kept in touch with what's going on.'

'Thank you.'

Sam left the room. As the door shut Mike spoke. 'Christ, he's been a player in his time. Why didn't you tell me?'

'You were too busy hating queers and blacks to listen.'

'Who is he?' Mike said.

'A man with some pretty good connections, never mind God.' Cal added some more detail.

'Remind me to learn to love the bas… I mean his holiness.'

'At least he's in the forgiveness business.' They laughed.

'Peace?' Mike said.

'Maybe. What did he say to you?'

'Not much. Enough to provide alternatives. Peace is an option and one I believe I'd like better than others.'

'Right. He's just had a big shock as well. The girl dying and his lost sister will take some handling.'

32

A BUMP jarred Eilidh into semi-consciousness. Blindfolded, she sensed people moving her somewhere strapped to a chair. Next, a diesel engine shook her as it started up and settled into a steady rhythm. Then someone rubbed her arm with cotton wool and again she felt the jab of a needle. Things began to blend voices, traffic noise and motion, until the world faded and a new nightmare clutched her to its heartless breast.

* * *

Next, another world. A civil servant told Eilidh she wouldn't be providing any more information. God, the disappointment was painful. Never mind, smile and say thank you, the contact had supplied excellent documentary evidence: dates, times, places, even a few names. Eilidh told herself to make a few notes and tweak her mind-map. She reached for her laptop just before it dissolved.

* * *

Something squealed and she returned to partial awareness as the vehicle jerked to a stop. Male voices buzzed and moved around. The sound of a bolt being slipped and a door opening was shockingly loud. A puff of manure-scented cold air burst in, followed by the grinding moan of a forklift. Awake but not fully conscious, lifted, moved and jerked about she became nauseous.

'Put her in the barn,' a gruff north-east English accent ordered.

33

CHARLIE JENKINS didn't like his brother questioning his business savvy, even if Bill was usually right.

Charlie had a tough self-image. His platinum hair was a fuzzy three millimetres long all over. A diamond stud sparkled in his left ear. Broad and flat, he had a face as hard as his fists and icy dark eyes. His thin lips had a permanent scowl which concealed bright white inward-facing jagged teeth like a shark. His physiology and psychology would readily be categorized as 'severe'. A bully by nature, he had broad shoulders, a slim waist and brutal hands. Keeping people in line came naturally. In his world, he was top dog.

One look and most men would stand aside, avoid his gaze or defer to him. He expected to get his own way.

Bill, his elder sibling, sat nearby, a bad day in prospect. He bemoaned the amazing stupidity of others, including his little brother, Charlie.

Bill possessed the same flinty expression and equally heartless eyes. As chubby as Charlie was lean, he affected business suits, loud silk ties and stylish hair. At one time his hands had been hard, but no longer, they were expensively manicured, nails smooth and pristine. Pulled tightly back, his blond mane was plaited and hung down between his shoulder blades. Cold green piggy eyes, which never seemed to blink, gazed with electric severity from his pasty face.

In the fearsome stakes, Bill enjoyed a chilling reputation more than equal to Charlie's. The legend told how, when younger, Billy had torn strips of skin off people who had earned his displeasure, using a knife and a pair of pliers, hence the nickname "Billy Pliers". People didn't cross Bill lightly.

Charlie and Bill made their living from criminal activities. Bill schemed and Charlie steamed, a partnership of strategy and enforcement. Two men in their early fifties, making money and enjoying life.

'Tommy is out of order,' Bill rumbled in his tough East-end accent. 'He's going to create trouble. There's plenty of money in everything else without moving into kidnapping and slavery.'

'Nah. It's safe enough. He picks 'em carefully. You get up to twenty-five grand for a pretty one, fifty for a princess. Don't need many of those to make a mint. He says he's already done twelve locally in the past six months. This is serious money.'

'It's bound to get rumbled. The press would love something like this.'

'Come on, Bill. He pays us twenty percent when he's on our patch. £250 grand for doing nothing. We're not traceable. That's good dosh. The girls disappear. The coppers don't know they're gone, and even if they start lookin', the tracks are icy cold.'

'I understand, but it's an ugly business. I don't like it. Is he still going for expansion?'

'Yeah. Says he's got new deals going in Nottingham, Leeds, Birmingham and Manchester. All the big cities.'

'What do we get?'

'Five a pop.'

'What's the plan?'

'Ten units a year from most cities, up to twenty from the bigger ones. We're talking about a million or two for us in a short time frame. Good money, low risk.'

'It bothers me. Not nice.' Bill would often come back to a point when he wasn't happy, the only person in the world who could disagree with his brother. 'Recreational candy is one thing. We're just the pipeline, logistics and distribution. These banker and Government types who support our transportation services are making life easy and low profile. Why take more risk?'

'Look,' Charlie spoke with exaggerated patience. 'It earns. It don't need effort. It's business. Who cares about missing people these days? The public's got a brain like a goldfish, they remember nothing. Anyway, we're not properly involved. We just get paid like serious businessmen.' Charlie knew Bill enjoyed being called a businessman.

'Charlie, you sure we're clear? No dirty connections?'

'No dirty connections. Not one.'

'Okay, I'm with you for now.'

34

'WE'VE GOT ONE victim in St Mary's.' Mike Swindon briefed a small investigative team. 'She had a real hammering, was raped and died a short while ago. This is now a murder enquiry. We think her name is Jenny Madden, aka "Jenny Joystick" or "JJ". Madden had some form and we'll formally confirm her identity shortly. She was a drug-user and had a lifestyle to support her habit: thieving, whoring and general ripping off. Let's see what more we can find out about her recent movements and who she's seen. There's a possible connection to Somerset or the West Country.

'You two start a *misper* file search, as far back as necessary. We need to find connections, any patterns. Check age, sex, background.

'You two, out on the ground. What's being said? There has to be some evidence. We've got three days. Report twice daily to me.

'The other is a missing person called Eilidh Duncan, that's spelt E-I-L-I-D-H. It's pronounced ay, as-in-say, lee. Any of you plods not know how to spell Duncan? She disappeared a few days ago, we think Thursday 17th May. She's a good girl as far as we know, not on the slippery slope, but you never can tell. She's been staying at Charlotte Street near the junction with Fitzroy Street, off Tottenham Court Road. Last seen at a club called the Neon Orchid located between Guildford Street and Theobald's Road.

'Inspector Cal Martin will be involved in the Duncan investigation. Dave Smiley and Flo' Binstead are assigned to work that one. Keep Inspector Martin in the loop. Give me a two-minute update twice a day. As you may have heard there is other assistance on this from outside the Met in the form of Colonel Sam Duncan, the missing girl's older brother. For now, we're cooperating with him. He has experience in counter-intelligence and investigation. In his retirement, he's become a fuckin' man-of-the-cloth, a vicar. *Best watch your language*.'

'Why's he involved, Mike?' One of the old sergeants spoke up.

'He's got good connections and I think it's in all our interests to work together. Here's some pictures of her. One last thing, guys, if nothing breaks in three days I'll be reviewing how we resource this. Superintendent Boyce is worrying about limited assets and results.'

General budget constraints had led to Superintendent Bobby Boyce stating they, 'weren't going to hammer this one for long.' Mike could remember his exact words. Somebody had given Bobby's bum a nip. *Bloody politics*.

35

THE FORKLIFT unloaded Eilidh in a dark, silent place. The container opened with a clank, she was unstrapped from the seat and led, still blindfolded and manacled, into a larger space. The atmosphere was cool but not cold. She was led to an old wooden chair and, thrust into it.

'Take some water.' She sucked greedily at a straw.

'Where am I?'

'Nowhere. Eat some food.' Someone pushed a pie into her mouth. She tried to eat and gagged slightly. Still, the man pushed the food at her, the greasy pie spread up her teeth and on to her gums. She couldn't resist the feeding.

'Easy,' another voice interrupted. 'She's to be kept in good condition, not harmed.'

'Feed her yourself then.'

The other man was gentler and it didn't take long. 'Do you need to go?'

'Yes.' She stood as a firm hand guided her. They walked towards a strong smell of stale urine. A door squeaked and the stench grew stronger. He took her blindfold off. He was stocky and wearing a black ski-mask.

'I'll free your hands and you can sort yourself. Any nonsense and you'll crap where you lie. Understand?'

She fought back tears. 'Yes.' Finding her way around a cluttered half-lit toilet, with stiff limbs was hard. She struggled to remove her overalls. The pot was icy, no seat and damp from other users.

She sorted her clothing wishing she could wash her hands. The man put her blindfold back on and led her to a cot, helped her lie down and handcuffed her again. The pillow smelt sour. The blanket itched with rough wool and straw. She thought she heard rats skittering about. An insect bit her arm but she couldn't scratch because of the cuffs. The captor followed a script before leaving.

'*Silly girl. This wouldn't be happening if you'd kept your nose out of matters that don't concern you.*' A cold rub of alcohol-soaked cotton wool then the prick of a needle. A damp, malodorous cover tucked up to her nose. The click of a key in a lock.

The nightmare followed her into unconsciousness. Her last thought was of Sam, confident he'd be looking for her … please God!

36

AN E-MAIL from the investment in Central Division pinged into Bill's mobile. What he called an 'investment' most people would have called a corrupt police officer. The person was high-level, ambitious and earned the money.

> *Interesting sniff. Mike Swindon of Team 5 is looking into the beating and murder of a girl called Jenny Madden, Jenny Joystick or JJ on the street. A team called Young Bloods delivered the pain. They've been very, very loud about a contract for the abuse and beating of JJ. It's a leak you may want to plug. Connects to the disappearance of one Eilidh Duncan. Her plastic was recovered in JJ's possession. Duncan's big brother is already in town and on the case, working with Inspector Calvin Martin. He knows about JJ and the credit card because the YBs missed it. Duncan's been spooky in his time and could be extremely dangerous if leads come back to your neck of the woods. He's pulling strings. Avoid direct conflict with him at all costs. The boat doesn't need rocking.*

* * *

Bemused at first, Bill started to generate steam. This sounded like Tommy Bain's work. Tommy generally made good moves, delivered cash and still would, even if the people trafficking stopped. Someone's brains were disengaged on this one. Why a fireworks display when a simple nipping of a bud would do the job?

You handled dropped balls and similar problems with discretion, a basic rule. Who'd set them on the girl? Tommy? Hard to believe, but he'd better check. Something had gone wrong. He picked up a phone.

37

'CLANCY'S BAR.'

'Tommy Bain there?'

The barman knew the voice. 'I'll get 'im.'

Tommy came on. 'Who's that?'

'Me. You have a problem. The YB bastards have given a caution to a person somehow associated with another missing person. The impossibility of a connection being made has happened.'

'Bill—'

'Don't interrupt, you stupid twat.' Bill's voice was icy hard, a sound to chill the bones. 'If the problem is yours, make sure it disappears. Sort out those YB bastards. Send a serious *fucking* communication. A brother of my acquaintance would be decidedly unhappy to know there's a problem here. He's done a lot of reassuring. Don't let him down!' The words dripped slow, deliberate menace.

'I'll fix things.' Tommy's adrenalin surged with fear and anger.

'See you do, Tom. See you do.' Bill hung up.

Tommy knew about paying his dues and sometimes 'taxes', as he thought of percentages. The taxmen were Billy 'Pliers' and Charlie, 'the flashing blade'. Bill was bad enough, but Charlie was evil, and he'd met a few. It'd be great to stick a flashing blade in him. Oh yes. His day would come!

He put the phone down and thought about things. God! He hated Bill and Charlie Jenkins, the nightmare pair. He'd better get moving and make a couple of calls.

38

'TAFFY?'

'Tommy.'

'You had a problem the other night you didn't tell me about?' There was a pause.

'Yes, Tommy.'

'So, tell me.'

'After the job, me and Gorki went for a spot of womanising. We picked up a young girl and she gave us a bit and we paid her. Her nickname's Jenny Joystick, JJ. Gorki forgot to dispose of the Duncan girl's stuff when we dropped her off at the warehouse. So we were shaggin' JJ in the van and she must've found the bag, and maybe some other kit. I didn't know till Gorki told me he'd missed the stuff. The girl nicked the bag when she left us. It was one of them small over-the-shoulder things.'

'Why didn't you call me?'

'We've been trying to get this sorted without dragging you in. I called Jackie. He fixed it, expensive bastard. Says we shouldn't show face for a time, people might remember us. We paid him a grand each from our own cash to cover the clean-up. We don't want to ruin our business relationship, Tommy.'

'It's affected, Bill Jenkins is unhappy and turning up the heat. The pair of you better take a holiday—not in the UK. Stay away three months. Leave tonight. Got that? God knows what damage you've done long-term. You're a pair of fuckwits. Staying around could cause you health problems. Am I clear?'

'Crystal. See you in three months.'

* * *

Tommy made one last call.

‘Jackie, you set the Young Bloods on that girl.’

‘Yes, Tommy. I fixed it like you told me to.’

‘Fixed it? Like fuck you fixed it.’ Tommy fought to control himself.

‘Tommy, Tommy. We got the bag back and it’s destroyed,’ Jackie soothed. ‘What’s wrong?’

‘Your Young Bloods missed a credit card, fuckin’ wankers. Now they’re sounding off about the contract in the street, playing like they’re big boys.’

‘They’re excited.’

‘Word got back to the gruesome twosome and they’re not best pleased. How much did you pay ’em?’

‘Pay who?’

‘The Young Bloods, you stupid twat.’ Tommy rolled his eyes and made a face at the phone.

‘600 quid, 200 a piece.’

‘You can use some of the £1,400 you’ve got left from the van-boys to make sure the YBs are sorted out and I never, ever hear any more about this. Understand?’

‘Yes.’

‘Don’t forget.’ He paused. ‘And by the way, there’ll be no grand from me, you greedy little bastard.’ He hung up.

‘Right, Tommy.’ Jackie wondered how Tommy had found out about the two grand. He’d be thinking about that for quite some time, but for now, the answer escaped him.

39

THREE YOUNG BLOODS boozed away in The Stork and Chimney, down a lane just off Shoreditch Road. To call it dingy would have heaped flattery on the place. They drank strong lager and verbally reviewed their 'sorting out' of a problem.

Replaying the girl's attempts to placate them and avoid violence seemed funny as they huddled together, enjoying a feeling of power and dark legitimacy. 'Man's gotta do who a man's gonna do' had become a shared punchline.

'Christ, she was funny when she was beggin' us to let her go.' The tallest of the three giggled, a thin, shaven-headed young man with a bad case of acne and a slightly squinting right eye. He wore tight jeans, big boots and a black sweatshirt like his mates.

'The scrubber begged and begged,' sniggered another, fatter YB. 'Please don't hurt me anymore.' He whined in an exaggerated way. His mates laughed. 'That punch in the mouth made 'er shut up. What a smacker. Boy, the way she sat down.'

'We're enforcers. We do 'em and they stay done.' Their leader a hard-faced, wiry, slightly older man, said. 'You made seventy-five quid each, the bitch takes a serious lesson, no one gives a fuck and we're havin' a good time.' The other two nodded. 'I reckon we'll get more contracts after this.'

In their self-absorbed talk, they didn't pay particular attention to three unremarkable types who walked in wearing hard expressionless faces and dark clothes. Anonymous.

'You the Young Bloods?' said one of the men.

'Yeah.'

'You do work for other people?'

'Sometimes.' The leader gave a hard stare. 'Who wants to know?'

‘We do. We’re looking for talent.’

The bar quietened. Four people put their drinks down and left. The barman confined his glass-wiping to the far end of the counter. His eyes formed an intimate relationship with the polished surface of the bar.

‘We are fuckin’ talent,’ said the fat YB. He began to guffaw in a harsh, hard man sort of way. His double chins belied his toughness as they squirmed against his tight sweatshirt.

‘Not enough.’ The statement arrived with a quick whipping blow from a cosh to the hinge of the fat YB’s jaw. The sound was similar to dropping a bag of marbles on a table. The blow smashed bone and dislodged several teeth.

Feeling no pain, the fat man collapsed straight down, unconscious, and toppled forward on to his face. A trickle of blood slowly spread on to the uneven surface. A white molar pushed out of the YB’s mouth with his first ragged snore.

The remaining YBs froze for a moment.

The skinny YB turned and tried to run but was cut off by two attackers. One of them grabbed him, slammed him into the wall and, as he bounced back, punched him in the throat and, twisting his fist into the back of his victim’s garment, held him up.

As the thin man gagged, the other assailant administered five solid blows with brass knuckles. Broke his nose. Gashed an eyebrow. Removed several teeth and splintered others. Smashed his lips and fractured his jaw.

The scrawny man made a mewling sound as he slid down the cheap plastic panelling. Blood and fragments of bone welled from his mouth. When his backside hit the floor he fainted and slid sideways to the floor, properly cautioned.

Acting on instinct, the YB leader, a seasoned if somewhat crude fighter, drove his half-empty pint glass straight into cosh-man’s face. The stunning reactive violence, almost impossible to predict, required the best of reflexes and awareness to deflect.

The glass broke against the ridge of cosh-man's eyebrow with a gentle chink and glanced downwards. It slashed through his eyelid before nicking his left eyeball. Next, it tore into his cheek in a squirt of blood. Blow completed, the boss YB pulled back his hand and rammed the jagged base into his victim's mouth.

The bubbling moan was as frightful a sound as a human can make, with the raw power of horror and agony. The damaged man stood wobbly and dazed, until a crunching head-butt dropped him.

The YB leader escaped through a fire exit at the rear of the bar by the toilets. A dark mixture of fear, adrenaline, anger and exhilaration lent him wings.

With their partner squirming on the tiles, the other two hard men eyed each other, nodded and left the pub.

Violence over, the barman dialled 999 and asked for 'ambulance and police'. One of the remaining customers attended the now unconscious YB by the wall, getting him into the recovery position. Next, he started on the glassed man, already well gone with shock.

Towards the back of the bar the fat YB, who had drunk a lot of strong beer lay quiet and ignored. He vomited. No one noticed. Unconscious, he drowned in a mixture of lumpy puke, beer, blood, teeth and snack remnants pooled into a small lake on the uneven floor. When more than his soul had passed, the stench alerted others to his plight, but it was too late.

Nine minutes after the trouble started the police and paramedics arrived. One corpse and two seriously injured men gave them pause. There were no witnesses.

40

'I COULD MURDER a fry-up.' Sam wore his dog collar.

Five minutes later he and Cal were in the hotel's diner, a counter with stools and direct service from a chef-cum-waiter who looked even older than the night-porter if such a thing was possible.

'Two full monties, young man.' Sam nodded at the balding cook in his white chef's jacket and blue beanie.

'Coming right up,' the man grinned, adding even more wrinkles and creases to an amazing relief map of a face. 'Fried bread as well?'

'Amen, brother.'

'I wasn't aware God let you Jocks represent him.'

'Only in the most heathen and debauched of lands.'

'I'd better give you extra toast to keep you going.'

'A thousand blessings on you.'

'Tea?'

'Please.'

'How'd you like your eggs?' They told him. 'Won't be a moment, gentlemen.'

An instant later two large steaming mugs, a jug of milk and a bowl of sugar arrived on the counter.

'Five minutes to further furring of the arteries, gentlemen.'

'Thanks, chef. I'm sure Him-upstairs won't consign you to hell for producing a fry-up.'

'Angel food right enough, vicar.' He made for the stove.

Ten minutes later, deep in conversation, they worked through well-cooked food. 'Okay. What have we got so far?' Sam said.

Out came Cal's notepad. 'Let's start with Eilidh. She lost touch with her family. She's missing. She met a new lad week-before-last: second date last Tuesday and another date on Thursday at the Neon Orchid. She didn't come back. Abby got our attention. Now we're ahead of the game in missing persons' terms.

'Understood. We believe she visited a club called the Neon Orchid, maybe more than once,' Sam said. 'There's further information to come from Mr O'Casey.'

'Checked him out, no form, has a colourful approach to life, the world and everything. Past connections with some paramilitary operations in the Emerald Isle might raise a glimmer of interest. No known activities over here.' Cal turned a page. 'As for Jenny, she's an addict. She hit the bottom and would've been dead within a year if she hadn't been murdered. She sold her body for money and stole things to pay for her habit. Jenny somehow got hold of Eilidh's credit card. Her beating wasn't a random event, the style doesn't fit with the MO we'd expect. Is there some connection with Eilidh's disappearance? Possible, might be indirect. It's probable she nicked more of Eilidh's stuff than the plastic.'

'So, what are the links?'

'Jenny, the credit card, the people who beat her and the bastards who hired them. The Neon Orchid because we assume she went there, but we need proof.'

'Think there might be a drug connection?' Sam asked.

'Maybe, but we've nothing to hang the hat on. Let's follow the leads.'

'Where do we start?'

'11 a.m. at the Waterloo Arches with Mr Stanley Parker. I think Mike Swindon is willing to send a couple of his guys to talk to people after we're done down there. We mustn't hold anything back from him.'

'We won't. Especially now he's inside the tent.' Sam winked.

'What'd you say to him?'

'Nothing much. Just a touch of interest alignment.' Sam smiled. 'How's that for political correctness? Mike enjoys and milks a tough reputation. He seems to be a good guy in a phone-directory-ripping sort of way. In fact, I quite like him.'

* * *

The phone vibrated in Sam's pocket. He checked the caller ID and sighed. 'Hi, Mum.'

'What's happening, Sammy?' Abby said.

'Cal and I are working on things. We'll know more soon.'

'Hec's coming back at lunchtime. We could come to London.' Abby's voice broke and a quaver started in her voice. 'Oh Sam, my wee girl.'

'Mum, the best thing you can do, for all our sakes, is sit tight and let us do our stuff. Karen will be happy if you want to go down and spend some time with her and the girls. I'll be back tomorrow. Keep your chin up.'

'I'll call Karen.' Her voice steadied. 'Bye, Sam.' She hung up.

* * *

'Cal, when I was on the dark side we used a wall and post-its to structure the parts of a story and put them in a time frame. What do you guys do?'

'We sometimes use walls, whiteboards, pieces of string and pictures. Nowadays, we even key information into computer outlining systems and query interlinked databases. The main thing you can't replace is the human brain. You going to change out of the vicar kit before you meet the Parker man?'

'No. I'm fine for now. I wore it to the hospital this morning.'

'I need to go to the office for half an hour. I'll catch you with Parker.'

'Sound.' Sam decided to walk to the meeting.

* * *

On his way to meet Parker, Sam switched on his phone. A text pinged in from Cal.

> *Got to attend a briefing down the nick. Catch up lunchtime.*

Sam replied.

> *OK see you.*

41

PARKER WAS WAITING when he arrived.

'Ah, the tartan holy man.' Parker's sonorous voice echoed from the hard brick walls. 'Where's your dark-hued friend?'

'Couldn't come.'

'Unreliable?'

'No, he's reliable. Just other things to do. Buy you a coffee?'

'I only drink coffee for breakfast.'

'What do you want?'

'A goodly glass of quality alcohol.' Parker spoke with a proper accent, pronouncing his words with a crystalline clarity BBC presenters would envy.

'That can be arranged. What's your poison?'

'West Coast single malt, brain food.' Parker's face showed anticipation, liquid brown eyes gleaming, inspired by the water of life.

'Know somewhere near here?'

'Of course. Follow me.' Parker kept up a surprising pace, his baggy trousers flapping in a breeze which had blown up, showing thin legs pressed against the shiny material. They walked for twenty minutes to an ancient pub on Park Street.

Sam bought a large Laphroaig with a half pint of Ruddles County for himself. They sat on the riverside terrace and let the world go by as they talked. Trains rumbled past on the railway bridge to Cannon Street Station. Traffic stuttered and honked on Southwark Bridge. Threatening clouds rolled up the Thames.

Parker sipped his whisky with obvious pleasure. 'Samuel Pepys watched the Great Fire of London from here. The new Globe Theatre is just around the corner. Dr Johnson worked near here from time to time. This place is steeped in history. Now, Vicar, tell me why you want to know about Jenny.'

'First the bad news. Jenny died this morning. She never recovered consciousness after her operation.'

'Give me a moment. I'm so sorry to hear that. I'd hoped she'd be saveable. Poor girl.' They sat in silence for five minutes.

* * *

'Now, Sam, explain your interest in Jenny.'

Sam gave a brief version, sticking to relevant facts. Finishing with: 'My sister's credit card was found in Jenny's shoe. Current thinking is she was attacked to recover stolen goods. Anything you can add will be useful.'

'Jenny did some petty thieving, this time from the wrong people?'

'Perhaps. What did you find out?'

'A bit. One of my homeless friends was all boxed up when the baddies came to call. He stayed hidden and didn't try to intervene. There were three of them. They called themselves the "Young Bloods" which, I have to say, lacks any sense of originality.

They used words like "bitch," "slut," "scrubber" … you know, the sort of language that justifies the misery they inflict. One of the attackers mentioned some names before being told to shut up: Tim or Tom, Thomas … maybe Tommy, and a Jack or Jackie. They informed her she was being punished. She gave up the goods she'd stolen, but evidently, not the credit card found in her trainer.'

'Any idea where this happened?'

'Yes. Some of Jenny's friends moved her when they realized she needed help. Took 'em two days to decide. They didn't want the police digging around in their cardboard city too much.'

* * *

'What are you doing here, Parker?'

'Justice.'

'For whom?'

'My son and my wife. Drugs killed my only boy, Jasper, and destroyed his mother as he faded away.' Sam heard the flatness of voice and noticed Parker's eyes were welling with tears.

'Tell me more.'

'I'm a lawyer, barrister, not a man of physical action. My world is the commercial side of of law. I have friends and contacts throughout the City. I am The Establishment. I was an innocent. I'm wealthy. My life revolves round deals and money. I asked few questions of myself, assured of my respectability, until my son fell off the world.' He paused and looked at Sam.

'Off the world?'

'Jasper died fourteen months ago. I didn't know him properly. Too busy. Gave him money. My connections provided work.' He halted again, gazing at the past.

'Go on.' Sam said.

'He went through the young idealist stuff in his teens, rebelled at university, still got a reasonable degree. His mother begged me to help and I said he was just growing up. By the time I realized he needed support it was too late. He called me an inaccessible, insensitive and pompous old fart, who only cared about business and money. I pleaded with him, but he left.'

'Ouch.' Sam said.

'He was right about me. I told myself he needed time. Of course, I was avoiding reality. Eventually, I had a private investigator track him down. By then he was too far gone with AIDS. He hadn't been getting treatment.'

'No treatment.'

Parker nodded, 'naturally, I arranged the best of medical help and support. Too late again. The end of his young life happened in a hospice. Nothing to be done, you see.' A tear trickled from his eye.

'You don't have to go on.'

'Maybe, but I will. The love of his life was a man called Barry.' Parker's eyes saw another time and place. He wiped his eyes with the back of his hand. 'Have you ever seen a person as thin as a stick, how big their eyes are? My Jasper was lying on a bed, in a loving space, tubes everywhere. Barry was with him, a lovely young fellow. We meet now and again.'

'Sounds like a nice person, Barry.'

'Yes, very nice.' A deep, slow sigh wheezed as Parker closed his eyes and shook his head with gentle sadness. 'Three weeks were all he had left. We talked and made up. He forgave me and asked my forgiveness. I was there when he died, Barry holding him tight and me clutching his lifeless hand, his mother sitting rigid at the bedside. You've no idea, Sam.' He contemplated Sam for a moment. 'Then again, maybe you do.' He sniffed, pulled out a hanky, blew his nose and wiped his upper lip.

'And then … ?'

'My wife died six months ago. Couldn't come to terms with Jasper's death. Reminds me of the old cliché, "broke her heart and she wasted away". I discovered how little I'd invested in our marriage. I couldn't build communication bridges with her after the fact. Her life ended as our boy withered away. She'd nothing left for me.'

Sam nodded. 'Tough stuff.'

Parker nodded in turn. 'At first, I fantasized about death. Then I realized what I could do. My reach and resources are considerable. Real people are damaging themselves and being damaged. I decided to do something discreet yet worthwhile. I've kept my finger in the legal pie. I'm quietly finding out what goes on from another perspective.'

'Challenging?'

'Of course, I come down here and work with the inhabitants. I behave, shall we say, otherworldly, strange perhaps, but now they accept and trust me. They talk and share. I watch the soap opera of life at the bottom, listening, finding out and becoming aware. I'm building a picture, discovering opportunities to help.' He stopped. 'That was an excellent whisky.'

Sam bought him another, this time a Bowmore.

'Good Lord, another splendid dram. Dr Johnson was wrong, my boy. There are two good things to come out of Scotland, the road to England and Islay Malt whisky.'

'You've had a tough time.' They sat in silence for a moment. 'Now Parker, I'd be grateful if you'd point me at the site of Jenny's beating. I hope you're willing to help as we go along.'

'Happy to.'

'Thanks. You think this might be a little dangerous, don't you?'

'Perhaps, I'm not sure.

'Cal is a policeman and we are looking into a tricky situation. You say you are establishing yourself with these people for positive reasons. What a shame if helping us affected your aims. We must avoid that.'

'Sam, are you a genuine minister? You seem less otherworldly than any man of the cloth I've ever met.'

'I thought I was cut out for the Kirk, a mistake. I'm ordained and still keep my hand in for friends, you know: baptisms, weddings, funerals and so on.'

Parker nodded. 'Here's a card. Now let me tell you how to get to the place where Jenny was assaulted. Go out of here and turn towards the river. Turn right under the railway bridge to Clink Street, then right again and first left into Winchester Walk. Here, I'll draw you a map. He pulled out a piece of paper from his inside jacket pocket, made his drawing and handed it over, 'Do, please, keep in touch.'

'I will, thanks for your help.'

As Sam walked away Parker took out his mobile and made a call.

42

ONCE PAST the railway Sam called Cal and told him about the meeting. 'I'm off to the Arches now.'

'Watch your back, Sam. Not all the people in the area there are good for your health. In fact, I'll join you. Be there in ten minutes.'

'Right-oh.' Some company wouldn't hurt. He walked on. It took fifteen minutes.

* * *

'Well met, oh mighty one,' said Cal.

'So where's the fifth arch, after the second arch with fancy brickwork on the left, Nathan Lane? I'm walking up and down this lane and can't find the fancy brickwork.'

'Nathan Lane or South Nathan Lane?'

'Hmm, let me look,' Sam said. He's written squiggle, Nathan Lane. You're right, South Nathan.'

'South Nathan is about 100 yards from here and runs off at forty-five degrees right round a corner.' They set off.

'Any news, Cal?'

'O'Casey phoned. He wants to meet you, says he's got something. Sounded quite keen.' They were near the left turn.

'Mike's briefed a team. We've got three days. He's put some energetic people on the case.'

'Is energy is all we're going to get?'

'Let's just say they're young officers.'

'I suppose four pairs of hands are better than nothing.'

'Don't blame Mike. He's getting no help from the ivory tower'.

They turned into South Nathan Lane. The Arches were on the right, old doors damaged and rotting, some timbers missing or snapped like discoloured, broken teeth. A scattering of dirty faces of indeterminate sex could be seen through the first entry and replicated in the next three.

'Number five and no one's home.' Cal caught Sam's elbow and pulled him past the opening. 'Just a sec. Let's check this is right.' They walked on. 'We'd best be prepared for a surprise. It's the only one with no people. Why?'

'Someone dump a vindaloo?' said Sam.

'Paranoia?'

'Are we going in?'

'Do you see a white hat?'

Both men changed their breathing rhythm, easing their muscles instinctively. The sense of expectancy heightened awareness and adrenalin had a comfortable familiarity. They entered the archway and stopped, letting their eyes adjust to the shadowy light.

'This must be the one,' said Cal. 'Maybe over there.' Above them the walls sloped inwards towards broken brick a darker hue of red because of the gloom. They increased the space between them and followed the wall Sam to the outside. They moved in a way that gave each of them a wider field of vision. Even though expected, when the voice came it was startling.

'Vicars and wogs. Now there's a new party idea!' said a gravelly voice.

'Vicars and wogs putting their noses where they don't belong,' a second man spoke, equally tough-sounding but more nasal.

'No, lads. Priests and witch doctors.' Yet another voice joined in.

'One black one, one white one. Where's the one with the fairy light on?' A fourth man sang in a tuneful tenor—not quite the rugby song Sam remembered.

'Enough of the humour, lads,' said raspy voice. 'What do you foolish people think you are doing in our manor?' In the twilight of the arch they could make out the faces of the four men ranged against them, each with a club of some sort in his hand.

'I'm looking for my sister. I wonder if you can help me?'

'You don't belong here. We are going to give you a memento of your trip to London and you'll leave town, never to return. That goes for you too, Sambo. We don't like Rastas here.'

'But we don't know you.' Sam said.

'You have caused offence, my son. And you will be punished. A broken leg for you and a sound spanking for Sambo.'

'Why do you want to hurt us?' The old concentration tuned in. 'Can't we persuade you to let us go and say no more about this?' Sam said.

'Nah, it's lesson time. Which leg?' He smacked his hand with his club.

'Pick one and make your move.'

"Rasper" charged towards Sam raising his cosh. His rhythm broke as his intended victim flowed towards him.

Sam pushed his left elbow inside the line of the blow then pivoted his forearm to the vertical, forcing his opponent's energy outwards and his centre of balance upwards.

He slid his hand up to his assailant's wrist gaining control by pressing his thumb on the man's knuckles then rotating the hand to lock the wrist. His right palm levered immense pressure on the attacker's elbow and upwards to his shoulder. The turn and leverage forced the assailant to bend downwards, the club falling from this hand.

He started to scream as Sam followed through and drove him into the ground. At the same time slamming on extra force with his left forearm.

The defensive move dislocated "Rasper's" shoulder and elbow, and fractured his wrist. The agonized howl ended abruptly as Sam's elbow strike to the side of his face, below the ear, knocked him out.

While Sam defended himself, Cal disabled another man who fell, dazed, to the floor. He swivelled to face a second assailant who tried to stop moving forward, a little too late.

Cal feinted in a couple of directions and sold a 'dummy'. The man slowed down as he fought to adjust to the changing movement, lost balance and bent forward. Cal inflicted a percussive strike, slapping both of his opponent's ears hard between his hands. Semi-conscious, the man wailed in agony, fell to his knees, handcuffed in a moment.

The fourth attacker, facing Sam, held his hands palms up, 'we didn't mean to hurt you too much, just warn you off.' The whine grated.

Sam said, 'I'm going to ask you a few questions. You will answer them.' The man turned to run and was grabbed by the collar. Of similar size to Sam but in the wrong league, he lashed out with his fists. Sam took a glancing blow on the shoulder, then slammed his forearm hard under his assailant's eyebrows smashing his nose. As the man staggered back, Sam grabbed his hand and twisted to lock his arm out.

'You've seen how this works. Got your attention? Now, the questions. Failure to answer will have repercussions. Who sent you?'

'Fuck off.' The defiance was surly, brittle and understandably nasal. This was followed by a scream as Sam dislocated one of the man's fingers. The dislocation made a juicy plopping sound.

'That's one little piggy. Lots more where that came from. Who sent you?' The man started to cry, blood running from his nose mingled with tears and dropping to the floor.

'Fuck off.' Then he screamed again. Plop!

'That's two little piggies. You won't enjoy hands, knees and whoops-a-daisy!' Cal saw the set of Sam's face. Chilling. 'I'll ask again, who sent you?'

The man sobbed. He spoke in a whisper, 'Jackie Steel.'

'Louder.'

'Jackie Steel.'

'Why?'

'I don't know!'

'Tell me more.' Sam took the next finger in his hand and started to twist.

'No, please. There's been a cock-up. Jackie says we're making our bones with some big people. I dunno anything else. I'm only a soldier. Please don't hurt me again.'

'Where do we find Jackie?'

'Shoreditch.'

'Anyone else?' He tweaked the finger.

'Tommy Bain.'

'Who else?'

'Nobody! Nobody!'

Sam gazed at him, quiet, for a few seconds. He nodded his head. 'Right. Sorry about your fingers. Let's see if we can reconnect them shall we.' The assailant looked dubious. 'Trust me, I'll fix them. Three days and you'll never know we had a run-in.'

* * *

The man didn't struggle and followed instructions. Sam turned him around, gripped the fellow's arm with his elbow and pulled the man's hand across his stomach. Then holding the wrist tight, grabbed each bent finger in turn and pulled it straight. 'Christ!' The attacker squawked briefly.

'Now, wiggle. Any easier?'

'Yeah.'

'Sit on the floor and stay put.' The man did as he was told, sat down and stared at the concrete surface. Sam turned to Cal.

The sound of police sirens wailing grew louder. 'I'll keep an eye on them. Go get your mates.' Cal left and, two minutes later, returned with Mike Swindon.

43

'HI, MIKE.'

'Reverend Duncan. I believe there's been a bit of a rumble with some hard men.'

'Pure self-defence. Minimum force.' Sam gazed into Mike's eyes, calm and cold. 'Ever heard of the name Jackie Steel? Seems he's the person who set up our little meeting with these hoodlums.'

'The man's an aspiring tadpole but lacks the brains to make a frog. He hasn't enough charisma, contacts or juice to make a prince.'

'Tommy Bain was the other name.'

'Ahh. A bigger fish.' Mike's face creased into a smile that stretched the scar tissue around his nose. He winced as the cut on his lip expanded. 'The good news is that you two are okay and there's confirmation something's going wrong for someone. They're getting twisted knickers and making bad moves.' He hesitated for a moment and looked at a man with a squashed nose clutching sore fingers.

'You arrived in an almost timely way.'

'Confidential tip-off, Vicar, from someone we both know. You two have a guardian angel, scales of justice in one hand and a telephone in the other.'

'Tell me more about the names, Mike.'

'Jackie works on the fringes of badness, dirty but unimportant work mostly.'

'And Tommy?'

'Tommy Bain. Bit of a nutter and tends to get away with things. He's shrewd and a frightener. It's bad news if you're up his nose.'

'Maybe we're up it, or about to be.'

'Take care then, Vicar. You're getting into an evil school.'

44

'GUESS WHAT Eilidh did?' Mike said.

Sam beckoned with both hands, 'come on, tell me.'

'She sent a photo from her mobile to her flatmate the other night. Shirl forwarded the pic this morning. Here, have a look.'

'Took her time,' Sam said.

'Eilidh emailed it. Her pal's been doing big shifts and staying at the hospital, only just checked her email.'

'Handsome guy.'

'I don't think he knew he was being photographed.' The snap was taken from table level pointing upwards capturing a good-looking olive-skinned young man with dark eyes and curly hair. He had a fairly square jaw and Cupid's bow lips. He was looking to the left, his right hand raised in greeting towards someone. His mouth was puckered to one side as if he was saying something or about to smile. In the background was a wall with some gilt light fittings and a few blurry people milling about.

‘They date and time stamp these things like e-mails’ Sam said.

‘Yes.’

‘When was this taken?’

‘The night we think she disappeared. Ten forty-nine.’

‘Where?’

‘Someone’s going round to the Neon Orchid to either confirm or eliminate it as the place. The picture enhanced pretty well, so we should get a positive confirmation.’

‘I quite like O’Casey.’

‘There you go being a vicar. Soft on the villains.’

‘I didn’t know he was a criminal, Mike. Got a secret you’re not sharing?’

‘No. I don’t like the nightclub culture. It hurts lots of kids. The herd grazes on Ecstasy and moves on to binge drinking, hard drugs and violence. I’d close the bastards down. We spend huge amounts on cleaning up after avoidable stupidity—waste of fuckin’ time if you don’t sort the cause.’

‘I understand.’

‘I’m heading back with the walking wounded. We’ll keep tabs on the hospitalized. Bye.’ With that he departed, leaving two officers to secure the site for the scene of crime people.

‘I want a private word with you.’ Cal’s face was serious.

45

THEY FOUND a quiet tearoom nearby and an empty corner table by a window. The physical tension of the conflict dissipated over a mug of tea and a couple of silent minutes. They gazed at a rainy street. The reversed window letters advertised wondrous coffees, cakes and light snacks. The hiss and swish of traffic tyres sounded like surf draining through stones on a shingle beach.

'Got something on your mind, Cal?'

'You're on my turf, you ruffle feathers, but you aren't a policeman. You don't know this world, Sam. I care about Eilidh. I care about you.'

'Thanks.'

'This afternoon, if you'd gone to the arch alone, there's a pretty good chance you'd have had a serious hiding. Parker must've had a similar feeling.'

'I buy that.'

'Sam, don't you think this is getting a bit hairy? You were an expert soldier. You've done some off-the-record thuggery, or should I say "special ops."'

'You saying I'm over the hill? Think I should join the twenty-first Mechanical Zimmer brigade?'

'That's not what I mean, this is important. Come on, Sam, horses for courses.'

'Time for me to lose all sense of heroism, aggression and my nail-the-baddies ethic?'

'Stop taking the piss. There are leads, some people to talk to and expert investigators. We're well resourced.'

'Glad to hear it.'

'You put the frighteners on that guy in the Arches big-time—and scared me too. You sailed near the wind there, mate, this isn't a war zone.'

'Surprised me as well, but we're talking about Eilidh here. Then there's Jenny in the morgue. We got two names out of the man. I won't apologize for doing what had to be done, sorry if it gave you pause.'

‘I’ll cut to the chase, Sam. We’ll do the looking and I’d be happier if you weren’t under our feet.’

‘I’m inclined to agree with you, Cal. Let me disappear for a couple of days. Got some things to do before I catch up with O’Casey, then I’ll take off. ‘I’ll be back for an update.’ He reached out and rubbed Cal’s tightly curled hair. ‘Tough to tell me you’re all growed-up now, isn’t it?’

‘Yeah. You being decrepit and all, Scottish wild man!’

‘One thing, Cal, I’m wondering how those guys were tasked to hammer us, knew where we’d be and all that good stuff. ‘*Vicars and wogs looking into things where they don’t belong*’. How’d they find out?’

‘Parker?’

‘No, why would he send the police to rescue us? If not him, then who?’

‘Fair question, Sam. Somebody got Jackie Steel focused. A low-life like him doesn’t have big connections. He does what he’s told and, in his case, tasks need to be explained several times and clearly numbered if they’re going to be done right.’

‘Okay. So who pushed Jackie Steel’s button?’

‘Someone who wanted things to happen straight away who is desperate enough to use Jackie. Look, to be honest, the Jackie connection doesn’t make a lot of sense.’

‘How come they were waiting for us where Jenny got hammered, and not where she was found?’

‘Someone involved had to know the place it happened. The police weren’t aware until either Parker phoned Mike, or you’d told him where we’d arranged to meet.’

‘I didn’t tell Mike.’

‘Okay. Our attackers came to sort us out. They waited for us at the exact place where the assault happened. You’re off your patch, the light’s poor, they’re expecting us. They don’t know you’re the law, but they do know about us.’

‘Who might be aware of us looking about the Arches, Sam?’

‘The bad guys, Macho Mike and some police colleagues, Parker. The people who saw us at Parker’s patch? O’Casey didn’t know about our Arches excursion. At least I didn’t tell him.’

‘Me neither.’ Cal said.

‘We’ve eliminated Parker and O’Casey for the moment, so that leaves the fuzz.’

Cal stiffened, his face hardened. ‘That’s seriously out of line. Mike’d never do a thing like that.’

‘I’m not saying Mike would. Others might.’

‘Let’s not go there. In an organization the size of the Met, there’s bound to be corruption, but not Mike, not our guys.’

‘Fair enough. I’m under your feet, and now I’ve offended you. Please keep it in mind. I could be wrong, but I’m staying open to possibilities.’

‘Can’t say I’m happy, but I’ll bear it in mind. I’d like you to leave town as planned. You do get up people’s noses at times.’

‘Yeah, Karen says that too, I told her you’d called me “pushy” now she’s calling me Mr Pushy.’

‘Karen’s got sense.’ A half smile.

‘Cal, I’m not trying to tell you your job. In your shoes, I’d be getting tired of me throwing my weight about and challenging loyalties, but we have to face all possibilities. I’ve been there. If there’s a leak, best be open to the prospect early on. It makes sniffing things out easier and less bloody.’

Cal’s shoulders slumped and he sighed. ‘Sam, I’m sorry, you’re right. We can’t exclude any possibilities.’

His mobile rang.

He looked at Sam. ‘Positive ID. It’s the Neon Orchid in Eilidh’s picture.’

'O'Casey here I come. There's a couple of hours before I'm off to Gatwick. Keep in touch.' Tired and a little fraught, they shook hands.

Sam paid the bill, went outside and caught a cab. Cal walked to the nearest tube station. On the way, thoughts percolating and infusing like a good brew of coffee, he realized how angry and yet controlled Sam had been. How gentle, yet scary. He enjoyed the protection of his job. Who protected Sam?

46

'TOMMY BAIN here. I arranged a caution for the YBs.'

'Tough stuff, Tommy, tough stuff. More than I expected.'

'I want to make amends.'

'We'll see.' Bill disconnected the phone. The stirrings of anger played with his jaw muscles, his normal response to frustration. Sure, Tommy was trying to please him. At the same time, he couldn't believe how inept the caution had been. The fiasco with the Young Bloods, one dead, two seriously damaged. A bloody horror story.

He sat in the rear of the car calming down, heading for his office in a new Dockland development he owned. The Docklands Light Railway was nearby and the City was easy to reach. The place had wonderful vistas if you liked docks. Glass doors led into a beautiful reception area staffed by lovely girls who added real quality.

In the back, through a security number pad, lay the offices and nerve centre of his business empire. He loved returning from a meeting, stepping out of the Rolls and walking into the executive area, class, *pure class*.

The office made a statement of power, control and style. He loved his eight-foot wide teak desk. His black leather seat had more cushions, cosseting more parts of the anatomy than a hedgehog had pricks. The phones (two), computer keyboard, mouse and thirty-inch LCD screen gleamed black and high-tech. Across from the desk, a low four-piece suite in black leather surrounded a smoked-glass coffee table.

The walls were covered with pictures and photographs of boxing stars and celebrities, all signed 'to Bill' with a little personal message of some sort. The deep-piled wine-red carpet colour coordinated with the blotters, coasters and writing pads. A 'proper' black Italian coffee machine in the corner matched a fridge and well-stocked bar. Beside his desk, a fifteen-foot picture window gave an unmatched Dockland view. He looked forward to getting back to his lair.

* * *

Charlie sat staring at the Dockland panorama, unfocused, brooding, concerned about the Tommy thing. He'd spent time persuading Bill of his ability to spot opportunities and make a contribution to revenues. Bill kept telling him 'discretion, Charles … to avoid the heat, just be discreet.' *FUCK!* Tommy was being about as unobtrusive as the QM2 in Southampton dock.

He felt insignificant beside Bill, useless, not a partner, a spare part. He sat at a corner of Bill's desk awaiting his return. His sense of inferiority catalysed the rage and emotion churning in his gut.

Charlie's laptop spoke in a breathless, sexy female voice. 'Ooh! Guess what I've got for you.' He smirked, in spite of his anger. It sounded so cool to him. He ran his finger along the trackpad and clicked on the e-mail. The message came from the investment, forwarded to him by Bill. Charlie's stomach started to churn.

Do you know this man? He has been ID'd as the likely abductor of a certain young lady. The Vicar was attacked and sorted out the attackers with a helper. The bad boys gave up the names Jackie Steel and Tommy Bain.

The Young Bloods thing is a disaster. Who arranged that? Murder and very serious assault. Sometimes punishment has to be resisted. One of the punishers is in custody. I don't think he'll talk, he's a pro. He'll probably walk anyway. The YB who escaped sounds like a wild man.

Batten down the hatches.

* * *

Charlie opened the picture. Mmm, a pretty boy. He liked pretty boys, a secret pleasure. He made trips to Spain and other places where he indulged the need. Women were okay up to a point, especially on home turf with little choice. He didn't recognize the boy but one of the lads would.

* * *

Bill walked into the office. 'Talk of the devil …' He took a seat opposite Charlie. 'The investment doesn't sound too happy.'

Charlie put on his stone face.

'I forward stuff to you, Charles. I keep you in the loop, don't I?' Bill, without trying, emphasized the facts of life: remember who's boss. Charlie's demeanour stayed sullen. 'Charlie, Charlie, I'm your brother. I'm good at what I do. You're good at your stuff. We've got to build on our strengths. We need to sort this out and learn.'

'Bill, I just want to help. The business is different from twenty years ago. I'm like a spare part. My stuff is hardly needed anymore.'

'Don't be daft. Of course you're needed. We must act before things unravel any further and manage the situation. Certain lines of enquiry need to be blocked. In fact, I think a spot of discreet erasure is needed. We may need to amputate some rotting flesh. Prune the tree. Bury some secrets, if you get my drift. Now, who's the bleedin' expert in that department?'

They looked at each other then laughed aloud.

'Right mate, we can plan this one together. Then you take the lead and fix the bastards.'

'We'll sort them, Bill, we bloody well will.'

'Let's start thinking now and meet around 4 o'clock to agree our way ahead.' Bill took charge as always. He nodded to Charlie who rose and left.

His eyes weren't smiling when the door shut behind his brother. What had got into Tommy Bain? He'd need to make sure his business partners didn't panic over the situation.

Bill believed City people were short on bottle in the world of illegitimate demand, supply and laundering. As for the contraband suppliers, they liked you to make your money quietly. They paid well for a reliable conduit: an invisible, quiet, ripple-free channel to market. Decisive action was needed. Stick to your core business. As for the rest, no trails, no links, not a voice to be heard.

How did you get a crazy vicar off your back? The investment—a Chief Superintendent—and he needed to talk. The direct line in the investment's office rang five times and stopped. This happened every ten minutes until an e-mail arrived.

Usual place. 10 a.m. tomorrow.

Bill and the investment seldom met, but they had a crisis in the making. Bill preferred to watch a person's eyes as advice was given. Thinking done and action planned, he leaned back and thought about some angry and devious people.

47

SAM MET O'CASEY in his office at the rear of the Neon Orchid. Both sat comfortably in easy chairs. A half-empty cafetière of excellent Colombian coffee added a delightful aroma to the atmosphere. There was a steaming stoneware mug in front of each of them. Chocolate biscuits dressed in bright foils lay in a scattered heap on a plate, untouched.

A gentle Irish brogue. 'I mentioned you to friends. You've played tough in your time, in the Troubles and all that awful stuff.'

'True.'

'Does the name Orin O'Reilly mean anything to you?'

'Aye. I remember him.'

'You killed him.'

'Yes.'

'My cousin was the priest who gave him the last rites, and you a hard time. Can you believe the experience took away any doubts he had about supporting the peace? He said you were a good man, even in our family too. He held you up—a British soldier—as an example of why the fighting had to stop. God, you must have put on quite a display. Wait till I tell him you're a man of the cloth now. He'll probably become a feckin' Protestant.'

'Father Brendan Haughey?'

'The self-same,' O'Casey said.

'He and I met a couple of times after O'Reilly's passing. He helped me understand the deep sense of injustice the Catholic community has experienced over the years, the anger and frustration of being second-class citizens. I liked him.'

'He respects you.'

'Now,' Sam said, 'to business. My sources tell me you're fairly clean. You dabbled in the politics of the Emerald Isle as a young man. They don't cast you as a problem, at least not anymore.' Sam let the words sink in and went on. 'Anyway, I'm not here to discuss politics, be a covert operative or anything else. I'm looking for my sister. What can you do for me?'

'We'll cooperate. We'll ask around. We'll keep your friends on the force posted.'

'Thanks, Colm. There might be troubled waters ahead, dangers we're not aware of, and consequences for you we can't predict. My water says there's a fair chance things'll get worse before they get better.'

'You're laying this on quite thick, Sam.'

'Any commitment needs the eyes to be open. I want you to be aware of a possible downside.'

'I understand. We'll still help. We can't have criminal kidnapping going on in our venue. Our eyes are open and our heads up,' O'Casey said.

'Thank you. Let's get to facts. What do you know?'

'One of our regulars may have been involved in the disappearance of your sister. The police made a positive ID on our premises on the likely night of that event.'

'So I hear,' Sam said.

'Our team has seen the young man around here on more than one occasion. Next time he shows we'll notify the police.'

'Thanks.'

'Your turn. You're telling me this may be the tip of an iceberg. Does this mean, possible connections to other nefarious activities by, shall we say, criminal interests? You suggest this could get exciting but you're talking about an excitement I'd rather do without. Then you equivocate. Any feckin' things you aren't telling me just now?'

‘No, of course not. This morning I stood by the bedside of a young woman and watched her die. At first, the police thought she was my sister.’

‘Nightmare.’

‘Yes. Four hours later, I was attacked.’

‘Ouch!’

‘I survived.’

‘How’s the other guy?’

‘Concussion, mild bruising, one or two fractures.’

‘No shit, Sherlock.’

‘Cal Martin is a beast when he gets moving,’ Sam said.

‘Yeah, right. So what are you going to do next?’

‘After we’re done I’m off home. I expect to return in the near future. Now, you wanted to talk to me about something else …’

‘Yes. My investors need comfort and this situation will worry them, to say the least. Promise me you’ll try to protect our interests. This is a good clean business with no troublesome reputation. We’re profitable. We’re getting investment lined up to start a chain of clubs in the UK and Ireland. It has taken a lot of hard work and I want to protect it. I mean every word I say about what we’ll do because it’s the right thing. If it leads to problems for me, will you help out?’

‘Of course. Any skeletons in this cupboard of yours?’

‘Nothing momentous.’

‘If the situation is as you say you can count on me. Anything murky, let’s agree to talk and clarify. No guarantees. You can always rely on my gratitude for your help with Eilidh. Don’t think I’ll sell out my friends, principles or the police.’

‘Thanks, Sam. No sell-out required.’ O’Casey smiled.

‘I expect the constabulary will be round soon to follow through on the investigation. Have you any security video?’

'Yes, digital. We have copies. The police are welcome to take what they want. We cover the main entrance and the two fire exits. One comes out in the lane at the back, the other at the front. Plus a new camera above the exit we bring stock through. We're preparing a copy of the footage for the last week.'

'Thanks. Not much more to say. I'll get out of your hair.'

They shook hands. Sam headed for the Tube, Victoria and the train to Gatwick. As he left the Neon Orchid, a watcher took around twenty high-resolution shots from a car across the street. An interested party received the pictures within ten minutes.

48

THE LAST FEW days had been hectic. Sam decided to switch off. With two hours to kill, he stopped in a pub for a sandwich and a pint.

Taking a paper from the rack, he sat down to enjoy a cool air-conditioned breeze in relative peace. An amorous prelate was being savaged for finding love in the choir. Trouble enough for the poor man, but even more so because he was involved with an all-male choral group. He chortled. Some interesting quotes kept him amused. His mobile vibrated with an incoming call

'Hello.'

'Are you Eilidh Duncan's brother?'

'Yes.'

'I'm Jamie Carron, her editor. What's all this about her having disappeared?' He spoke with a slight lisp in a squeaky high-pitched voice.

'She's missing. Hasn't been to her flat for days. We're rather concerned. Can you cast any light on this?' Sam said.

‘Eilidh has been working on a story with real potential.’

‘What’s she researching?’

‘Can’t say. Confidential.’

‘Are you free just now? Could we meet?’

‘Where are you?’

‘About a ten-minutes from Victoria.’

‘Sorry, too far, I’ve no time available. Will you be back in town soon?’

‘Yes.’

‘Phone me when you get back.’

‘Some things have come up. Can I have your number?’ The other end was silent. Jamie had rung off, his number was blocked.

Sam texted Cal:

> *Spoke to Jamie Carron, E’s editor. Not helpful. No contact information. Knows what she’s working on. Big story. Won’t tell.*

* * *

The fun drained out of the article. Sighing, Sam closed his eyes and imagined his sister in the protective bubble of light. She had to be alive. His phone vibrated, Cal’s reply:

> *We’ll look into him. Speak later. Watch your back.*

49

SAM CALLED Cal from the Gatwick Express. ‘How you doin’?’

'Tense. We've stumbled into a complicated situation. The Young Bloods, the yobs who hammered Jenny Madden, were in a fracas in Shoreditch last night. One of them is dead, I'll know more later.

'Ouch.'

'One thing concerns us. The bad guys are ahead of the game. They must have good intel, they're moving fast, way too fast.'

'They're well informed.'

'Right, maybe a leak. Shit!'

'Tough one, Cal, but a strong possibility.'

'Right. Madden is dead, you and I attacked, and the Young Bloods get a doing. All this in two days. Talk about crazy, reactive and fuckin' dangerous. Mike has a lead on pretty boy. He should be able to tell us something. What we don't know is the reach of these people, but their moves are scarily good. You get the drift?'

'Danger outside of London. Maybe in the provinces?' Sam said.

'Spot on. You're heading in the right direction. In your shoes I'd want to keep my family safe. These guys are violent, in a hurry and we've no idea how we're hurting them or what they're trying to protect. The simple fact is they seem to be overreacting everywhere.'

'You're right. The violence is frightening. The action is happening crazy quick and disjointed, it's barely controlled. I wonder how many interested parties are sticking their oars in.'

'Let me finish, Sam.'

'Sorry.'

'If you've pissed in their soup, with luck they'll only focus on you as long as you're in London. Perhaps you're jumping up and down on a raw nerve and they'll try to take you out. We don't know. Don't take chances,' Cal said.

'I'll talk to the boss and get back to you. Take care.' Sam said.

'You too. Bye.'

50

'HI, FUSS.'

'Hiya, Sam. How the fuck are you?' Fuss sounded well, fruity language pouring out as ever. A voice murmured in the background, his voice became faint. 'Sorry, Sadie.' Then back he came loud and clear, 'I'm tryin' hard with the swearin', Sam, sometimes it slips out and Sadie kicks my scrawny arse.' There was another murmur. 'Wait, Sam, I'll take the phone to the kitchen, hold on.' The sound of feet in a corridor was followed by the closing of a door. 'Where are you?'

'Gatwick, in Departures, about to fly home. Wanted a quick chat.'

'Word is you've been adventurin'.'

'Unusually well-informed, Sar'nt Major.'

'Inspector Martin of the Yard called me. He's somewhat concerned.' Fuss took a loud breath. 'What the fuck have you been up to, Colonel Duncan?'

'Nothing much. Following a lead or two in search of a missing sister.'

'Stepped on some sensitive toes, have we? Got up a nose or two? Been indulging in fisticuffs? Going home for some TLC and then heading back, after a few days R 'n R, for another pop at the baddies. How's that sound, Sir?'

'Spot on. Of course, I'm not looking for trouble.'

'Course not. Trouble's lookin' for you. Want some help?'

'You working or still retired?'

'Casual stuff. Pension is just enough. The odd job buys fine holidays and strong drink. I asked if you want some help.'

'I'm beginning to think Karen and the girls should take off for a few days. Perhaps send them to Abby's tomorrow or the day after. A spot of oversight would be good. The answer is "yes" to your kind offer and as soon as possible.'

'Bag's packed, I can be in the car in ten minutes, ETA your place two hours. Sadie's happy enough to see the back of me.'

'I'll call Karen. Please get moving.'

'Aye, you've got to talk to the lass. Fuckin' wives have ideas and opinions. More's the fuckin' pity.'

'I'm not sure what we're involved in. One thing's definite, some evil people are taking an interest.'

'Sammy, I feel like I'm fuckin' Superman to the rescue. On my way. Catch you later.'

51

'MIKE?' Cal said.

'Pretty boy from the picture. We've found him.'

'Is he talking?'

'Not unless you can recommend a bloody good medium, my son. He's had a meeting with Stanley.' Stanley was a short-hand for an extremely sharp box-cutter.

'Shit. How bad?'

'Terminal. Ear to ear. We're processing the place at the moment. He's been dead less than six hours.' Mike was clinical and professional. The horror of the scene echoed in his haunted tone. 'First pass by forensics suggests he got hit fast, just inside the front door, surprised by the looks of things. The chap who killed him grabbed him quick. The struggle was on the brief side. A small table and a couple of chairs were kicked over.'

'You're saying him.'

'Yeah, him. Okay, I-must-be-an-objective-investigator and politically-effin'-correct but if it was a her, she'd need to be built like the bleedin' Terminator. His chin was lifted and the knife was really pulled round. I mean under the fuckin' jaw and all the way in, carotid, windpipe and everything else in between at a stroke. Hard to believe the head's still attached. The blood sprays are well up the wall. Looks like he was held by the killer until he died, mate. He had no chance at all.'

'Hold on, Mike, we had a similar MO about six months ago. Drug stuff. There was a slight trace of semen on the trousers of the victim, not his. Came out on forensics. Killer got off on the deed and leaked the needful DNA through his pants.' Cal experienced the tingle of hair standing up on his neck as he told Mike.

'Well remembered. We'll check things out. What a sorry bloody world.'

'Yeah,' Cal said. 'Someone out there is worrying, big time.'

'When you worry and you'll kill, you're either not rational or you're protecting something valuable. We're in some serious waters here, Cal. Kidnap. Rape. Assault. Murder.' Mike paused and drew a deep breath. 'Throw in a warrior-vicar-cum-spook with a big bloody Scots spurtle. Add the cast of Psycho, an ex-IRA club owner and some establishment spookery and we've got the beginnings of a proper little conflict here.'

'TFR,' Cal agreed, *too fuckin' right*. 'Another important thing is the speed they latched on to Sam and me at the Arches.

Parker's call saved our bacon. If we hadn't been able to handle the attack, or the bad guys had been more expert, we'd have faced a seriously hairy time.'

'As they say in the Army, your pal Duncan acquitted himself well. He's tough. He got his man *and* some information. Not that I want any details, you understand. That gangster was mucho twitchy, and he'll tell his friends. When we get right down to it, this is getting scary.' Mike and Cal were silent for a moment. Mike broke the spell. 'What's the plan with the holy man?'

'Home tonight, thinking about coming back on Tuesday or Wednesday.'

'Will he behave?'

'Probably,' Cal said.

'… and if the chips are down?'

'He'll take action. The time you get to know a guy like Sam is when the action starts.'

'How so?'

'In action, you find the true man.'

'True man?' Mike said.

'The warrior. He's survived the hardest of schools. When it's time to rock 'n' roll pulling punches just isn't part of the mindset.'

'So what's the bottom line?'

'He's a killer, investigator and intelligence operative. He's been there, done that, worn the tee-shirt and had the blood transfusions. He'll be a bit rusty but you'd better believe he's been working on some moves since this started. He was lethal at the Arches, and it's family.'

'Cal, he's a fuckin' vicar for Christ's sake.'

'Right enough. Mike. He is technically. He means well. And there's another thing.'

'Make my day.'

'He's licensed to carry.'

'You don't say.'

'Ex-spook and all.'

'Will he?'

'Who knows? He might if things get sticky. A friend tells me he's done range time.'

'I wonder what he's thinking.'

'Me too.'

'He needs to be careful.'

'He's been told. One last thing.'

'Yeah?'

'I hate to say this, but a leak in our side of things is beginning to seem likely.'

'Sad to say, I've got to agree with you.' His voice rose signalling the end of the conversation. 'Right, Cal. Catch you later.'

'Bye, Mike. I'll speak to Sam.'

52

WHEN THE CALL with Mike ended Cal found he enjoyed the improved professional contact. He texted Sam:

> *Pretty Boy murdered. Leakage probable. You are known about. Hide the family.*

A reply came back with surprising speed.

> *Fuss is minder. Will talk to Karen before deciding action.*

53

'COLONEL DUNCAN, please.' A feminine, polite and clear BBC London accent.

'I'm sorry, he's not here at the moment.' Karen spoke in loving spouse auto-pilot.

'When do you expect him?'

'Later. Who should I say called?'

'A friend. I'll call back. Thanks. Bye.'

Karen felt uncomfortable. She dialled 1471. The automatic voice told her: 'You were called today at 16.33 hours. The caller withheld their number.' She made a note of the time.

The phone rang again and she jumped out of her reverie.

'That you, love?' Sam's voice was soothing and calm.

'Who else? Today's Saturday. Jeannie is playing basketball in Carlisle and won't be back until 8.30. Al,' (Alice liked the nickname) 'is away hill-walking with Julie and her Mum and Dad over by Moffat. She has a pass until 9.30.'

'No one home but you. Put your feet up and forget housework.'

'Easy for you to say, Mr Tidy! When are you getting back?'

'The flight's been delayed half an hour. Allowing two and a half to three hours after landing, I should be home about 9.00 to 9.30, sooner if we make up time,' Sam said.

'The girls are missing you.'

'Lovely. I've business planning to do on the plane. The facts are okay, just got to produce some waffle to link the key points. Bloody Bankers. I'm glad we'll soon leave borrowing behind.'

'I've had a strange call from an English-sounding lady-friend of yours. Wouldn't give a name. She'll ring back later. Nothing on 1471.'

'Oh, my mistress. I've told her not to phone when you're in.'

'Watch it, buster.'

'You shouldn't smirk when you threaten me. Can we do serious for a minute?'

'I'm listening,' Karen said.

'Fuss should be with you in a couple of hours. It's probably nothing, but this Eilidh business is more complex than a simple missing person. I'll brief you as soon as I'm back.'

'Fuss is coming down? Run this by me again.'

'Think of it as a safety measure. I'm not convinced there's danger, but can't take any chances. We had a wee dust-up with some people. I'll tell you the whole story when I get back. Cal sends his love. Fuss'll be there soon.'

'A wee dust-up? Sam Duncan! I need more information. Don't hang about.'

'Yes, Ma'am. I'll be with you as soon as I can. I'll text from the airport. Love you. Bye.'

'Bye.' Karen shook her head. A wee dust-up indeed. A chill wriggled up her spine.

54

THE PA SYSTEM announced the Edinburgh flight was available for boarding. Sam texted Fuss.

K uptight. More bad news from Cal

Just before he entered the plane his mobile beeped.

There in 10.

Once in his seat, Sam spent the trip preparing for the business meeting.

As the plane completed its approach, he leaned back and shut his eyes. He recalled with Fuss when he returned to duty after being wounded in Bandit Country during the Troubles.

* * *

'I'm a fuckin' Catholic and I'm related to half the fuckin' population of Belfast. Half my fuckin' cousins talk gobbledygook about the 'Cause', fuckin' prats. Hardly any of the fuckwits have a fuckin' scoobie about what a Cause is. Everyone knows fuckin' criminals are involved as well. You've got priests and ministers siding with their own brand of fuckin' terrorist. Whatever happened to love one another, for fuck's sake? What I'm sayin' is the whole fuckin' situation is crazy. All the factions are fuckin' about trying to achieve their goals. Not one of the fuckers gives a shit for the folk they claim to represent. The only ones sufferin' are innocent members of the public and us.

'Old father James Murphy, the priest who taught me the Bible, was a fuckin' wild man. He drank like a drain and was the reddest-cheeked and loudest man I ever saw. He preached a message of love, forgiveness and pragmatism. He told us the world wasn't perfect. He said we were sinful wee buggers, and we were. His bottom line was God doesn't care if you're Catholic, Protestant or anything else. Love one another. Be kind to one another. Forget all the shite about an eye for an eye. Okay, he didn't use the word "shite". He also said we aren't fuckin' perfect and can be forgiven.

'You know, Sammy, after that youngster was killed by my lads in Armagh, I went to confession for the first time in ten years. I didn't go because of guilt. The wee fucker deserved to die. I went because I was glad he got it. I felt fuckin' triumphant. That scared me.

'Father Murphy said, "I've known you since you were a tiny wee hard man fighting your brothers and everyone else in the street for your place. Now, you're a soldier. You didn't make the war. You're just rendering unto Caesar what is Caesar's. That's your job. Maybe you're right to be happy you triumphed, you lived." He asked if I hated the dead boy now. I said "no". Then he said, "Take from this that you aren't an evil man. You're a normal man who's a soldier. Until you retire your life is the life of a servant and potential killer for your country. Try not to hate. Do your duty. If a member of the Orange Lodge happens to appear in the crosshairs when you're over by, and you have an accidental discharge, come to me again. I'll straighten things out with the Lord."'

* * *

They both howled, slapping each other's back, their bond of friendship as strong and deep as it gets. Four days later Sam killed a seventeen-year-old terrorist in a tricky operation, Fuss's words were a consolation.

55

SAM RETURNED to reality when the flight attendant asked him to put his tray up as the plane started its final descent into Edinburgh.

Two text messages arrived before he left the car park. The first from Fuss:

Home secure, K OK, J home, Barney and me had walkies.

The other from Cal:

Checking for leakage. Watch your back.

* * *

Forty-five minutes later he drove into the Borders, the diesel engine thrumming gently. He changed from his usual route taking the A68 down north of Jedburgh, over to the A7 at Hawick: two hours in all and safely home.

Pulling into the drive, he parked fifteen yards away from his normal spot. The interior lights stayed off when he stepped out of the car. He snatched his grip from the passenger seat and strode to the house.

The door opened as he reached for the handle. Fuss jerked his head towards the kitchen. Sam dropped his bag at the foot of the stairs and went through.

'Sam.' Karen walked quickly up and hugged him. He could feel her tension and sensed strong emotion kept in check. He rubbed her back and kissed her.

'Yo, Jeannie!'

'Hi, Dad. You're too old to "Yo" me.' She was both happy and irritated to see him, hormones being what they are.

'No hug?' She gave him a hug.

'How'd the game go?'

'We lost by five points. The coach is ecstatic.'

'So she should be. Wonderful result. Where'd the black eye come from?'

'Elbows under the basket.'

'How's the other guy?'

'Aching.'

'You'll save on make-up.'

'Funny! Ha! Ha! I'm off to watch the box. Mum, when's supper? I'm starving.'

'About half an hour,' Karen said. Jeannie went off to the lounge.

Sam nodded to his old friend.

'Thanks for coming, Fuss.'

'No bother, Sammy. You're lookin' well for a man straight from the fleshpots of London. Any chance of an update?'

'Of course. Let's make a cuppa. You want to hear too, love?' Karen nodded, brewed a pot of tea and filled the mugs. As usual, Fuss had three spoons of sugar.

'Here goes.' He covered the story briskly and soon was talking about the photo from the phone. 'Eilidh took a mobile phone picture of her lad, we call him "Pretty Boy", caught him unawares and emailed the pic to a pal. A handsome young man if you're into dark Latin looks and all that.' He wiggled his eyebrows at Karen who smacked his arm. 'Also the picture shows features which identified the nightclub. Any questions so far?'

'You sound a bit of a fuckin' Sherlock Holmes, Sammy.' Fuss looked at Karen. 'Oops.' He started to colour up. 'Beggin' your pardon, Karen, I'm tryin' not to swear. I manage fine with youngsters but forget in adult company. Sadie will shoot me if she hears I've been on the curse down here.'

'No problem in front of me. In front of my girls, I'll shoot you myself!' Karen lightened up.

'Understood, Ma'am.'

'Moving swiftly on,' Sam said, 'some questions and loose ends are starting to appear. What happened to Eilidh and why? How did Jenny get Eilidh's credit card? Why was Jenny beaten up? Who arranged the attack on Cal and me? Why? Some of this must be over-reaction and appears less cool and objective than you'd expect from professional criminals, which makes it even scarier.

'I met with the owner of the nightclub before catching my plane. He's an ex-IRA guy and knows of me from a killing that happened years ago. His cousin's the priest who was around that day.'

'When you nailed the assassin?'

'Right, Fuss. The good father has been singing my praises and I'm not in bad odour. He's a guy called O'Casey and truly concerned to avoid damage to his business reputation. He's helping the law. The police are reviewing his security tapes.' Sam paused and took a swig of tea.

'As I was heading for the plane I heard from Cal. Pretty Boy was murdered, by the sounds of things, this afternoon. Throat cut. O'Casey's folk ID'd him, said he'd been there a couple of times. On top of that, the police are following up the names we got when we were attacked. We'll learn more later.

'The cops think we've accidentally stumbled on to a rather dangerous situation, complete with multiple players and agendas. These people aren't taking prisoners. We don't know how or if Eilidh fits in yet. I called Fuss to get us protection. I believe the family should decamp for a short while as a prudent precaution. Maybe up to Fife and stay with Abby? What do you think?'

The house phone rang. Karen answered. 'Cal, hi. I'll get Sam.' She gave him the handset, lips tight, pale.

The briefing paused while Cal spoke and Sam listened making one or two cursory remarks before saying goodbye.

Sam gazed at Fuss and Karen and sighed. 'The latest news is that the guys who beat up Jenny got beaten up themselves. Pretty seriously by all accounts: one's dead, one's in intensive care and one's missing. Some enforcers were involved—hard men. One of them was glassed and blinded in one eye. A broken glass was rammed in his mouth. Not a pretty sight. Won't be doing much talking or kissing for a while.'

'Ouch.' Fuss said.

'He's a hard man with lots of form. They don't expect him to be communicative, even if his gob was in good working order, but it gives Cal and the team leads and connections. I'll find out more in due course.'

'Imagine, at least two lots of crazies on the loose, probably more. The Fuzz think the action is connected, yet somehow disjointed and disorganized. Cal and his colleagues want us to leave town and quickly. They're now pretty sure there's a leak in the Met. That means the bad guys know who I am, where I live and what my background is.'

Karen was pale. 'Are you sure Fife is far enough for hiding?'

'Not now.'

'Include me in, Sammy.' Fuss spoke quietly, seriously. Sam could have warmed his hands on the warrior aura emanating from his friend.

The phone rang again.

56

SAM PICKED UP the handset on the kitchen table.

'Speaking.' His jaw tightened and he went a little pale. He left the room. Fuss and Karen exchanged glances.

The woman had an attractive English voice. 'Mister Duncan you're not welcome in London. Don't force us to take reprisals against you or your family. Just keep your nose out and enjoy the rest of your life.'

'What about my sister?'

'If you want her to be safe you'll stay away.'

'I want her safe, and that won't go away. Maybe if your criminal right hand knew what your psychopathic left hand was doing we wouldn't be talking at all.'

'That's as may be. We don't care about your sister, not in the least. We'll know if you come back. Heed this warning and nobody need get hurt.' The caller hung up. 1471 produced the same result as for Karen. No number. The call was timed at 22.06 hours. He'd pass the information to Cal. Sam walked rather stiffly back into the kitchen.

'Who was that, darling?'

'The woman who called earlier, Karen. Threats and a confirmation. I think she knows about Eilidh but isn't fully up-to-speed on the other stuff. She told me to stay out of London or else.'

'And you can't do that, can you, Sam?' Her eyes moistened. 'I wouldn't want you to.' Sam took hold of her. He glanced at Fuss, raised an eyebrow and shook his head. Fuss left quietly to watch TV with Jeannie.

'We agreed you'd go to London but never dreamed of a mess like this.'

'Right, love. You guys must be safe, full-stop. The weird mix of players gives us no choice but to hide you.' Bending forward Karen sobbed into his neck for a moment. Then taking his head gently between her hands she gazed into his eyes with great trust and confidence and gave him a solid kiss. A tear ran down her cheek and jawline. It splashed on to her blouse, leaving a temporary dark stain. They were silent for a long moment. She turned away from Sam, tore off a sheet of kitchen roll dried her eyes, blew her nose, walked back to Sam and hugged him hard.

'I'll get the girls packed after dinner,' she said.

'They'll enjoy a break, even guardians about.'

'You mean quiet men with silly names?'

'Silly names? The criminals are calling me the Vicar in London.'

'Quite.'

They found themselves chuckling in spite of the tension—maybe because of it.

* * *

Barney barked a warning. Sam pressed Karen against a kitchen unit, signalled for her to stay put and went through the door keeping close to the wall. Fuss, at the lounge door, signalled for him to stop, then moved to take the handle without showing himself in the glass. He opened the door.

'One eager walker returned safe and sound. Sorry we're late. Got to dash.'

'Thanks, Harry,' Sam called after him, 'cheers.' Harry had already turned back towards his car, oblivious to anything unusual.

Alice came in and Fuss closed the door. 'Hi, Al. How's my wee girl?'

'Fine, Dad,' she jumped up and gave him a big squeeze. 'Hi, Uncle Fuss, you're a nice surprise.' She grinned at the grizzled ex-soldier and ran to him for a big hug as well. Fuss was average height and had a marathon runner's body with an extra a layer of muscle up top.

His craggy face beamed, light brown eyes bright with delight. He pushed her back holding her by the shoulders and smiled into her face. 'You're getting more beautiful every time we meet.' Alice blushed, he could tell she was pleased. 'You're lovely like your Mum,' he nodded, 'much better than taking after your ugly old dad.'

Karen called out. 'Girls, come to the kitchen please, I need to speak to you.' After their powwow, everyone enjoyed a late meal in an atmosphere of subdued excitement.

* * *

Hundreds of miles away, bad people were thinking of them.

57

A WEIGHT MOVED on Eilidh's chest. Dawn lit the window behind her.

She dropped into another reality of swirling memories and random faces. Then it was bright daylight and still the weight lay on her, a rat? She hardly dared peek. A kitten mewed and rubbed its scrawny body against her chin.

'Hi, kitty.' She smiled, touched by the warmth and rubs of furry affection.

The small feline purred and gave some unconditional love before settling down again across her throat. She liked the warmth and drifted back into unconsciousness.

* * *

A sharp pain made Eilidh squeal. Her throat took a nasty scratch when a hardened hand seized the little cat who tried to stay securely attached. She heard the spitting, wailing scream of the kitten as it was thrown to the side.

'Only one pussy allowed in here.' Nasty man chortled and tapped the side of her face. Features hidden by a red balaclava with a white stripe down the middle, he showed her the syringe. '*Silly girl. This wouldn't be happening if you'd kept your nose out of matters that don't concern you.*' He sneered as she faded away.

58

SATURDAY BECAME a preparation and planning day. Business was brisk and enjoyable at BorderStory. The manager and two supervisors came planned cover for Sam and Karen's absence.

The key to the business was making sure the logistics side was nailed down with someone to cover the phones and filing, a role often taken by Karen.

All agreed on Willie Aitken, a retired Minister, as an ideal choice, if he was available. Willie had been firm friends with Sam since he trained for the ministry and had supported him when he resigned his charge. They kept in frequent contact by e-mail and once or twice a month on the phone.

Willie understood scheduling, coordinating transport and contracting coach services, a world he'd worked in before his call from God. The team knew and liked him as he'd covered before for sickness, and sometimes when Sam and the family were on holiday. Minimal disruption was expected.

Sam rang Willie and offered him three weeks of operations and office dogs-body work. Willie gave an enthusiastic *yes, please*.

Next, he called James Smith the Session Clerk of Westerholm Parish Kirk to tell him Willie would be around for a while.

'Think he'd step into the pulpit while he's here?' asked James, eager to get Willie into harness. Pulpit supply ministers were scarce.

'I expect so.'

Sam called Willie again and told him he could have preaching and pastoral work if he wanted it.

Willie was delighted and excited. 'I'll warm 'em up with a spot of "turn or burn".'

'Up to you, Willie. They're about as middle-of-the-road as can be. Mix old and new hymns fifty-fifty. Wear the full uniform. Tell a couple of appropriate jokes. No prayers longer than three minutes. Hold on, you wrote the drill! Anyway, you can give James Smith a ring and he'll sort things out with you. He's aware you'll be staying at our place.'

'Sounds good to me.' Willie's happiness gushed from the phone. 'Since Elspeth died, I've been under-utilized, after all, I'm only sixty-nine and bursting with health. D'you think I can make a comeback like those stars on Big Brother?'

'Willie Aitken, the Come-back-to-God Kid. Might work.'

'Karen's made you up a bed in the usual place, the blue door on the right at the top of the stairs. Towels, sheets, anything you need in the airing cupboard. Loads of food in the freezer.'

'Excellent, I'm familiar with the luxurious surroundings of your home and will thank God for this opportunity later.'

'Karen's prepared a pretty comprehensive note for you.'

'She's thorough, BorderStory wouldn't work without her administrative abilities.'

'Don't you start. One other thing, a worthy member of the community will give you a tidy up on Tuesday, Thursday and Saturday, laundry twice a week, as you require.'

'I take back any snidey remarks, Sam.'

'In which case, you'll find a bottle of Baillie, Nichols and Jarvie second shelf up in the cupboard in my study. A wee dram, feet up on the old recliner is a fine way to end the day.'

'You're sure to get to heaven, young Sam.'

'Amen brother! Thanks again for your help.'

'Nothing at all.'

'Why not stay on for a few days when we return?'

'Love too. By the way, how's Barney the wonder dog?'

'Fine.'

'Don't put him in kennels. Leave him for me. I'll enjoy walking him.'

'Excellent. I'll call you on Tuesday to make sure you're settling in.'

'Thanks, Sam. You can't imagine how much I'm looking forward to this. Bye.'

59

THEY DISMISSED staying at Sam's mother's house as a bad idea. It was easy to get at from all directions, with too many houses, streets and people round about—plus the beach. Their rationale gave them the answer.

After a phone call, they decided to decamp to Mweenstor Island near Carna in Connemara, County Galway.

Relations owned a place on the island where they'd spent two happy family holidays. The locals were delightful people. The house was available 'any time', a lovely cottage facing the wild North Atlantic of Western Ireland. At 04:30 on Friday morning they planned to go to Prestwick Airport via Dumfries. The family would catch the morning flight to Shannon. Hec would bring Abby across from Fife to travel with them.

Sam summarized the thinking. 'Taking the causeway is the only way on to Mweenstor. An attack from the sea is unlikely, the coast is as rough as guts and takes no prisoners. If anyone wants to get near us or makes enquiries we'll be informed, the benefit of a relationship with the locals. The house has all mod cons. The shore and garden are a safe place for the kids to let off steam and go walkabout. And the big thing is we haven't told anyone where we're going. The customs will get a record, but after Shannon, we'll just disappear. A friend of a friend has arranged the rental of a people carrier, local registration, couple of years old and suitably nondescript. I'll head south when we've dropped you off.'

Karen eyed Sam. 'Heading off? No surprise there then.'

'No love. Kind of scary tuning into the old ways again. I made a guy talk the other day.'

'Is he okay?'

'Yes, of course.'

Karen responded with support. 'Man's gotta do …' A chill touched her stomach.

'Yeah, rather too easily. I think I rattled Cal.'

* * *

At 20.00 Karen walked into the study. Sam looked up as he finished cleaning his Browning Hi-Power (modified hammer and a customized trigger). She touched his arm and sat down. 'Is that going to be necessary?'

'Not sure. This beast is in fine nick. The clip springs are okay, mechanism's fine. I fired off a couple rounds with a similar beastie in London the other day. I'm still good. This gun has saved my life.' He looked up and caught her eye. 'Our family is threatened, what am I supposed to do? I'm not too happy about being armed in London. For now, better safe than sorry.'

Karen left him to finish his preparation. Her heart ached a little as she remembered Sam's sadness at the killing of the 'Irish Assassin', as she referred to Orin O'Reilly. Sam's nightmares had introduced her to O'Reilly on a nightly basis for months.

Working mechanically, Sam loaded two clips with Federal Hydra-Shok 124g ammunition. He fitted a clip, chambered then ejected a round. Fully operational. Having put the clips and pistol into his Bianchi case along with the gun-cleaning kit, he was about to lock up when Fuss came in.

'Let's have a look.' Fuss examined the gun. 'Clean and in good shape.' Fuss returned the Browning. Sam secured the pistol.

'Excellent teacher, Sar'nt Major.'

'Freaky should arrive at Mweenstor late tomorrow morning, Sam. He's going overland and prepared. Mutual friends have provided what is needed. You remember when we got him out of the shit in that NI thing. He's not forgotten. He'll give us oversight, big time.' Oversight meant surveillance and sniper skills. His presence would not be easy to spot.

'Hard man to forget, old Freaky.' Sam remembered a loyal and tough, uncompromising man he'd worked with on operations a number of times. They became friends in the way people sharing danger do. A medium-size, unremarkable man. He earned the name 'Freaky' because he did anything but freak out when under pressure. So people started calling him 'Freaky Fred' to get under his skin. They failed. He said Freaky was a fine name and it stuck.

'He's still geared up for the survival life. Teaches coping skills to fuckin' desk jockeys and stays out on the hill half the time by all accounts. His wife seems happy enough,' Fuss said.

'He keeps in touch with me, too. Thanks for bringing him in. Any comms kit?'

'Aye, walkie-talkie: five handsets, two-mile range, one for the house and the others for the watchers, Karen and Abby. We've a digital camera for recording the people who come about the place and some night-vision stuff, just in case.'

'Does this mean he'll be crapping in cling-film?'

'No. I'll make sure he's regularly relieved. What're you laughin' at?'

'What're you going to do? Stick a pail under his jaxie?' Sam said.

'You know what I fuckin' meant. And one other thing, he'll be sittin' outside with a fuckin' M85.'

'The sniper's delight. We'll be safe.'

'Safer than most.'

'Are we over-prepared?'

'You can never be over-prepared, son. Not any time. We never lost a man because we over-prepared. You nearly died when those brass hat fuckers in the Falklands hadn't prepared properly.'

'You're right.'

'Oh, I almost forgot … speaking of relieving.' Smile. 'Bilbo should arrive tomorrow midday.'

'Fantastic,' Sam said.

'Freaky and Bilbo will share the watching: one floating, one close-by. We'll nail a routine down. I'll float.'

'So, speaking of relieving, you're gonna be a floater too.'

'Fuck off, stupid fuckin' Rupert.'

'Thanks for your help and support. I can't say how much this means,' Sam said. He reached over and shook Fuss by the hand.

'You're worth the effort, even for a fuckin' Proddy priest.' The planning went on.

60

'GOOD EVENING, Mr Duffy, I'm DI Martin. You spoke to one of our constables this afternoon.' Cal had been ushered into a tidy, sixties style living room.

'Yes, there have been goings on out the back. We've had enough of it.'

'You say these disturbances have happened more than once?'

'Yes, four or five times.' Mr Duffy looked at his wife. 'What you think, old gal?'

'I'd say at least five.' Mrs Duffy said.

'What exactly happens?'

'A van comes into the lane. They park and sit with the engine running, the smell of fags and exhaust pours in our window,' Mr Duffy said.

'Annoying,' Cal said.

'You're not kidding. We're old and need our sleep. The window's open for fresh air. When the door from the club opens all the noise comes out. I got up every time it woke me and seen a young man helping a drunk girl out to a van. They're lucky someone collects 'em when they're so sozzled. Unable to put one foot after the other. Is the collection a service from the management?'

'I'll find out. Thanks. You say you witnessed a girl being helped out at exactly quarter to one in the morning?'

'Yes, through the fire door,' Mr Duffy said.

'She sounded Scottish,' Mrs Duffy said. 'She said something like she hadn't drunk much and didn't understand what was happening to her.'

'Did you see her, ma'am?'

'Yes, shoulder-length hair, maybe blonde, certainly light. She had jeans and a blouse on. He dropped her you know. Didn't seem to care.'

'Called the others to help him and they put her in the van, like a sack of potatoes. The boy's an Italian type, dark skin, gelled hair, tight pants and a shirt open showing off his chest,' Mr Duffy said.

'How does this picture compare?' Cal showed him the photo from Eilidh's phone.

'Yes, I think that's him. What d' you think, Floss?' He handed the print to his wife.

'I'm ninety percent certain. Darkness is difficult, the further they come away from the door light the harder it is to see 'em. He's awfully like the young man. In fact, I'm sure.'

'He's been helping girls to the van?'

'Yes, a few. Never two the same. He's there every time,' Mr Duffy said.

'How many is a few, sir?'

'I dunno, maybe four or five. Sometimes we've woken up when the fire door slams shut.'

'Thanks. You're saying all the women you've seen were different?'

'Yes.'

'Did you think it strange, them always being brought out to a van?' Cal said.

'Not really. People get drunk and need to be helped home.'

'Perhaps. Let's talk about the van. How many people in the van?'

'I think two of them.'

'Yes, two men,' Mrs Duffy said.

'They park in the shadows over beside the downpipe and the broken end of the wall. Both of them smoking, but their faces weren't clear. They wore overalls.'

The questions went on for a further twenty minutes. When he'd finished, Cal called for a crime scene team to secure the area and begin a detailed examination. The parking space might provide clues. *Please, God.* After thanking the witnesses, Cal next went into the Neon Orchid to interview O'Casey.

* * *

'Hello, Inspector,' O'Casey shook his hand.

'Mr O'Casey, we've been making enquiries. We now believe a number of girls were abducted from here.'

'Christ! More than one?'

'At this point, I'm considering whether or not to continue our conversation under caution, but I'll let that go for now. Please be honest and clear. First, tell me about your security arrangements.'

'Full alarm, video surveillance and recording system.'

'What are your times of operation?'

'24 x 7, needed for insurance purposes.'

'Where are the controls?'

'The main control is in the back office. We have a small panel at the rear exit to switch the alarm off for deliveries and that sort of thing. Our cellars are down some stairs at the rear exit. Everything comes in there.'

'Who has access to the controls?'

'Me, the security team and the bar manager.'

'I'll need a word with everyone.'

'Of course. The team'll be here around six. Good Christ, I wonder if someone's been letting things get out of hand. Would also explain some of the shrinkages, nicking bottles mainly.

Started to rise over the past few weeks. It's not too bad compared to the trade in general, but our stock control is good and we want to keep our standard high.'

'How many security cameras, and where are they located?'

'Four, the main entrance and the fire exits. We put a new one in above the door into the lane a few weeks ago. Copies of videos are kept for three months and backed up with the rest of the computer stuff. Keeps the insurance companies happy.'

'We'll need copies.'

'Already prepared. Mr Duncan said you'd want them. Another thing, anyone doing anything on the security system must log on. We should be able to find out who did what. Let me speak with Stevie, my main bouncer.'

'Before you do, listening to you, I'm getting the impression you don't check your videos every day.'

'Not unless we've got a reason. We'll be having a bloody serious inspection later today.'

Cal thanked him for his time and left.

As he left the club, a dozen pictures of him were transmitted from across the road.

61

At 19:15 Jake Stills, a bouncer, owned up to putting the alarm off a number of times. The log showed three nocturnal switch-offs in three months, between midnight and 00:45. They found four recent afternoon openings not associated directly with deliveries. He had logged in on each occasion.

Stills was arrested, cautioned and taken to the local police station where Cal gave him another formal caution. Detective

Constable Flo' Binstead accompanied him. They noted some bruising on Stills' forehead and a swollen upper right lip for the record. Nobody commented or appeared concerned.

DC Binstead switched on the twin tape machine, stated the date and time, identified herself and Stills, cautioned him. 'Mr Stills, I have given you a formal caution, you are under arrest. Do you understand that?'

'Yes.'

'You have a right to legal representation. Do you wish to have a lawyer present?'

'No. I confessed to turning the alarm off, what more do you fucking want?'

'That's three times between the hours of midnight in the last three months.' Cal read out the dates. 'Is this correct?'

'Yes, it's logged. I didn't think they checked. The Irish are thick mate, fucking thick.'

'But the logs were checked?'

'Yes.'

'You acknowledge four recent instances of the door security system being switched off by you during the day, on each of the last four Thursdays.' Cal read out the dates. 'Again, you logged on for this. Is this correct?'

'Yes.'

'This is not part of the present inquiry, but may be the subject of further investigation at a later date. Do you understand?'

'Yes.'

'Mr Stills, I'm going to show you a photograph. Can you please indicate if this is a person known to you?' Cal showed him the picture of 'Pretty Boy.'

'Yes. That's Lou Aramente. He paid me to open the door on those nights.'

'Mr Stills, do you know Lou Aramente?'

'Of course, I do. We went to school together. Bit of a self-employed businessman.' Stills then gave Aramente's mobile number and street address. 'He'll tell you it was a nothing deal, I think he was meeting some people out back and wanted privacy.'

'To be absolutely clear, I want to confirm that you switched off the alarm and opened the fire door and, each time, Lou Aramente paid you.'

'Yes.'

'Louder please.'

'YES.'

'You never checked the picture to find out what was happening?'

'No. Ask no questions hear no lies. He asked me to switch the alarm off and then told me when to switch on again. It'd be off for about five minutes. I mean an easy thirty quid. No questions. Drinking money, that's all. Ask him, he'll tell you. Nothing bad happened.'

'Was Lou Aramente alone when he went out on these occasions?'

Silence. 'I'm not sure.'

'Mr Stills, Jake, you've admitted to being there, switching off the security camera and opening the door.'

Stills started to sweat. 'I suppose I did.'

'Is that a yes?'

'Yes.'

'Was he alone?'

Silence.

'Mr Stills we need an answer.'

'No.'

'Louder please.'

'NO.'

'Who was with him?'

'A woman.'

'The same woman each time?'

'No.'

'Louder please.'

'NO.'

'Did Lou Aramente come back in later?'

'Yes.'

'Did the women return with him?'

'No.'

'Louder please.'

'NO!'

'What do you think happened to them?'

'They went home.'

'What did Lou Aramente say occurred?'

'He said they were bit pissed and a friend collected them. Is this more serious than I thought?'

'This is part of our enquiry, which we can't discuss at this time.'

'Look, Inspector, I'm cooperating, aren't I?'

'Yes you are and we're appreciative. I would like to speak to you further, but I am not able to do so at the moment. This interview is now over. You will be remanded until a court hearing. We'll notify you of the next step in due course.'

DC Binstead stated the finished time and date of the interrogation, then called a PC who took Stills away.

'Well, Flo', the questioning was as painless as any I've had. Wish they were all like that?' Cal said.

Flo', a trim, powerful blond with a gentle and steady set to her mouth, nodded. 'Me too, sir. I wonder how he got a job as a bouncer.'

The good feeling of a job-well-done would soon evaporate.

62

'THE PROFITS are starting to flow, and just as we benefit from our investment, somebody drops the ball. Why?' Maybelle Jones, an attractive plump person, didn't suffer fools and made people aware if she wasn't happy. She tended to talk more than listen, as one could in a top post at the Home Office. 'What's happened? How can we be under pressure?'

'Calm down, Maybelle.' Devlin Forsyth, a specialist in trading and banking, and a highly regarded government adviser, spoke with practised firmness. Maybelle stared at him, considered a retort and controlled herself with a big sigh. 'Our plans are working out. The fly in the ointment seems to be a simple journalistic glitch which we thought we had isolated and resolved—wrongly as it happens—but a problem our new friend Bill Jenkins can resolve tout de suite if we ask him.'

'I'm not happy and now we've widened the need to know,' Maybelle said.

Devlin said, 'Come on, Maybelle, we decided to frighten the girl off and haven't widened the need to know. I enjoy a business connection with Mr Jenkins, a well-known godfather who aspires to move his interests into legitimate areas. As far as he's concerned, I represent a group of influential businessmen he'd like to join. That's all. He understands we made private arrangements to avoid any mud getting on his shoes, and so on.'

'Maybelle, as Devlin says, we agreed what we'd do: a low visibility application of stress and trauma that we'll follow up to make her even more circumspect,' Gemma Smythsone said.

'Remember, we discussed all possible action up to and including termination, before taking our decision to frighten her off. And now we're paying the price for squeamishness,' Jim Thomas interrupted. He always managed to sound angry. A Geordie, his north-east accent carried distinctly different edge from the others.

His three colleagues and 'guest', Sir Marcus Attenwood-Leigh, contemplated Jim Thomas, a top player in MI5, and heavily involved in the National Security Secretariat. 'What's your take, Jim?'

'Recruitment is going well, Marcus. We're selecting capable folk, cleaning up blemishes in their history and making them fit for purpose, squeaky clean.'

'Nothing like a spot of productive head hunting, Jim. A couple of keystrokes and, hey presto, useful people, pure as the driven snow.'

'Close scrutiny might cause a problem, but our trail is well hidden.' Jim said.

'Pity we can't besmirch people the same way.'

'Too tricky, too risky, Marcus.'

'Sadly.' Sir Marcus' smile straightened. 'You'd have done the journalist thing differently.'

Jim took a hissing in-breath, 'Yes, but I went along with our decision.' Maybelle Jones nodded to him.

'Your spook bones said something else.'

'I've been a long time in MI5, much of it in the field …' Jim paused and thought. 'There are times when you simply have to do something … maybe something awful, just to solve a problem … make it disappear.'

'This is one of those times?'

'Yes.' A clandestine operator of many years experience.

Devlin said. 'As agreed, I cut out middlemen to ensure need-to-know only. I left the Jenkins brothers out of this. Evidently, our contractor, an expert in disappearing people, experienced a slight quality problem, which is being fixed at the sharp end. That should be the end of it.'

'One unfortunate thing, Devlin,' Jim said, 'is the unexpected appearance of one Colonel Sam Duncan.'

'Who's he?'

'Something of a spook and black ops man,' Jim said. 'He turned up in a conversation in the intelligence community the other day. Our journo is connected to him, big brother no less.' We've given him a stay-out-of-it call and made threats against his family, but I don't think he'll back off.'

'Jim, I threatened him as you asked.' Gemma said.

'He can be taken care of inside twenty-four hours.' Jim said.

'Shouldn't the Board have been involved in this?'

'No, Maybelle, we delegated to Jim. Jim received intel he believed he had to act on. So he talked to me and I agreed to make a threatening phone call. Jim?' Gemma said. 'I called him last night and put the frighteners on. I'm not sure I scared him off, he sounds a determined type.'

'He's a danger to us and it won't change. Not now, not ever.' Jim said.

63

They completed the cross-country drive from Westerholm via Moniaive, over the Ayrshire hills by Dalmellington, Patna, and round the Ayr bypass to Prestwick Airport. Sam parked at the bag drop-off beside the terminal. With two trolleys and Abby in attendance, Hec was waiting for them. The girls sprang from the car shouting, 'Granny!' and dashed over to hug her, followed by more robust displays of affection with their robust uncle.

A larger version of Sam, Hec was six foot three, eighteen and a half stone, most of it muscle, with sandy hair and the same penetrating eyes. He lifted both girls effortlessly, one under each arm, and twirled them around. Alice squealed with delight. Jeannie, older, seemed to consider her dignity for a few moments before starting to screech with delight. The rest of the family hugged and exchanged warm greetings. Fuss had a quiet word with Hector.

Sam made the organisational noises. 'Come on you lot, let's get the bags sorted. We've got ten minutes before I'll need a parking ticket.' Everyone chatted as they loaded their trolleys and moved off towards the terminal.

* * *

With two hours to departure, Sam drove away to leave his car off-site. He had a friend with a caravan park, back towards Troon, about a mile's walk from the terminal. He didn't plan to use the car again short-term. Hiding it made sense.

He said a brief 'hi' to his pal, left the keys, and received a promise the battery would be kept in good fettle, and the tyres turned.

* * *

The walk to Departures took twenty minutes. The family were checked in, the kids excited and their Granny fully occupied with the minutiae of supervision, conversation and good humour. Karen looked stressed. Fuss was discreetly watchful.

'Sooner we're through security the better, Boss.' The command chain was operational.

'Aye, Fuss.' He hugged the kids, reminding them of the serious reasons for their departure and to do what Fuss or their Mum told them without question. They nodded.

The hug from his mother was stoic and she looked at him, a glint of steel in her eye.

'You sort out your sister. We'll look out for the girls and Karen. Fuss has lined me up with a wee twelve-bore. Any nonsense and kaboom.' Abby had been an excellent rough shooter in her day.

'There will be three professionals, Ma, listen to them. Do what they tell you and don't get between them and action. We don't want someone dying because you got in the way. Plonk the gun somewhere handy. Maybe stick cartridges at discreet points around the house if you'll feel better. Leave it unloaded, only takes a moment to gear up for action. Clear?'

'Clear, son.' She mock saluted and hugged him again.

* * *

Sam and Karen stepped aside for a private goodbye. 'Nobody knows where you're going. We know the area and that helps us set up our defences. I've walked it through with Fuss. Hopefully, this'll be over soon.' As he spoke he could see her emotions and fear for him. He raised an eyebrow, gazed into her troubled eyes and opened his arms.

She stepped into the hug and squeezed him tight. 'Come back in one piece. You've got a growing family to support.'

He gave her his slightly lopsided grin. 'I look after me and you take care of everyone else. The usual.'

'What are your final plans for heading south?'

'Hec and I will pick up my things at the car. I'll head off later.'

'Take care.' A tear escaped down her cheek only to be dried by a gentle finger from her husband. She sniffed, firmed her face, suppressed her tears, kissed him firmly, then turned to the family bright and strong. 'Right, everyone. Let's get through security. Passports, boarding passes, single item of hand luggage each. Off we go.'

'Bye, Dad.' Two swift hugs from his daughters.

'See you, Sam.' Fuss hugged him. 'Good luck, take that fuckin' pistol with you. I've a queasy feelin' on this one, son, fuckin' queasy.'

64

'TELL US SOMETHING about this man Duncan, Jim.' Maybelle Jones said.

'He's a former Tier 1 operator. Quit the life and became a Minister in the Church of Scotland and he's been off the radar ever since.'

'That isn't all you know. Come on, give us the goods.' Devlin smiled as his hands beckoned for more.

'Okay. This tale must never leave this room. He's a decorated soldier, officer, and spook. He served in the Falklands, Northern Ireland, the first Gulf War and other theatres. Was wounded a few times. He managed to get up the nose of some of the Republican Mafia in Belfast, involved in a raid on a bank robbery team in one of the towns. Three paramilitaries were killed. He was one of the killers. The father of one of the deceased was both a serious player and a double agent. He called in a marker and certain information was provided to support a revenge killing. Duncan's details were fed to the bad guys.'

'You mean our side sold him out?'

'Who knows, Maybelle. Unlikely to be us, but a bribe or a sympathizer is a good possibility. Covert operations is a tough and dirty business.'

The awkward silence made time drag. The reality of being Bizz made an uncompromizing demand.

'What happened? Why is he still walking about? Bit of a swift second-coming, don't you think?' Devlin's tone was light.

'He got the drop on the killer they sent after him. The assassin died.'

'They didn't try again?'

'Before they could, he rotated out and, because he'd been marked, he never returned to that theatre. His identity was protected. The godfather in question lost the plot somewhat and was killed by his own people a couple of years later. Life moved on. Things changed. The Peace Process happened. No more pressure.'

'So, where's the problem?'

'In the detail. Our supplier cocked up. Danger man is dragged in through his family connection. He has motivation for a serious investigation and is a competent investigator with friends in the Met. We're getting word of other ripples from the cock-up. Probably Maybelle can get some clarity for us on that, as it does sound somewhat bloody. We didn't want this, anything but. He's had a call to warn him off but, sad to say, he's not known as a quitter.'

'So why put the frighteners on?' Maybelle said.

'Good idea before everything went pear-shaped. Young family, exposed in a small community. Best he protects 'em on his own patch.'

'And if he doesn't stay put?'

'Unfortunately, I don't now believe he will. With his track record, I think we'd be well-advised to terminate him. We know where he is. We don't want to lose sight of him. We must make sure the criminal cock-ups stop and loose ends are tidied up,' Jim said.

'Sounds harsh.'

'Sometimes, Gemma, harsh action saves lives and lots of money. We're in this for the cash. It may be the unacceptable face of capitalism, but shit happens when noses get stuck in where they're not wanted.'

'You're saying we kill him?'

'Not necessarily us, Gemma,' Maybelle said. 'We own a contact in the Met who has a connection with the people we mentioned earlier. Perhaps we can bounce them into taking action for us. Maybe all we need do is stir things up, sow some fear and uncertainty and leave them to it.'

'It could work, but if this man needs to go I suggest we commission more of a certainty than our gangster friends appear able to deliver.' Jim spoke quietly, they listened. 'I can put an ex-special forces asset on to this if needed. We must decide quickly, tomorrow at the latest, can we meet then?'

They all nodded.

'We're agreed as Jim outlined? Nothing to happen before Monday's meeting. If we decide to do it we leave the action to you, Jim.' Maybelle said.

'Fine.'

Bizz shared a collective sigh and a moment's thoughtful fidgeting as their first-ever murder was almost certainly sanctioned. Jim hid feelings of elation behind a poker face.

* * *

'Now to business, how are we doing?' Maybelle said.

Devlin provided a brief procurement report. 'Three more contracts worth £57 million were awarded this month. Income from this of nearly £2.9 million will be paid into our offshore mechanism over the next twelve months. That brings total contracts for the past 6 months to slightly over £570 million which, at 5 percent, is £28.5 million per annum. Running total for sales to-date is £678 million, and we're on course for our £5 million a month, eh, our procurement and consultancy target.'

'What about the National Infrastructure Plan?' Jim Thomas said.

'We're in there and well placed. We also have assets in the Home, Foreign and Cabinet office planning groups. Positive noises, networking and so on.' Maybelle said.

'And the EU?' Gemma said.

'Goldmine. An ever dripping roast.' Sir Marcus said and giggled. 'It's a bull market, Westminster is woefully short of expertise, and, what they don't have, they'll pay for.

'How will we handle the workload?' Jim said.

'Who cares?' Maybelle said, 'Growing team, growing workload, drip-drip-drip.' Her smile gleamed.

'We've on-boarded several new partner organizations with more in the pipeline. Demand escalates our growth and bigger bangs per buck. Our people are trusted and near the procurement coal-face. We're getting busier and busier. Dividend prospects are even more exciting.' Devlin beamed, triggering light chuckles around the table.

Maybelle said. 'The income from Customs avoidance side is on the up, but we expect procurement will overtake it by procurement later this year. Funds are off-shored as earned and being invested in property and other holdings with relevant commercial partners and consortia.

'Don't you love Panama?' Sir Marcus said.

'The sooner the Land Registry is privatised, the better.' Devlin said.

Maybelle raised a finger. 'I have to say, for a virtually risk-free proposition, we do really well for ourselves and,' she made air-quotes, 'our "off-piste" helpers and our international supporters.' She paused and looked at each of the team in turn. 'This is a fantastic success. We don't make as much as some bankers, but we've grown and are making a bundle. And zero tax!' There were more chuckles and bright-eyed nods.

Sir Marcus nodded. 'Growth is wonderful.'

'The Border lot are already snowed under. Opportunities abound.' Maybelle said. 'Minutes from you, Gemma?'

'No problem, Chair. Tomorrow morning, usual smokescreen.'

* * *

'Right, smokescreen over, let's get to today's official agenda for the rest of the morning.' Maybelle picked up the phone. 'Sarah, we're ready, please ask Colin to come in to take the minutes?'

Moments later a young man entered, and during the pleasantries he grabbed a coffee. He sat down with his pad.

'Ready Colin?' Maybelle said. 'We've finished our preliminary chat. Now lady and gentlemen, the Commercial Oversight and Security Working Group is in session. Our first agenda item is the security of the new banking monitor and the acceptability of the proposal to the City. Devlin, I wonder if you could lead off on that.'

'Certainly Chair. Following consultation with the big players I can report …'

Bizz met in a high security Home Office meeting room, where they met regularly to do official work and sort out the unofficial operation of their criminal agenda.

Key contacts attended their meetings with guaranteed privacy for discussions, a real benefit to them and their country. Enterprise.

Three hours later the meeting ended. 'Right everyone, we're close to delivery on this project, the Minister will be pleased.

They all nodded and left. Jim and Gemma exchanged nods at the door.

65

SAM STOOD, a wistful set to his face, as he watched everyone disappear into the secure area. He turned to Hector. 'I've stuff to collect from my car, Hec.'

'Aye, Sam. No problem. Now, why don't you bring me fully up to speed? I'm feeling left out. Mum's been emotional and quite hazy about things.'

They set off for Hec's Land Cruiser Amazon, a huge practical workhorse parked not far from where Sam had dropped the bags off. An hour later they were through the Clyde Tunnel heading for Hec's apartment in the West End of Glasgow near the Botanic Gardens. Sam briefed his brother on the way in.

'Our sister kidnapped and the guy who took her killed. What's going on Sam?'

'No idea, except she's in the mire.'

'How so?'

'Hec, I simply don't know the whys or hows, but I will find out. I'll do anything to bring the minnow back safe and sound.' Sam and Hec had privately referred to Eilidh as the minnow since her birth. 'The crazy thing is the threats to me and the family. I don't get it and neither do the police. There's something we don't know.'

'Hold on,' Hec said, 'I met Eilidh down in London a few weeks back. She's been doing some journalistic research for an investigative article, something to do with politics, City money and crime links.'

'Interesting.'

'She was bouncing with excitement. Maybe she's been getting somewhere and been found out. You know, corruption and all that.'

'Could be.'

'Anything more I can help with in London?'

'No. The flat's enough. Nothing else for now, but I'll keep you posted.'

'I know a couple of guys on the fringes of crime up here, maybe I could ask around.'

'No Hec, thanks all the same. You might tip off some bad people in the Smoke. I'll be in touch. Please don't do or say anything unless we've talked about it and agreed. Promise me.'

'Okay. See and keep me up to speed.'

'Done deal.'

66

HECTOR ARRANGED TRANSPORT through a friend with a trucking business. At 23.00 Sam was on a large articulated lorry, heading for Birmingham.

The Birmingham leg of the trip was a non-event. Sitting chatting and dozing was easy for Sam. In no time, they arrived in the truck stop at Hilton Services on the M6. The driver, a pleasant man called Ishmael, nudged Sam once the wagon was parked up.

'Wake up, we're here.' Ishmael was a handsome, slightly plump Asian Scot with a broad Glasgow accent. 'I'm away in for a spot of breakfast, then off Bristol way in forty-five minutes or so.'

They ate with little chat, Ishmael having got hold of a paper which he read, making occasional remarks about the news. Finally, it was goodbye.

Sam said he'd find his way to North Wales, wished Ishmael a safe journey and watched him depart.

* * *

Using a new pay-as-you-go mobile he texted Tonka. Forty-five minutes later he was picked up in the north-bound area. They looped around from the next exit, heading south using country roads. At last the arrived at a cottage beside Tanworth-in-Arden.

'Great to see you, Sam.'

'Likewise Tonka, or do you prefer Peter now?'

'Tonka's fine mate.' Tonka radiated calm and competence.

'How's Sally?'

'Dead.'

Sam jerked forward with surprise. 'Dead? What happened?'

'Cervical cancer, three years back. Missed in the routine tests. By the time we knew something was wrong, too late. Quite shitty and ironic, we couldn't have kids and it was the plumbing that killed her.'

'Why didn't you get in touch?'

'Not much to say and she didn't want people to see her. She never could abide a fuss … except for that bloody wild sergeant pal of yours from the Gorbals.'

'Glasgow?'

'Glasgow, Gorbals, Ardrossan, it's all the same to me, mate. Apart from professional contacts, I've only got one Scottish friend and that's you. Fuss is a wee hard man. Don't like the breed.'

'I suppose one out of two is a pretty good hit rate.'

'Fuck off,' accompanied by a short laugh.

'Right-oh, but if you ever get the chance, give Fuss the benefit of the doubt. THere's more to him than the cover, believe me. I've been to the wire with him a few times. He's okay.'

'I hear you.'

'Okay. I'm so sorry to hear about Sal. She didn't half put up with some of our nonsense.'

Sam gazed at his tough featured friend who had the look of a classic Roman aristocrat: aquiline nose, light eyebrows, chiselled and characterful chin, all slightly battered. Thick, cropped grey hair and eyebrows with patches of black and grey, set-off his alert, tawny eyes. His big hands were calloused and rugged from regular manual work.

'So, what's the score here?'

Sam told him, finishing with the threatening phone call.

'Woman's voice you say?'

'Aye, clear, precise, pretty and cold.'

'What have you been getting yourself into, Samuel?'

67

'GEMMA SENDS her apologies.' Maybelle Jones went straight to business, not even a welcome for Devlin Forsyth and Jim Thomas.

'What's up?' Jim said.

'Some sort of crisis for one of her big clients. Do-or-die thing and being unavailable isn't an option.'

'Understood. Bad news, Devlin,' Jim spoke. 'Maybelle and I swapped notes. We've got ourselves into the middle of some bother. Not of our making, I hasten to add. Our contractor is in poor odour with our gangster friends and, in trying to clean up the mess, achieved a rather unhelpful reaction.'

'Unhelpful reaction?' Devlin managed to sound both frosty and quizzical. Dressed in a city pin-stripe, he wore his dark hair parted on the right, like a fifties' schoolboy.

'One, maybe two dead, according to our police source. Also appears to have been a fracas involving Duncan before he left. We now believe he acquired intel we'd rather he didn't possess.'

'Are we beyond frightening him off?'

'Damage limitation time, I'm afraid, Maybelle. The risks are mounting.'

'You told him to stay put and so on?'

'Yes, Gemma did as agreed. She spoke to him and, as far as we know, he's taken heed.' Devlin said.

'That's true, Devlin, but it doesn't give us much comfort now.'

'Fair enough, Jim. But is our man staying away as instructed?' Maybelle said.

'He is, but for how long? On top of the potential leads, some weirdo cut the throat of a person linked to the kidnap of Eilidh Duncan. Police interest has gone from low-level to sky-high. There'll be problems suppressing a murder enquiry, especially with the added media spice of a lovely young man with his throat cut from ear to ear.'

'What are you saying, Jim?'

'I'm saying very, very reluctantly, we should take him out before he regroups or comes here and causes serious trouble.'

'But he is staying away.'

'I return to the question: For how long? The whole family has decamped to Ireland. He didn't travel with them. The risk is becoming major and getting worse by the hour.'

Devlin said, 'Come on, Jim. Moving his family may be a reasonable response to some unexpectedly violent events. Who knows what he's been told? He's connected to the police, with friends in your world. On the other hand, are we on his agenda? Can we risk an enquiry by a well-connected investigator, a loose cannon with contacts? You say he's had involvement in the intelligence side of things?'

'Yes. Here, in the US and in Europe. He's a top-class operative. From time to time he's played hardball, so won't deflect easily and *this is* his family.'

'Jim might be right, Devlin. We can control most of the enquiry events from our side, but a serious wild card? Is the risk so great we should remove it?' Maybelle asked.

'I've no problem with silencing a problem person. Still, I'm reluctant to go after this man. My trader's antennae aren't twitching yet. Are both you and Jim sure this is the best course?'

'I am,' Jim said.

Maybelle nodded. 'Shouldn't we consult Gemma?'

'I had a quiet word an hour ago, Devlin. She supports us if we decide to go ahead,' Jim said. 'Risk management has been discussed several times now. In isolation, I'd avoid going for termination, but Duncan is one fire we can put out … tomorrow. He's joining the dots. Taking him out keeps them separate and, with any luck, us off the radar.'

'Okay. Reluctantly, I agree.' Devlin paled. Chancing your arm on the market as a trader was one thing, sanctioning a hit, quite another.

Maybelle said, 'it's only business.'

'I'll set things in motion.' Devlin said.

'Thanks, Jim. I'll apply more pressure to the criminal fraternity. Who knows, maybe they'll do some other sorting out of their own.' Maybelle smiled grimly, her skin showing a slight sheen of sweat.

Go button pushed, the meeting ended without any minute-taking or further informal business. Jim Thomas strode down the corridor whistling a quiet tune. Outside he sent a text:

> *Sorry for the delay in getting back. Can't make it. Hope you have a great party.*

68

WILLIE AITKEN enjoyed a super day. After breakfast, he'd spent some time relaxing, walked Barney, went to the office, then joined the Session Clerk, James Smith, for lunch. This was followed by an hour back at work, getting himself organized to start the next day. Afterwards, he took a wonderful nap, then out for afternoon tea with a local friend. It was all so much fun and generous.

Tea, delightfully, meant another foray into good cooking. Willie's return to pastoral care boosted his morale and energy. Tomorrow, after a morning's work, he'd be attending the lunch club in the library meeting area where he would sit down with the more advanced in years.

He'd spend the afternoon in the office and, in the evening, the choirmaster expected him to attend the rehearsal and meet the team. Thursday night involved the Rotary, as the guest of a local businessman and Kirk elder. He'd soon be coming here for holidays. He smiled inwardly at the thought.

For the past two hours, the work on his sermon had been rewarding him with a clear message and the enjoyment of creativity. When you were on a roll with a discourse, you felt a real sense of accomplishment. It was like pottery, experiencing the joy of seeing the artefact emerge from the clay. A whisky was getting nearer.

A press on the doorbell snapped his train of thought. Willie scribbled a few reminders and rose, happy to have a visitor.

He switched on the porch light and unlocked the door, opening it with a wide welcome on his face. A man was stood pointing at him. Pointing, why?

He didn't hear the plop of the bullet that shattered his teeth, severed his spine and blew the lower half of his head off. Nor was he aware of his fall straight backwards onto the hall rug, some blood and brains spattering on the phone stand and wall.

Another round in the skull and the two in his chest were completely unnecessary.

In the kitchen, Barney started to whimper. The assassin went through and called him over. Looking doubtful at first, the dog's tail tip wagged a little with unease and hopeful optimism. He approached the killer who fired a round through his head, then one more once he'd stopped twitching. Force of habit.

The killer put the porch light out, pulled the door to and went away.

Later, his shoes and clothes disappeared into a waste disposal site near Hexham. He liked easy money. Ten grand, tax-free, for slotting a simple target. Killing people meant nothing to him. Pity about the dog.

* * *

At 10.00 next day, Liza Clark arrived to do the cleaning and laundry. The horror she discovered would haunt her dreams for life.

69

BREAKFAST, planned for 08:00, started at 10:15, both of them sleeping on: Sam exhausted, and both somewhat hung-over.

'I want to be in the London area by tonight,' Sam said, 'got to get sorted.'

'Where're you staying?'

'Kensington. I have access to a flat, care of my brother and one of his business connections.'

'Sounds posh.'

'Probably is. The owner's in Dubai for six months. I have a key.'

'I'll drop you off in The Smoke, mate. Least I can do.'

'Not necessary.'

'I'd like to.'

'Okay, thanks, thanks a bunch. Let's go. Why don't you bring an overnight bag? There's parking at the flat.'

They decided to watch the news headlines. The first report was a predictable less than optimistic piece about the Credit Crunch and home repossessions. Next was yet another politician being caught exploiting expenses and allowances. The third story silenced their conversation after a double take.

'*... reports are coming in of the murder of a Minister in the Scottish Borders town of Westerholm. Early information suggests this bears the hallmarks of a contract killing. The police report they are not in a position to provide any details other than to confirm a murder enquiry has been launched ...*'

'Oh shit!'

'Christ! The story you told me yesterday is growing legs, mate. You're caught up in something.'

Sam switched his mobile on. 'Got to call Karen.' He rang a number and got no reply. 'Bloody poor signal where they are.' He sent a text then switched the phone off. 'I'm in a shooting war.'

'No, *we're* in a shooting war. I remember Eilidh. Cheeky little monkey. My diary is clear, my sinews are strong, my loins are girded and you need some serious help. Sorry about your friend, if it's him.' Tonka said.

'It's Willie. Lovely man. I'll grieve later. Job to do first.' Grieving later. How many times had he put off the grief at the sharp end? A pocket full of pain, stored up for ages, sometimes years.

'Let's get moving,' Tonka said.

After driving for twenty minutes in silence, 'Know something?' Sam said.

'What?' Tonka flicked his eyes sideways quickly, attentive yet focused on the road.

'Bit worrying when someone's prepared to assassinate you to stop you looking into your sister's disappearance.'

'Yup, killing and disappearing people is a serious step. One thing, mate. The easy answer is at the other end of the chain. Why not just kill Eilidh?'

'Why not indeed? Want to go home, Tonks?'

'Nah. You need help, mate.'

70

A STONE-WALLED causeway joined the Irish mainland to Mweenstor near Carna. Once over, they reached a staggered crossroads which demanded a right-left manoeuvre before going straight ahead, up and down over a small hill, towards the rugged shore.

Fingers of vicious skerry reached out to grasp the sea, interspersed with patches of bright sand and glinting shingle. Rock pools abounded with a careless scattering of seaweed clusters. In the distance, the yellow wheelhouse of a Spanish trawler, wrecked years before, provided a reminder of the power of the North Atlantic. With an abrasive wind stroking the face, the salty tang of the air and a distant roar of thesurf, this place engaged people whether they liked it or not.

Around 100 metres from the shore, on the right, lay the house. The L-shaped building possessed a staunch gable end and stout double-glazed windows. There were stalwart dormers along the upper floor interspersed with large skylights. A short drive and parking of beach gravel, pebbles and dirt lay beyond a rustic five-bar gate. The main entrance stood just three metres from a right-angled bend where the other part of the 'L' made inroads into the garden. 'Garden' seemed too benign a word to describe an area of wind-blown rough grass and wildflowers surrounding the drive, but one couldn't deny the rugged beauty.

Once unpacked, Karen enjoyed sitting on a worn bench below the windows facing the sea. The cottage held many pleasant memories for her and the family. The girls knew the area well and were happy to spend days on the beach. She had explained enough of the situation to help them understand the importance of staying close to the shore side of the house and no further from the house itself.

The two watchers (as she and the girls called them) never spoke beyond pleasantries. Karen only bumped into them as they came or went off watch, stopped in for food and other creature comforts. Sometimes they watched together. One was always awake. The 'off-duty' watcher crashed out and slept for most of his spare time.

She tried to absorb a book on meditation and the benefits of the less-cluttered life. It wasn't working.

Abby applied herself in the kitchen, churning out scones, cakes, soups, sandwiches, as well as three square meals per day. She stayed busy, running the heart of the home, it eased her tension. She rubbed her hands on a cloth as Karen came in.

'Hello, dear. How're you bearing up?' Abby looked suitably granny-like in a big blue, shapeless dress and a white apron. Her strong arms were bare below the elbows and the smell from cooling scones and a brace of cakes improved morale.

'Thought I'd pop in for a cuppa and listen to the midday news.'

'Good idea,' Abby said. 'Lunch at one-thirty. A scone'll tide us over. There's ten minutes to go, so we've just time to make some tea and butter some scones. Fuss, are you around here somewhere?'

'Aye.'

'Want a cuppa and a scone?'

'Yes, please.'

'Ready in two minutes.'

'I'll be right through.'

Karen switched on the radio and came into the middle of the weather report. The presenter droned out an encouraging forecast.

'Good for the girls,' Abby smiled.

'Yes.'

'Marvellous how they've settled into the rhythm of life here so well, considering the situation.'

'They're a fine pair. I just wish they'd stop fighting half the time.'

'That's natural.' They talked family as the headlines started. Shock stopped the conversation.

'… begun enquiries into the assassination of a Church of Scotland Minister in the Scottish Border town of Westerholm last night. Early reports describe this as a gangland-style killing. Police are tight-lipped regarding circumstances and say a woman found the Minister mid-morning…' The reporter's voice was impersonal.

They did a double-take, staring at each other, mouths agape with shock. Karen stumbled to a chair, hardly comprehending the words. Abby dropped a plate in the sink where it smashed.

'I got that, Karen, Abby. I'll head into Carna. There's a signal near the shore.' Fuss seemed business-like and calm. They couldn't see the lightning flash of adrenalin shoot downwards from his throat to his gut.

Leaving the house he tripped the walkie-talkie. 'Boys, the news just headlined an assassination in Westerholm. I'm hoping it's not our Sam. I'm sure he was heading off. He gave no details. You know the drill. I'm off to Carna.'

'Roger that. They're covered.' Freaky said. Bilbo waved as he went into his hide.

Working hard to stay calm and focused, Fuss switched his phone on and drove off. Almost a mile later, on to the causeway a text pinged in. He pulled over and read:

> *I'm alive, tell Karen and Abby. Willie gone. Baddies probably don't know they didn't get me, yet. Bit scary. With Tonka. Don't reply to this number. Out of use. Karen to Milo's bar for 19.00. I'll call. S.*

Fuss laughed aloud, punched the steering wheel, turned around and darted back to Mweenstor.

'That was quick.' The walkie-talkie blurted.

'Good news. Good news.'

'Telepathy was it, you scrawny Scots git?' Freaky said, he couldn't keep the smile out of his voice.

'No, a fuckin' text, you English twat. The banter stopped. 'The bad news is Sam's minister mate was slotted.'

'Fuck!'

'Yeah, a war's started. I'm goin' in to tell the lassies about Sam and sad stuff about their pal.'

'Tough one.' The tone once again impersonal, focused.

'Aye.' Fuss parked and hurried into the house. Abby and Karen were hugging each other, both pale and shocked. They hadn't moved since he'd left barely ten minutes before. 'Sam's okay. I had a text before I got off the causeway. Sam's okay.' An audible and prolonged sigh escaped from the women who released the tears they had been struggling to hold back. 'There's also some bad news.' Fuss felt the old, sad, familiar pain of communicating painful information. 'Sam's pal, Willie the Minister, is dead. They killed him.'

'Ohh!' Karen sobbed in earnest. 'Poor Willie. Sam loved him like a father. Poor, poor Willie.' She paused. 'Where's Sam?'

'I've no idea, but he says to be in Milo's for 7 o'clock and he'll call you.'

'Right,' Karen said, 'not a word or sign of this to the girls. Tell the boys, Fuss. Are you okay, Abby?'

'I'll hold up. I'll go and wash my face,' Abby said. 'Sam was right to get us away.'

'We're well out of the way.' Fuss said. 'We'll take some tracking down.' He didn't like lying but sometimes it's the right thing to do. It wasn't what he said to the lads.

71

THE ATMOSPHERE BOILED-over, tense and angry—business as usual for the Jenkins brothers. The initial exchanges boomed away like adolescents having a row: swearing, posturing, accusations, counter-accusations and, as the anger burned out, the ability to listen and engage the thinking part of their brains returned.

'Come on, come on, let's calm down. You told me everything was squeaky clean, Charlie.' Charlie leaned forward and made to speak before responding to a stop gesture from Bill. He sat back, compressed his lips and listened some more, arms crossed firmly on his chest. Bill continued. 'I've just talked to my City contact and he tells me this human trafficking lark that Tommy is working on is bad news … ba-a-a-ad news.'

'I never expected this to be a problem, Bill, I'm horrified, bro' … horrified.'

'You're not alone, my son.'

'You say the Vicar got topped?'

'Yeah. The asset says the people involved are seriously big players with a long arm, and we should avoid any further attention to this matter. I said we're not responsible for the problem. That Bizz lot created trouble for themselves by taking his sister. They cut us out of the loop, did a deal with Tommy, and shouldn't start blaming us when things go wrong.'

'Blaming us, that's not fair.' Charlie sounded hurt.

'How many of the people we lean on would say we're fair?'

'Yeah, gotcha.'

'For now, we've got to go along to get along, but we don't forget this, not ever. We're being mugged or used as an excuse. Still, something's wrong.'

'So, where are we?'

'Charlie, we must break any links to Tommy's human trafficking. Did you tie off the loose end?'

'Yes. Sorted him personally. No extra people in the loop. I wore a plastic suit, incinerated with all my clothing afterwards. No bloody DNA, squeaky clean.'

'Right. Good job. We need some risk management. Our core businesses are being threatened by this sideline. Duke Earl should be fine, let's keep him onside. Are Tommy and Jackie liabilities? Got to ponder.'

'At least somebody sorted out the Vicar for us.'

'Yeah.' Bill nodded, but he didn't share his worries. 'Charlie, don't do anything without us chatting first. Got that?'

'Yes.'

'Fine. Now, one last thing. I've set an investigator on the business contact who called the hit on the Vicar and expect to know more soon. Let's eat lunch and come back to decide how to get clear of this minefield. Jason and Martine are popping in for a bite with Dad and their favourite uncle.'

The mood changed instantly with attention now being paid to the family. 'How's Jase doing?'

'Pretty good. He's been running his division well, the profits are super and the growth potential gold-plated, especially with our Mick friends in Dublin. That time he spent with Andy G in the States paid off. He learned management and enforcement from business-like tough guys. He's quite a frightener when he needs to be, but he'll learn to use diplomacy. He's got some good lads on his team and they go about their work without drawing attention to themselves. He's developing a sound business head. I'd like to bring him in on this after we eat. You okay with that?'

'No problem, Bill, good to see our enterprise taking root.'

They relaxed into lunch mode. Then, on cue, the phone rang and the receptionist told Bill the family had arrived and were starving.

They left as if they lived in another world, which they did with family and friends. Jason knew the score and wouldn't discuss business in front of his sister. His dad admired his developing skills and hoped he'd be the man to take the firm all the way to legit.

72

SEVEN O'CLOCK appeared on the elderly quartz clock in Milo's bar. Fuss and Karen were sitting at a table near the door. The mobile in Karen's bag sounded. She pulled it out and answered.

'Hello.'

'Hi, love.'

'Oh Sam.' Her eyes misted. 'Where are you?' She walked out, past a cluster of smokers at the entrance and into the car park.

'The Smoke, and I'm fine. How are the girls?'

'Okay. The weather is good and they've been spending their time on the beach. Just the occasional nippy words and emotional outbursts. You know.' Karen didn't notice Fuss move to lean against a wall watching the main road. Nor did she see the weapon covering her and the car park from between two bushes. She sat down on a stone bench.

'Don't I.'

'Fuss keeps the security tight. Fred spends a lot of time being invisible. He seems decent enough.'

'He's sound, old Freaky. He'll keep you all safe or die in the attempt.'

'He brought a friend along, quiet fellow, big hands, Norman or something. He does invisible well too.'

'Good old Norrie. We call him Bilbo because he kept reading and re-reading The Lord of the Rings. Another seasoned man. We couldn't ask for better protection. How's Abby?'

'She's taken charge of the kitchen and is operating a production line. She supplies constant soup, sandwiches, meals and hot drinks for the men. We just help ourselves when we're hungry. She's cooking up a storm.'

'Nobody will starve then.'

'Makes me a spare part. I've got time to think and worry. Poor old Willie. He didn't deserve to die like that.'

'I'm sad I'll not speak to him again this side of the grave. I've another bad piece of news.'

'Worse than Willie?'

'Barney. There's no easy way to say this.' Sam's voice broke. 'Whoever shot Willie killed Barney at the same time. Johnny Lucas has buried him on the hill.'

'Oh God!' Silence. 'I'll tell the girls.'

They were quiet for a moment.

Karen said. 'What are you doing in London?'

'Keeping things moving with the police. All the action seems uncoordinated and knee-jerk. Something's gotta give.'

'What a fright I got when the radio reported the assassinated minister in Westerholm. Poor Eilidh. Do you think she's still alive?'

'I'm not sure. Between us, okay?'

They talked on intimately, verbally touching and holding each other, caring for the kids and crying for the dog.

'Okay love, can you put Fuss on?'

'I think he's still in the pub.'

'Nah, he'll be nearby.'

'I see him.' Karen signalled Fuss who walked over.

'Hi, Boss.' The gruff Glasgow accent a real change of tone.

'You're well organized.'

'We are that. They're both well hidden. Bilbo is less than thirty metres from the house with a good view when he's not relieving Freaky. He's got a shortened and suppressed Ruger

10/22 with a twenty-five shot capacity, goes full auto as well. Right now he's forty metres away covering me and the missus.

Freaky's 400 metres out, he can cover the causeway too. The fields of fire are spot on. The house is covered both sides. They have night vision. Always one on watch, often both. We're sound.'

'There'll be some tears when you get back.' Sam said.

'How so?'

'They killed Barney the wonder dog along with Willie.'

'Fuck.'

'Karen'll tell the girls.'

'Okay. I'm sorry to hear that, I know how much you loved him.' A wistful silence, then business.

'Right. We got you away in good time. They may get inside information on our movements.'

'We're ready for 'em.'

'No surprise there then. Food okay?'

'Fuckin' fab-dabby-dozey. That old lady of yours can cook.'

'Which one?'

'Both of them. You're no' trappin' me, Sammy boy.'

Back to business.

'Check for a text every two hours, okay?'

'Got it.'

'Regards to the lads.'

'Roger that.'

'Bye.'

Sam felt alone as he prepared for his next move.

73

TENSION CRACKLED at the Bizz board meeting. The hit sparked a national wave of publicity and speculation. Comfort in short supply, blame apportionment laced the talk.

'Well, Jim, not exactly a discreet assassination.' Maybelle Jones said.

'No, eliminated the enemy and sent a serious signal to our criminal friends, particularly the godfather types, about getting their house in order.' Jim Thomas said

'Didn't we cut them out of the loop on this one?'

'Yes. Yes, we did. The hit used an asset from the North-East. What I mean is there's a lack of structure on the criminal side. Stupid mistakes should be avoided.'

'Thanks, Jim. I'm worried the murder of this man Duncan will cause us trouble downstream,' Gemma Smythsone said. 'I shouldn't have backed the killing.' Devlin Forsyth gazed at her impassively, secretly enjoying the fact that they had an on-off affair. Their colleagues knew about neither the relationship nor the links they shared with other powerful people.

'Maybe you should make sure you attend meetings.'

'Relax, Maybelle,' Devlin said. 'We decided to remove Duncan because he represented a serious threat to our business. There was no choice. The deed is done, the problem gone and the godfathers warned. Your job is to use your Met asset to apply pressure keep the godfathers in line.'

'I'm doing that. My asset is sowing the seeds of misdirection, and helping us achieve some level of invisibility.' Maybelle said.

Devlin said. 'We've done what we had to do. Jim discussed his plans with me following the meeting and I agreed with his logic. Still do. His operative was back on his own turf before the hit was discovered. There is no tie-in to us. The payment for the service was arranged from outside the EU by funds transfer into a private account after blind transactions. Contacts are as secure as the intelligence services can make them, one of the benefits of our cabal. Job done. I'm sad we were forced to terminate a man of the cloth, but business is business.'

'Sorry folks, this is a reality I hadn't expected. I'll get over it.' Maybelle's round face still showed a mist of perspiration although her features were more composed. Her dark suit and lilac blouse with the lace ruff remained smart and pristine. There she sat, every bit an executive who had to cope with, and move on from, upsetting news.

'We are where we are, and I don't care for termination either. Having said that, I do like the profits,' Gemma said. The others nodded agreement. 'I'd prefer to keep killing off the agenda if we can.'

74

The whole world was trying to give him a bollocking.

'Now, Tommy, this breach of security caused grave embarrassment to high powered people of my acquaintance. Everything was to be handled as sweetly as possible. You were paid well to collect, process and deliver the merchandise. What, exactly, went wrong?'

Tommy knew that lying was not an option with these particular people. 'The help, Mr Forsyth. The drivers decided to stop for light recreation with a young woman before they completed the disposal of traceable materials, and some of the stuff got nicked.' Devlin glared. 'I found out after the trouble started and took corrective action.'

'Where are the drivers now?'

'Abroad. Three months minimum.'

'Can you arrange to retire them?'

'You mean permanently?'

'Yes. What would be the likely cost of that?'

'Twenty grand for the pair. I'll make special arrangements with some professional operators.'

'Please see to it.'

'Consider it done,' Tommy reassured him.

'Now, regarding the question of your own situation …'

Tommy couldn't hide the tremor in his voice. 'Yes?'

'You are safe, provided no more major balls are dropped. Do you understand?'

'Yes, Mr F.'

'How soon can you make the retirement arrangements?'

'Within forty-eight hours.'

'Quicker if possible, there's a good chap.'

Tommy, listening to the patronizing tones, experienced the joint sensations of being put down and inadequacy—an angry brew. Not something he'd forget.

'I'll do what I can.'

The edge in Tommy's tone earned an immediate manipulative response from Devlin, who began to soothe a bruised ego.

'The money will be wired to you tomorrow. Oh, and by the way, may I say this is, in my humble opinion, just a temporary glitch in a strong and developing business relationship. The top men are impressed by your savvy and effectiveness. This dangerous situation, with the potential press involvement, is causing concern. Believe me, I stood up for you and explained how effective you are. There's a bright future ahead, Tommy.'

'I'll sort the problem.'

'Of course you will. Every confidence.'

Devlin hung up and prepared for another, related call.

75

TOMMY PHONED a man in Puerto Banus. Ten minutes and £12,000 later the deal was done.

* * *

The van-men headed for a party at the kind invitation of one of the retired criminal types (£1,000). They boozed with him enjoying the pre-party warm-up. When they were well-oiled, he called them a taxi to take them to the shindig. They sat in the back and were driven to an underground car park in a new development (£1,000).

Wobbly and bleary-eyed with booze, they got out of the taxi and were met by two cheerful men who apologized for the building site. The 'fiesta' was, '*over this way … sorry for the noise but the builders are still working in places … fuck me, they're pouring concrete …*' They walked up some cast steps to the side of a fairly deep pit and, without even having time to turn and ask questions, each received a bullet in the back of the head and a push over the edge (£8,000 for the two). Their still-twitching remains lay in the foundations of a shortly-to-be-erected block. A concrete river engulfed them as they lay in their last resting place (£2,000). Job done.

* * *

Tommy received a call twenty minutes later.

'The two items in question are sorted.'

'The payment will be made in the usual way.'

'Thanks.'

'Is a return consignment due anytime soon?'

'Around a week.'

'Any to spare?'

'Some.'

'What are we talking about?'

'Ten, maybe twelve.'

'Ten will do.'

'Agreed.'

'Price?'

'£200 K.'

'Deal.'

'It's good doing business with you.'

'Yeah. Fantastic, mate. Speak soon.'

Two calls followed the conversation. The first to Bill Jenkins from Spain. The second to Devlin Forsyth from Tommy.

Different viewpoint, similar subjects: dead men don't tell tales.

76

'WELL NOW, how's your good self, Sam,' O'Casey said. He spoke warmly, having opened the fire door into the lane. 'You can't be the minister assassinated up north.'

'True.'

'A delight to see you alive and well.' They shook hands.

'Thanks. Good to see you too!'

'Shall I assume the killing is coincidental and unrelated to your recent visit down here?'

'Anyone's guess, but I'd appreciate you not broadcasting my being around. As regards calls to find out anything, just lie. Haven't seen him since last week. Who? Either should be fine.'

'I'll do that. What brings you back?' O'Casey secured the door and led Sam through to his office.

'A feeling. You asked me about Orin O'Reilly and your cousin Brendan Haughey. Have you some information?'

'Twitchy stuff, Sam. I need your discretion.'

'Of course.'

'How do you think you got picked for killin'?'

'Don't know. Random? Spotted coming out of barracks or a cop shop? I've no idea.'

'If I was to tell you that you were fingered by one of your own, would you be concerned?' O'Casey's expression was dead serious, lips straight, eyes focused on Sam.

'I'd be shocked, but if you say so, I'll bear it in mind.'

'What were you working on?'

'Not a lot.'

'Were you getting anywhere?'

In Sam's head, the wheels turned, but he couldn't respond with clarifying information. 'I can't discuss any of that, sorry.'

'What happened to you afterwards?'

'I was removed, posted from Northern Ireland, never to return. What are you telling me, O'Casey?'

'I'm telling you I've been told that your own people gave your picture to the killer. They might even have told him where you were and kept him posted. I think I'm sayin' they set you up.'

Sam's face paled and he shut his eyes. 'Ouch! Oh dear, oh dear, oh bloody dear! If you're right, we have a thread going back over twenty years.'

'Don't say I'm not good to you.'

'I hope you're wrong.'

'I'm inclined to think my sources are sound. Somebody will be thinking you're a hard man to kill. In their shoes, I'd be worried.'

'Fear makes for stupid moves, happens all the time. Let's go through this again, from the top. I need to take notes.'

Sam pulled out a small notebook and the conversation continued. The longer they spoke, the greater his unease. Later, when he went out through the back door, he thought of his family. He turned left and exited the lane a block away from the public entrance to the Neon Orchid. He wasn't seen.

What was the connection to the past? To the Troubles?

77

DISCUSSING MURDER can be a pleasant conversation. Two people, who knew each other well, enjoyed an international chinwag between England and Spain.

'How's life in the Costa, Del?'

'Super, Bill, super. Sun's always shining. Women always willing, beautiful and know when to bugger off.'

They both chuckled.

'Things seem to be complicated for you at the moment.' Del said.

'Somewhat complex. Untidiness earns its own rewards.'

'As do secure lines,' Del said.

'Too right mate. Too right.'

'Tommy is bringing in a consignment in the next week or so.'

'We'll take him over.'

'Done wrong?'

'Nah. His guys screwed up and the people we're dealing with are worried about security. Can't say I blame 'em. They cut our firm out of a loop and are paying the price. There are still some loose cannons about, a tidy-up is happening as we speak. Left town, they say. Probably won't be back if they've any brains.'

'You think that's concrete?'

'So I hear. Makes the best of a bad situation and the main business is too good to lose … at least the inward half.'

'Poor old Tommy. He won't be happy with the takeover.'

'Toughl. One more screw up and the entire operation is toast. If we don't step in, the deal will be dead in the water. We've been examining the business for a while and making approaches to the right people. The middle men over here are comfortable. We'll secure lots more market share at the right time, and the rest is just supply, demand and greed,' Bill said.

Del knew the way such takeovers worked. It was a simple choice for Tommy. 'You're gonna make him an offer he can't refuse?'

'Yeah,' Bill replied. 'I won't be dealing with Tommy myself. Our friends are taking responsibility, something of an apology for a lack of consultation.'

'Nothing damaging for you with this, Bill?'

'Nah. Tommy made the contract on his people and we'll help him grow. We're clean and well removed from the day-to-day. Insulation. It's the best way of keeping the heat out.'

'Excellent. Come out and see us again soon, old son.'

'Will do.'

They ended their conversations with the usual family pleasantries and chit-chat.

78

'MR FORSYTH?'

'Ah yes, Tommy.'

'Job done.'

'I knew you'd deliver, thank you. You've received the payment?'

'Yes. Thanks.'

'Must dash, but thanks again. I'll be in touch again shortly.'

Tommy hung up, feeling pleased about achieving a difficult deadline. His latest consignment of young women was due to land at its destination late evening. The return shipment would be despatched in twenty-four more. Things were swimming along.

Too bad for the van-men, but those were the breaks. They had screwed up, there would always have been doubts about them and now, with a simple bit of action, they'd never be seen again.

79

'JIM, YOU SAID our friend had been eliminated.'

'Yes.' Even the wrinkles on his ill-fitting shirt frowned with unease.

'So, what do we think took place, Jim?' Maybelle Jones managed an acidic and patronising tone.

'Duncan moved fast and left the area much quicker than we expected. He arranged for a pal to cover some of his work and put him up at his home. Our intel confirmed one man in the house. Correct information, wrong man. The hit was utterly professional: right place, right time, as planned.'

'So we killed an innocent bystander.'

'Yes, Devlin.'

'We cocked up?' Maybelle said.

'Yes.'

Silence reigned as Maybelle, whose dark eyes bulged under pressure, fixed a glassy stare on Jim Thomas. The hush demanded explanation, adding more pressure with every passing moment.

'In the best-run operations we always risk collateral damage, people get hurt. Last thing we want. I can't say how sorry I am. At least it's a clean situation. The killing should be untraceable and I'd stake my life on that being the case.'

'Quite.' Maybelle: a seasoned blamer. Another pause, less ominous but still uncomfortable. 'So where is the Vicar?'

'Hard to say, but we do know where his family is.'

'Anywhere nice?' Maybelle said.

'Maybelle, enough of the blame game! It's a cock-up. I can't deny it, alright, *ALRIGHT?* It's a bad mistake and I've held my hand up, *OKAY?* Now's the time to plan our next move. Don't just sit on your lardy arse being pompous. You need to get your head, no, we need to get our heads around what we should do next to retrieve the situation.'

'You've no right to be personal and rude.'

'Hark at her. Who are you going to report me to? This isn't PC country! *We*, I say again, *we* got it wrong. *We* must sort it out.' Jim said.

'Jim, I think we're listening,' Gemma Smythsone said. 'People are understandably upset and disappointed. It's a ghastly situation, but it's real.'

'Spot on, Gemma,' Devlin Forsyth said. 'We're concerned, we must act and we're in your hands, Jim.'

'Thanks, Gemma, Devlin. Sorry, Maybelle. The facts are that our man flew the coop with amazing speed. We put the frighteners on him and, clearly, he moved in a direction we hadn't expected. He got his family out and sent 'em to Ireland first thing on Monday. That's bloody quick. Assets at airport security recorded their departure to Shannon. They had transport pre-arranged and headed north, somewhere past Galway. We thought he'd returned home. There's no real surveillance cross-country between Prestwick and where he lives. Enquiries are ongoing through assets who won't point fingers at us if things get tricky again. One of the target's old military friends is with the family, riding shotgun. We'll know more by tomorrow morning, maybe later today.'

'Can our enquiry be traced back to us?' Maybelle said.

'No. The airport information is low-level, widely available and easy to access. We add risk if we show more than a normal interest. Enquiries are being made outside of formal channels, via people we pay for information. They'll be excluded, shortly, as we hand over to our criminal friends and they, in turn, use their own networks. There are people in the Republic who are well plugged-in, and enjoy useful little earners from the wild men of Dublin.'

'Why are we so deeply enmeshed with these gangsters? Our main business is a white-collar proposition,' Maybelle said.

'Let's remember our arrangement with Bill Jenkins is a huge contributor to our income. We've built an expanding, quality relationship with him, on customs avoidance, and it's growing quickly.'

'Right, Gemma. We wanted to frighten a pain-in-the-arse journalist off our case. The options were kill or scare,' Jim said.

'We chose scare,' Maybelle said.

'Right, Maybelle. We didn't use Jenkins because it's not up his street and we don't want a major criminal knowing too much about our activities.'

'So, we used someone else.'

'Right again, Maybelle. Making the Duncan woman disappear needed certain specialist skills. Devlin knows a man who specializes in that sort of thing. The disappearance went like clockwork, although with unforced errors by our contractor,' Jim said.

'Sounds risky,' Gemma said.

'Risk is inevitable and we contain it. We're close to, but not enmeshed with, some rather bad people who we do good business with,' Jim said.

'… who think we are even more seriously criminally-connected than they are,' Devlin said. 'They've taken the blame for the mistakes. They may not yet know the Vicar fellow escaped our net.'

'And the men who disappeared our journalist?' Jim said.

'Gone abroad, never to return.' Devlin said.

'Guaranteed? They could be another loose end.'

'No, Maybelle. They'll not be back, I promise you.' Devlin said.

Jim said. 'Never?'

'Never.'

'You mean permanently never?' Maybelle said.

'Permanently.' Devlin nodded with an authoritative scowl on his face. Silence.

'Now, to our vicar … where were we?' Maybelle said.

'As we know, he's moved his family to a remote part of Ireland, and put them under some sort of guard, although one old ex-squaddie doesn't sound like much,' Jim said.

'Don't underestimate these people. We've done it once and an innocent man died, a parson no less.'

'Quite right, Gemma. Got to keep our noses clean. Any risk from the asset you used, Jim?' Devlin said.

'None, Devlin. I guarantee absolute discretion. He's available when needed.'

'That's good enough for me, Jim. Let's aim to be a step removed from any further action. Agreed?' Devlin said.

Maybelle peered over half-moon glasses like a judge at the Old Bailey. 'Do enlighten us.'

'We make millions a year with much more to come. We can apply resources to pay for help and insulate ourselves from action or investigation,' Devlin said.

'Amen to that,' Jim said.

'Agreed and relieved.' Maybelle signed up with a smile that raised smiles all round.

'Let's keep our hands clean and continue to act through third parties. I'd like to work with Jim as a colleague on any action, because it will be a useful learning experience. Jim?' Devlin said.

'Fine.'

'Right ladies, are you both happy with this?'

'Okay with me,' Maybelle said.

'Fine,' Gemma said, 'but no more collateral damage … and report back regularly.'

'Yes report back regularly,' Maybelle said.

'The first step, Jim, is to find him.' Devlin said.

'Right.'

'Maybelle, assuming Jim is free, can we stay on here for an extra hour or so after the other business is done?' Devlin said.

'No problem.'

'Thanks.'

With that they went back to the proper Government work they were paid to do.

* * *

An hour later the planning of Sam Duncan's permanent termination began.

80

'NOW, BILL, this fellow could cause us untold harm and is jeopardizing our business. Tommy couldn't fix him. My contacts got the wrong man, damned bad luck. The hit was as professional as they get, but the Vicar managed to be gone before people knew,' Devlin said.

'One vicar more or less doesn't make a big difference. They all believe in Heaven, so what if they arrive early?'

'He's ex-military. Bound to be able to handle himself,' Devlin said.

'Put a scare into some local hard men I understand,' Bill said.

'Sorry?'

'The people sent to scare off The Vicar by one of the less bright local contractors. I think it's called "role reversal". The Vicar made them reveal all.'

'Oh.'

'So, what do you want from me, Mr Forsyth?'

Devlin noted a change in the tone of respect, a move towards less. He became uncomfortable. 'My contacts can sanction another attack straight away, but we wonder if you'd be more comfortable resolving this yourself, following our dropping of the ball last time.'

'Why should I give a fuck if they decide to kill off a poxy vicar?' Bill said.

'Because he may be on your patch, or heading your way.'

'My patch? They want me to fix their problem for them, do they?'

'Possibly.'

'For possibly I read definitely. What's in it for me to sort this out for you?'

'Goodwill and support in high places.'

'Like what?'

'Like useful intelligence. Avoiding hassle like the seizure of 200 keys of coke a few months back. They can give you heads up on a lot of that stuff.'

'Mmm ... might be useful. We lost a lot on that deal, money and manpower. Three men will be doing lengthy time. What must I do for this help?'

'Sort the Vicar.'

'As in …?' Bill said.

'Sort him. Take him out.'

'Top him?'

'Yes, find him, neutralize him and benefit from the gratitude of my contacts. I'd like you to be a full board member. It'll add a million a year to your bottom line over the next few years.' Devlin Forsyth said.

'Sounds good. The family's in Ireland?'

'Yes.'

'We have close associates in Paddyland. The way to a man's heart is through his family, I always say.' Bill laughed, a smug sound. 'The Irish can be quite forceful. They'll lend support. Are the family located?'

'We're close. We managed to get a line on them. They're north of Galway town. You know, probably an isolated house somewhere.'

'I'm sure I can finger 'em in no time.'

'There are two girls, a mother, a grandmother and a retired soldier. Should be straight-forward. Obviously, it's up to you to gather intelligence and avoid surprises.'

'Leave this to me, Mr Forsyth.'

'Devlin.'

'Leave this to me, Devlin. Any problems, I'll come back to you.'

'Ideal. Thank you.'

'Any word on the Vicar?' Bill said.

'Not by the sound of things.'

'Scare 'em, shall we? That should bring him out from wherever he is.'

'I suppose so, let's open the batting.'

‘I’ll keep you posted, Devlin. We’ll get on the case. We might even manage something quite soon, all things being equal.’

‘Thanks, Bill.’

The call ended and thinking began.

81

EILIDH THOUGHT she was in her flat. She came to partial awareness thinking of Norman Brown, from Hull, telling her about William somebody or other. The name lay somewhere in her papers. The man, who visited Brown’s boss, had a posh accent. They’d been chummy and had spent a lot of time together. A senior official in counter-terrorism, it was natural for him to review ports of entry.

After the first visit, Brown’s boss began dropping in at the ‘coal face’.

In a dreamy half-aware state she wanted to check her notes. This man, William, had also shown up in a procurement contract review, the team thought it a poor bid, but the service supplier won. What was the big man’s his last name?

She was near to the answer when her right breast was grabbed roughly.

‘Got beautiful boobs on her.’

‘Leave her alone.’

‘I’ve half a mind to give her one.’

She began to cry.

‘Leave her be.

‘If you weren’t my brother I’d thump you.’

'You and whose army?'

'Better keep your eyes on her.'

'If you touch her, I'll shop you to the big boss in London.'

'Fuck you.' The leaner man, wearing a ski-mask, stormed away.

'Sorry love. It'll be over soon.' He paused, '*Silly girl. This wouldn't be happening if you'd kept your nose out of matters that don't concern you.*' The injection stung. As the world drifted away, Eilidh remembered a detail from the auditors' report. It pointed to criminality.

The paper in her mind morphed into Sophie's screaming, distorted face as the nightmares came shrieking back.

82

BILL DECIDED the Irish trip would be a safe chance for Jason to flex his muscles as an enforcer.

'Jason, come in here, I have a job for you.'

They spoke for around ten minutes.

After the chat, he made a called his Dublin business associate, Denny O'Martin.

'Bill. What can I do for you?' Bill told him. 'No problem. An old fart sergeant and a cluster of women. Just send your boy over and consider the evil deed done. There'll be wheels and men ready in Shannon, 11.00 tomorrow morning.'

'Thanks for this. I won't forget.'

'No problem.' Bill would never be allowed to forget the obligation, no bad thing in itself, as obligations and services to others built and strengthened relationships. 'Well, maybe one slight issue, one of the lads I'll send hates the Brit military.' The Irish brogue was warm and comforting. 'Would there be a problem if the old soldier popped his clogs?'

'Not for me, my friend. Do what you have to do.'

Four hours later, O'Martin confirmed an ex-soldier type of man, two kids, a woman and a granny on Mweenstor just over the causeway from Carna. As a communication channel, the drug supply network worked well.

83

AT 10:30 the following morning Jason Jenkins arrived in Shannon Airport. He cleared the arrival formalities and strode on to the concourse. As instructed, he stopped at the meeting point.

'Mr Jenkins?'

The voice was gentle and articulate Irish, a stark contrast to the rugged, sandy-haired man with hard, penetrating black eyes who spoke.

'Yes.'

'I'm Strangford. I'm here to transport you to a meeting. I've brought two colleagues along to provide gravitas.' Close up Strangford's countenance bore the evidence of more than a few blows which had altered the angles and planes of his face. The loss of symmetry added character and a hint of danger.

'Pleased to meet you, Mr Strangford.'

'Strangford is fine, Mr Jenkins.'

'Right, Strangford. Are we ready to roll?'

'Undoubtedly.' Waiting in the car park opposite, a black Mercedes Benz S Class 5.0 litre started. Strangford raised his hand and the Mercedes cruised over.

They climbed in the back and, in near silence, headed for Galway and onwards to Carna then Mweenstor, confirming the action they would take.

With his enforcer head on Jason dictated the show. Rough up the kids, feel up the mother and a black eye for the grandmother. Simple really. The old soldier would be killed and his body disposed of before they returned to a hotel in Limerick and dinner. A tough message would go to the Vicar. Jason would fly home the next day at nine o'clock. Easy.

The roads were fairly busy and the journey slow, taking four hours. They drove confidently past the farm machinery shop, turning on to the causeway and the crossroads. They did the zigzag over the angled junction, up a small rise and the house was in sight.

84

FREAKY'S VOICE SQUAWKED from the walkie-talkie. 'Possible contact. Big Merc and four gorillas.' Fuss, sitting at the kitchen table, put down his mug of tea.

'SitRep Bilbo?' Fuss said as he fitted the earpiece, aligned the mic and pocketed the communicator.

'Ready.' Bilbo said.

* * *

'Cellar please, Abby.' Fuss said.

Abby turned off the cooker gas, wiped her hands on a dish towel and hurried to the cellar door, switched on the lights, picked up the shotgun from its shelf, grabbed a handful of cartridges and descended. Fuss closed the door behind her.

'Where's Karen?'

'Three-quarters of a mile, on the beach, far side of the bay,' Freaky said.

'Karen, over,' Fuss said.

'Karen.'

'We have bandits, repeat bandits.'

'Roger,' Karen said. She distracted the girls and involved them in shell hunting. Ever watchful she looked back frequently.

'Right lads, show time.' Fuss said.

'At the gate.' Freaky said.

'I'm coming out.' Fuss said.

'They're parking.' Freaky said. 'You're covered.'

Fuss walked out the front door. 'Don't fuckin' miss.'

'Roger.' Freaky said.

The rules of engagement were basic. Wound where possible, any doubt at all and "extreme prejudice" applied.

Fuss neared the car.

Two men got out first and opened the rear doors for the other two. All wore dark suits. The men from the back seats stepped forward and made it hard for Fuss to see the two soldiers from the front seats.

'They're tooled up. Right rear has a Mac10.' Bilbo said. He was invisible yet only thirty metres away.

'Mac10 acquired,' Freaky said, eye to the telescopic sight.

The four men stayed close to each other. The big red-haired man faced Fuss. He looked like the leader and a piece of work to boot. He made eye contact, standing tall with hands clasped over his groin, close as a cricket box. His attention never left Fuss.

The other man at the front, probably in his mid-twenties, wore an expensive pin-stripe. A puff of wind lifted the corner of his jacket revealing a red silk lining. Black brogues, a white shirt and a blue-spotted tie completed his ensemble. His face was impassive yet somehow cocky and confident, surrounded by dark hair, short on the sides and gelled fairly upright. With a well-squashed boxer's nose. His thin-lipped cruel mouth, over a strong chin, did nothing to change the severity of his face. His ears stood out from his head. He said:

'You're a Jock, mate.' Fuss didn't reply. 'You're helping the Vicar,' (he gave the word a clipped, harsh sound) 'who is out of order. He must desist.' The cockney accent was clear and affected.

'I'll tell him.'

'Not good enough, old son. I want a word with the lady of the house.'

'No can do.' Fuss said.

'That's not good enough either. NOT-GOOD-ENOUGH!' The angry young Englishman pulled out an automatic which he held down by his side. Even though the day was fresh and the sky filled with puffs of white cloud, a thunderous tension grew.

'Don't lift the gun, son. You'll get hurt.' Fuss said.

The red-haired man stood stock still and made sure to keep his hands in plain sight. 'Jason, careful, they're prepared.' He said.

Lost in his own macho fantasy, Jason wasn't listening and started to lift his pistol.

'Stop, son.' Fuss put his hand up like a policeman directing traffic.

'Fuck you.' Jason said. Three red dots splatted on to the back of his hand. He squealed and dropped the pistol. The small-calibre bullets had torn through his skin, flesh and bones, splattering blood around.

As the gun fell the red-haired man raised his hands to chest height, palms exposed and rolled his eyes.

'Don't any of you move,' Fuss said. The man at the back lifted the Mac10. 'Don't son. DON'T!' The top of the shooter's head seemed to ripple. A red mist puffed as the round from the M85 burst through his skull followed almost immediately by the whiplash of a high-powered rifle. The bullet struck just behind his ear killing him instantly, destroying his motor function and spraying blood, some brains and bone over the rear of the car. He crumpled straight down on top of his machine pistol.

'Don't any of you move.' Fuss said.

The uninjured survivors gave him maximum attention. Jason made a sobbing pained sound and clutched his hand.

'Now, you.' Fuss pointed at the red-haired man. 'Are you carrying?'

'Yes.' He said.

'Slowly now. Pull out your gun, two fingers, lay it on the ground and kick it towards me. No wrong moves.' Fuss said.

'No wrong moves.' The curly ginger mop nodded as he complied.

'You at the back. Drop your gun and kick it away. Any more weapons anyone?' Fuss said.

'No.'

'You?' Fuss nodded at Paddy, the boss's son.

'No.' Paddy said.

'Now, lads, time to pack up and go. Take your dead friend with you.'

'You bastard, you haven't heard the last of this.' Jason, humiliated, couldn't contain his bluster.

'You've lost this battle so just shut it and go. Leave the gun. Talk to your friend here. He knows the score.'

'Strangford's got nothing to do with it. You'll pay for this.' The man called Strangford rolled his eyes.

'Shut up or take the consequences.' Fuss said.

'I'm coming after you, you fuckin' Scots git. I'm going to …'

A red dot appeared on the meaty part of his leg above his right knee. There was the slap of a small-calibre bullet striking home. He squealed, sat down and, after a moment, vomited on his lap.

Fuss made bemused eye contact with the Strangford who nodded. 'More lip and you'll be travelling in the boot with matey, so shut it.' Jason, white-faced, shut-up.

'Okay, Mr Strangford, you need to go. Leave the hardware. I'll drop out a bucket of water to swab the car. Blood and snot won't sit too well with the Garda. Stay within ten feet of the vehicle or die. No fancy moves, got it?'

'Understood.' Strangford said.

'Tell whoever you work for we didn't look for this. It's about an innocent family being dragged into danger by some bad people over the water.' Fuss said.

'I'll tell them.'

Fuss went into the house, updated Abby and then contacted Karen.

'Problem solved. Stay where you are for now.' Fuss said.

'Roger.'

He got a bucket of soapy water and returned to the car. Strangford and his uninjured colleague had stuffed the dead man in a body bag and were wrestling with the zip.

Fuss eyed the bag. 'Who was that for?'

Strangford looked him in the eye. 'You.'

‘Mmm.’ Fuss looked at the dead man. ‘Take out the old soldier?’

‘What can I say?’ Strangford shrugged. ‘He didn’t get his wish.’

‘Good. Any more of that ilk?’

‘No comment.’ Strangford said. Fuss half-smiled.

Jason sat on the gravel. Body bag zipped, Strangford picked up the bucket and gave the cloth to Jason who wiped the vomit from his trousers. Next, Strangford cleaned the gore from the rear of the car, carefully holding his jacket away from the surface with his left hand.

Fuss went back to the house and returned as Strangford put the pail down. He watched Paddy and Strangford stow the body in the boot and then help Jason into the back of the car. He handed Strangford two ampoules of Morphine. ‘Here’s a present, Mr Strangford, it should shut that arrogant shit up while you drive.’

‘Thanks.’ Strangford’s light green eyes communicated professional respect. He went to the back of the car and jabbed an ampoule straight through Jason’s left trouser leg.

‘Ouch, watch what you’re doing! That bloody hurt!’ Jason scowled as he spat out the words.

‘Not for long, laddo.’

‘Fuck you, Strangford.’ Strangford rolled his eyes and sighed. Fuss shook his head.

‘The message from this end to your master is simple, eh, Mr Strangford. We’re not looking for bother and only responded to extreme threat. Boyo got himself shot because he made a threatening move. Motor-mouth here’s alive because we could neutralize him with minimum firepower. We didn’t want to kill anybody. Your Mac10 man needed to be taken out before he harmed anyone. The brain shot protected you as much as us.’

‘I’ll pass word along.’ Strangford said.

‘You needn’t be involved in the trouble over the water. Don’t escalate action like this. The outcome may not be to your liking.’ Fuss said.

‘I’ll pass that along too.’ Strangford said. ‘Don’t threaten us.’

‘No threat intended. I’m only making observations and aiming to clarify things. Dead man got any connections we should worry about?’ Fuss said.

‘Don’t think so.’

‘The other guy has a gun back of his pants. He dies if he pulls it out. Acquired.’ Freaky said.

‘Your other lad is thinkin’ about a move. Stop him. We don’t do second chances.’ Fuss said.

‘Paddy, you listenin’ to the man?’ Strangford said. Paddy held his hands out.

‘Two fingers, drop the piece. NOW!’ Fuss said.

Wry-faced, Paddy pulled the pistol out and threw it away. Strangford raised one eyebrow and made a small shake of his head in acknowledgment and apology. Fuss gestured at the car door. The three men entered the Mercedes.

‘In case common sense doesn’t prevail … you’re in a kill-zone and will be even after you’re out of sight of us. If you stop, come back, do anything other than leave town you might all die.’ Fuss said.

‘Got it. Think about leaving town yourselves.’ Strangford said.

‘Yeah.’

85

STRANGFORD BECAME THE DRIVER, Paddy sat in the front with him.

The big Mercedes started, turned around, left the yard and took the road to Carna. They drove on to the causeway and slowed for a van coming the other way.

'Strangford, you honestly think we're covered out here? They won't get the jump on us a second time.' Jason said.

'They will. They'd kill us in a heartbeat.'

'Stop a minute.'

'He said, "don't stop."'

'Stop the fuckin' car. I'm in charge! Your boss told you that. Do what I say!'

'Okay.' Strangford stopped the car and held his hands up. Paddy did the same.

'I want to go back …' He didn't finish the statement because the wing mirror blew apart with a crash. '*Fuck!*'

'He did say …'

'Fuck you.'

'No, he said "don't stop" and we're not going to.'

Tyres squealed as the black car accelerated away.

86

FREAKY EXPRESSED SATISFACTION with his mirror shot, 600 metres and bang on. 'The big geezer put his hands up.

Didn't want a round through his skull. Jason has clout. He mouthed off before they stopped.'

'Right!' Fuss said. 'You okay with the killin'?'

'Righteous. If he'd got the zip gun up there'd have been a body count.'

'Yeah.'

"They were geared up for a walkover, didn't expect a fire-fight. Don't think they'll be back today.'

'Right, only two women, two kids and a rusty old fart … no danger. Even brought me a body bag.' Fuss said.

'Bastards. We're still alert.'

'Somebody fingered us. I wonder who the local druggy is. Let's find him. I'll talk to Sam.'

With the big car gone, Fuss took the garden hose and washed the gore and soap suds away through the gravel. The way the man had gone down had kept him upright. He'd do most of his leaking in the bag.

Clean-up done, he asked Karen and the girls to return to the house and called Abby out of the cellar. By the time the kids and their mum walked back from the beach all signs of the trouble had vanished.

Karen took Fuss aside. 'What happened?'

Fuss told her like he'd told Abby.

'One dead, one wounded?' Karen said, shaking her head and biting her lower lip.

'Why not tell the girls we had a drill?'

'No, they sensed my fear.'

'Okay, hold back the details,' Fuss said.

'Yes. Fair enough. I'll tell them some unwelcome people came to call and you and the guys chased them away.'

'True story.'

'Abby won't say anything, but she'll be under pressure.'

Karen entered the kitchen.

'Come on, Gran. What happened up here? Old Fuss looks pale.' Jeannie was interrogating Abby as her mother walked in. Alice looked on.

Karen said, 'Okay, I'll explain. In a nutshell, some men came to scare us today. Fuss and the guys saw them off.'

'I wish I'd been here.'

'Well, you got a chance to protect me instead.'

'I thought I heard a gun,' Jeannie said.

'I don't think so.'

'So, all your scaredness was a waste of time?'

'Maybe, but I'm your Mum, and I'm supposed to worry, aren't I?'

'Oh, Mum,' Jeannie said. 'You're soooo parental.'

'Right. We'd better pack. Your dad will be concerned when he hears about this.'

The girls went upstairs. Packing started with the clattering and banging noise of the young.

Fuss returned and talked of leaving. 'Tomorrow morning, Karen. After those boys get back where they're going, sort out the casualties and prepare for war we'll be long gone.' Her glance quizzed him. 'Dublin plates.' We don't need to hare off. Best we do an orderly retreat. Must talk with Sam and we've got to ensure a leaky person is silenced.'

'Not killed?'

'No, we're only for necessary killin'.'

'Excellent,' Abby said. 'Enough of the Rambos for one day. Anyone for a feed?'

The tension eased. 'Too right, Abby. This excitement makes me hungry,' Fuss said.

'Grub's up in one hour. Off you go.' She shooed them all out of the kitchen.

87

Once they left the Causeway, they kept going.

'Why'd you put your hands up?' Jason Jenkins said.

'To confirm who was calling the shots … them.'

'They shot me.'

'Rather you than me, sunshine.'

'My dad'll learn about this.'

Strangford said. 'You tell him. I've done what I was told and you're in one piece, more-or-less. Doesn't change the fact you're a fuckwit.'

'Fuck off.' Jason's weak and whiny tone invited more.

'You kept your mouth going when you should have engaged your brain, and that's why you've got a sore leg.'

'It hurts.'

'Lucky you, at least you can feel the pain.' Strangford said.

'There'll be payback.' Jason said.

'Take your medicine, Mr Jenkins, we've been up against pros. They were waiting for us and they're ready for us now … if we turn back.'

'Are we heading for Shannon?'

'No, Dublin.' Strangford watched Jason's eyes become heavy as the morphine took hold. He turned to Paddy. 'Call Michael and get him to arrange a funeral for Davy and a doctor for Jason here.' He waved his thumb towards the back seat. Paddy made the call.

A very relaxed Jason sang. 'In Dublin's fair city …'

Strangford scowled. 'Give him the other shot, Paddy.'

'Right. What do I do?'

'Read the instructions and stick it in him.'

With Jason's noise from the rear dying down Paddy turned to Strangford. 'The old man won't be happy.'

'No. At least his blue-eyed boy saw the light and managed to stay alive and uninjured.'

'He'll want payback.'

'Maybe, but he's a pragmatist. The information from London was poor.'

'Sorry, I ran off at the mouth. I was angry.' A woozy Jason chimed in from the back seat.

'Angry doesn't beat these guys. They could've taken us all out in seconds. The fact we're alive is a sign we ought to read.' He eyed Paddy. 'I hope you pay attention.'

Jason snored.

The mobile in Paddy's hand rang. He talked quietly, then broke the connection.

'We're to go to Molly's near Athlone. Davy will be taken from us and suitable arrangements made for his interment. Wide-boy is for a quack at Tullamore. We're to wait with him and meet the old man when Jason is sorted. We will drive him to town and put him in a fancy hotel in the city centre.'

'Right.' They settled down for the next two and a half hours of their journey. Within five minutes Paddy slept, which was more than could be said for his father who had a tricky phone call ahead.

88

'AH, SAM. Sam Duncan.'

'Ben Charlton? How the hell are you?'

'Retired but active, you might say.'

Sam remembered his former CO. Well-respected, proper, wild sense of humour after some gins, a strong and creative thinker.

'Thanks for calling. Good thing, text messages. Called your wife, she texted you. You called me. You're doing secretive, big time, at the moment.'

'No choice. My family's under threat. I'm making money for the pay-as-you-go brigade.'

'Yes, I spoke to your wife eh, Karen?'

'Yes, Karen.'

'Having something of a time in Ireland, I believe.' Charlton said.

'She told you?'

'No, her tone and anxiety was eloquent. Remember I met her several times before you upped sticks. Finding out about her nearness to Carna in the west of Ireland was straightforward after the call.'

'Sure.'

'Now, Sam. Am I on the side of light or darkness?'

'Good question, Ben. I know what I hope.'

'I'd say the light. Will you trust me for now?'

'Keep talking.'

'We're concerned about some naughty people. Your friend's assassination the other night, condolences by the way, is worrying.'

‘Yes.’ Sam said.

‘Can we meet?’

‘Why not.’

‘Where are you?’

‘You must know from my cell.’ Sam said.

‘I want you to come and talk. I’m not monitoring you.’ Charlton said.

‘I’m in London, low on the radar, looking for my wee sister.’

‘Yes, heard something about that, Sam. Your enquiries entered and irritated some nasal passages, rather scary ones at that.’

‘Quite.’

‘Are you acquainted with a man called Parker?’

‘Yes. Met him recently.’ Sam said.

‘I know him quite well. We became friends a while back during some legal to-ing and fro-ing. When he lost his boy, I attended the funeral. He investigates the low-life world, wanders the bottom rungs looking for facts and leads. In the way of things, we met, enquiring into unusual people and events, routine: commercial crime, old boy, not your style.’

‘No.’

‘But, you’re in the crosshairs … ’

‘Without a doubt, Ben. When would you like to meet?’

‘Later today, if possible.’

‘Where?’

‘Let’s say the pub where you last met Stanley Parker, and don’t tell anyone else.’

‘Okay, how about 20:00? I need a couple of hours.’

’20:00 is fine. Are you secure?’

‘I believe so, but no guarantees.’

'I'll bring minders. This white-collar badness smells somewhat and is pretty dangerous at the moment.'

'How can I verify your credentials?'

'Talk to Parker.'

'I'll do that.'

'À bientôt, Sam.'

'I hope I'll enjoy the meeting, Ben.'

89

'GOOD AFTERNOON, Parker.'

'Ah, Sam, come in, come in.'

Sam moved panther-like across the small office past several shiny brown leather high-backed chairs in dark stained wood. Nearby, a small side table in matching brown had some magazines splattered on its top. The walls wore a dingy cream emulsion. The door was half ripple glass. They sat at an old table facing each other.

'Thanks for seeing me at short notice.'

'No problem, my boy.' They shook hands. 'Client meeting in an hour, I need twenty minutes beforehand to tune in. What can I do for you?'

'An old army colleague of mine, Ben Charlton, made contact. I believe he's something of a spook now.'

'Eh, yes.'

'He says you'll vouch for him.'

'Yes. He phoned earlier and said he'd been in touch with you.'

'Have you mentioned me to him before?' Sam said, holding Parker's eyes.

'Yes. I called the police after we met in the pub the other day. I rang Ben and expressed concern for you after that.' Parker looked almost saintly as he explained himself. 'You might say that my experiences of life at the bottom, and of some of the bottom feeders made me concerned for a possibly naive country type, quasi-holy-man. Ben wasn't worried for you in the least. He told me you were a big boy, but he was interested in your situation.'

90

DENNY O'MARTIN spoke with the warmest, softest southern Irish brogue. His voice sounded like a smile. 'Bill, how the hell are you?'

'Fine, Denny, fine.'

'Some news from our side of things. Not good I'm afraid.'

'*Jason?*' Bill said.

'He could be worse. He got himself shot.'

'Christ! Is he badly injured?'

'No, painfully wounded more like. Nothin' life-threatenin'. At least two snipers we weren't aware of. '

'God! Sounds like he's lucky to be alive.'

'Sure, but he was shot with a small-calibre gun. It's his pride hurts most. They killed one of my lads,' Denny said.

'Not your boy?'

'No, praise be to the Holy Mother, one of my tough guys. The one who hated Brits and planned to take the old soldier fellow out. He ran up against some hard men.'

'Where's Jason?' Bill said.

'He's recovering from a spot of treatment and should be in a hotel in town tonight, all wrapped up and snug. A nurse and so on is arranged.'

'Good of you, thanks.'

'We're trying to keep this under the law enforcement radar. You may want an alternative to a public flight to bring him back. Security might be stressful.'

'I'll send a plane.'

'Good.'

'Now, tell me what happened.'

Denny spoke for ten minutes. '… that's it. I sent three people to meet Jason, including my number two, who is ex-Foreign Legion.'

'They were prepared for us,' Bill said.

'Yes. Snipers are impressive. The big gun was quite a way off. They used radio communications and managed the shooting zone like professionals. My man reckons they're special forces. Describes them as cool, respectful and hard as nails.'

'What warned them? Have we a leak somewhere?'

'I hope you're not suggesting …'

'No, Denny. God no, not you. Apologies, *apologies*. No, I'm thinking of over here. Got some daft stuff going on close to my business interests.'

'Does this include the family at Mweenstor?'

'Somebody kidnapped a young lady and the next thing her rather difficult big brother is looking for her. He's a vicar and ex-military. You visited his family this morning.'

'Got you.'

'We didn't expect they'd be so organised and, of course, we didn't get the leverage to make him stop being a nuisance.'

'A bloke I know has invested quite heavily in a nightclub in London. He's worried about some abduction shenanigans going on. Seems like young women have been disappearing for a while, nasty business. Ring any bells for you?'

'Yes,' Bill said.

'Is it connected to this?'

'Might be.'

'Any decent man would want to protect his sister.'

'Right.'

'So he gets his family out of the firing line and starts searching.'

'Exactly. He got another fuckin' vicar to take over while he was gone. The man was topped within a day or so.'

'Tough stuff.'

'Now, we turn up to scare his family and help some powerful people, but without the full story.'

'Shit, that's feckin' wild. What can he do?'

'Not sure, but he's still active. The situation's a mess. Invisible people are dabbling and interfering. We're investigating.'

'Any impact on our merchandise deliveries?' Denny said.

'Better not be.'

'What should we do about the Mweenstor lot?'

'Can you keep tabs on them?'

'Will do. We own a small-time fellow out there. He found them for us when we started looking. He'll keep us informed.'

91

THE LID BLEW off Karen's emotions after breakfast. She stalked round and round in an area near the beach with a good mobile signal. 'Karen, love… slow down a bit.'

'It's bloody hard, darling! Four men came to our secret place today. Three left alive, one of them wounded. They've blown away Willie and our dog. I'm scared for my kids and your mum, never mind myself. What are we into?' She sat on a rock with Fuss standing some thirty yards away. 'The girls and I were on the shore when Fuss called me on the walkie-talkie. Imagine trying to be a happy mum and wondering if a killer is heading your way,' she sobbed. 'We're exposed here. Our kids are in danger. Eilidh is missing. You've been assaulted. What are we going to do?'

'Move you again.'

'What do you think we are? Pack-and-go?'

'No, you aren't safe. Those men went away with their tails between their legs and they may come back mob-handed. Someone got killed, remember? I'm so sad anything happened at all.'

'Yes, yes.' She gulped air and puffed-out a hissing breath. 'Sorry darling, I needed to sound off. Anyway, it's what husbands are for.'

'How soon can you be ready?'

'We've started. Maybe an hour. The girls are uneasy. They heard shots and the explanation is *rather thin*.'

'So you need to improve your lying skills!' Silence. 'Joke.'

He could visualize the dangerously pink cheeks. 'Careful.'

'Are you okay?'

'Yes.'

'Is Fuss handy?'

'Yes.'

'Please wave him over and put him on. I think you should go out by road and back to Scotland via Larne to Troon. Can you face Westerholm? We've been promised protection by the police and more discreet elements of the security services.'

'How did you manage that?'

'Sold my soul.'

'You'll be safe?'

'As is possible in this crazy world.'

'I'm not ready for Westerholm yet, not after Willy.'

'Didn't think so. I'll get something fixed up.'

Karen absorbed the sea view, almost grey because of cloud and a slight mist. The distant cries of the gulls and smell of seaweed soothed her. 'God, Sam, I need you.'

'Thanks, good to be needed … I hope that didn't sound too schmaltzy.'

'What's wrong with schmaltz? My temperature's rising.'

'Put Fuss on, please?'

'Hi, Fuss, he wants a word.'

'Bye, love.' Karen handed the phone to Fuss.

'Bye, darling.'

'Don't darling me you fuckin' part-time soldier.'

In the background, Karen cackled.

'I need all the love I can get, you old war hound. We need to agree the next move.'

'Aye.'

They talked routes and tactics.

'We've got two vehicles with Freaky's. It's enough.'

'Great.'

Fuss sat back and shut his eyes for a moment and took a deep breath. 'Only one problem. We think there's a leak close by, the local drug dealer. He's bein' paid a visit as we speak.'

The dealer was well-known and not greatly liked. He talked in his Guinness and had let slip some facts which had been communicated barely half an hour before by a neighbour.

'He lives on the shore near Carna and we're having a wee chat for clarity on the leakage. After that, he'll meet Mr Morphine for a lengthier time-out. He might make an evening pint tonight. When he wakes up, we'll be long gone.'

'Sounds good.'

'Take care, Sammy.'

'And you.

The connection broke and Sam looked thoughtfully out the window of Ireland West Airport. This'll surprise the girls. He bought a packet of biscuits and a coffee and made another call after a hot sip of caffeine.

92

THE KITTEN proved itself a sneaky, delightful visitor, snuggling up and vanishing when someone came. Eilidh found the visits from the tiny creature uplifting, both healing and an anchor to the real world.

In the midst of her befuddled confusion, the little creature provided a brief sense of love and support before they drugged her again. The warmth of the small body on her neck, the purring, the swift move away when someone came. A furry little lifeline to sanity, a touch of hope and a connection to a world she knew.

Sam, please find me.

He'd never find her there.

93

Sam arrived at Ireland West Airport at 08:30 that morning via Stansted. It meant an early rise.

The car and a minder came for him at 05:00 and made easy work of the journey travelling in the opposite direction to a building rush hour.

He had always liked the sense of space at Stansted, and having a bodyguard along was a novelty. He checked-in and went straight to security. The minder left him at the entrance.

He remembered Charlton's briefing. 'You're valuable, Sam. We'll keep tabs on you until you go through security. Unlikely there'll be any threat after that.'

'So, what precisely makes me valuable to you?'

'As a rule, villains try to hide from us. In your case, they're looking for you. You're a magnet.'

'A sacrificial lamb more like.'

'Mmm, fair enough, but not right now, and certainly not in an airport or some obscure part of Ireland. We don't think they know where you are, but let's take no chances.'

'Tonka is down here.'

'Oh, you mean Waberthwaite, top-notch operator. Lost motivation, I believe. We spoke to him two or three years ago, no interest. Wife died, took the puff out of him.'

'He's got his puff back.'

'Excellent. We'll talk more when you get back. Family first.'

* * *

Once in Ireland West airport, he relaxed, read a paper and enjoyed the lack of bustle.

When the Zafira arrived, he sneaked alongside.

'What kept you?'

'Daddee!' Alice shrieked, her spontaneous joy warmed him. 'I've been queasy.' He made a sympathetic face.

'Hi, Al.' She leapt from the car and slammed into his arms. Jeannie followed, trying to look cool, if swift. He hugged them both. 'Boy have I missed you two. Queasy, Al?'

'Yes, queasy. Mum says it's the bendy roads.'

'Can you take some more?'

'I suppose so,' Alice said. Her attempt at a stoic face failed, belied by her bright-eyed bouncy energy and aura of happiness. She beamed. 'Dad, I'm loving this holiday.' She danced a little jig on the spot. 'I can't wait to get on the ferry. Neither can Granny.' A thoughtful expression slipped on to her face. 'Will Barney be in heaven?'

'He's there already. One day we'll see him again.'

'I cried about him.'

'So did I.'

'Did you?' He shared a sad-smile and nodded.

Jeannie grabbed his elbow and took him aside, serious. 'Dad, Mum and I were talking about the sex education stuff. She admits you sometimes … er … you know.'

'Uhh Huhh.'

'Aren't you a tad old for that sort of thing?'

'Nope. Woody Allen said it's the most fun he ever had without laughing.'

'Oh, Da-a-ad.' She strode away blushing, turned around and came back. 'They killed Barney, didn't they?' Her eyes were bright with emotion.

'Yes.'

'We're in danger, aren't we?'

He paused and thought. 'Yes. All this moving around is aimed at protecting you all.'

'You'll protect us, won't you, Dad?'

'With every bone in my body.'

She looked into his eyes, lips twitching as she wrestled with her emotions and the words she needed to say. 'I do love you,' her mouth pursed, 'even when you aren't cool.'

'Come here.' They hugged hard. Jeannie buried her face in his neck and sobbed for the dog. When they separated she sniffed, gave him a shy smile and blew her nose on a tissue.

Karen came over and gave Sam a solid kiss. The excitement of meeting was infectious. They separated slowly.

Abby, waiting her turn with characteristic patience, grabbed him in a grizzly bear hug. 'My wee boy.' The love seemed to ooze from every pore in her body. His spirits warmed.

'That's me Ma, wee Sam.' They stood back and smiled at each other needing no further words.

Karen came back over and held his hand.

'Hi Fred, Bilbo.' Sam shook their hands. 'You're men I can count on, bless you.' They seemed to grow taller. Their faces remained impassive, eyes watchful.

'Fuss, a quick word before we go, please?' They stepped about ten yards past the cars. 'Is the songbird silenced?"

'Quiet for a while yet, three ampoules worth. He was the leak, for sure, sang like a …' gulp … 'canary straight away.' He glanced at Karen.

'That's quite a speech impediment you've developed.'

'Just …' gulp 'off you …'

'I should get that seen to.'

'Let's get the' gulp 'out of here.' Fuss looked serious, then he smiled with an out-of-character radiance, the expression of a man rediscovering a sense of usefulness and enjoying time with the family. He became the Sergeant Major once more.

'Come on you lot. Move!'

They moved. Sam drove the Zafira. Fuss beside him in the front, Abby and Karen in the middle and the girls in the rear. After half an hour, Jeannie complained of stiffness, They pulled over and transferred her into Freaky's Discovery.

Everyone was upbeat. Sam's mobile phone rang. He pulled over and stepped out of the car. Freaky pulled over 50 metres further on. A shape left the car and moved up the hill, a long shape in hand, and dissolved into the hill side.

Ben Charlton's crisp English voice. 'Are you safely over, Sam?'

'Yes, arrived as planned.'

'How's the family?'

'Shaken. My wife and mother are somewhat distressed. The girls are suspicious about what happened.'

'Where are you heading?'

'Larne to Troon. Karen's not ready for Westerholm yet and we need to find a safe place of some sort.'

'Divert to Belfast International,' Charlton said. 'You'll get a lift from there, then a break on Arran, the Scottish one. Sound okay? We have a safe cottage near a place called Sannox. The mystery men train in that part of the world, know the terrain well, and have rapid reinforcement from Prestwick and other places if needed. Supposed to be exceptionally beautiful, if a tad lumpy.'

'I holidayed there as a kid. Sounds good to me.'

'I'll confirm arrangements the moment we're finished. Teams are in place to provide surveillance and security. Your men can be engaged or not, as you decide. They know the score and are in good odour, possibly admired!'

'Good guys,' Sam said.

'Please get here first thing tomorrow. We need to irritate some people.'

'Understood.'

'A chopper will pick you up.'

'Thanks.'

'Speak soon.'

94

CHARLTON LEANED BACK in his twenty-four-seven chair which had more hydraulic levers than a tractor. He shaped his hands as if to pray before pressing his fingers to his lips. It was tough on Sam, a good man, dragged into a lethal, unravelling situation. On the upside, he now had a deal to protect his family and, conceivably, get his sister back. He hoped she was still alive. What had happened to her?

When Sam arrived in London they'd get down to putting the picture together. It was both worrying and quite exciting. Clear thinking would build the model about the whos, whys and wherefores, adding the snippets of information as they came in. Sam had skill at that sort of thing.

Tonka might be a strong asset too, if that worked out. Hard bastard.

95

SAM CALLED Freaky's car via the hands-free. 'Change of plan. We're heading for Belfast International. We'll go to Dungannon for a spot of lunch and then on to the airport. We should arrive for 17.00. Our friends believe we can make the next port of call quickly and safely from there.'

'Got that, Freaky said, 'we'll follow you.'

'Sound. Fuss will liaise.' Sam said.

He saw Bilbo return from cover to the Disco as he drove off. He smiled, safe for now.

'Why the airport?' Karen said.

'They've arranged a secure transfer for us to a beautiful secure location. They want me in London promptly after that. Their aim is to keep us all safe. More security people will be involved once we arrive. Oh, and one other thing, we're transferring by chopper.'

'Chopper, Dad?' Alice was quick on the draw, 'You mean helicopter?'

'Yes.'

'Faaaantastic!' Jeannie and Alice chorused, abuzz with excitement and expectation. Sharing between two cars at fifty miles an hour. Sam caught Karen's eye in the mirror as she appreciated the spontaneous brightness of the girls. He raised one eyebrow conspiratorially at her and winked, being rewarded by an increase in the happy-wrinkles round her eyes.

Fuss kept quiet, looking forward. A chopper wasn't provided lightly. The decision to drag Sam away signalled an urgent operational need.

'Roger that, ready for lunch. Speak later.' Freaky ended the connection.

Alice broke into Fuss's thought, 'Fuss, have you ever been in a chopper?'

'Aye, Alice.'

'Exciting, isn't it?'

'Aye, love. I've had some exciting trips on choppers.'

'I can't wait.'

Turning and smiling at her, Fuss nodded. 'Yeah, it'll be fun.' His face wore a serious expression once he faced forward again. 'Loads of fun.' His voice tapered away as he remembered some chopper trips that had been no fun at all.

* * *

Dungannon passed uneventfully. Lunch was large even by Irish standards. They arrived at Belfast International without incident. Driving towards the terminal a policeman waved them down and asked them to follow a marked-car. They went through a series of gates and entered a temporary two-storied office building. Uniformed personnel helped with the luggage.

Sam spoke to the security people. 'There are some unusual items of baggage.'

'Not unexpected, sir, I presume you mean items involving Messrs Sig, Sauer and Browning?' A regional accent and a note of humour. 'I would suggest the ladies in your party go straight inside and we can deal with any unusual items.'

'Thank you.'

'No problem. The chopper is due in an hour. In the meantime, an officer has dropped in from Belfast to see you. The receptionist will direct you.'

'Right. Fuss, can you handle things?'

'Aye.'

Sam turned to the official. 'Thanks again.' He walked to the beige-grey building. His womenfolk were clustered together and chatting. He went over. 'Someone wants to see me. Back shortly. We've got about an hour here.'

They nodded and kept talking. Jeannie came out of a washroom and Alice rushed in. Karen caught his eye and smiled before turning back to talk to Abby, who apart from lunch, had slept for the entire journey. He went over to the reception window and knocked on it gently.

'Hello, sir.' A young woman who was probably a police officer put her finger in the hole and pulled the glass wide.

'Hello, my name's Duncan, and I've been asked to see someone here.'

'Yes sir, that'll be Superintendent Molloy, he's popped down from the city. I'll buzz you through. Room twelve, three up on the left.'

'Thanks.'

96

THE LOCK BUZZED like a wasp in a jar, clicking open when Sam pushed the hand-plate. He went down the corridor to door twelve and knocked.

'Come in.' Sam walked in and looked at a face that, although slightly florid and filled out, was instantly recognisable. He recalled their last meeting over the bloody body of Orin O'Reilly. He scented the cordite and heard the screams for a moment.

'Don't tell me … Peter Molloy.'

'Pete.' Molloy extended a mechanical shovel of a hand. 'I'm told you retired.'

'Sort of. Temporarily back in harness.'

'With the family too, eh … Mr Duncan.'

'I can't explain just now.'

'Understood. The main reason I came down to meet you is curiosity. I'd like to know the end of the assassination story involving you in '94.'

'A hard day to forget.'

'Aye, memorable for all the wrong reasons. Anyway, please have a seat.' He waved to a chair and picked up the phone. 'Pot of tea for two, please, and some biscuits.'

'The abridged version is: my cover was blown and I moved on to other things. In 2001 I left the military, found a new career and wasn't involved in any way until the last few days.'

'Sure, you moved on. You had to. I'm interested in the picture story.'

'Picture?'

'Yes. O'Reilly had a copy of your official file ID.' With a growing chill in the pit of his stomach, Sam remembered O'Casey's briefing. 'I sent the photo to the MI5 contact: no comment or feedback. I followed up, hit a stone wall and let the sleeping dog lie.'

'I never knew anything about this until last week, when it came from a source in London.'

'Well yes. You'd been working with Sean James and Brendan Docherty on a number of bank raids and their connection to the paramilitaries.'

'That's right. Lovely guys. How are they?'

'They aren't,' Pete said.

'Aren't?'

'They're dead. Dead a long time. Brendan was a bloody good cop and a close friend. Bottom line was Sean was dead days after you left. Brendan, virtually brain-dead, followed Sean three years later.'

'We were investigating a series of bank robberies. I was the military liaison, we worked well as a team. I'll need some thinking time to remember. Give me contact information and I'll get back to you. How'd they die?'

'Surveillance. Their car was shot to pieces from behind, with a burst into each of them for good measure. They were assassinated.'

'My ID photo was in the hands of O'Reilly, the assassin?'

'Yes. It was recovered from his clothes by forensics.'

'Who'd you send it to?'

'Pulled the record when I saw your name heading our way this morning. Chap named James Thomas of MI5.'

'Rings a bell.'

'Not surprising. He was a link man for a lot of the counter-terrorism and organised-crime work we did. A scruffy bugger and quite arrogant. I worked with him once or twice.'

'Why would the three of us be targeted?'

'Maybe you stumbled on to something.'

The woman from reception knocked on the door and came in with a tray.

'Possible. Wait a minute, we'd had intelligence about a raid on a bank in Bangor and we were planning to ambush it. The name of the informant escapes me. I'll note it for my recollection exercise.' A shared smile.

'Does Rupert O'Callaghan ring a bell?'

'Sure … . He was the asset!'

'He died two days before the hit on you. We found his body a week after he was killed. He'd really been worked over. We thought the violence was down to hatred and nothing else. Christ, this joins up better than I dared hope. I only found out O'Callaghan was an informer about four years ago when we were looking into something else. Two cops shot up in a car is one thing, but add you and the informant and we have a conspiracy. This guy Jim Thomas better still be alive.'

'Hard to say. I'll soon be in a position to mention his name in high places.'

'I thought you said you'd retired to a new career.'

'Yes. I did. Something came up and, as I say, I've been temporarily re-engaged.'

'You're being treated like royalty, Sam. I wonder how long temporary is.' He reached into a square metal-framed briefcase on the desk. 'I brought along a copy of a file I made up on this. I'd appreciate it if you'd come back with your thoughts.'

'Give me some time, but I'll get back to you,' Sam said. 'One other thing, in '93 I was involved in a raid on a terrorist cell. In the firefight I killed one of the bandits. The story always told to me and my commanders was that the attempt on my life in '94 was to be a revenge killing. You've got me wondering.'

'Here's my card. Keep in touch. Good to meet you again.'

'Aye, you too.' Sam rose, shook hands and went back to the reception area a thoughtful man. The receptionist gave him a large envelope to seal the file in.

97

EILIDH LAY COLD, dirty and damp. She had no idea of the date in the constant nightmare of partial awareness, weird visions and unconsciousness.

The kitten leapt away and she became more aware than usual. Her minders were a couple of hours late attending to her. They came in bickering.

'So we're just going to dump her?' nasty-man said.

'We're doing a favour. It won't be forgotten,' nicer-man said.

'Okay, let's get the little cow moving.'

'Go easy on her.'

'Fuck off. We're druggin' her an' dumpin' her. I'll fetch the car.'

A blindfold was put on her. Nicer-man's fairly gentle hands released her from the bed.

'She's ready,' He got her to her feet. 'What's in the files you mentioned?'

'What files?' Eilidh said.

'The other night you were raving about computer files and talked about a memory stick.'

'It's just my writing. I think I've lost a pen drive.' In her stomach, icy fear and total confusion. Just what had she told these people?

'Well, you're a lucky girl. We're letting you go. Maybe you'll find it.'

'I hope so,' she said.

Nasty-man returned. 'Let's get movin',' he said. 'This is the only prick you'll have today.' He snickered as he jabbed a syringe into her thigh. 'That'll fuckin' keep you quiet.'

'That looked more than usual,' nicer-man said.

'Waste not, want not. A double dose'll make sure she behaves.'

She faded fast as they put her in the car.

'What have you done, Ned?'

'She'll be fine. Look she's sleeping like a baby.'

Ned? Then she drifted through hellish visions into the nothingness of deep, merciful unconsciousness. The next thing she heard was a siren.

98

HE SAT DOWN with his girls and talked. They were excited about the helicopter and asked about Arran. He told them stories of his childhood holidays there.

'Arran is one of the most beautiful places on earth,' Sam said. '"Scotland in miniature," is what they say. It's peaceful like Mweenstor, but a lot lumpier.'

'Do you mean mountains, Dad?'

'Yes, Al, rugged mountains and glens. You'll be staying near Glen Sannox. I spent holidays there as a boy.'

'I can't imagine you as a boy, Dad.'

'Probably just as well, Jeannie.'

'What's that supposed to mean?'

'I'd get even more cheek and rebellion from you, you big red-haired Valkyrie.' He reached out, wrapped his arm around her head, pulled her into a playful headlock and messed up her hair.

'Oh, Dad!' She blushed and he realized other people were looking on.

'Only dads are allowed to do that. Boys wouldn't dare.'

'Sort her out, Dad,' Alice said. She squealed when she realized she was next for messing, but couldn't escape a quick lunge.

'You pair. Your hair's a mess!' Eyes bright, they hugged him. From her seat opposite Karen enjoyed the fun. Abby, sitting beside her, patted the back of her hand.

The receptionist came round to speak to Sam. 'Excuse me, sir.' He nodded. 'Your flight is in and will be ready to board in about five minutes.'

* * *

On cue the roar of an engine increased in volume as the aircraft came closer, sideways. Fuss, Freaky and Bilbo arrived. Freaky's car was being transported for him and would arrive the next day.

Moments later they were flying. They landed after twenty-five minutes. An obliging pilot took them over the ridge between Cir Mhor and Caisteil Abhail, the dizzying drop away into Glen Sannox caused shrieks of delight from the girls which sounded again as they flew level with the Witch's Step and over the shoulder of Suidhe Fheargas, and down to North Sannox Burn car park. Two large 4x4s waited for them, their darkened glass adding an element of menace to their imposing bulk.

The winch-man opened the door as the rotors wound down.

A man stepped forward, 'Colonel Duncan?'

'Yes.'

'Please bring your party, sir.' They disembarked straight into the vehicles, their luggage stowed by each driver, with two more protectors on sentry. In a short space of time they drove up the single-track lane, forking left over the bridge and upwards to the road, the steep flank of Suidhe Fheargas standing like a jagged tooth above them.

99

THE CARS EASED down towards the and and the Firth of Clyde smiled through the trees. As Sam stepped out of his vehicle, his mobile rang.

'Hello.'

'Ah, Sam, you've arrived.'

'This minute, Ben.'

'Do get your family settled in. Be ready for extraction at 05.45.'

'Okay.' He stepped aside from the group and covered the phone and mouth with his hand. 'Before you go, can you get a discreet line on a former, maybe current, MI5 bloke called James or Jim Thomas? Something came up before we flew out. Gathering a few facts before we meet will be helpful.'

'I'll find out. Not so he'll notice of course. Enjoy a happy time with your folk.'

'Thanks. See you tomorrow.'

Security arrangements were explained, people introduced and ground rules detailed. The evening was pleasant.

Sam enjoyed a romantic interlude with Karen and all too soon, it was time to go. Later he thought of the farewells. A quiet conversation with his wife when he awoke. Had she been lying awake for hours? He felt for her. She was silent as she hugged him, hanging on hard for a moment, lips fluttering. Dry-eyed and smiling when he finished dressing, she showed a positive face to the world outside.

When he stepped into the hall, both Alice and Jeannie emerged. They'd been waiting for a while, concerned and quiet. Their hugs said it all. He whispered 'love you' in youthful ears. Their mother returned with them to their room and closed the door. In the kitchen, Abby waited with a cup of tea, her face drawn yet composed.

'I'll keep an eye on them, son. We're safe here.'

'Thanks, Mum.'

'Find your wee sister for me.'

'I'm trying hard.'

'It's awful pressure, Sammy, but you're all she has.' She cried then, like a sudden squall, briefly and with an incredibly deep sob before drying her eyes on her dressing-gown sleeve.

She regained her self-possession as if the recent outburst was a figment of his imagination. She gave him one of her strong hugs, a kiss, stroked his cheek, and left for her room without looking back.

* * *

Emotions churned as he drank his tea, then settled as he became focused and energized by duty and love. He stared out the kitchen window towards the jagged peaks of Glen Sannox and the grandeur of the Devil's Punchbowl, changing swiftly from silhouettes to staunch three-dimensions. He sighed, walked across to the Aga range and topped up his cup as Fuss came in.

'Off again, Sam?'

'Aye.'

'Always hurts a bit. Fuck, I even miss Sadie after a couple of days. Don't concern yourself about here. These boys are experts. I'll stay on for a few days. Freaky and Bilbo are heading over to Argyll for a spot of wanderin'. They'll stay handy for a time, but they don't want to cramp the style of the minders.'

'Okay. Ask them to delay on Arran until they're debriefed, which should happen today or tomorrow. I aim to catch up with everyone when this is all over and have a bash. Please tell them thanks again.'

'Will do.' Fuss appeared thoughtful, mouth clenched and turned down at the sides … waiting … Sam didn't make the invitation. 'You're in the right place here, Fuss.'

Fuss gave a bleak smile. 'I enjoyed the rumble over by. The excitement never goes.' A nodding head responded eloquently. 'Good luck, Sammy. Remember the Duke Street dictum: Do unto others before they do unto you. Forget the holy man bit if you're under fire. Shoot first and save souls later. Sleep well.'

* * *

A quiet knock at the door summoned Sam.

'Ready, sir?'

'Aye.'

Karen hugged and kissed him, brave, hair tousled from making love before his shower.

'By love.' She gave him a love you-hate you-but mostly love you glance and climbed into bed. She pulled the covers up to her chin and blew him a kiss, lips twitching gently.

He grabbed his pack, chucked it over one arm and marched into the sharp morning air, the sound of surf a distant hiss from beyond the dunes.

'Chopper'll be here in fifteen minutes. Pick-up is past the point. Let's go, sir.'

Ten minutes later Sam was on the shore, 200 yards beyond the measured mile pole, the base of the old sea-trial finishing line. Against this measure nuclear submarines and surface vessels alike, had proven their performance capability by surging through their paces, bow waves sticking out like sprinters' chests striving to burst a tape.

The increasing sound of a Sea King heading straight over from the Ayrshire coast overtook the peace. Minutes later he was airborne. He hoped the family would get back to sleep.

They were now truly safe and he'd have to earn the rent the hard way.

100

THEY ARRIVED AIRSIDE, at Glasgow International. A security vehicle transported Sam to a door near the gate for the 06.45 BA flight to London City. Handed a boarding pass, he confirmed he only had hand luggage. They took him through a security door and up some stairs. Twenty minutes later he was airborne. Given an aisle seat, instead of dozing he spent the trip being jostled and bumped by flight attendants' hips and occasional trolleys. Forced to stay awake, he got hold of a paper and read the current news covering the credit crunch, jihadi trouble, political ineptitude and questionable practices. Routine stuff.

A grisly article described how two bodies were discovered in the foundations of a Spanish apartment block. The corpses came to light because a human hand, sticking up through some ready-mix, was spotted by a pouring team. Early evidence suggested a criminal hit and a buried-alive victim who had struggled to get free.

A pleasant feminine voice instructed passengers to put up their trays, straighten their seat backs and fasten seat belts securely. The plane flew past Canary Wharf landing at London City Airport with a gentle bump. It taxied back from the end of the runway rotating on the apron until the door faced the terminal. Five minutes later, Sam walked briskly on to the concourse. The man who'd seen him off to Ireland the previous day met him.

'Morning.'

'Morning, sir. Good flight?'

'Yes, thanks.'

'We're going straight to the office.'

They slipped through the airport in moments and into a black saloon. Barely ten minutes from stepping off the plane he was in the car. Things were moving.

The minder closed the rear door and stepped into the front. The driver wished him good morning. They took him to an office on West Ferry Road. The male receptionist produced a visitor card on a chain when Sam signed in. Along the wall to the left of the desk was a solid-looking white plastic door with frosted glass and a smart card entry system.

As they neared the entry, the lock buzzed allowing access to a carpet-tiled waiting area with a few seats, doors and a corridor straight ahead. The gentle aroma of coffee oozed from a brewing machine on a small table. A notice board displayed formal documentation including policies, Health and Safety notices and other required bills and certificates, clear evidence of compliance with legislation. Everything looking pristine and unread.

The minders left him with, 'Help yourself to a brew, Colonel.' Sam took a sachet of Columbian. He picked up his drink, took a seat and relaxed, letting his shoulders fall with a sigh.

* * *

'Morning, Sam.'

'Ben.'

'Come through.' Ben led him into his office. 'How's the family?'

'Safe.'

'Excellent.'

God! Three hours from the peace and calm of Arran to business in one of the world's major cities. Sam half-smiled.

'A lot going down for you, Sam.'

'It's been a while since I've felt so operational. The family threat kept the stress levels up. Now they're safe and I'll be able to relax more.'

He was surprised to see an ordinary-looking window. Ben noticed his surprise. 'Aluminium oxynitride,' he said. 'New stuff from the States. The coating stops people seeing in and also stops most rounds up to armour-piercing fifty calibre. These walls are armoured as well. I'm glad you can relax on the family front, we've business to attend to. Two bodies found in Spain may be connected to this situation.'

'You mean the men in the foundations? I read about it on the plane.'

'Yes. Happened a couple of nights ago. A Spanish police undercover man got the intel. Fingerprints connect them to the London criminal fraternity. Their van turned up yesterday in a street in the East End. Routine surveillance, unfamiliar vehicles are cause for concern these days. It was examined as part of a normal anti-terrorist security check. There was some blood and other bodily fluid traces inside. Our police friends put us in the loop, and the tyre print links it firmly to an area behind the Neon Orchid. The fingerprints on a cigarette packet in the van match one of the concrete men. We'd like a DNA sample from you to match to some unidentified samples recovered.'

'Of course. Samples of what?'

'Blood and hair. I'm sorry.'

'Yes, understood.' Sam looked out the window for a moment.

'We also found a street security video of the van leaving the lane at the back of the nightclub with, we believe, your sister on board. All good timeline stuff. Swindon and Cal Martin are doing excellent work. It won't go unnoticed.

'So, we have confirmed the van is linked to Eilidh's disappearance and other messy aspects of this whole mystery, such as the rape and hammering of the Madden girl, and the fight in the pub in Shoreditch with the idiots who hurt her. Events expose layers of action and initiative. Why did your sister disappear? Who disappeared her? What motivated this?'

'She's a rookie investigative journalist who uncovered something.'

'Good probability.'

'My brother said she was excited about things some weeks back when he saw her down here. Maybe she stood on some toes.'

101

TALK ABOUT a screw-up. Sam's mobile rang interrupting the conversation. He looked at the display turned pale, hung his head, rolled his eyes heavenwards and signalled he was going to step out of the office, Charlton nodded. He went to a chair near the reception desk which was vacant, cringing. 'Boy, Hec, you must be mad at me.'

'You're not bloody kidding. I'm in Mweenstor and there's nobody home. What the hell's going on, Sambo?'

'Give me a chance to explain.' Sam told the Mweenstor story.

'Christ, near one.'

'Aye. Can't talk more over this line. Get back to where we dropped the folk off. I'll send an email by then. I'm sorry for forgetting to contact you.'

'Understandable. I might forgive you one day.'

'Thanks.'

Sam returned to Charlton's office and related the chat with Hec. They both smiled and sympathized. Charlton offered Sam a webmail connection on his computer and within five minutes the Arran information was on its way to Hector.

102

CHARLTON POINTED at a large whiteboard on the wall. 'This is space for us to capture and structure our intel to build up a picture of what's going on. The story suggests at least four groups of criminals, five if you count the Dublin lot.

'We set up discreet surveillance at Shannon after your family's arrival. Jason Jenkins, son of the fearsome Bill, came from London to be met by a man called Strangford from a Dublin criminal gang and two colleagues in a big Mercedes. There are photographs, for review by your team.'

'Two will head off soon,' Sam said.

'Not before each of them studies the photos.'

'Right.'

'By all accounts, young Jenkins received a painful lesson at the hands of your man with a small-calibre burp gun.'

'The idea was not to kill anyone,' Sam said. 'The chap who died had a Mac10 and was making moves to use it. He was taken out to prevent serious bloodshed.'

'Understood.'

'The photos may give us an ID.'

'We already know who the people are: two Irish gangster soldiers, one now deceased, fortunately not the godfather's boy, one injured aspiring London gangster, and, lastly, a fairly serious criminal operator from Dublin who goes by the name of Strangford, very cool and calm, ex-Legionnaire no less. Not to be underestimated and, by all accounts, dangerous. Your people will confirm IDs and make statements we can use in court if we need them. Your family's safe, so now let's get down to planning, tactics and some cage rattling.'

103

AN ABUSIVE CALL from Denny O'Martin shook Colm O'Casey. The smiling psycho raged having lost a man and a chunk of face along with him. Denny took persuading of Colm's innocence, and the fact he was as much a victim as anyone else, paranoid swine. Colm emphasized the legitimate nature of the business. Like a flicked switch, Denny moved back into charm mode.

'Holy Mother of God, what are these wild men up to?'

'Not much good, Denny, and have limited wit or wisdom as far as I can tell.'

'This vicar man they're banging on about. Tell me more.'

'Been a player in his time. He killed a Provo assassin one-on-one during the Troubles. He's now an ordained minister of the Church of Scotland.'

'The fucker. A firebrand like that old bastard, Paisley?'

'My cousin gave the last rites to the assassin. The killer went to eliminate the Vicar and got the tables turned. I'd say he's a polar opposite to the likes of Paisley.'

'An angry daddy is bending my ear. He wants revenge.'

'Let it be for now. A lot of security people are crawling around.'

'His card is marked. He'll be pushin' up feckin' daisies if he sets foot in my patch ever again. Warn him, Colm. Warn him off.'

'I'll do that, sir. I'll do that,' Colm said, pouring a little oil of humility to soothe the bruised ego of a powerful man.

'Be sure you do.' A long sigh. 'Now, you say the profits are okay in spite of the recession? …'

The rest of the call was business-like and friendly, but he couldn't avoid a niggling doubt. Denny was good to do business with. The vindictive part of him meant he didn't forget lightly those who crossed his plans or sensitivities. Sam's people had made the Dublin crew look ineffective. They'd engineered a result against Denny's team, bad news stark and unavoidable. Young Paddy was of the same ilk as his dad and he'd be eager for a pop at Sam.

Colm wanted to keep his own nose clean. He hoped Denny would steer clear while the situation resolved itself, but they'd never forget and would go for payback one day. Pity the idea of forgiveness and moving on proved difficult for people in a crime lord's position.

* * *

The phone on Colm's desk rang.

'Colm, Sam.'

'Talk of the devil.'

'Can you spare me a minute around nine tomorrow morning?'

'Back door?'

'No, the front door from now on.'

Having hung up, Colm realized something had shifted. He didn't make any calls.

104

BILL FEARED for Jason. His boy spent an extra day in Dublin under medical observation. With his unaccustomed worry came a sense of powerlessness which, for him, meant anger close to rage.

His son, shot by some jumped-up soldiers. He'd find them, they'd pay. And, this bloody vicar! Just who the fuck did he think he was? He remembered his missus telling him to take deep breaths when he was angry. Today he did and, sure enough, he began to ponder more easily.

'When Jason gets in I want to talk to him,' he told his PA Annie.

'Yes, Mr Jenkins. Been upset, haven't you?'

'Yes, Annie.'

'Want some comfort?' He gave her a warm glance. She'd been giving him comfort for ten years. A smart looking girl, she earned her bonuses.

He could feel the beginnings of excitement in his groin, but business first. 'Comfort would be good, love. Maybe in an hour. A few things to attend to. Mr Forsyth will be dropping in shortly.'

'I'll bring him in when he gets here.'

'Thanks, Annie.'

The first call was a straightforward tongue-lashing for a small-time criminal who'd overstepped the mark. In a voice cold as slush he uttered frosty threats and implanted icy fear.

Devlin Forsyth arrived on time.

'Devlin. How are you?'

'Not terribly happy, Bill.'

'Me neither. Our friends tackled the Vicar's family and they got away. One of the Irish men died, my boy is injured.'

'Not badly, I hope.'

'Bad enough, but he'll be okay.'

'Two people killed in Spain surfaced from forty tons of concrete. Bain blew it again.'

'Can't blame him. The arrangements were good, I checked, the implementation and the plans were good. The contractors are responsible for the screw-up.'

'We're not sure about him.'

'What you decide is okay by me.'

They talked about business and plans of action for an hour. Their charity work was well known in the Docklands commercial community and being together would raise no eyebrows, even if the content of their discussions might. By the time they'd finished talking they had agreed to sort problems out as opportunities arose.

'Yes, we'll take the situation by the scruff of the bleedin' neck,' Bill said. They shook hands. Bill watched Devlin go and wondered …

105

A SECURE CONFERENCE ROOM held Devlin Forsyth's next meeting in one of the towers at Canary Wharf, near the Underground station. Inside two people waited one Asian of Chinese extraction, Kenneth Chen, a top banker and the other a Member of Parliament and the Privy Council, Sir Marcus Attenwood-Leigh.

'Devlin, old boy.' Sir Marcus stood up, walked over and offered his hand, a slim slightly stooped man about six feet in height, perhaps sixty years of age. He spoke with the practised, not necessarily sincere, warmth of true power, and dressed as always in a Reid and Taylor pin-stripe and old-school-tie. He offered a well-manicured hand. 'Lovely to see you.' At least the welcome sounded warm.

'You too, Marcus.' A nod to the side. 'Ken.'

'Devlin.' Sir Marcus led off. 'We are becoming concerned about recent events.'

'Understandable.' Devlin said.

'The network, Bizz included, is powering forward. People are extremely satisfied with their earnings and the quiet discretion with which things happen. The mechanism works divinely. Our cell system operates with speed and security. Everyone is delighted with progress and profits.'

'Fantastic.' Devlin smiled.

'The projections get better and better. We're talking billions, and it's early days.' Sir Marcus' eyes changed. His accent became clipped and icy-British authoritative. 'You are our man on the ground, Devlin. What are you doing to sort things out?'

'The best I can, Marcus. Things started to unravel when a journalist was disappeared. In fact, we weren't aware of a certain family connection that is causing difficulty. Sad to say, decisive remedial action hasn't worked out thus far.'

'Yes, didn't work out. Things must be resolved and quietened down. Silence and invisibility are all we ask. We want profit and a peaceful, harmless existence.' No threat was needed, the requirement clear.

'From your lips to the ear of God, Marcus.' Forsyth's sarcasm had bite. Sir Marcus coloured. 'No offence, dear boy. I don't think you'll be displeased with the action. As for the rest, I'll sort it.'

'Thanks old man, thanks. Anything to add, Ken?'

'No.'

After the usual end of meeting pleasantries they stood, shook hands and Devlin left. Sir Marcus turned to Ken.

'He's a good fellow, a bit out of his depth in an operative role.'

'Give him a chance, Marcus. He is riding a stormy sea with more than a few ships steering different courses. He hasn't got where he is by being ineffective. He'll sort things out and stay low. Our oversight is important but we mustn't be too controlling.'

'Fancy some lunch?' Sir Marcus said.

'Always.'

'Gemma Smythsone will join us. I'd like her view. She wanted to leave the journalist alone, you know. The man Thomas persuaded the rest. They hurried the risk assessment.'

'Power affects people strangely and becomes a lethal plaything in the wrong hands: people die, plans are threatened and sadness fills hearts.'

'Sadly.'

'Yes.'

'Lao Tzu?'

'No idea.'

They chuckled and left for a splendid lunch.

106

JACKIE CLEANED his small office, everything lifted off his desk and on to the floor, in all a phone, pens, a notepad and his PC. He dusted with thoroughness and replaced the items, giving each a wipe. The routine of cleaning relaxed him and, within the bounds of his capability, it gave him time to think. Truth to tell, given long enough, Jackie was every bit as competent a thinker as the next man. He only suffered from incomplete consideration when time-poor, a frequent occurrence.

He operated the vacuum cleaner and hoovered the carpet. The sound of the door opening passed him by until the power was switched off and suction stopped.

'Ziggy, old son. How are you?'

'What do you think?'

' Nothing I could do, Zig, out of my hands.'

Ziggy's eyes stared. 'We got ambushed by those bastards at the Stork. We did what we was told.'

'You didn't recover all the gear.'

'Did.'

'Nah,' Jackie spoke with authority, 'You missed some stuff in her bleedin' trainers. Her trainers, Ziggy. Helped the fuzz.'

'Did you arrange the attack?'

'Nah.'

'Who did?'

'Leave it alone, son.' Jackie gave good advice. He nodded and put on a half-sympathetic smile. Ziggy seemed to lean sideways and smashed him across the knee with what the police would call a 'blunt instrument.' There was a crunching sound. Jackie made a mewling noise from deep in his throat as his leg gave way and fell sideways to the floor, face deathly white.

'Who ordered it, Jackie?'

A realist, even through his agony, Jackie told him, 'Tommy Bain. Christ that hurts.'

Ziggy held a piece of lead-filled antler in his hand, about eight inches long with a thick brown leather thong. 'It's called a priest, Jackie. My uncle got it in Scotland where he went fishing. Came to me when he died. They use 'em to brain the salmon they catch. Some sort of joke about the last rites. Tommy Bain. He's a bit of a tough man I hear.'

Jackie hissed in agony. 'Yeah, hard as nails.'

'Who sent him after us?'

'Can't say.' He raised his arm to protect himself as Ziggy swung again breaking his right forearm in several places. He began to cry. 'They'll kill me and they'll kill you.'

Ziggy just looked at him as he made a connection. 'Billy Pliers! Big man. This must be serious.' Ziggy shook his head thoughtfully. 'Don't worry about them killing you, old son. I'll take care of that.'

Jackie died before lunchtime. Ziggy would later tell himself he had been firm when he needed to be, but not cruel, and that Jackie had died painlessly once he had given up his information … as painlessly as blunt trauma allowed.

107

TOMMY LOVED a sandwich and a pint at The Steaming Train on Battersea Park Road near the junction with Albert Park Road. He knew the locals. They'd been having an ongoing conversation for over ten years. They all thought he ran a small business, which he did. They didn't need details.

He'd enjoyed a juicy slab of a rare roast beef sandwich with nippy English mustard, a plate of salty chips and a wonderful, rich and hoppy pint of bitter.

He felt good. Yesterday the conversation with Forsyth had been difficult. It had been necessary to tell him where to get off, bloody posh bastard. He'd be conciliatory today, straighten things out and return to normal. The fuckin' journalist had caused a lot of trouble. And who had ordered her removal? Who'd rocked the boat? None other than bloody Forsyth himself. His anger bubbled away.

He drained the last of his pint and nodded thanks to Gino behind the bar. 'See you tomorrow, lads.' They all waved or grunted or said 'Bye, mate.' Fine bunch. He turned left out of the door heading for a walk around what he called 'the loop.' He believed the exercise kept him healthy.

As he turned into Latchmere Road, a man came up from his blind side and propelled him between two trees. He fell none too gently and started to get up as two gentle putting noises sounded. He partially heard the first but not the second. 'Double-tapped', his body collapsed backwards on to a wall and, sliding sideways down the brick, crumpled in on itself. His heart pumped desperate squirts from his ruined head before giving up on him.

His killer fired one more bullet into his heart and strode away.

Tommy was found two and a half hours later by some children playing on the way home from school.

By that time, the killer was whizzing through Stevenage on his north-bound train, enjoying a coffee and reading a thriller.

108

CHARLTON ENTHUSED. 'Well, my boy, we've got a few horses running now. This man Jackie Steel sounds a real possibility for a bit of sweating. The Met will pick him up later. There's been serious effort put into stopping you. Why? You're only looking for your sister. What we're having trouble understanding properly is the connection between the criminals and the commercials. We seem to have some high level, white-collar crime here, but the raison d'être and structure are unclear.'

Sam's mobile rang. He read the display, unknown number. He glanced at Charlton who nodded.

'Hello.'

'Hi. I'm looking for Eilidh Duncan.'

'I'm her brother. Who are you?'

'Jamie Carron, a commissioning editor. We spoke last week. She's now a bit behind with some deadlines and we want an update on progress.'

'Tell me more, Mr Carron. We need to talk.'

'I didn't give you my number, sorry. With me abroad for a few days, it's been difficult to communicate. Eilidh is providing a well-researched investigative piece for publication nationally. Her basic work is excellent and her delivery has been reliable as clockwork. Now she's gone offline. She isn't responding to messages to her mobile, her e-mail or at her flat. I finally managed to get her flatmate, Shirl Johnstone who gave me your number. Hence my call last time. I need to contact your sister.'

'Mr Carron, you know she's missing. I told you last week.'

'Well sort of. People don't kidnap journalists in the UK.'

'Where are you based, Mr Carron?'

'Wapping.'

'Let's meet. I'm over past Canary Wharf.'

'Is there a problem?'

'Yes, there is. I wasn't kidding when I said she was missing.'

'Sorry, I only got back yesterday. I'll come over. Where are you?'

'West Ferry Road.' Sam gave him directions. 'We'd like more information about what she was working on.'

'Okay, but you'll need to tell me what's going on before I'll give you anything.'

'Not over the phone.'

'I can be with you in about forty-five minutes.'

'Wonderful.' Sam terminated the call and looked at Charlton. 'Eilidh's commissioning editor and a connection to

Eilidh's investigation. At last, a lead to her work. I'll be interested to hear what Jamie Carron says for himself.'

'Cool head, young Duncan, cool head.'

* * *

'Now, until Jamie Carron gets here, let's look at the timeline we're assembling. Your friends Martin and Swindon are coming in later to show us how this should be done. I thought we might make ourselves a preliminary structure to the investigation.'

'Good idea.'

'Let's put some dates and content on the grid before they get here.'

'I'm glad they're willing to come so far from their patch.'

'They're seconded for the time being.'

'Seconded?'

'One of the joys of power. We're connected to the Serious Organized Crime Agency, SOCA, in a low-profile sort of way.'

'So, the enquiry is gathering status?'

'Yes, my boy. We enjoy clout and, hopefully, your sister's disappearance and your spontaneous investigation shook a rather poisonous tree. When small people rattle big people's cages, they're squashed. All good public school stuff.' Charlton was known for his egalitarian view of life, having been born to a miner's family in the Durham coal fields. 'You know the toffs, keep your place and all that. Boots and doormats. You either walk on others or they walk on you. Only Her Majesty gets to walk on everyone without having anyone to walk on her.'

'I see.'

Charlton harrumphed and became business-focused once more. 'I digress. Let's do our timelines and analyse the factions.'

They talked, put notes on post-its and began the foundation for building their understanding of the occurrences up to the present. Dates ran left to right across the top of the board and events and players down the left side as they began to structure their input. Both hoped Jamie Carron's information was going to be worth having. They discussed and added information on the wall. Then Carron arrived.

* * *

'Show him into the interview room please, Colonel Duncan will be through directly. He's all yours, Sam. I'll listen in.'

'Fine.'

Sam went into the reception space, found the door marked 'Meeting Room', knocked and went in. He pulled the slider on to the 'engaged' position and closed the door.

109

'SAM DUNCAN.' He offered his hand.

'Jamie Carron.' He shook Carron's limp, sweaty hand. Carron was dressed in a fairly macho style, medium length sideboards cut as short as the hair on the side of his head. He wore black clothing and a bright green tie. His long spotty face sported a snub nose topped by a high intelligent forehead and strong brows. His gelled hair stood erect. For all his lack of taste, Jamie had presence and an air of intellect and capability.

'What do you do here?'

'Nothing much. A desk from an old colleague, useful when I'm in town.'

'Before we start, let's be clear that journalistic privilege is sacred.'

'Of course, but we are talking about my sister here. Her life and well-being are sacrosanct to me and hopefully you as well.'

'Sorry, Sam, she is the most important part of this whole thing.'

'We have some facts to convince you the story will benefit from an exchange of information, plus the return of my sister as soon as possible. But, we must be certain disclosure only happens when both her safety and any necessary public interest or policing issues are well-protected until her release is agreed. I'm sure you're familiar with the general idea.'

'Yes,' Jamie nodded and then opened a transparent pink plastic folder with a button-down flap. Within twenty minutes some serious cards lay on the table. 'Her outline shows two broad strands. Here's an edited copy, scribble on this. I can't give you the meat.'

'Understood.'

'She began with information about procurement fiddles on an industrial scale. Insiders and businesses making loads of money from *almost* legitimate contracts. The second strand is an organized blind eye to contraband coming through our ports.'

Across the road, a pair of eyes watched the journalist enter the building. The surveillance had not gone unnoticed and his picture was taken several times. When he moved on, his departure would be noted and his movements monitored.

110

MAYBELLE STARED at the ceiling, eyes unfocused. An extremely capable person, she had a good degree from Manchester Business School and a Masters from Harvard. These had helped her shape a winning, fast-tracked career.

She enjoyed Bizz but had never considered a time when the decisions would involve life and death, nor how complicit she might be in the process. Fantastic money eased the pain. A large attractive person with all the normal urges and appetites of a liberated woman in her late thirties, she loved being abroad and spending with abandon. The 'company' credit card gave her purchasing power outside of her previous experience. How she enjoyed a private lifestyle, luxuriating in the good things and avoiding any risk of money passing through her usual accounts.

She poured a glass of well-chilled Chardonnay, sitting in the 'designer' living room of her flat, surrounded by comfy furniture, professional lighting, with some nice art on the walls. Almost distraught with mental anguish, an earlier conversation with Devlin weighed heavy in her thoughts. He had told her about a 'little rumble', as he put it, in Ireland. He reported the gangsters in London had partners over there and had set the dogs on Sam Duncan's family in the place they had gone to escape trouble. Jim had obtained security information on their landing and where they were heading, which he had passed on. The Irish had done the rest.

A confrontation occurred and the family disappeared. All the gangsters were unhappy, naturally enough. Dominance vanished with a bloody nose, no leverage and no idea about the disposition of the enemy. The trail to his people and Duncan himself had vanished at Belfast International.

The pressure was on Maybelle, with her police, security and customs connections, to find out what had happened. Accustomed as she was to the rigid hierarchy of the Civil Service, the lack of structure and control stressed her, as did the stark expectation of delivery, now. To top it all, her high-level asset in the Met reported that Duncan was back in town. Two senior detectives had been seconded to an anonymous quasi-autonomous agency. The advice to keep a low profile had been given again and with firmness. It wasn't fair. Constant companions, butterflies fluttered in her tummy. IBS twisted her gut tight.

* * *

The phone rang. She jumped. 'Hello.'

'Hello, Maybelle. I'm secure, are you?' A cold male voice.

'Yes.'

'Somcone in the Audit Commission, a friend of ours, tells me this pesky news-bitch has other contacts we didn't suspect. Promoting the woman to the Foreign Office was an excellent idea and she's settled well. Fewer worries about her.'

'At least that worked.'

'The problem is she leaked stuff to the Duncan girl before her move. One or other of them passed information to the Audit Commission people, who are assessing and looking at some contract payments and efficiencies, which could be compared with official reports.'

'How exposed are we?' Maybelle said.

'Hard to say, but we're on the case.'

'Thank goodness.'

'Unfortunately, or fortunately, depending on your point of view, the audit official person handling this had a major car accident at the weekend and, sadly, didn't survive.' The frosty Oxbridge tones of a Deputy Director in the security services betrayed no sympathy.

'Oh God.'

'The journalist must go. Make her disappear.'

'I'll give the instruction, William.'

'That's my girl.' He hung up. *Patronizing bastard.*

* * *

She rang Jim Thomas and told him the news.

'Oh Christ, Maybelle. Our contact Tommy Bain died this afternoon, like we agreed. Eliminate loose ends. He's gone. I'll have Devlin speak to Bill Jenkins. Maybe Jenkins knows more than he's telling.'

* * *

Devlin's call drew a blank at first. Bill might privately enjoyed the difficulty they discussed, but knew nothing. He made some enquiries and came back inside fifteen minutes saying the move had been organized through people up north, known only to Tommy. They didn't know how she'd been transported or by whom.

The deal was that Eilidh would be set free somewhere in a few days' time. They'd need ears on the ground to latch on to her when she surfaced. Devlin updated Jim Thomas.

* * *

Jim Thomas told the Chair. 'Maybelle, no luck, with Tommy Bain dead, we have a missing link to the people who have the journalist. Nobody knows where or who she's with.'

'I'll report back.'

* * *

Maybelle updated William, the mandarin. 'No luck. The only thread was severed this afternoon. We can't access her until she's released as planned.'

'That's unfortunate. We don't know what she's got and it might be dynamite.'

'Understood.'

'Just an added pressure, my dear. Don't worry your lovely self.' He didn't smile as he hung up.

111

'WILLIAM, MAYBELLE TELLS ME the news is bad and the journalist is beyond reach for now.' Sir Marcus said.

'Yes, so she says.' Talk about frosty.

'The Duncan woman is going to appear in the North as far as we can tell. Can your connections get some people in the field?'

'Doubtless, old man,' William said, 'I'll have a word about preparations for her reappearance.'

'Thanks.'

'How's the divine Gemma doing?'

'The grooming is coming on well. Ken thinks the world of her. She's beautiful, sharp and ruthless. Definitely got a future.'

'Excellent. Succession planning is such an underrated art.'

'Indeed.'

Succession might become critical. William's eyes glinted.

112

THE MEETING on the timeline and players involved was forthright, detailed and solidly tested. The discussions had included Mike Swindon and Cal Martin, who had been assigned an office two doors down from the conference room. When Sam returned from his encounter with Jamie Carron he went straight to Charlton's office. Quentin Billings, an old contact from the

Troubles and some other clandestine activities, was with Charlton.

'Charlton, Mike, Cal.' Sam walked over to Billings, smiling broadly. 'Quentin, lovely to see you again.'

'And you, Sam. An unexpected pleasure.'

'Any more surprises, Ben?'

'One, Sam, but she can't get here for a couple of hours, by which time we can give her a helpful start on the structure.' Charlton continued. 'Indira Shastry is one of the best database people in the business. Whatever happens, she'll bring superb thinking support and insight as we go forward. Quentin and Indira will help us structure, assess and interpret the information and intel we get. Some experts call it mashing.'

* * *

They talked and shared. Facts started to link as the jigsaw came together. Quentin took notes with thorough persistence, stopping people and asking for repetition where necessary. The fog around the factions started to clear. The varied interests, players and organisations suggested chaos, yet the confusion provided investigative opportunity.

After two hours, Charlton wiggled two thumbs in the air. 'Interesting confirmations. Intriguing. Let's review the photos of the players together. When Indira gets here, this content will be structured into a database. A yellow diagonal stripe indicates that the person shown is no longer breathing.' He walked along a cluster of photos, tapping on each with a pen as he briefed about them.

'Let's replay the recent conflict. There are other connections and at least one fifth-column. Here we go then. The attack on Sam's family provides a major connection and takes us ultimately to Denny O'Martin, one of the Dublin crime lords. By all accounts, a hard, vindictive and unstable man.

'There is a tough, capable fellow who goes by the name of Strangford, yes one word. He's more than an enforcer, probably number two in the family. With Strangford is Paddy O'Martin, son of Denny, reported to be a violent, spoiled wastrel, not a player. Last of the Irish connection is Timothy Hartson, who gave up the ghost trying to bring a Mac10 to bear on Sam's team. He hated us Brits and was a strong supporter of the Republican Movement. Hardly surprising he wanted to start shooting, I wonder if that means he had permission to kill some British military. Don't think he'd shoot without prior authorisation.'

Sam said, 'Fuss Cathel confirmed they came with a body bag for him. Hartson had permission.' Charlton nodded.

'Now, Jason Jenkins.' Charlton said. There was a red marker line to another cluster. 'Son of Bill Jenkins, an East End gangster with modernising and legitimate-business pretensions.' Charlton's plummy tones made him sound like an Oxford or Cambridge don giving a lecture. 'Jason was wounded during the Mweenstor event. Reported to be a legend in his own lunchtime, a bully and a future head of the corporation. Spoiled rotten, well-educated at the best of schools and allegedly bright when his testosterone isn't in control.

'Now, let's consider his dad. Bill is trying to make his business at least appear legitimate. He can be as ruthless and cruel as they come and, conversely, by all accounts, he's socially adept. Don't underestimate him. His nickname is "Billy Pliers" because as a young hoodlum he actually tore strips of skin off a couple of people who had earned his displeasure using, you guessed it, pliers. He is greatly feared. Next to him in this London group, is Charlie Jenkins. He's not considered stable or, indeed, a pleasant person in any situation. He may have, shall we say, deviant appetites. Aka the "flashing blade" and is suspected of at least two killings. I'm sure you can guess with what.'

Charlton went on listing players and putting factions together around Tommy Bain (three of whom had recently died: Lou Armente who had kidnapped Eilidh, and the two van men).

Jackie Steel and Duke Earl were next. Jackie's team included Danny Trimble who gave up Jackie to you, Sam, and Si Twentyman who had been knocked out during the confrontation in the Arches. Then, of course, there was the link to the Young Bloods.

There was one picture with a yellow line for Timothy Smith aka 'Blob', one picture without a yellow line for Rick Noble aka "Nobble", he was still critical in hospital. Finally, a blank picture space for someone called Ziggy, leader of the YBs. He was thought to be responsible for the severe injury of one of Duke's men.

Duke's 'cautioners' were displayed around him including a picture of 'Bone' Marrow, who had received ghastly injuries after the pub fight. Marrow, a seasoned criminal, seemed unlikely to spill any information in the immediate future. There were two blank frames for the men who'd escaped.

Gradually, the representation of factions and players became a helpful visual story. It grew quickly as they talked and would expand as the investigations continued.

* * *

'The pictures are useful.' Charlton moved to the table at the front and sat on the edge supported by one leg, the other dangling. 'We also have some unknown people we can't ignore. We'll call them 'Invisible' and 'Secrecy'. We can infer their existence using questions. How did the criminals find out about Ireland? How was Sam's involvement and personal information discovered? Who was the woman who phoned Sam to make the threats? Who put out the contract on Sam and killed Sam's guest? Who initiated Sam's sister's disappearance? What created the situation where different criminal elements, who know each other, seem to be working in conflict? And, why?'

'The interconnections make for an interesting enquiry. Someone has to be reaching out and building connections and relationships across the boundaries,' Sam said. 'Does everyone say yes? What happens to the people who say no?'

Charlton nodded. 'One thing, which is sensitive and top secret, and it won't appear on this board. A potential one-to-watch, raised by a security connection, Superintendent Molloy of the PSNI, is a senior MI5 person, James Thomas. Thomas is somehow mixed up in the killing of some police and informants in Northern Ireland between 1994 and 1996. There may be a cover-up involving criminal interests, he might even be on the side of the angels. Is there a possible link to the assassination of our people at that time?'

Charlton continued, 'Sam survived an attempt on his life back then. He was compromised and whisked away to other work immediately, and didn't know two of his police colleagues had been assassinated. A low-profile investigation into Thomas's routine, contacts and working connections is in hand, Quentin is the owner. Quentin?'

'We have a couple of "ears" in the vicinity. I'll keep you posted.'

The complexity and emerging scale of the challenge was not lost on anyone. 'Now, our structure: Quentin, you coordinate everyone except Sam who is mine. Mike, Cal you work for Quentin. One of you will act more senior. We'll sort it out as soon as possible. I'm sure I can count on whoever doesn't get the nod to support his colleague.' They both nodded. 'Secrecy is essential. We must not provide information, beyond need-to-know, to anyone outside our team without agreement. Please log all interest and from whom. Anything, however trivial, must be reported to Quentin, who will ensure proper input to our database. We are concerned about a leak in the Met as you probably know. There may be some other interested but doubtful parties on the security side of things.'

'One last thing. Each of us will carry a tracked, secure mobile phone 24/7 when we're working or on call. No exceptions. Tracking is good enough for cars and more than good enough for people.'

'Excuse me, sir,' Mike Swindon spoke up. 'Why is it essential?'

'They give us supporting evidence and the safety of knowing where you are if you need support. Those yellow marks on the photos. Count 'em. One dead Irishman, four dead Brits and a historic link to other murders. Add a couple of attempts on dear old Sam here, including the killing of a friend of his. Serious murder. Anything we can do to provide support and protect our people will be undertaken. This is part of it.'

'No exceptions?' Mike said.

'None.' Charlton fixed Mike with a frosty eye. 'Their reach is impressive. We didn't lift Sam out of Ireland because we thought it would be jolly good fun and make his kids happy. He and his were in jeopardy. We mustn't underestimate the opposition.'

113

CAL PICKED UP his vibrating mobile. He glanced at the screen, held his hand up and signalled he needed to step out. Charlton nodded. Moments later Cal returned looking serious. 'Something for us, Cal?'

'Bad news, sir. Jackie Steel has been found beaten to death. The people at the scene estimate three to four hours ago. Blunt instrument. He didn't die quickly, poor sod.'

'Sad indeed. Five dead Brits.' Charlton paused and they sat silent for, perhaps, ten seconds. 'But it may provide leverage for our investigators. It could frighten some of the bad people into cooperating.' Everyone nodded. 'This is moving from scary to terrifying. Sam, are you still willing to be out front on this? You are going to be exposed. I'm prepared to sort out a new strategy. At the risk of being clichéd, can't be anyone here who wouldn't understand if you want to back off.'

Sam looked thoughtful. 'This is scary. If it wasn't for my sister I'd ask for a new arrangement, but we can't simply drop this and re-plan around no bait. It won't work. I accept the risks. I am counting on you guys to guard my arse. Can we involve Tonka to watch my back?'

'If he'll do it.' Charlton said.

'He will.'

'Excellent, he's in.' Cal's phone buzzed again. Once more he read the screen. 'Take it in here, Inspector.' Cal answered, listened, thanked the caller and switched off. He looked up with a stunned expression.

'Tommy Bain. About four hours ago. Professional hit. Found by school kids. Double tap in the head and one through the heart.' Everyone stayed quiet, looking thoughtfully at each other.

'This is turning into a spaghetti western,' Charlton said. 'Let's get moving.'

'I'm off,' Sam said. 'I'll brief Tonka and be on the ground rattling cages first thing in the morning. I hope your IT wunderkind, Indira, is as hot as you say. That tracking could be important.'

'She's that good, don't worry, and we've got some surveillance all over the place.'

Sam grinned. 'No fuckin' fear then, eh lads?' Laughter echoed.

The humour faded to a thoughtful silence, then with a rustle of paper and moving feet a chorus of good lucks was accompanied by everyone filing out except for Mike. ‘A word, Sam.’

‘Sure, Mike.’ Sam glanced at Charlton who nodded. ‘Let’s use a meeting room.’

* * *

‘I’m worried about the tracker, Sam.’

‘What are you up to?’

‘I’m having an affair, probably going to leave my wife. Being monitored is a bit worrying.’

‘This is a secure operation. You’ve told me your situation, only two people need to know, Charlton and Quentin. Nobody else. You may require the extra protection the tracking gives you. Our movements will be monitored. If you can’t face this I’ll support you pulling out.’ Sam looked at Mike with no expression. Slowly they both grinned at each other.

‘You’re not thinking I’m a fucking stupid idiot are you?’

‘Who’s to say?’ Smile. ‘You’re a human being and you have a life. It’s your business. I won’t judge you.’ Steady nodding through the last sentence was reassuring. ‘Let’s go and tell the boss. You still in?’

‘I’m in.’

‘Good.’

* * *

The meeting with Charlton and Quentin was brief and to the point. Mike Swindon would wear the tracker. They guaranteed to protect his records. Mike left.

‘This place must have a back door, Ben.’

‘Of course. Let me check what is happening with the watcher.’ He spoke briefly on the phone. ‘He followed that editor fellow. Someone else is on shift for the watchers, opposite the front door. They’re under surveillance and we’re investigating.

We have two other exits. The one you can use tonight will take you out on to the road between here and the South Dock. A car will pick you up.'

'I'd prefer to get some exercise.'

'Right. In that case, take the car just the same. Jump off at the quayside on Admirals Way. That first half mile gets you clear. It makes all the difference between security and exposure. There's a footbridge you can cross, which leads to the Dockland Light Railway at Heron Quays, or you can carry on to Canary Wharf. You can also get the Tube at Canary Wharf. Either way ,you'll be in the city pronto. Someone will cover you.'

'Thanks, Ben.'

'Good luck. Speak to you soon.'

'Bye.'

As ever the parting was immediate and unsentimental. The watcher over the road stayed vigilant.

114

BILL STAYED in placatory mode. 'Calm down, Denny. My boy got shot. I'm delighted Paddy escaped unhurt and Jason's on the mend.'

'I'm absolutely livid, Bill. Those people we went after are bloody experts in warfare. Timothy Hartson hadn't a chance.'

'Yes, but the Scots guy warned him. Jason told me he was told to stop lifting the gun and he didn't listen.'

'So I hear and, actually, I couldn't give a fuck about Timmy. He wanted to kill some Brit military, had a go and got himself killed, stupid bastard. No, my problem is loss of face in a world where fear and respect keeps wild men in line. Must be the same for you.'

'Yes, I understand. Face is important.'

'Where are the people from Mweenstor?'

'Gone.'

'Gone? Come on, Denny. You traced them to Belfast airport.'

'Right enough. We also questioned the fellow who took their car back. Your pal, the Vicar, disappeared with his entire family.'

'You sure?'

'Positive.'

'He doesn't half get about,' Bill said.

'His friends include special forces. Three other men arrived with the family. What sort of mess are we into?'

'Some powerful people over here got an independent contractor of our acquaintance to kidnap the Vicar's sister. When the Vicar came looking, another independent contractor tried to give him a hiding and failed. Must've got his juices flowing. The bigwigs I told you about, promised to leave him alone if he stayed away, and within a day attempted to kill him. They got the wrong man. Who wouldn't put every effort into protecting his own?'

'Sweet Mary Mother of God. These people gave serious provocation. A saint would have trouble turning the other cheek.'

'The two independent contractors were killed this afternoon.'

'In the name of the wee man. Our lads were lucky to get away with their lives. You think he was responsible?'

'Search me. We don't know enough yet. One thing, the man's a player.'

'We must stop him. He's a problem for both of us. I'll send Strangford over to help you.'

'Thanks. I'll provide some muscle.'

'Good. A driver would be helpful.'

'Goes without saying. Get him to fly to City airport.'

'I've got plans for our vicar friend.'

'You sure that's wise?'

'No fuckin' man, however strong the justification, will piss on me and my patch.'

'Up to you, Denny. When will your lad be over?'

'Tomorrow, by lunch.'

'Speak soon.'

'Yeah.'

* * *

In Dublin the comment as they disconnected was, *arrogant English prick.*

* * *

In London, *thick Irish twat.*

115

'STRANGFORD, GET IN HERE.' Denny was jumping mad, similar to hopping but an order of magnitude more pissed-off. Strangford came in.

'Denny.'

'What's all these sheets and things?'

'Redecoration.' The walls had plastic sheeting taped to them, with covers on the floor around the desk. 'You asked for this some weeks ago.' Denny thought for a moment and refocused, humming with anger, an irate hornet. His rages could be frightening and had occasional terminal consequences.

'You're going to London. I want this vicar fellow dead. Got that? Tits up.'

'Are you sure this is a good idea? Bodies everywhere.'

'So? One more won't make any fucking difference.'

'You're making their problem our problem, I think it's a bit dangerous.'

'Don't you dare second-guess me. I tell you what to do and YOU WILL COMPLY!' The volume rose towards operatic levels.

'Sorry, Denny.' Strangford looked at the carpet. 'You're upset.'

'Course I'm fuckin' upset. They could've killed my son.'

'They didn't.'

'God, I'm so angry, so, so angry.'

'Come on, Denny, you're wiser than this. These guys are tearing themselves apart. That represents a business opportunity at the right time.'

Denny O'Martin sighed. 'Fuck the niceties. I promised them you'll go and, go you will. Got that?'

'Loud and clear.'

'Kill the Vicar. When you find him make him dead. No ifs, ands or maybes. He has caused major embarrassment to me.'

'He's been forced into this, Denny. Why not stay out of it?'

'No fuckin' way. He hurt me and he has to fuckin' die. Go and kill him. If you won't do that, you and me have a problem. Terminate him or take the consequences. What do you say?' The insane light in Denny's eye allowed only one response.

'Will do.' Strangford bowed his head in submission.

'Take Paddy.'

'I'd prefer not to, I'm heading into danger and he needs watching.'

'Don't fuckin' argue. He goes. He's angry too. He'll be your master after me.'

'As you say.'

'Good.'

'If he gets hurt, don't blame me.' Strangford turned his back and fiddled with something.

'I'm getting tired of you making things sound difficult. Stop dissenting from everything I say.'

'Sorry, Denny.'

'You're a fuckin' jumped up so and so. What're you doing?'

'Putting on a suppresor.'

'Why?'

'All the better to kill you with.' Strangford turned, pointed the suppressed Sig at Denny and blew his brains all over the wall. 'Your day is over, you stupid, stupid man.' He went to the phone.

'Paddy, could you step in here a moment, please.'

Paddy joined his father moments later. Strangford made another call.

'It's done. Send the lads in and tidy up. Get Stevenson at the Garda to sort out the forensics. I'll handle contact with the O'Martin family as planned.' As he started to tremble, he knew he'd taken the right and only option. The majority of the gang had agreed. All would approve now, or else.

He wouldn't be off to London in the morning. He'd be occupied consolidating his new business. He felt exultant in spite of the adrenal shakes. Colm O'Casey's view had been spot on. Too much would happen in London to make him want to be around, especially when the shit hit the fan. He'd enough to do in Ireland.

Good luck, Vicar, you're going to need it.

116

The conversation at the Jenkins' office in London was nowhere near as lethal as Ireland. After letting off steam they built their own idea of what had been going on.

'Why did Devlin and his cronies decide to frighten the journo girl?'

Charlie said, 'Why does anyone, Bill? Fear, mate, fear. When we get scared someone will grass we are fearful. What do we do? We put the frighteners on them and make them more scared of us than anything. Devlin's lot are fearful.'

'Good stuff, Charlie. Why are they fearful?'

'Why indeed. Must be to do with their world. It's not the same as ours. They talk money and business, but they don't know our world. They don't know what to do. Think about the Duncan girl. She got moved without a thought for the consequences. They didn't involve you. A lot of loose cannons started firing off. They dragged the Vicar in. Jason got hurt.' Charlie thought Jason deserved the pain, a good lesson in life. The arrogant upstart needed taking down a peg.

'Yeah, mate, they may have powerful friends, but they are new to this. It's a serious opportunity. Let's chat with Tommy Bain. We ask him nicely and he'll tell us the score.' Bill said

'Right, I can hear him singing already.'

'If anyone can make him talk it's you.'

117

'YOU'RE IN.' Sam said.

The pleasure in Tonka's voice was unmistakable. 'Good.'

'Meet you in forty.'

'Sound.' The call ended.

* * *

Thirty-five minutes later Sam arrived. He had taken the DLR to Tower Hill Gateway and changed to Tower Hill on the Central Line. Like any competent invisible man, he held up and read a paper all the way.

They met in Mabel's Kitchen in Wright's Lane beside the Tube. Sam came briskly out of the side exit from the station and into the cosy interior, 'Hiya.' He spoke over a solid buzz of conversation.

'Been busy?'

'Yup.'

'What're you having?'

'Americano and dash please, and one of those bilberry muffins.' Almost immediately an attractive young woman came over and took their order. They hunched over the table, heads together.

'This is turning into a shooting war. Two more got slotted today. Doors being closed.'

'Sounds interesting, especially as I'm now your minder.'

'Yes. My back needs guarding.'

'When does the action begin?'

'Tomorrow morning.'

'Where are we starting?'

'A nightclub.'

They talked and planned before their meal.

118

THE MEETING with the police members of the team happened in the evening after Sam left to meet Tonka. Charlton updated the group. His plummy, clipped style added a frosty seriousness to the proceedings. His delivery both energized and focused people.

He walked through the timeline and connections board. He took questions and invited observations at any time. Always positive about contributions and listening, he created an atmosphere to invite input and sharing. 'Any thought is important. No idea will be dismissed out of hand. The quality of our talking, listening and thinking—our communication—will make us successful. With the database, we can capture anything, drill down to the smallest detail and screen out dross. The computer system will be up and running within the next couple of days and fine-tuned within the week. Anything you want to add, Quentin?'

'No. Very clear so far.'

'Right. Any questions?' No one spoke and Charlton continued. 'Our colleague Sam Duncan, who the criminal element call the Vicar, has become something of a pain to the people we are investigating. God knows what would have happened to his family if a lunatic with a machine gun had managed to pull a trigger. Tomorrow morning he starts to rattle cages. He has a minder, but the two killings yesterday make the threat level stratospheric. Your investigation is extremely important to increasing his safety. We need your contribution.' Quentin raised a finger. 'Quentin.'

'Going to mention the leak?'

'Yes. We think there's a leak in your division. You must not, repeat must not talk outside our task force. Report back any unusual interest, in fact, any interest at all. Your team leader is Mike, he is now an acting DCI. There will be other promotions as our team grows. Go and get me some juicy information, something we can sink our teeth into. Mike?'

'The death rate is unheard of. They even topped the lads who drove the van. Let the world know that Jackie Steel is critical, he has no real family, and he's getting better gradually and is being guarded 24/7. Let's squeeze the fuckers,' Mike said. 'We've got Sergeant Bob O'Neill coming in to support us and co-ordinate police activity. He will work closely with Quentin and Indira.'

The investigators left, eyes gleaming with the excitement of the chase. Already facts were starting to emerge and, with the diligence of their kind, would be fitted together piece by piece.

They started straight after the briefing, working in twos, Cal and Flo' Binstead, Mike and Dave Smiley with one further partnership. Mike agreed and assigned work to the pairs.

Across the city, Sam and Tonka slept, ready for a risky day.

119

'SAM DUNCAN for Colm O'Casey.'

One of the staff came to the door. Sam entered. Over the street a surveillance team recorded the scene. A transmission streamed to an interested party.

'Sam, fresh as a daisy this bright and early.'

'You're looking well, Colm.'

'Taking no hurt and much happier now the business of the police investigation is passing. How are things with your sister?'

'Nothing, Colm. Still plugging away. What news?'

'Employees of one of my main investors encountered some of your kin in Ireland a few days back.'

'Yes.'

'They had a slight misunderstanding.' O'Casey said.

'Not sure I like your choice of word.'

'Sorry, my friend, but I'm going to speak in fucking code.'

'Go on.'

'There's been a change of management at one of my main investors. I'm told there is no interest at all in further involvement in this unfortunate situation. The people concerned are anxious to enjoy a positive, lengthy and proper business engagement in the UK.'

'Thanks, Colm. I'm on message. Now, could you do some decoding, please?'

'Honour's even. No threats, no anger, no nothin'. They will not take this further. Hands are washed.'

'No conflict, no revenge?'

'None. Get on with your life. For ourselves, here at the Orchid, we shall continue to provide full cooperation to the police and authorities in the investigation.'

'Excellent.'

'Off the record, Sam, I am surprised. Also relieved and delighted. It doesn't compensate you for a missing sister but closes a problematic and distracting avenue for me. Now, how about some coffee and craic?'

'Please. Before we lose ourselves in chat, Colm, do remember to watch your back. The wild men are restless at the moment and people are dying.'

They had an interesting and enjoyable conversation about anything, but the situation.

* * *

After half an hour Sam left. Door closing behind him, he thought the visit had taken long enough to interest any watchers. He made the pre-arranged signal and set off briskly towards Leicester Square. The narrow cobbled surface of Lisle Street, with its profusion of Chinese restaurants and shops stayed greasy after some showers. He went through Little Newport Street, across Charing Cross Road and into the Tube. Sam's phone vibrated for an incoming text message.

> *Probable camera. Address sent on. One follower now sleeping. Something of a dish. C U next stop.*

Adrenalin churning, Sam enjoyed the edginess of the moment. He connected to the old days. Inside the concourse, by Leicester Square Tube entrance he paused and made a call.

120

'BILL JENKINS, please.'

'Who should I say is calling?'

'The Vicar.'

'Hold on.' Silence. 'Putting you through.'

'We talk at last, Vicar.'

'Thank you.'

'What can I do for you?'

'Meet me at your office in about forty-five minutes.'

'Why?'

'Why not?'

'Okay. We'll put the kettle on.'

'Thanks. See you soon.'

121

BACK IN LISLE STREET, an unfortunate surveillance operative experienced a strange world as she struggled back towards consciousness. At first, in a daze, she seemed to be dreaming about a wonderful Chinese meal. Then her hands began to feel slippery.

The taste in her mouth was confusing. An awful headache exploded. She reached out to pull the covers back. No bedding. Eyes open with shock she struggled, swimming in and ingesting a tide of food waste. What an overpowering smell. She spat out food scraps and congealed sauces as her terrible headache pounded away.

Five minutes later, clothes ruined and covered in a wide variety of meats, vegetables, rice and noodles, no mobile, she threw up. Looking every inch a mess she found a public phone and called in. The promised car arrived after ten minutes. She'd be living the day down for a while with her colleagues. Some, more wise in the ways of surveillance, thought she'd escaped death.

Her boss started a heated conversation with his manager.

122

SAM DIDN'T want to give the Jenkins brothers early warning, yet he believed the anticipation of his arrival would generate, with luck, a little tension. He reviewed what information he had on them.

By all accounts, Bill was a bright and aspiring person, but also a ruthless criminal, clever, capable of extreme violence and cruel if he had to be. He didn't appear psychopathic. He'd get to know him. Surveillance pictures showed a rather chubby, open-faced man with regular features, a full head of tied-back hair, almost gentle brown eyes and a clear taste for flashy suits.

The nature of Bill's brother and partner in crime was much clearer: a dangerous nutter and reportedly a gay man who repressed his feelings and slaked his needs abroad. Suspected of two murders, in his youth he had served three prison terms. Since then, he had managed to be discreet. The photos of Charlie dripped machismo: leather jackets, jeans with big buckles, silver-tipped and plain cowboy boots, silky shirts and sleeveless vests. His appeared lean and fit. His face, longer than his brother's, had a vertical scar on his right upper lip. His rather large nose had been battered several times judging by the almost unnatural straightness of the bridge.

Sam meditated on the DLR. He noticed Tonka come in behind him and sit three or four rows back. He felt protected. Shutting out the noise of the train and the buzz of conversation, he imagined a thread of light flowing upwards from his head into a place of strength, light and support. As he visualized and his body relaxed, the tension eased. He prayed for his sister, and for all his folk in a cluster of positive thoughts. He made a mental note to talk to Karen and the kids that night. Action time.

* * *

He exited the DLR at Crossharbour, down the steps to Pepper Street. Turning left he went under the building, which sat like a medieval gateway before the bridge between the inner and outer Millwall Docks, then along Muirfield Crescent and down Greenwich View Place towards the offices of the Jenkins brothers.

The entry lay past some parked cars and landscaped gardens. The door, a wide glass affair, opened silently as he approached. He knew Tonka was now backed up by other operatives from Charlton's department. With all the help around, the butterflies and increasing nervous tension didn't go away. Entering reception he asked for Bubble and Squeak Investments.

'Who are you here to see, sir?'

'Bill Jenkins.'

'Who should I say?'

'The Vicar.' She studied a screen, tapped some keys.

'He's expecting you. Please take a seat. Help yourself to coffee.'

Sam sat, picked up a magazine and browsed. His sense of engagement and focus came fully into synch. His heartbeat steadied and the adrenalin started to work for him. Calm and ready he sat poised.

'Hello, sir. I'm Annie, Bill Jenkins' PA. Follow me, please.'

They went over to a lift and up one floor. The doors opened into a spacious area where a large man stood with a metal detection wand. He signalled for him to stand — 'Won't take a mo', sir.' — ran the device over him and frisked him thoroughly. Tonka had his tracker, picked up from a wall by the station.

Check finished, Annie beckoned him and turned left towards a solid-looking black double door. She took a plastic card from a little holder at her waist and touched a sensor which beeped and freed the door lock with a click. 'I'll take you in, sir.'

123

TWO MEN stood near a huge desk.

Bill, recognizable from his picture, walked confidently towards Sam, offered his hand and fixed him with an appraising stare.

'So, you're the Vicar.' Sam held the eye contact, smiling diplomatically.

'So they tell me.'

'Been rocking boats, Vicar?'

'I wouldn't know.'

'Your sister is missing, I believe.'

'Yes.'

'And you're looking for her.'

'Correct.'

'We may be able to help.'

'That would be much appreciated.'

Bill waved his hand towards his sibling who moved towards Sam. 'This is my brother and business associate, Charles.'

Charlie grunted, barged past Sam and stalked out of the room. The ease and strength of his movement suggested a high degree of fitness.

'Forgive him. He's having a bad day.' He gestured towards a chair in front of his desk. The surface was so large Sam thought of an aircraft carrier. He sat down.

'He's forgiven. I could even put in a word if you like.' Behind him, the door clicked and he heard a swift movement.

* * *

Across the dock, a camera man muttered 'Oh fuck!' and pushed his comms button. 'Camera five! Camera five! Holy man red. Repeat red.'

Charlton watched the video. 'Alert! Alert!'

Charlie halted behind Sam with a large knife. Sam sat stock-still as a seven-inch blade came down past his eyes. It settled under his chin and a hand grabbed the back of his head.

'Charlie!' Bill's eyes bugged with horror.

'This bastard shot Jason,' Charlie said. The sweaty, shaking tension in his grip communicated craziness and danger. The blade scraped like a razor.

'Who's Jason?' Sam said.

'Our boy.'

Bill seemed more shocked than Sam. 'Put the bloody knife away, Charles. Stop being an idiot and do what we agreed. This man didn't shoot Jason.'

'I want him scared,' Charlie said

'I'm frightened. Okay?' Sam said.

The tension eased. Point made, the knife disappeared. Sam sighed in nervous relief, cheeks puffing out. Charlie stepped over to the desk, radiating a more controlled anger. He shook with energy, his eyes blinking rapidly. He tapped the desktop with his knife point, sounding a slow rhythmical beat. His face developed a half-smile.

* * *

Bill spoke with something close to sincerity. 'Please accept my apologies.'

'Accepted.' Sam slowed his breathing and quelled an angry urge to sort Charlie out. So, Bill kept Charlie in check, what if Bill had been out? Another deep breath. 'Now, about my sister, Eilidh …'

The camera operative shook his head. 'Stand down.' Charlton's crisp voice spoke in the teams' headsets. His sigh of relief wasn't broadcast.

'Yes, your sister. Now, before we get to that I'd like to sort out a few things.' The shocked pasty white colour remained round Bill's cheeks and neck. Charlie sat back, cleaning under his nails and looking smug.

'I want collateral comfort,' Bill said.

'What's that?'

'Guarantees.'

'What can I guarantee?'

'I'm not sure. You must have some sort of back-up. The Irish stuff couldn't have happened without help.' Sam didn't give much back.

'Old comrades.'

'Will they leave Charlie and me alone?'

'Not if he kills me. Leave me and my family alone and I guarantee no danger for either you or Charlie from them.'

Charlie said. 'You're on our manor, son … our manor. You've got no power here. Talk about threats, bullshit!'

Ignoring Charlie, Sam focused on Bill. 'My sister?'

'Tommy Bain took your sister. If you want to communicate with him you'll need some of your heavenly connections. He died yesterday, a professional hit.'

'Ouch.'

'He kidnapped her at the request of some people she's been investigating. I can't give you names.'

'Pity, names would help.'

'Sorry, we don't know any more than this: the people she's been annoying wanted to make sure she got the frighteners but without physical damage. The reason I'm telling you this, Vicar, is too many people are dying. It's crazy.' A pause and wry smile. 'It must stop.'

'Nobody wants killing,' Sam said.

'So, the good news is she's still alive. There is not-so-good news, unfortunately. I expect you know Tommy traded in people. We recently decided to close him down.' Sam raised an eyebrow. 'No, not kill him. We're shocked he's dead. The police were tipped off about his holding facility yesterday. Several girls were rescued.'

'Aye. Last night's news.'

'Your sister wasn't there. However … however …' Bill repeated himself like a politician, holding his finger up and shaking it, 'a source confirmed she's still alive and somewhere in the country.' Sam nodded.

'The country? Where?'

'Maybe the north-east. Whoever they are, they're scaring her off and, as I say, last I heard, she was still alive. We don't know any more.' Bill opened his hands. 'It's all I can tell you. I hope you find her and she's well. I have a family myself.'

'Thanks,' Sam said, 'every bit of information helps. Let me give you some in return. The incident in Ireland was regrettable. I understand your son may have been hurt.'

'Shot.'

'I'm sorry.'

'He's recovering, but I'm really concerned.' His brows knitted. 'In fact, I'm fucking angry.'

'Of course, any father would be. I'm glad he's recovering.'

'Thanks.'

'A small-calibre weapon was used. The intention was to warn, not permanently harm. Far more damage could've been done.'

'Doesn't change the fact my boy was harmed.'

'Of course not. As a man of God, I don't condone or support violence. Nor can I deny some experience of it.'

'Yeah, I heard. Had a bit of a rumble the other day, didn't you,' Bill said.

'Self-defence.'

'Broke some fingers and noses I hear.'

'Better than necks.'

'Much better.' They shared a fleeting smile.

Charlie snickered. 'You're just a wimp, Vicar. A fuckin' wimp.'

Sam stood and nodded to Bill.

'Thanks for your time and help, Mr Jenkins. Charlie lacks your wit and charm, poor fellow. Bless him.' Sam looked at Charlie and saw the insult strike home.

Bill glanced at Sam with a touch of apprehension then, sighing, rolled his eyes as his brother came round from behind the desk.

* * *

Sam walked towards the door. Charlie stepped in front of him and stood, full-square in his path, scowling. Sam stopped about three feet from him. Charlie moved up close and took a cocky rocking stance, sneering and childish.

'You're lucky my brother's protecting you, Vicar. Left to me you'd be converted into haggis and shipped back north. As for your sister, she's a tart and deserves a good spanking for causing trouble.' He brayed a laugh, feeling the energy and humour of imagined power.

Charlie's head rocked forward, only to stop when the top of Sam's forehead connected firmly with his nose, crushing the cartilage and crunching into the eyebrow line. He stumbled, stunned. As he clutched his face Sam stepped level with him moving his left leg and body forward, close beside Charlie.

Sam's right leg remained extended behind him, knee bent. Levering his power through his leg, trunk and accelerating arm, he slammed his right palm upwards into Charlie's groin, crunching the loose flesh. As his hand rebounded from the pubic bone Sam grabbed the undefended genitalia hard and, gripping tight, jerked the soft tissue down about six inches. With a whistling sigh, Charlie collapsed on to the floor, holding himself and moaning quietly, barely conscious.

Bill came round his desk. Sam turned, ready. Bill stopped and backed up, shocked by the implacable set of Sam's features and the flat light in his eyes. He knew fear as he faced a stone-cold killer.

Across the dock, the cameraman laughed out loud. Charlton stayed tense. 'This isn't over yet. Keep focus.'

'I was coming to protect you, Vicar.'

'Thanks.'

'You don't need my help.'

'No, not now,' Sam said. His eyes eased a little and a touch of humour flitted across his lips. 'Apologies, Bill. I didn't know what he'd do. No way I could have him fired up and behind me when I left.'

'Accepted. He won't forget though, you know.'

'I hope he does.'

'So do I. You've got some blood on your forehead.' Sam pulled out a handkerchief and looked questioningly at Bill.

Bill took the cloth and wiped the smear away. 'Okay, all gone.' He returned the hanky.

Sam nodded, folded the material and put it in his side pocket.

'Thanks for the information.' He turned and left the office without looking back. Bill released a tense sigh and continued over to Charlie.

The camera recorded Bill giving his brother a solid kick in the ribs.

'You're a bleedin' liability, Charlie. A bleedin' liability.'

Through the door, he heard Sam speak. 'Annie, do you want to show me out or should I find my own way?' It was just as well he couldn't see the suppressed humour in Sam's face.

'Follow me, sir.'

Charlton told the team to stand down.

* * *

Outside, Sam called Charlton. 'Am I safe to walk back?'

'No. Move towards Pepper Street. There's a car coming for you. It'll be with you shortly.'

'Right.'

124

'SPEND A LITTLE time in the loo, did we?' Mike took Sam aside before the meeting started.

'Get to my age and you'll have more frequent trips. Also, a competent young lady wanted to relieve me of a hanky with a blood sample for forensics.'

'I think you've let yourself down a bit, Sam.'

'How so?'

'You were supposed to do some cage rattling, not knacker rattling. Can't you follow instructions?' His beam of pride shone. 'Bloody good show. We should release it on YouTube.' The team murmured agreement.

'No comment. I'm a man of the cloth.' Both pleased and wistful Sam remembered occasions when celebrations had been tempered by things not working out so well. He wondered if he could have found a different way to sort the Charlie problem and realized he'd enjoyed the confrontation and its release.

* * *

Charlton started the meeting, 'Right, everyone. Brief and clear, please.' Each team presented the outcome of their investigations thus far. Sam quickly outlined the fact the Irish had opted out (or so they said). He reported Tommy Bain's responsibility for kidnapping Eilidh, the involvement of 'City types' in starting the Eilidh situation off and Bill Jenkins' information.

Quentin and Indira sat still, listening hard and making notes. Charlton chaired. Mike summarized the police investigation.

'The strands turned up some common names. Mostly we know them well. However, the name Forsyth came up from both the Jackie Steel and Tommy Bain threads. It seems that Jackie — he wasn't such a bad little bastard — said Bain does business with a City player called Forsyth. This squared with one of the men involved in the murder at the pub in Shoreditch. So, we have a name. The bigwig we know of is one Devlin Forsyth, a non-executive director at a major bank and a number of golden blue-chip companies. He's a consultant, including to the Government.'

Charlton summed up. 'Interesting stuff, thanks. As you know, we already have the name of James Thomas to play with. Indira has done some data research and come up with some helpful facts for us. Indira?'

Indira said. 'Both Devlin Forsyth and Jim Thomas sit on a project preparing a report examining ways to increase probity and value for money in Government procurement. They have meeting facilities in the Home Office under a high-level official named Maybelle Jones. The fourth member is Gemma Smythsone, a City lawyer with Brumous and Dingle, a solid establishment firm. Both Forsyth and Smythsone had separate meetings with Sir Marcus Attenwood-Leigh MP and Kenneth Chen, a major international banker, yesterday. Sir Marcus is a hugely well-connected politician who sits on one or two select committees. He's recently suffered minor press criticism of his probity above and beyond the expenses scandal.'

'Hmm, a useful and powerful collaboration,' Quentin said. 'We've got two surprising new links. I'm awaiting feedback about some surveillance resources that may have been used slightly off-piste by the other side.'

Sam said. 'My minder mentioned a woman following me after my first meeting this morning. Somehow she became unconscious and fell into a Chinese restaurant waste container. It may make for a traceable morsel.'

Quentin chuckled along with some of the others and made a note. 'Thanks.'

Charlton said, 'I wonder if we might tickle a corrupt cop and get 'em to tell their paymaster in a way that can uncover them? Anyone asking from your end, Mike?

'Not so far, but we haven't been back in the old office since we came here. What would you like said?'

'How about we think there's a high-level link that connects to the disappearance of a journalist and a murder, and we're following up leads. And there may be a North-East connection? Any disagreement?' None.

'Right. I'll leak it later today.'

'Good. Indira make a note please.' Indira nodded, her black hair glimmering like a gentle wave reflecting light. 'Starting a hare running is fine. The downside is the risk of pre-emptive action and more danger for you, Sam.'

'Accepted. Could we also allow an evil person to spot an inept surveillance, perhaps close to the next time the committee meets?' Sam said.

Mike said. 'Sounds good. How do we find out when they are meeting?'

'We can check the Chair's diary and feedback,' Quentin said.

'I can get that now,' Indira said.

'Excellent.' Charlton summed up: a leak would happen that afternoon, and a noticeable surveillance would be mounted on Devlin Forsyth when he attended the next meeting of the working party.

'The next meeting is tomorrow morning at ten,' Indira said.

'How often do they meet, Indira?' Charlton said.

'It was about once a fortnight until around a month ago when it became weekly. It's now every other day.' Charlton looked over her shoulder at the monitor.

'Seems to coincide with Eilidh's disappearance, Sam.'

Sam shrugged with a slight smile. 'Something must be keeping them busy.'

'Thanks everyone.' Charlton closed the meeting.

125

MAYBELLE RECEIVED a communication from the asset.

> *People have been seconded from here to a task force. They are following up the links to the disappearance of the*

journalist and at least one murder. There is thought to be some connection to the North-East. Be very careful.

Nausea gripped her again. As the pressure mounted she had retreated into alcohol and sex. She used to enjoy her fun with Edmond, a man in his early twenties who loved the larger African woman. Now her mind raced and fear gnawed away at her bowels. Negative fantasies surged through her mind. Half a stone had melted away in the past week, unnoticeable in the grand scheme of things, but significant to her.

Time to get to the Bizz meeting. She took the lift down to the third floor and went along to the room. They were all ready.

* * *

Devlin said, 'Good morning, Maybelle. How are you?'

'Fine thanks, Devlin. You look happy.'

'Couldn't be any other way. Our income has trebled since those big transport contracts were awarded. We're enjoying a significant in-flow of merchandise month-on-month through our informal channels. We're awash with cash and our cells report happiness.'

'Excellent news, but a police asset has raised a concern. They are linking the journalist girl's disappearance and a murder. They also think there may be a North-East connection.'

Jim Thomas spoke up, looking as self-confident as ever. 'Funny this should come up. Devlin had a word with me this morning about being followed. He took a wander down near our office and I clocked him for half an hour. He is being followed.'

It never occurred to Jim, in his arrogance, to find this all too easy.

Devlin asked, 'How have they got on to us? Or indeed, are they on to us? The main connections are pushing up daisies.'

'Relax, Devlin,' Gemma soothed. 'Let's face our problems together and resolve them.'

'We can't go on killing people. Look how that's backfired,' Maybelle said.

The meeting descended into recrimination.

126

AFTER THE MEETING, Gemma took a taxi and met Sir Marcus.

'The decision to eliminate the Duncan fellow was a terrible misjudgment, but understandable as we find our feet. His sister's disappearance happened at arm's length. Is there another agenda here? I can't think what. I need to talk to Jim.'

'Maybelle is wobbling. I wonder if she'll do anything silly,' said Gemma.

'Maybe, but she won't risk damaging her own reputation. She is too much of an arrogant self-lover for that. She's a blame-shoveller like many of her type, and this is not a particularly easy buck to pass.'

'That leaves Devlin.'

'He's yours. Use your wiles and make him believe. He's mostly sound and at his limit for this sort of thing.'

'He's not much of a lover.'

'Shut your eyes and think of luxury.'

'When will we enjoy another tryst?'

'How about the next big get together? It's only two weeks away. You'll be joining us?'

'I can't wait.' Gemma sounded eager and noted the glint in Sir Marcus' eye. She smiled. Certain lies were always appreciated and believed.

127

'AH JIM, dear boy, do come in. Take a seat.' Jim braced himself for trouble.

'Thanks, Marcus.' They were in a small meeting room in the Commons.

'We need to chat about Bizz. It can't be allowed to go pear-shaped now.'

'No.'

'Talk me through the truth of your reasons for recommending Duncan should be killed.'

Jim Thomas sat and thought for a few minutes. He started talking with reticence, warming up gradually, then speaking with relief, ridding himself of a long-standing burden.

'I was compromised in Belfast by a loyalist group, a sex thing. I couldn't come clean and decided to turn. It also paid handsomely. They were recketeering, basically the whole range of gangster activities, like many of them did. They'd been doing a series of bank raids as well. A small intel team I was linked with put a picture together. Duncan, two RUC detectives and an undercover man were involved. We decided to off the lot of them.'

'Off?'

'Kill. I leaked information to the Provos. Gave them Duncan. They put a top assassin on to him, but he failed. Duncan killed him and was immediately reassigned. Another policeman found the official ID for Duncan on the assassin's body and passed it on. The link was never made.'

'Duncan escaped.'

'Yes, and he's been no trouble until now.'

'And the others?'

'Using my information, the gang eliminated the undercover man the night before they went after Duncan. The killer was the man who Duncan nailed. I set up the two police by disclosing the location of their surveillance and the vehicle they were using. The wild men didn't need a second chance. They killed the investigators.'

'Pretty evil.'

'Yes, but at the time, and at arm's length, options were limited. It was the only way forward as far as I was concerned. I regret it now. With Bizz, I wanted to finish the Duncan job. Having him come back into view after all those years … what a shock. He's a link to a bad, vulnerable time for me. This situation landed in my lap, like a godsend. He is and will continue to be a danger to Bizz. I honestly believe that and convinced the others he should be terminated. They have no idea of the history.'

'And you single-handedly exposed our enterprise to extreme risk!'

'Not true, I recommended termination to avoid risk.'

'You imagined God would send you one of his shepherds and you could kill him readily?'

'No. If you construe this as a big mistake, forgive me. I don't believe in God. The police don't believe in coincidences. Imagine how I felt when I saw the picture of Duncan as he showed up to investigate the disappearance of his sister. I apologize, yet believe I did the right thing. It's self-evident we should have killed the sister and Duncan. If we'd done that, there'd be no problem.'

'I understand better. There are plenty of bodies littering the stage just now. You live alone, no family …'

'Yes.'

'You openly enjoy sex with S&M specialists. There's no one we or others can use to pressure you. You're just a pariah, Jim, with a grubby past. On the upside, you've enjoyed a strong career in intelligence. You are pragmatic, intelligent and ruthless.

Your main flaw may be bad judgement where your own interests are involved. How do we correct that?'

'My interests and the interests of Bizz are aligned. I will keep my nose clean and win forgiveness.'

'Thanks for your candour. As you say, keep your nose clean. Your social life is your business. I'll recommend absolution and get back to you.'

'One piece of information, Marcus. Some quasi-official surveillance on Duncan stopped today. Somebody took out one of our people.'

'Took out! Permanently?'

'No. Just knocked out and dumped in a skip of food waste.'

'God! Someone will sort out the problem.'

Jim smiled inside. He would be able to continue his life. At fifty-eight he wanted the other few years before he had to retire. He'd find a way to neutralize Sam Duncan. He believed he could trust Sir Marcus.

128

THE VISIT from the Vicar unsettled Bill. Charlie was at the doctor's having his nose straightened and his testicles checked … served him right. The phone rang, piercing Bill's gloom.

Annie, his assistant said, 'I think you should take this call.' She explained why.

'Put him through.'

'Mr Jenkins?'

'Yes.' Bill said. His voice dripped icy cold menace.

'I'm a man who did Tommy Bain a favour with a journalist.'

'And you are?'

'Arthur Bailey, Mr Jenkins, from up north.'

'Got that. What can I do for you, Arthur?'

'I'm told Tommy's dead.'

'Yes. Lead poisoning.'

'The woman mentioned something I want to pass on. Tommy said your brother is a business partner but he's not at your office at the moment. They put me through to you.'

'Get to the point, Arthur.'

'She talked about files and records and I think they're why she was taken.' He took a nervous breath. 'She rambled a lot but mentioned them a couple of times. We dropped her in Carlisle on Wednesday evening, as instructed. I thought someone ought to know in the absence of Tommy.'

Bill's spirits lifted as Arthur Bailey shared more interesting information. Now he owned a useful nugget of intelligence, pure gold. 'You did exactly the right thing, Arthur. Thanks for that.'

'Any time you need help in the north, I hope you'll think of me.'

'Of course, I will. Leave your details with Annie. We appreciate the call.' He transferred Arthur back to Annie and sat back.

So that's what was worrying the amateurs. They were vague about what she knew and a major dossier and copies existed. To cap everything, he knew her rough location. He could deal himself good cards with that. Bleedin' dynamite, wonderful stuff.

* * *

Twenty minutes later an e-mail arrived in the police asset's inbox:

> *There are files possibly paper and electronic with a lot of evidence and information that relate to the missing journo.*

She has been released in Carlisle. This might interest some people you know.

Fifteen minutes after that, an e-mail pinged into Bill's PC.

Thanks. Communicated without attribution.

Bill smiled. Nothing like a spot of fear, doubt and uncertainty to get the knees jerking. And, of course, jerky knees often revealed people and interests in a helpful way. He called in two of his top men and issued some instructions about personal protection and low-profile information-gathering.

* * *

The police asset passed on Bill's information to Maybelle Jones who raised it in Bizz. Jim Thomas looked on with interest. Gemma would report up the tree when the meeting ended.

A top person in Bizz's UK parent "company" received the information second-hand and enlisted allies from outwith the usual suspects. She started a process of consultation to make sure doors were closed, lips sealed and critical buttons pushed. No more frightening people off.

If in doubt, sever the head.

129

'THE CHINESE FOOD story was too juicy to hide. Gossip and laughter surfaced the details and participants. We've linked the surveillance team to Jim Thomas, no surprise there. We managed to extract the information as the portcullis came down,' Charlton said.

'Cover up, Ben?' Sam said.

'Yes, but more of a buggeration factor. The word from on high is hands off. And, while the confusion and mistakes getscleared up, every trace of evidence will vanish with people thoroughly cleansed of sin.

'Same old, same old.'

'Right, we're standing on such important and sensitive toes, I've been told to reel our neck in by the Cabinet Office. We're not compromised, but we've managed to get up a large proboscis.'

'Power play?'

'Yes. Put in place an hour after the intelligence operative climbed out of the skip. She's been sweet-and-sour about the whole thing by all accounts.' Big smiles. 'Inter-team banter and gossip confirmed things.'

'Will they confront us?' Sam said.

'I don't think so.'

'Do they know of us?'

'Quentin?'

Quentin said, 'not much clear detail, but they'll know there's a grey little operation out there. The vagueness helps. Thomas's lot may also be aware to some extent. We suspected the tail was theirs, now confirmed. Their power players may check us out, but we're not quite line-of-sight. The Border Agency is their prime focus, plus giving assistance to other divisions. Our secret little task house has informal links to SOCA and crime bodies. We report to the Prime Minister.'

Charlton watched Sam. 'Penny for your thoughts.'

'I'm concerned we're only somewhat invisible. That explains the surveillance on the editor fellow, our front door and, I suppose, me.'

Charlton said, 'Yeeeesss.'

'You say we have permission, resources and initiative.'

‘Correct. They need to prove justification for stopping us at the centre or we can carry on. We must follow procedures to untangle the web and receive profuse apologies, probably from an innocent official. At least one unidentified person, maybe two or three, have impressive access to our police friends’ communications and operations, which is a key concern.’

‘Can we communicate disinformation if we choose to?’ Sam said.

‘Fair point.’

‘The unseen enemy needs to be smoked out.’

The phone rang.

‘Mike?’ Indira handed the handset over. Mike listened, his posture changed.

* * *

‘Your sister’s found.’

Sam’s face broke into a huge grin. He punched the air. ‘Where?’

‘Carlisle. They picked her up on Wednesday, drugged out of her mind.’

‘Condition?’

‘Dunno, but she’s alive and in hospital.’ Sam couldn’t help thinking of young Jenny’s death. ‘We received the news not fifteen minutes ago.’

‘I’m glad I didn’t know when I was on the spot with the psycho twins,’ Sam said. ‘Ben, can we step out a moment?’ Charlton nodded. They entered the reception area. ‘I need to make arrangements to travel. Get over to the flat, get a bag and get going.’

‘We’ll sort the tickets to Carlisle. Keep your head down. Any more intel will be passed on. Now, Sam, before you dash, what about protection? Tonka still with you?’

'Yes.'

'Excellent, he's a sound operator.'

'The best.'

'The Chinese take-away was a fabulous show. Call me when you're moving.'

'Will do.'

'Good luck.'

* * *

Sam texted Tonka and left after him. The car dropped him at the bridge to Canary Wharf. Tonka, in position, covered his back. With their kit collected, they made for Euston Station. Tonka, on board the train well before Sam, cleared the area. Two single first-class seats, facing each other, had been booked. Tonka took his seat five minutes after departure as the coach picked up speed.

'I'm enjoying this,' Tonka said.

'You can't keep going round sticking female operatives in food scraps. People will talk.'

'Yeah, they did.'

'Thanks for the cover.'

'No problem. Fancy a wee scotch?'

'You English buggers can't pronounce wee. You always make it sound like a bodily function.'

'Fine … what about a large one?'

130

THE TRAIN RATTLED on through the night. Sam stood alone at the end of the coach, talking.

'Are you coming back soon?' Karen said.

'Very soon with any luck, but you've got to remember the commitment with Ben Charlton lasts until we solve murders, corruption and various forms of criminality.'

'Piece of piss for Mr Pushy.' A smirk.

'Naturally. With the pushnik on the case, we can't go wrong.'

'Got the jockstrap over your trousers now, Sammy?'

'There's no alternative. Superheroes have to dress right.'

'At least you know how it's hanging.' *Cheeky*.

'I'm missing you and the girls.' He paused. 'Eilidh's been found.'

'Eilidh?'

'Yes. I'm going for her now.'

'Oh, darling, fantastic. How are you?'

'Elated and feeling the pace. Keep this news under your hat until I confirm the identification. I can't forget that poor girl in London'

'Of course.' Karen sensed his emotion. 'This sounds much more hopeful.'

'Yes. This line is breaking up. I'll call you later.'

'Take care. I'll pass your love on.'

'Bye.' Sam took a deep breath and returned to the table.

* * *

On Arran, Karen sat in silence for a few minutes, washed her face in the room sink, patted it dry and soothed her eyes with Optrex. Finally, she went back downstairs to be the all-singing-all-dancing mother, daughter-in-law and lady of the house.

* * *

Less crowded after Preston, the Pendolino entered Cumbria around nine o'clock. The journey through the Westmorland Fells in setting sunlight was delightful. After Penrith Sam switched his phone on and in moments received a text:

> *Two reservations at the Cumbria Town Hotel. Take care. We'll settle the bill. Call this number when you get to the hospital and someone will meet you. Expect a police presence on arrival. Inspector Graham Joyce, six foot two, blond, scar through left eyebrow.*

* * *

Once the train manager announced the approach to Carlisle, Tonka picked up his backpack and moved two coaches up the train.

The express stopped at platform four allowing immediate exit from the terminal into Court Square. Tonka stepped off and checked the platforms, back across the footbridge and forward into the ticket and retail sales area.

Sam delayed his exit to give Tonka time. Stepping on to the platform, a tall blond man approached him.

'Mr Duncan? Inspector Joyce, Cumbria Constabulary.'

131

SEEING SAM with the cop described in the text message, Tonka crossed the road and took a cab to the hospital. He was dropped off opposite the main gate. He walked up the drive, wide-aware, and dissolved into the night.

* * *

‘Good to meet you, Inspector.’

‘I’ll take you to the Infirmary.’

‘Could we delay a little while?’

‘Minder?’ Sam nodded. ‘We can tour around for five minutes. When we realized the situation, we automatically raised our security. There’s an officer outside her door at all times and a team of four on patrol.’

Nearing the infirmary, Sam clicked on the number in the text. ‘Yes?’

‘I’m the person with the sister who is ill.’

‘Come to the reception area.’

‘Thanks.’ They made for the front door.

‘Here’s the doc now.’ Joyce raised his hand. A shorter than average, plump figure waddled towards them dressed in blue jeans, trainers and an Aran sweater.

‘Mr Duncan?’

‘Yes. Dr Khan?’ As they shook his hands the doctor eyed Sam up and down.

‘I was twenty-three when she happened along. My parents surprised everyone, not least themselves.’

Khan smiled. 'Please come with me.' They took the lift. Tonka observed them from the atrium floor as they left the elevator and headed for the Intensive Care Unit.

At the ICU, they used the antiseptic gel dispenser, rubbing the ubiquitous anti-bacterial lotion into their hands and feeling the cool evaporation. They entered a small office.

The doctor gestured towards a seat at a light grey circular table. Sam sat down, Graham Joyce beside him.

'Gentlemen, thank you both for meeting me at this late hour.' They nodded. 'Mr Duncan, I'm a psychiatrist.' Khan had a Cumbrian accent. 'I was called in by the police, to assess your sister. We've been working with her for nearly thirty-six hours now. There is concerning news for you. As you listen, please remind yourself we have a strong positive light at the end of the tunnel.'

'Okay.'

'Perhaps you could give some background, Inspector Joyce.'

Joyce spoke. 'At one a.m. yesterday, Eilidh was found in Botchergate, that's to the right of the station as you look out. Drug-taking is not uncommon in the area. When officers assessed her, they noted the bruising on her wrists consistent with having been restrained, realized she was critical and called for medical assistance. Bystanders said she was pushed out of a car, a dark Vauxhall Vectra estate. We have pictures from a surveillance camera. The registration checks out with a stolen vehicle from the North-East which was recovered, burnt-out, earlier today near Hexham. We need more intelligence before pursuing enquiries. Over to you, doctor.'

Khan spoke in a matter-of-fact way. 'Your sister had a cardiac arrest in the ambulance. Her heart was restarted and medical steps were taken to flush out her system. When testing for what she'd been taking it became clear that she did not self-administer the drugs. She has serious bruising on her upper arms and thighs in a way that would be unusual if one was self-administering. The other factor is the additional use of Rohypnol and Midazolam.'

'Bottom line is she was given a cocktail of drugs sufficient to keep an average person subdued for many hours at a time. We believe she received a double dose before she was released and, as a result, her life was endangered.' He glanced at Inspector Joyce.

'We are treating this as attempted murder.'

Dr Khan continued. 'If the police hadn't called the ambulance, she would almost certainly be dead.' He nodded back to the policeman.

'The first task was to allow the doctors to stabilize and treat Eilidh. We needed time and finally managed to get some sense out of her early today. Finally, she gave us her name and mentioned London. We made further checks and contacted the Met who confirmed their interest mid-morning. We finally spoke to acting DCI Swindon, around five-thirty this evening. He told us you were on your way.'

Sam said, 'A six or seven-hour delay between notifying London this morning and getting a response.'

'Sometimes delays happen. I have no explanation,' Joyce said. 'However, when we realized the seriousness of the situation we put a full security operation on place. It is good to have an excuse to practice.'

'Thanks for that Inspector. How is she now Dr Khan?'

'Physically, pretty well after a good clean-up. Mentally, she is distressed and disorientated. One of her captors, a man called Neddy, has threatened and sexually abused her. Not raped her, but caused her great distress. A good thing seems to be a kitten who kept her company. She needs some careful psychiatric nursing, but should recover well over the next few weeks, a month or two at the outside.' Sam was pale and stern-faced.

'Can she be moved?' Sam said.

'Yes, if you arrange a nurse. It would be best to sedate her for the journey.'

* * *

'Could we break for a moment, please? I'll make a call, I need privacy.'

'We'll step outside. You'll get a line by pressing nine.'

'Thank you.' Khan and Joyce left the room. Sam called Charlton using a secure line code.

'Charlton.'

'Sam.'

'What news, Sam?'

'She's improving. Not bad considering she's been drugged, abused and nearly died. The prognosis is fair, but she has mental problems, not thought to be permanent.'

'Thank God.'

'Yeah. I need to get her to Arran.'

'Can you take her by road?'

'No problem.'

'I'd like to stay low key if possible. Short of a helicopter, car to the ferry is the quickest way.'

Sam said, 'I know the routes up to Ayr well. We'll take an unobtrusive path. The mid-afternoon boat is the one to go for. I'll return to London day after tomorrow unless you want me sooner.'

'Right.'

'A psychiatric nurse is needed for up to two months.'

'I'll make arrangements. I'm so pleased to hear she's safe.'

'Me too. Hold on a moment.' Sam put the receiver down, stepped out of the office. He asked the doctor for contact information, received a card and read the numbers to Charlton.

'I'll get on this now. We'll have a nurse available by mid-afternoon tomorrow.' Charlton said.

'Excellent. One last thing …'

'Yes?'

'The news about Eilidh was delayed around seven hours before it reached Mike.'

'Ouch. Seven hours?'

'Worth checking I'd say.'

'We'll investigate. You concentrate on the task at hand.'

'The good news is the local police are running a major security operation and she's fully covered. The place is crawling with plods.'

Sam went to the door again and waved Khan and Joyce back in.

'Thanks for your patience, gentlemen. Dr Khan, you'll be called concerning the transfer of Eilidh to my custody. I expect the call will come between seven and eight tomorrow morning. A psychiatric nurse is being arranged. When would be a good time to pick her up?'

'Nine-thirty at the earliest, subject to discussions and agreement with your medical people. We'll sedate her and prepare her for travelling. How long is the journey?'

'Six hours maximum,' Sam said.

'She's asking for her mother. What is the situation there?' Dr Khan said.

'Mum and other family members are at the destination.'

'Just what she needs. It'll help her to re-orientate. Now, you'll want to see her.'

'Please.'

132

THE AIR SMELLED of disinfectant. They went through the ward to a private room. The atmosphere was hushed with an occasional squeak of shoes on the spotless floor. A viewing window in the wall showed the figure on the bed. A policeman sat opposite the door which was open. They walked in.

Sam said, 'It's Eilidh. She looks peaceful. Thanks for everything. May I sit with her for a few minutes?'

'Of course. Try not to disturb her too much. You can hold her hand,' Dr Khan said. 'Now, if you'll excuse me, I must get away.' He shook hands with Sam and Inspector Joyce then left.

Sam said, 'Thank you for your time and help, Inspector.'

'No problem, sir. We'll guard her until you take her in the morning. We have re-doubled security and with armed officers on watch in the area.'

'We haven't detected your minder.'

'He's here, and an exceptional operative.'

'If you need assistance these are my numbers.' He gave Sam a card.

'Thanks for that.'

'You're welcome.' He left quietly, nodding to the constable as he passed.

Sam sat back, took Eilidh's hand and, releasing a deep breath, gave thanks. She came almost to consciousness and murmured a few words, eyes partially open but not focused.

'Everything's fine. Sam's here.'

'Sam … I can't find you.' She moved erratically in a slow motion of confused distress.

'I'm here.' He passed his hand near her eyes so she could sense the shadow.

'Sam?'

'Yes.'

She relaxed visibly. 'I'm safe?'

'You're safe, and Mum's waiting.'

She cried and her nose started to run. 'Ned's a swine … a filthy bastard.' Sam took a tissue from the bedside table, dried her tears and wiped her nose.

'You're safe now, Eilidh. There's no Ned here.'

'Mum?'

'Yes, you'll be with Mum later. Off to sleep, Eilidh.' He stroked her forehead with fraternal gentleness. With a big sigh through a slack smile, she fell deeply asleep. He rose and left, nodding to the guard.

He thought he'd like to meet Ned one day.

133

IN THE ATRIUM Sam called one of the taxi numbers by the Freephone in the foyer and arranged two taxis, one immediately and the other in ten minutes. Midnight had passed. The first car arrived. Tonka glanced and nodded as he left for the hotel where he'd check the lie of the land. While he waited on his cab, Sam texted Karen. Once at the hotel he found his room and had a deep, dreamless sleep.

They met for breakfast. Sam knew Tonka had been alert all night and, as always, found it hard to comprehend how he coped with such little sleep.

'Had a better relax than usual, Sam. The police had us under protective surveillance.'

'Were you snoring for England then?' Sam ate a large chunk of Cumberland sausage.

'Hardly, I walked the halls like an old ghost between naps.'

'What's a spook to do?'

'You're a fine one to talk.'

'Shut up and drink your milk.'

'Tea.'

'Whatever.'

* * *

Breakfast on board, Sam called Arran on his room phone. Karen answered.

'We should be picking her up in about an hour. Can you hold off telling anyone until I'm absolutely certain we're getting her? I'm pretty sure she'll be released, but best not to disappoint.'

'Okay, but hurry up.'

'You want any shopping?' She gave him a long list including wine, cheese, various foods, cereal, fresh vegetables, toiletries and so on.

'Got all that. I'll go to the shop now and call you again when we're nearer the boat.'

Once checked out, Tonka and Sam waited in the garden area. Their rental car was delivered just before 09.00, a Vauxhall Zafira with a powerful diesel engine. Tonka opened the passenger door, reached into his bag and produced a rear-view mirror with wide-angle wings which he stuck to the top of the windscreen. 'Extra eyes.'

The Zafira suited Sam. With loads of space for Eilidh and the supplies, the trip would be comfortable. Starting the car he realized he was barely twenty-five miles from home. Talk about full circle.

They drove down to the main road and turned right for the nearest supermarket. Forty-five minutes and two loaded trolleys later a text arrived:

> *You should have the car by now. You are booked on the 15.15 sailing from Ardrossan. Arrive an hour early. The nurse will meet you there.*

Sam texted his thanks. Leaving the store they turned left, back towards the city centre, down Stanwix Bank, following the signs for the West. The ancient bulk of Carlisle Castle lay squat and implacable on their right. Five minutes later they were parked in front of the hospital at the ambulance area.

'Dr Khan.'

'Good morning, Colonel. We can release your sister. I have spoken with the nurse who will be caring for her and her psychiatric supervisor, both excellent professionals. Eilidh is going to be well cared for. Medicine has been arranged at the other end.'

'Thanks for all your help.'

'You're welcome. Porters can take Eilidh to the car. She is heavily sedated as we want to avoid anxiety. She'll be out of it for around six hours. All things being equal she'll have professional supervision before she needs medical attention.'

'Right.'

'Inspector Joyce sends his apologies and good wishes, but he has to be somewhere else. Now, I must go and become a bureaucrat once more. Goodbye.' He signalled and two attendants brought Eilidh out in a wheelchair, head lolling. A policeman came watchfully behind Eilidh and the two helpers. Dr Khan vanished into the building.

'Where you putting her, marra?' The first porter asked, using the West Cumbrian for "mate".

'Nearside, back seat,' Tonka said. Sam made sure Eilidh was handled with proper gentleness. They put plastic sheeting on the seat, with plenty more to protect the interior in case she sprang a leak. The child lock was set to closed. Then they lifted her in, wedged her at a slight angle, pulled down the central armrest, tucked pillows around her, wrapped her in a blanket and shut the door, a professional transfer.

'Thanks, lads.'

'No problem, marra.' The two porters nodded and walked off.

'Thank you, constable.'

'Sir.'

Sam and Tonka climbed into the Vauxhall. 'Warm for a coat, Tonks.'

'Never know what'll happen next, Sam.' He referred to the weapon he was carrying.

'Concerned?'

'We never sleep, boss, we never worry. You Ruperts do the sleeping and don't worry enough.'

'Once we're rolling, you can snatch a nap.'

'No, not until Arran. Don't worry. I've taken the wake-up pills.' In the car he unslung the mini-assault rifle, took off his coat with an exaggerated sigh. Rolling his eyes at Sam he checked the safety and put the weapon in the foot well. He had a good look round and said, 'Let's get out of here.'

'Okay, We'll avoid the M74 and head over the moors to Ayr and on from there.'

'You know the patch, Sam.'

134

At 10:15 in the morning the journey past Carlisle Castle, and up to M6 Junction 44, was a breeze. By 10:35 they were on the slip road, heading north. Ten minutes later, after the Scottish Border, they exited the motorway following signs for Dumfries. The banter was happy as they stayed alert. Eilidh slept in the back, face relaxed, sometimes snoring loud enough to be heard.

'There's route that'll make a tail easier to spot,' Sam said. They left the A75 at Rigg, aiming for Annan.

'Still bothered?'

'Aye, gut's going. Probably nothing. We've time.'

With Annan passed, the route followed the B724 through Cummertrees, Clarencefield and Mouswald.

After ten minutes Tonka said, 'we've got at least two tails. A Volvo V70, light green, and a Fiat Punto, dark blue or black. They've been behind us three times each. Minimum two people on board. One was with us when we joined the main drag. Appeared again by Clarencefield. The Fiat turned off at Mouswald.'

'I made the Volvo. Call Charlton and see what you can find out. He's in Contacts, under C.' Sam handed Tonka his secure company mobile.

'Hello sir, Waberthwaite, er, Tonka here …' Sam lost track of the conversation as he concentrated on driving, with frequent glances behind. He maintained an even unsuspecting pace. 'Thanks, sir.' Tonka paused, then he said, 'they've no knowledge of the tail. They can't provide close support. Charlton thinks the description of the surveillance suggests limited resources, probably our own people. He'd prefer us not to kill anyone if it can be avoided.'

Sam snorted and shook his head. 'Unbelievable.'

'We're on our own until we get most of the way north. They'll send cover to meet us near Ayr, but don't hold your breath.'

'Right. Let's avoid killing people if we can. But Eilidh's safety is paramount.'

'Just our luck to be in a godforsaken part of the country.'

'Beautiful.' Sam said.

'Okay, beautiful and godforsaken.'

'Same problem for the bad guys,' Sam said. 'The first thing is to find the Fiat … or not. We're almost at the A75. The Volvo took a right moments ago.' Sam braked hard, did a U-turn and went back to the junction where the Volvo had turned off. 'They'll be expecting us to show up at the next junction in a few minutes. There's a way across country to the A76. It's some miles up from Dumfries but not far off our route. Can you make the satnav work?'

'Yeah.' Tonka pushed the start button.

'I'm going up to the A75, turning left then right aiming for Torthorwald. I'm sure I've seen that sign from some of the other roads near Dumfries. There was a sign half a mile back. First thing though, we stop and check the car for a tracker. We didn't do that at the hospital, did we?'

'No. My job. Sorry.'

'Our job,' Sam said.

* * *

Once they crossed the A75, they pulled on to a farm track. Tonka pulled out a mirror from his bag, adjusted its telescopic arm and started a detailed search outside and inside the car. Sam raked through the shelves and cubby-holes. They didn't find anything. Tonka asked for Sam's cell phone. 'Batteries out, SIM cards out, put 'em in the glove box. What about Eilidh's stuff?'

'There isn't any. She had nothing when they found her.'

‘She’s got a new sponge bag,’ Tonka said.

‘Dig in.’

Tonka searched it. ‘Unusual for a comatose person to have a switched-on phone.’

‘Chuck it out the window.’ They drove at pace towards Torthorwald.

The satnav came to life as Tonka read the map. ‘Head for Tinwald. First left in the village for the A701. Then pull in again.’ Tonka started to learn how to scroll around and operate the navigation system.

Sam followed the instructions. When they stopped, Tonka said. ‘Head for Duncow then Dalswinton, find and follow signs, watch out for Auldgirth.’ Tonka pressed some buttons on the satnav. ‘OK I’m ready, where are we headed?’

‘Moniaive and over the moors to Carsphairn.’

‘If you can fuckin’ spell it, I’ll programme it in.’ Tonka checked the map. Sam found simultaneous spelling and brisk driving a challenge. ‘There we go Carsphairn via Moniaive.’ The disembodied English lady spoke, calm and clear.

Do a U-turn when safe to do so.

Tonka checked the trip on a map. ‘Straight on. Straight on. Ignore the bloody voice.’ They drove on at pace, tense and watchful. Finally, the electronic voice said to head for Auldgirth.

‘Okay, Sam, take a left on the A76, go over the bridge and then first right. The satnav should keep us moving after that. I need to concentrate more outside the car.’

135

IN 200 YARDS turn left. Turn left.

Tonka kept his running commentary going. 'We'll cross the bridge soon.'

'Thanks, Tonks. The satnav has taken it on.'

In 200 yards turn right. Turn right. Then turn right.

'You know how these systems sometimes send you down a road you can't get through. I'm double-checking with the map.'

'Heads up, Tonka. What's that in the lay-by ahead?'

'A dark blue Fiat.'

'Shit!' Sam smacked the steering wheel.

'Do they want us to see them?' Tonka said.

'Makes sense. He's waiting for us. Puts the pressure on and herds us forward.'

In 200 yards, turn left. Turn left.

'We can't lose them. Let's take 'em out.'

'Right.'

'Yeah.' Tonka studied the map. 'Ignore the satnav. Take the next right. It goes to a reverse 'Y' junction. Take the turn, drop me. Go twenty metres and block the road, I'll be behind them. We'll secure them, get an idea of their equipment. I want to know what we're up against.'

If you can, make a U-turn do so now.

'They're 200 yards back.' Sam said. The bend would be sideways. Bushes hid the turn. He checked the satnav display for alignment. 'It's a sharp corner. Five, four, three, two, NOW!' With a hiss of deceleration, ABS clicking and releasing in a chatter of electronics, the car spun left on the handbrake. The seatbelts clicked as they locked. Tonka and Sam swayed against them. Eilidh grunted in the back. They wobbled and weaved but made the turn. Then Sam braked hard.

'Go!'

Tonka jumped out and moved into cover.

Twenty yards down Sam blocked the road and got out, pistol in hand.

In 200 yards, turn right. Turn right.

Almost instantly the Fiat came round the corner, turning briskly but not as savagely as Sam's Zafira. They skidded to a halt at the roadblock. Driver and passenger were talking when two bursts from Tonka's gun took out the rear tyres. In a blur of movement, Tonka appeared at the driver's side shattering the glass with his gun barrel. 'HANDS ON HEADS! NOW!' He jammed the gun-sight hard into the man's head, cutting him and starting a trickle of blood.

'MOVE! MOVE!'

Reluctant hands went on heads.

'ONE HAND! OPEN THE DOOR! ONE HAND!'

The doors opened. Sam covered the passenger. The driver gave Tonka a sullen stare.

'Hi, Keith,' Tonka said. 'You work for the opposition now? No fancy moves. Not one! We don't plan to harm you. Do what I say and you'll be okay. I will kill you if I have to. Understand?' The man nodded knowing Tonka spoke the truth – he wasn't dead. Moments later his wrists were secured.

Tonka took the car keys and frog-marched Keith round to the other door where Sam held the passenger's face against the roof grinding his pistol barrel into the man's neck. They cuffed them in seconds.

'Right lads, go to the telegraph pole.' Tonka jabbed his finger in the direction. There was a clear space at the base. 'Sit down.' The passenger complained about the rough nature of the surface. Tonka delivered a rib-cracking poke in the ribs. The man complied face twisting with pain. 'This will be the most painless fuckin' lesson you'll ever get, sunshine. Now face each other and put your legs around the pole.' They obeyed. He secured them ankle to ankle, both sides of the pole. With hands cuffed behind their backs, they would be there for a while.

'That should keep you two quiet for now.'

Tonka and Sam searched them and produced two Sig Sauer P226s with twenty round extended magazines. Sam rummaged round the car and came up with a telescoped C8 assault rifle with a M203 grenade launcher.

'Armed for bear.' Sam said. 'Well, it's good to have an equalizer. Three HE and three CS gas loads as well.'

'Useful. Let's tidy up.' Tonka climbed in and drove the other car half-way off the road, as if parked. He examined the equipment on board. 'They're using the government's private security network. We must have some trackers on board.' He fired three bursts into the security equipment. 'We need to move. That Volvo's around here somewhere.'

136

THEY RETURNED to the Zafira. 'Let's go for five minutes and do a tracker check.'

Eilidh slept on. The C8 Assault Rifle went under a blanket on the floor.

They drove on.

In 200 yards turn right. Turn right.

'For goodness sake turn that bloody thing off.' Sam said. Tonka pressed a button. 'Who's Keith?'

'A guy I trained a few years back.' Tonka said. 'He's good. He'd have killed us if ordered to. He'll be anxious to catch up with me for a chat. We get on pretty well. The "opposition" remark will have him thinking. He's a decent man for a stone-cold operator.'

A few minutes later they turned on to a rugged dirt and gravel lane. Tonka searched the car. Sam stood guard with the assault rifle.

'Eilidh's well wrapped up. Hmm.' Sam said. He handed the weapon to Tonka, opened her door and, leaning her against his leg and gently patted her down. She lay limp as overcooked spaghetti as he felt round the side of her body and along the seat. 'Gotcha.' He pulled out a small oblong case. 'Seen one of these before?'

'S100. Powerful device,' Tonka said. 'Keep searching.' He remained watchful, eyeing the road in both directions.

Sam worked with speed and dexterity coming up with a second S100 under the squab of the back seat. 'They've been thorough.' He said.

'We haven't much time. There may be another one somewhere, but we've got to keep moving.'

'What should we do?' Sam said.

'Take the Volvo out if it shows up. The business with Keith back there was lucky. Things worked out exactly right. Next time they'll be ready. Let's get rid of these trackers on to another vehicle, let them follow that.'

'Okay, you're the expert. Let's be visible to the next village and attach them to a vehicle. They've got to come this way.' Tonka nodded agreement. 'Do you think our secure phones are secure?'

'Hard to say. The firm's one should be okay.'

‘No chances mate.’ Sam said. ‘We best find a pay phone and update Charlton.’ They drove on. ‘We’ll use the secure one in an emergency.’

‘The bugging was fast and fuckin’ professional.’

‘Yeah,’ Sam said. ‘How’d they get access to this car? How and when did they find out? Who from? Where it was?’

‘They moved fast.’ Tonka said.

‘The intel about Eilidh’s release was delayed in London for some hours according to Mike.’ Sam nodded. ‘You’re right, Tonka, they moved bloody fast.’

‘ … and have reach. You don’t get folks like Keith and his mate coming out quickly on small-time surveillance. There are at least two cars, a powerful tracking system and a fair old arsenal. The tracker means these people have a good fix on us and we’re all in danger.’

‘On the upside,’ Sam said, ‘we’re not being chased by a proper team or there’d be loads of extra cars and technology. They either haven’t had enough manpower available up here or, more likely, they can’t risk putting any further assets on our tail if they want to avoid creating questions they can’t answer. Two cars may be the best they can do. Still, it’s bad news.’

‘Okay.’ Tonka said. ‘Right now we’ve got to get out of here in one piece, regardless of the odds. We handle one crisis at a time until there aren’t any more.’ The car rose and fell over humps in the road. G-forces made them sway as they took corners.

‘You’re right about the here and now Tonks, humour me for a bit longer. Why did we get Eilidh back? If they wanted her dead, why not kill her? She was out of sight for over a week, for goodness sake, easy to knock her off and bury her somewhere … anywhere. Some of the evidence suggests there are criminals, mandarins, bankers, national security … all in cahoots. Eilidh’s investigation joins big dots.’

‘So they let her go? No way, Sam.’

'A link must've broken somewhere. Two of the early players were murdered. Bain did human trafficking. Bad-man-Bill told me Eilidh was taken to the North-East. She gets dumped in Carlisle. The suspect car is burned out near Hexham.'

'Fits together. The people in the know are dead and the original plan gets followed. The new plan is lethal, but Eilidh's gone.' Tonka said. '*Need to know*, a spook's best friend.'

'So she got lucky and they couldn't prevent her release. Now they want to kill her and maybe nail irritants like you and me if they get lucky.'

'Works for me.' Tonka said.

'Anyway, as you say, whatever the story is, right now we're in the shit and need to extract ourselves.'

'And Charlton says we mustn't kill anyone. When we get to the wire Sam, what are you going to do.'

'Save Eilidh.'

'I smell blood.'

137

THEY DROVE ON, free of the satnav's monotone instructions. In the village of Kirkland on the A702, Tonka attached the S100s to a police pursuit BMW parked outside a shop. They chortled as they moved on. At Moniaive, Sam called Charlton from a pay phone.

'Sam, how are you?'

'Wired. We've removed one car from the reckoning and sidelined the people on board.'

'Injuries?'

'Pride and some bruising. We think they're Government operatives. Tonka trained one of them. Name of Brian Keith,' Sam said.

'Noted.'

'Are our company mobiles secure?'

'Should be. I'll make doubly sure.'

'We found two Ocellus S100 trackers in our vehicle: one under the back seat and the other tucked in with Eilidh.'

'Where are they now?' Charlton said.

'On a jam sandwich.'

'A police car?'

'Yes, the high-speed pursuit model.' Sam said

'That should get some laughs.'

'Hopefully. On top of that, someone managed to smuggle a sponge bag with a switched on mobile into Eilidh's things. Our security isn't watertight,' Sam said.

'Understood.'

'The phone left the car via the front window.'

'Right.'

'We're heading over the moors to Ayr. There's at least one more pursuer about. Might be worth checking who Inspector Joyce from Cumbria spoke to in London.'

'We're on that,' Charlton said.

'Good.'

'Two protectors caught the 11.00 boat and are disembarking about now. They're meeting up with two more from the mainland and are tasked to provide cover for you. Should be coming your way in about forty-five minutes. Can't say exactly where you'll meet. Dot-dot-dash.'

'Dot-dot-dash. Got you,' Sam said. Tonka nodded. The headlight flash code was a quick and useful means of identification.

'Regarding your remark about security, there is a leak down here. We're working on finding it,' Charlton said.

'Good luck. We better move.'

'Understood. Keep in touch.' He hung up.

'Roger.' Sam hung up and walked to the car.

He nodded to Tonka standing guard beside the car. 'Let's go.'

138

IN LONDON, the tension rose as the dangers of the journey became clear.

'They've dealt with one tail and will take action if another appears. Two powerful trackers were found. Now attached to a police pursuit car.'

'I never heard that,' Mike said.

'Mike, what have you learned on the timing of the information about Eilidh being found?'

'Delayed about seven hours, sir. I talked to Inspector Joyce of Cumbria Constabulary, helpful man. He mentioned one of our own, Jane Lawick.'

'What happened?'

'CS Lawick spoke to me after we were informed yesterday. She was pumping me in a friendly way, and apologized for an administrative blunder. I didn't realize it was so long. I'm due to meet her in about an hour, in the City. What can I tell her to help us determine if she's leaky or not?'

Charlton said, 'Impressive, harmless and non-strategic information.'

'We've already hinted that Jackie Steele isn't dead but recovering in hospital and has information. There are no close relatives. Nobody seems to be bothered about collecting the body.'

'That would work.'

'Maybe we should find a genuine replacement.'

'Who could play act him?' Charlton said.

'Needs to be a lean, shortish person. Someone prepared to take a risk'

'I know just the man.'

'Experienced?' Mike asked.

'The best. I'll sound him out. Give me a moment, then pop back.'

* * *

Twenty minutes later they reconvened.

Charlton said, 'Our man has agreed and should arrive in London tonight. We're making travel arrangements. Steele's body has been removed to a secure place and the paperwork modified. The detail will check out if someone cares to look. We'll give our man a make-over when he gets here. We can make him appear like Jackie. Jackie alive, may bother some people. Right, now there's CS Lawick for a start. What do you think, Mike?'

'Good idea. I'll leak it when we meet.'

'Excellent.

139

'I KNOW this bit of road Tonka,' Sam said.

They turned on to the B729, heading for Carsphairn. Soon they were travelling steadily upwards, towards the moors. The road dipped and twisted, widened and narrowed. Sam worked hard to balance speed with safety and smoothness. Mist blurred the vista as they passed between two hills, still climbing.

As the light changed the moorland colours altered from bright golds, browns and greens to sinister washed-out hues. The car's engine growled through the gears, as if responding to the ominous transformation outside. In the rear, Eilidh muttered briefly, then fell back into silence.

'Headlights behind, Tonks. Might be a Volvo. Been catching us up for five minutes. They're moving quickly. Let's check 'em out.'

Tonka buried his head in the map again. 'There's a bridge with a hard left turn about three miles up from here. We'll have to ambush them. Unlikely to be so easy now their mates have disappeared. HE or CS gas?'

'CS, HE as a last resort.' Sam said.

Tonka laid the C8 mini assault rifle on the floor and told Sam to use it if needed. He pulled the larger C8 carbine over the seat, loaded a grenade into the launcher and checked the magazine. 'Any shenanigans, we deal with them.'

'Okay. Let me flag them first.' Sam said.

'Roger that. Don't take a bullet for your pains.'

The pursuer was about 600 metres away and closing fast. Twenty seconds max before he arrived. Sam executed the turn over the bridge, Tonka exited the car as planned, keeping low, moving quickly to get a good field of fire angled on the corner. He found cover and knelt, safety off, supporting the rifle on a stump. He gazed through the scope. Sam walked to the left side of the bridge.

Tonka watched Sam, thirty yards from his position, wave to the car. The car braked hard but came through the bend. The driver's window was open as it slowed and a pistol came out firing three shots at Sam who fell to the ground.

The car stopped at an angle on the corner, facing Tonka who was twenty yards away. He fired a burst between the driver and passenger, diverting attention from Sam.

'Stay put. DO NOT LEAVE THE CAR!' Both leapt out. The passenger ran for it and Tonka, overriding many years of training, shot him in the legs. He fell over screaming.

Sam popped up, weapon in hand, shoved the driver backwards against the car and said something emphasized by the mini C8. The woman dropped her gun and got down on her knees, hands on head. Tonka walked over and knocked her cold with his rifle butt.

'Not a word Sam. *Not a fuckin' word.* Secure the bastard and hide her beside the bridge.' He threw some plasticuffs to Sam, who knew when to keep quiet. He secured the unconscious woman and dragged her away.

Tonka returned dragging a moaning man. 'I'll patch him up.'

'I'll move the car. Someone could come along any minute.'

Tonka set to work by some trees. Sam drove the Volvo off the road beyond the Zafira.

'How's our injured friend?'

'Bone's nicked in his right leg. The other's got a splendid hole. Arteries are OK. He needs attention fairly soon. I've packed the wounds. I had to engage, Sam. No choice. All I could do not to slot the pair of 'em.'

'I know. Thanks, Tonka. Any morphine in your kit?'

'Nope.'

'Our pal here will be hurting for a while longer. Let's get going.'

Tonka noticed the hole in Sam's jacket. 'You hit?'

'Bugger winged a love handle.'

'Show me.' Sam pulled his shirt up. Tonka gave him an annoyed stare. 'That's not a wing, it's a bloody hole. Be thankful it's not bleeding too hard. We're lucky you're not well gone with shock. You have to drive and I need to be ready to fight.' He plugged the wound and taped Sam securely.

'The nipping will keep me awake.' He blew out a painful breath and grimaced. 'I'll live.'

'You better had.' Tonka said

'We need to call in again. There's a T junction up ahead. Maybe get a signal near the main road.'

They drove on. Tonka reloaded the assault rifle and returned it to the floor. He checked the Mini and laid it on his lap. 'That bastard tried to kill you. From now on we shoot first and ask questions later.'

'Ooh! You're a warlike old bugger.'

'Too fuckin' right.'

Sam glanced at Eilidh in the mirror. 'OK, its war.'

140

'AFTERNOON, SIR. We've had a small fire fight.'

'SitRep?' Charlton said.

'Two of theirs secured and one of ours leaking. He's still driving, but he'll be sore in about an hour.'

'They shot first, nicked Sam. We could've killed 'em … didn't. Patched up the wounded man and secured his mate. They're available for recovery.' He gave a map reference. 'We're still moving. *Where's the fuckin' cavalry?*'

'En route. Good luck. You best get on.'

The connection broke. Tonka smiled, there are times when you can swear at a general and it's accepted. *Stroll on.*

* * *

Driving and losing focus, Sam was admiring the view as his adrenalin flow kept him going. 'That's Loch Doon down there. Bonny area this.'

'Yes. How're you doing?'

'Sore. Glad to be alive.' Sam said.

Tonka stayed alert. A large dark 4x4 was catching up as the road descended towards Dalmellington. 'Big beast moving up behind.'

'The protectors made good time.' Weakened thought processes a tad slow, Sam finally got it. 'No fuckin' way, Tonks. They're coming from the wrong direction.'

'Shit.'

The Mitsubishi Shogun pushed into the rear of their car, putting them into a barely controllable swerve. Sam slammed his foot down. The vehicles disengaged, the Zafira shooting forward. 'Hang on.'

Tonka checked the mini assault rifle. 'First lay-by on the right, pull over and brake hard. Try to keep square.' He turned to the back, pulled the pillows from under Eilidh and pushed her over until she was flat along the seat. She moaned. He opened his window.

The big car closed.

'Empty lay-by coming up, 400 yards on the right. No traffic. Dodge in and try to match speeds. Emergency stop when I tell you.' He checked the mirror. 'Shooters in their car will be on the wrong side — they're aiming to blow us away.'

'Okay.' The Mitsubishi pulled out as if to overtake. Sam spotted movement on the passenger side. 'No cars coming, bad guy closing on the right. Going RIGHT, RIGHT into lay-by. THREE, TWO, ONE!' Tonka braced himself in the window. 'GO!'

They swerved across the front of the SUV and decelerated rapidly. The big car had to pass on the left marginalising the pursuers' ability to fire with accuracy. They exchanged broadsides like men-of-war: two bullets glanced off the Zafira's windscreen. A third round whipped behind Tonka's head, punched through Sam's head restraint and out through the glass in his door. A concentrated burst of rounds splattered into the rear door and window above Eilidh. A safety-glass blizzard sprayed round the interior. More strikes hammered the back.

Sam adjusted his speed to the attacker's. Tonka fired bursts into the driver's window and door and then the rear of the Mitsubishi.

'STOP! STOP!' The ABS clicked and the Zafira squirmed under ferocious braking. Tonka replaced the magazine, leaning hard against the dash. The SUV swerved left, crashing and grinding into a dry stone wall. Metal groaned as the vehicle came to rest with its front angled slightly upward, front wheels in the air.

The Zafira rocked in a stinking haze of rubber smoke. Tonka steadied himself, reloaded and fired several shots into the road-facing wheels of their attacker, destroying the tyres and shattering the alloy.

'Stay on the right-hand verge. Stop level with their rear.' They arrived in seconds. Tonka leapt out, moved swiftly to the back of the big car and pulled the Diemaco into firing position. Weapon held snug to his shoulder he glanced into the 4x4 with a darting head motion. A second glance and he fired two short bursts into the rear. After another scan, he reached in through the driver's side window and took the keys.

* * *

Tonka started back across the road when, tyres shrieking, a second SUV slalomed as it braked, trapping him near the wall.

Tyre smoke swirled away from the front of the large vehicle. Tonka bolted to the side, rolled over the broken top of the dyke, and disappeared. Angry bursts of fire from open windows cracked on stones, blowing chips and dust around. In the brief silence after the shots, the flat sound of rocks falling and clacking together echoed across the road.

Before the shooting stopped, Sam was moving.

He dropped out of the car, opened the back door, punched the seat belt release and dragged Eilidh into the ditch at the roadside. She groaned and mumbled. He reached back up and pulled the C8 assault rifle from the floor.

As the attacking vehicle stopped, the doors of the SUV sprang open. Two men exited. One sprayed bursts at the wall where Tonka had disappeared.

The other man levelled an AK47. Automatic fire slammed the other side of the Zafira. Rounds burst through the back of the car, the bullets punching raised, jagged holes in the metal of the door a foot above Sam's head. He winced as another burst riddled the rear and back door. Orange juice, milk and wine poured from the gashes. So much for the shopping.

Staying low, Sam dragged Eilidh along the drain through water, mud and undergrowth. About five metres past the front of the Zafira, Sam raised his head slowly, peering through the grass at road level. A grenade rolled under the rear of the car. He pressed Eilidh's head down, pushed her tight to the bank and lay over her. The bang and zip of shrapnel were loud and proximate. His ears hissed and rang. Tonka popped up around fifteen meters along the wall. He fired single shots and ducked back as the two attackers engaged him. Sam retreated further up the ditch. One man's fire raged against Tonka as the other turned.

Hunched up, rifle in his right hand, Sam dragged Eilidh to a tree a further five metres up the gully. More gunfire slapped into the hapless car. He pressed his sister into a dent in the ground. She moaned, mumbled and then fell back into her drugged slumber.

Eilidh secure, Sam took deep breaths and eased into a prone position leaning on a shelf of root beside the tree trunk, legs braced against the slope of the ditch. He sighted towards the back of the riddled car as a curl of smoke started to rise from its rear windows. A blade of grass, flicked by the breeze, tickled his face as he lay motionless. The shooter's face appeared at the now glassless rear window, weapon in attack position. Sam fired two rounds through the man's skull.

A loud exchange of fire across the road, near the first car grabbed Sam's attention. He rose, behind the tree, with painstaking slowness and assessed the situation. A wounded man lay prostrate, flapping weakly like a fish out of water, his weapon on the road about three metres from him. A third attacker was partially concealed at the rear of the Mitsubishi. Sam fired the CS gas grenade from the launcher. The assailant jerked upright as it landed. A burst in his upper body knocked him down. Sam put two more through the man's head which exploded in a welter of blood and brains. Eliminate the risk. He aimed at the wounded man …

'Ceasefire, Sam. *HOLD FIRE!*' Tonka waved from behind the wall, jumped over and plasti-cuffed the injured man and turned. 'Welcome back wild man.' He said.

Released from the tension Sam looked at the men he'd killed. 'They asked for it.' His face hardened.

'Too right! Stone cold, Sammy. Only way. I saw you pull Eilidh out. Well done for getting the long gun.'

'Yeah,' Sam said. 'What's the tally with the first lot?'

'Driver's dead. Front passenger's out cold and now cuffed. Back passenger went for a shot.' Tonka shrugged, no words required. 'You nailed those two, mate, and we have an interrogation prospect. Now, we need to move.'

'The Zafira's going nowhere. We'll use the Disco.' Little damage was evident. The engine ticked over, calmly, like nothing had happened. 'I'll fetch Eilidh.'

Sam put the assault rifle on the rear floor and crossed to the ditch. Eilidh slept. He lifted her gently, carried her across to the big car, placed her on the back seat, strapped her in and pulled down the armrest.

Tonka pulled the dead man from the road into the undergrowth, leaving a wet red trail. Next, he dragged the wounded man to the vehicle on the wall. He groaned in pain as he was manacled to the tow bar. He wouldn't be going anywhere soon.

'Right, now let's get the fuck out of here.' Tonka said. The Zafira burst into flames.

Sam engaged gear and the big car accelerated away. 'They hammered our car. The fire and the grenade were directed at Eilidh. Hardly a bloody bullet came our way at first.'

'They meant to kill us, fuckin' bastards.'

'Well they failed,' Sam said.

'They'll try again, Sam.'

'Yeah.'

141

A POLICE CAR and ambulance rushed up the hill past Dalmellington. The constabulary were beginning a roadblock a mile further down. They raced past. There was no attempt to stop them.

'Fuzz'll be having a busy day,' Tonka said.

Next, a red and grey rescue helicopter went over the hills from Prestwick. Down the road after Patna and before Hollybush a black Range Rover came towards them. Dot-dot-dash flashed. Sam signalled back, waved his hand and beeped the signal on the car horn. He pulled over at the next lay-by. Tonka got out, weapon ready. The big 4x4 arrived.

'Just a precaution, lads. We've seen some action on the way here.'

Sam watched the process of recognition, then the shaking of hands and people looking at him. He relaxed with a sigh and started to lose consciousness. Next, he heard wireless traffic and Tonka on the phone, rather like a radio play.

'Waberthwaite again, sir. We've had another encounter. Ambush: two vehicles and six men. We had an exchange of fire. Four out of the six dead, I'm afraid. The first two cars herded us towards the ambush. The first two prisoners were definitely our own people … doing a spot of pole-dancing … Yes, sir …'

Sam lost the rest of the conversation, fading in and out. Someone woke him and helped him out of the driving seat. He moaned at the sharp, tearing pain as he moved, face screwed up and teeth gripping his lower lip. Strong arms led him back to the big black Range Rover where, seated once more, a shot of morphine produced a spreading painless warmth. He smiled as they connected a drip to his arm. Tonka came over. 'The police have closed off the road. An ambulance will collect you shortly. More security people are coming.'

Sam said. 'Stick with Eilidh, Tonks.' Tonka nodded. 'How is she?'

'Still asleep. Looks pretty angelic, but big brother made her all dirty.' Tonka said. 'They're getting the glass off her at the moment and then she'll go to the ferry. Believe me, after what we've been through, there's going to be serious protection.'

'See her safe, Tonks. I'll be okay. She'll be with her mum in a couple of hours. Don't forget the shopping …'

'None left.' Sam faded out again.

He heard the sound of the ambulance, sensed movement round bends and then more darkness.

Next, he was between clean sheets.

Time after that, a doctor stood beside the bed.

142

'YOU'RE A LUCKY MAN. The bullet blew out a chunk of fat (which you'll not miss) and, of course, drilled a hole in your skin which is now stitched up. Minimum damage because the Harris Tweed absorbed a lot of the shock. We removed all the cloth, other contamination in the wound and some obviously destroyed tissue. You've cleaned up well. Your jacket is a mess and won't recover.'

'Pity. I liked it.'

The doctor nodded in sympathy. 'You'll be with us for a few more days. In a couple of weeks, you'll be good as new. Any questions?' Sam shook his head. The medic walked away.

* * *

Karen arrived and visited for two hours. Sam tried to play the martyr, but couldn't get the smile off his face or the joy from his eyes.

'Oh Sam.' Karen took his hand, serious. 'Shot again.' She struggled to stay composed.

'I'm so sorry for the worry, love. We were well set up.' His face showed grief. 'I killed two men and almost took out a third.'

'Rather them than you.' She didn't flinch. 'Us or them, darling.'

'You're right. I am what I am.' A thoughtful expression crept on to his face. 'I never wanted to kill again.'

She listened, squeezing his hand. 'No choice, lover.'

They talked for half an hour: giving and taking emotional support, easing pain. Soon with Karen's help, Sam felt balance returning.

'Voulez-vous coucher avec moi … soon?' Sam said.

'What would I do with a horny middle-aged man?'

'How about … mmm … be patient, energetic and pushy?'

Karen laughed, leaned across the bed and gave him a long, passionate kiss. 'I have to go, wild man.'

He nodded. 'I'll be back soon.'

She left for Arran with two minders.

* * *

The window stared at a wall. Although clean and military the room provided a TV and radio for passing the time. Someone had put flowers in a vase.

One of the security guys from Arran popped in to say hi. 'We'll be around, sir. Fancy a sail fairly soon?'

'Sounds good to me.' Alone again, he sighed deeply and fell asleep, safe and, somehow contented.

143

'HE WALKED in here and broke my nose.' Charlie's surly indignation looked comical with his two black eyes and a nose wrapped in support bandaging around the bridge and nostrils.

'Come on, Charles. You deserved all you got. You stayed in his face the whole time.'

'Don't call me Charles!' His voice sounded shrill. Bill struggled not to laugh.

'Careful you don't sound like a queen, Charlie. What do you want to do? Kill the Vicar or make money?'

'Both!'

'Charlie, Charlie. Calm down.'

'He better not cross my path.'

'I'll say. We must sort out Tommy's legacy. The banker lot say the goods-inwards business is ours. Some hit that, stone-cold.'

'Yeah. When they get the right person, the job gets done.'

Bill turned to Charlie, 'Can I ask you and Jason to give the good news to Tommy's boys? No more date-rape disappearances, they must concentrate on the filthy lucre, white gold. This intermediary business makes us loads of money at minimal risk. I'll sort out the retail end.'

'Right, Bill.'

Bill did not understand the fragility of Charlie's self-esteem or where that might lead.

144

MAYBELLE READ and re-read the e-mail.

> *Remember security. Today there is a question mark about a meeting you attended with Forsyth, Thomas and Smythsone. Something set the investigators off.*

With no sleep for some nights, her IBS raged and gurgled away. She'd had a nippy call from Gemma Smythsone, challenging her authority.

She placed a plump, trembling hand on her desk, then shook her head. In her mind, a fearful fantasy of publicity strengthened. Having watched the revelations and exposure of MPs, she knew what would happen should she be called to account. God, the humiliation! The staff would be gloating.

Bizz had been an excellent idea. She'd worked, recruited and spread the cell mechanism, and she'd become wealthy. It had never occurred to her that she might be a useful figurehead for other, less visible players.

Her phone rang. 'A Detective Chief Inspector Swindon, Ms Jones.' She waited for the click of connection.

'Thank you, Jessie.' Always good to make people aware you had lackeys, were a person with power and not to be trifled with.

'Inspector Swindon? What can I do for you?'

'I wonder if you could spare me time for a meeting, Ms Jones.'

'In connection with?'

'Some enquiries which I'd like to discuss in person, ma'am.'

'Must it be me?'

'I'm afraid so. You may be central to our investigation.'

'Into what?'

'As I say, I would rather discuss this in person.'

'Is next week okay?'

'I'd prefer sooner.'

'I've got the Home Secretary tonight and tomorrow. Friday? 2 p.m.?' She separated the p and the m, pronouncing them with arrogant clarity. Then she added a suitable degree of Civil Service frost. 'This had better be good.'

'Understood, ma'am. Thank you. I'm certain you can help with our enquiries. Could you please confirm your address?' She did and hung up without a goodbye. Her stomach churned worse than ever.

Sitting all alone and exposed, something snapped.

* * *

Maybelle stood up, left her office and walked to the lift area, and travelled up to the top. When she got off the elevator, she entered the roof garden, a place she enjoyed and where she had spent peaceful times.

Tears ran down her cheeks.

With not inconsiderable effort she managed to clamber over the safety railings and, without even a by-your-leave or pause for thought-provoking words, she stepped off the building.

* * *

Maybelle shook her head and let the fantasy slip away. How desperate was that, imagining killing herself? She sighed. A policeman carrying out an investigation, what did he know? She got on with her work, letting the problem simmer quietly in the background.

Forty minutes later she called a colleague. Ten minutes after that, she spoke to a friend of that contact with a mind to warn-off the policeman.

She told herself that creating a ripple would give Inspector What's-his-Face some pause. Almost immediately she believed she had better control of the situation and tuned in to her work more positively.

145

'MARCUS, dear boy, how the devil are you?'

'I'm good, William, thank you.' Sir Marcus's natural bonhomie gushed from the phone.

'Careful as well?' A Deputy Director of the Home Office Counter-Terrorism group, William Wardle spoke pure Oxbridge.

'Cautious as can be.' Sir Marcus sounded less cheerful almost immediately.

'Our small low-profile enterprise, which we all love, risks becoming visible. There is, what shall I call it, a "secret body" we are dimly aware of, closing in on our adored business.'

'I see.'

'One person is listed for an interview with a member of the law enforcement community on Friday. She has made enough noise to reach the ears of one of my people who keeps me informed about potentially embarrassing ripples.'

Although Sir Marcus felt a jolt of fear, his voice didn't betray him. 'The weakest link, would you say?'

'Yes, dangerously weak, stressed and jumpy by all accounts,' William's upper-crust drawl was icy and condescending in equal measure.

'Worrying, William, worrying.'

'Risks our bigger picture.'

‘Awful.’

‘You helped the spook come clean to us. I believe he’ll be fully onside for the foreseeable future. He is redeemed.’

‘Good. He’s a useful man,’ Sir Marcus said.

‘The City type is tainted.’

‘Alas, yes. Act we must. Bad enough that the kidnapper of the journalist passed away before we could discover her location. Such stupidity. A permanent disappearance would have been most beneficial. Sadly, evidence ties our City friend to the abductor, and we can’t allow the connection to be the subject of an investigative interview.’

‘No.’ A chill seeped into his abdomen.

‘Can you solve the problem or do you need help?’

‘Best I resolve things. Our tame spook uses a good man.’

‘Excellent, dear boy.’

Sir Marcus returned fire. ‘The noise from the south of Scotland fiasco will echo for some time. Galling for you.’

‘Yes, our American friends were most helpful at short notice. Sad about the mess. The action still builds our international links, although the macho obsession with payback is somewhat non-European. I’m assured the captured men won’t talk. Professionals do the right thing and, of course, monthly income flows to their families. We take care of our people.’

‘How about a drink soon?’

‘Love to.’ Sir Marcus didn’t believe him. Hanging up the phone he called Jim Thomas.

Within two hours plans were laid and payment terms agreed.

146

THE NEWS travelled fast.

'Mike, give me a moment.'

'Yes, sir.'

'Close the door. Our little exercise worked rather well. The lady you spoke to is causing ripples and made the mistake of calling one of our friends, seeking information and wanting pressure applied to you. Bit hasty. Shows inexperience. Good to confirm we're on to something though.'

'I still aim to interview her.'

'I'd expect no less. Our compass bearing can only get better.'

'Heard about Sam, did you?'

'Yes.'

'He'll return in a few days.'

'That soon? You sure he'll want to come back after all this?'

'Certain. His sister and his family will never be entirely safe until we close this down. I hope Eilidh can share what she knows.'

147

QUENTIN DEBRIEFED SAM at the base near Prestwick.

'The last attack didn't come from the usual suspects. You were all meant to die. They link to the spooks chasing you somehow. Two of the dead were American ex-military, one a

South African, the other an Israeli. The people being interrogated are South African and American. A cell structure seems likely. They get instructions, get paid and don't ask questions.'

'They were aggressive, Quentin,' Sam said.

'They tried to kill you.'

'Targeted Eilidh more like. They directed fire at the rear of our car.'

'Why?'

'I'm not sure. Something she's done or knows, or they fear she knows, is causing serious concern.'

'The last attack raised questions and gave no answers. The shooting and personnel involved have caused real concern for Ben Charlton and the London team. They're searching hard for links, people and leads.'

Quentin had been debriefing Sam for two days. Although recovered enough to go to Arran a couple of days before, they'd agreed to do the work away from the family. Sam exercised and received physio every day which was helping his progress.

'The information on the last team of attackers is standard stuff. Sound like Black Ops assets having a paid holiday. They arrived at Prestwick from Malaga the day you went to Carlisle, probably assigned by the time you received word to collect your sister. The Shogun and Discovery were stolen in Glasgow, by whom is a mystery. The plates were changed and both were delivered to the pursuers' hotels. They stayed near Prestwick the night before your encounter. We haven't identified the source of their weapons, but they're all mainstream.'

'The pay-as-you-go mobile in the vehicle took a knock during the firefight but the call log is okay. We acquired the number and can build intel from that. They programmed their satnav from the hotel in Prestwick to Carsphairn. Someone primed them. As I say, the transmission analysis should be prepared soon.'

'Transmission analysis?' Sam rolled his eyes in wonder.

'Yes, to establish the time of the incoming calls, so we can compare it with the timings of outgoing calls. We've started with our own "usual suspect" intelligence services and will work our way around all the telecom switches in London if necessary. I hope we won't have to search UK-wide or further. We're already working on the mobiles of the second lot of chaps you interdicted.'

They talked on for another couple of hours, with Quentin getting Sam to go over his story time and again. The hospital porters and the trackers were reviewed. The porters had been detained and quickly admitted planting the two trackers for fifty quid each — didn't see anything wrong with it. Examination of the car had found a third tracker.

'Imagine tucking a third device in with the spare tyre. Our investigators checked the car hire place, and one of the rental firm's security cameras took video of an unknown woman both in and looking under the car. We've got time, date and a reasonable picture of her face, but I expect she'll look different without make-up and a wig. We have in-street security footage of her getting into a car and are trying to track her. These things take time. We know she followed the delivery of your car to the hotel. It gives us a pinch point to work around.'

'Can I see the pic?'

'Of course.' Quentin produced a small tablet, touched the screen a couple of times and showed Sam the face.

'I don't know her,' Sam said. 'What about the woman who shot me?'

'She was nursing a sore head in secure accommodation not two miles from here for a couple of days.'

'Is she one of ours?'

'Yes. She wasn't hugely communicative and her partner is still recovering from leg surgery.'

‘She shot me.’

‘Not surprising really. You were targeted as an armed and extremely dangerous Irish terrorist group. Think about it. When they caught up with you they believed you’d already taken out one of their teams and, when you jumped up, gun in hand, she tried to pot you.’

‘Shoot to kill?’

‘They couldn’t possibly comment,’ Quentin said. ‘At least you’re pretty well okay, and our spook colleagues are still alive.’

‘Wonderful.’

‘The important questions run along the lines of: How did they learn where you were? Who knew? How did the information get out?’

‘For me, start simple. How secure are the office and phones we use?’

‘Should be like Fort Knox but we’re checking, Sam. So far we’ve nothing. Everything seems fine.’

‘It may seem okay, but what you’re saying suggests a leak from within the team. Sad thought.’

With a ding, Quentin’s mobile signalled a text. He read briefly. ‘The signal to the third lot of attackers came from Grosvenor Square. Handy for the US Embassy I’d say.’ They looked at each other in thoughtful silence.

‘I better talk to Charlton,’ Sam said.

Quentin left for the airport.

148

‘THE PLOT THICKENS if we have a Yankee connection, Ben.’

‘I’ll wait until Quentin communicates,’ Charlton said.

‘Thought-provoking.’

‘Yes, but that’s for later. We’ve won round one, got your sister back and, apart from minor injuries, the team is intact. Time to regroup, take stock and plan.’

‘I’ve an old Yankee contact from my spooky days. We keep in touch. I think he’s quite senior now.’

‘Who?’

‘Bob Fogarty. I worked with him in Iraq 1, and a couple of other projects. He has integrity and may still be a player.’

‘Why would he help you?’

‘We’ve had some fight time. He’d say I saved his life.’

‘Okay, you can follow up later. I want our internal review over before you or anyone else talks outside. Quentin has debriefed you, now go home.’

‘You sure?’

‘Home, Sam. More debriefing from the protectors, plus family time. Sometimes striking when the iron is cold works pretty well.’

‘One last thing, Ben. Debriefing can be a two-way street. With Quentin it was. I’m finding it hard to ignore the real possibility of a leak from within our direct team.’

‘Tough one, Sam. We’re on it. Now off you go.’

‘I’m gone.’

He left for Arran two hours later.

149

SAFE ON ARRAN for the past week, Eilidh's progress was slow. Although visibly damaged, Alice and Jeannie's natural bounce helped brighten her gloom.

She spent hours hugging her mother. Therapy continued. They expected she'd improve.

Six days after the chase, Sam took an afternoon sailing to Brodick, Isle of Arran, on the MV Caledonian Isles. The mountains of northern Arran stood pristine and clear against a blue sky, stone slabs gleaming like armour plating.

He spent the entire crossing leaning against the bulkhead in the forward viewing area, relaxed and watching the island get nearer, ever more in touch with his family. He'd holidayed on Arran for ten years of his childhood and spent many happy days on the hills above Sannox and Corrie.

The security people who delivered him to the ship stayed with him until he walked down the gangplank.

The ferry tied up at Brodick Pier with hardly a jar as she settled against large fenders. He merged into the gentle aura of Arran's calm as he stepped on to solid ground, and walked to the arrival area where Karen waited with a minder. She gave him a hug that made him wince. Abby must have been teaching her.

'We need to move, sir.' *See these security people*.

'Come on, love,' Karen said. A Range Rover drew up and they got in. The vehicle moved off as soon as they were on board. 'How's my recovering little angel?'

'Not bad. Could have been much worse. I've already had five days of physio, remedial exercise and massage. I'm a lucky man.'

'The leader of the protection team wants to debrief you.'

'I thought you wanted to do that.'

She slammed an elbow into his ribs. 'Oh! Missus.' She flashed a glance of concern. He winked and smiled. She smacked his hand. He grinned.

'He'll ask what we did, who we did it to, what they did, where things happened, how we decided and so on … always the detail. Then he'll swap notes with Quentin.'

Sam relaxed, sat back and fell asleep resting his head on Karen's shoulder. She snuggled close and held him.

150

SAM AWOKE at Sannox surrounded by family. He'd slept late. They spent a happy, talkative two hours together over soup and sandwiches. He'd missed a visit from Hec two days before. His mother sat in a comfy chair in the farmhouse kitchen, overjoyed to be enveloped by her folk. She said little and listened to the chatter as if it were fine music.

'Come on, Dad. Let's play some ball on the beach.'

'I'm tired, Alice.'

'We'll play gently then, won't we, Jeannie?'

'Dad, stop being a bore,' Jeannie said.

'Okay, okay. Just remember I've got an injury.'

151

BACK FROM the beach after a tiring run around, Sam was ready for a mug of tea and a sit-down. Eilidh sat at the kitchen table.

'How you doin'?'

'I don't know,' Eilidh said, 'I've a head like a pound of mince and can't think straight. It's frustrating.' Her eyes filled.

'Mum says you're remembering more every day.'

'Yes, disconnected snippets. All night I dream horrible things. It's weird and scary, a full-time ride on a ghost train. I can't get off or stop it.'

'At least you're here, and for real. The ride is stopping.'

'Yes … *here!* The fucking Isle of Arran. This isn't my world. Last thing I properly remember was a nightclub in London, then that awful man groping me. The rest is flashes of a trip on a roller-coaster with you and Tonka talking, shouting and big bangs. Everything else is a blur.'

'What about your research?'

She sat up, tense, briefly lucid. Her beautiful eyes wide and momentarily clear. 'Pen drive. Green folder, soft plastic. Carrier bag.' She shrank into in her chair and started to shake. 'I can't remember much. I don't know how it fits. Trucks and pin-stripes. Alphabet soup, all jumbled up. I'm lost, Sammy, lost.' Her voice broke and she started to cry, inhaling ragged gasps and expelling long wracking sobs. Sam held her tight.

The nurse came in and gave Sam an enquiring glance. He nodded. She took hold of Eilidh's wrists. 'It's okay, Eilidh. You need some rest.' She led Eilidh off to her room. In two minutes Eilidh was on her bed, face drawn and pale.

Abby came in, lay beside Eilidh and hugged her. Eilidh calmed immediately and fell asleep. The nurse and Sam left the room.

'No need for medication when your mum's around.'

'Rough time.' Sam's eyes were flinty.

'Horrendous. The pain comes more from the drugs than the kidnapping. She had a dangerous cocktail administered by ignorant people. A sexual assault is likely, but the story's hazy. She was a mess when she was found, both physically and mentally. It's good she's improved as much as she has already, a little kitten may have helped.'

Sam was quiet. He nodded. 'I'm glad you're here, Sheila, you're making a big difference.' He turned and walked towards the kitchen. The nurse didn't see him screw his eyes shut for a moment and shake his head gently as he walked down the passage.

The nurse returned to Eilidh's room where Abby lay fast asleep as well. She picked up her book on her way through the lounge. She took a seat in the garden, available as needed.

152

Tonka slouched by the kitchen range, mug of tea in hand. He nodded, 'Sam.'

'Hello, Tonks.'

'Eilidh?'

'An inch away from a basket case.' Tonka stayed quiet. Sam stared at the floor looking up and locking eyes with his friend after a few long seconds. 'They damaged her, Tonks.' Sam shook his head slowly. His mobile rang and broke the intense atmosphere. Sam sighed.

* * *

'Hello, Ben.'

'Your chum Fuss is being transformed into a London villain as we speak. He's not terribly good with the local accent.'

'So, that's where he went.'

'Yes. Physically he's a reasonable replacement for a man who was murdered.'

'I advised him to stay out of this.'

'He wants in and can help. He's aboard.' Charlton said.

'Right. Sorry, if I'm not enthused.'

'How are you?'

'Getting better, wound clean, a few twinges.'

'Eilidh?'

'Not great, but at least she's alive and in good hands.'

'Everyone else okay?'

'Yes. Karen's as solid as ever and the kids are on holiday with handsome protectors as far as they're concerned.'

'Right, I'll be in touch. Have a good break.'

'Thanks.'

153

'FOR CHRIST'S SAKE, Maybelle, blame isn't the name of the game here. We've made decisions, screwed some of them up. It's the real fucking world, not some puffed up pass-the-buck bloody fantasy. We need solutions, not bullshit.' Jim Thomas edged towards rage.

'If you'd killed the Duncan man, as we agreed, this wouldn't be happening.' A grey pallor masked Maybelle's face. Her hands shook.

'Fuck that, you moronic bitch.' The volume continued to rise. 'You're not hanging the rap on me. If you'd not done the nicey-nice thing and we'd bumped off the Duncan girl when I said, none of this would be happening.'

'How dare you speak to me like that?'

'Because I'm tired of your buck passing pomposity. You …'

'… Jim, Jim calm down. You're right, we need solutions not blame.' Sir Marcus made soothing gestures and sounded much calmer than his heart rate.

'Sir Marcus is right, Jim, Maybelle,' Gemma gazed at their eyes, back and forth, as she spoke, 'we can fix this, but not if we fight.'

Devlin sounded tense. 'We must do something to seal off the problem. We can't risk any more unravelling.'

'Absolutely right.' Gemma and Sir Marcus nodded like toy dogs in the back of a car.

'Of course, we mustn't be in conflict. Maybelle, I apologise for speaking as I did.' Jim avoided eye contact.

* * *

Maybelle's mouth was opening to speak when a firm knock on the conference room door interrupted. The thump made her start.

The handle turned and two large smartly dressed men walked in. More people stood, visible, in the corridor.

'Ladies, gentlemen, I apologize for interrupting your meeting.'

'How dare you come into a private meeting like this?' Maybelle did indignant pomposity to perfection.

'I can only apologize ma'am but in a moment you will understand the reasons. I am Acting Detective Chief Inspector Swindon and this is my colleague Detective Inspector Martin.'

'You called me the other day. We're meeting on Friday afternoon.'

'Yes, ma'am. I wasn't going to mention it and look forward to our meeting. I am here on police business.' He turned and looked at Devlin. 'You are Devlin Archibald Forsyth?

Devlin's face blanched. 'Yes.'

Mike Swindon held up a folded document. 'This is a warrant for your arrest.' He nodded to Cal. 'Inspector Martin.'

Cal walked over and stood near Devlin Forsyth. He laid a large paw on his shoulder. 'You are under arrest on suspicion of criminal activity. You do not have to say anything. But it may harm your defence if you do not mention when questioned something which you later rely on in court. Anything you do say may be given in evidence.' Forsyth stood up. 'Turn around sir.' Cal produced his handcuffs.

'Chief Inspector.' Sir Marcus spoke with the authority of power. 'Mr Forsyth is not a violent criminal. Surely you could spare him the embarrassment of being taken out of here in manacles.'

Mike paused, a thoughtful frown on his face. 'You are, sir?'

'Sir Marcus Attenwood-Leigh, Member of Parliament and an occasional member of this committee. There's no question that you must do your duty. Whatever Mr Forsyth has done or not done, please treat him with respect.'

Mike nodded. 'Acceptable to you, Inspector Martin?'

Cal stood massive and impassive. He seemed to think for an eternity. The silence was deep and palpable. He sighed 'Yes sir, fair point.' He took Forsyth by the arm, just above the elbow.

'DC Fullerton.' A young man entered the room and walked across to Cal. 'This is Mr Forsyth who is under arrest. He has been cautioned. Please take him away.'

'What about his right to legal representation?' Gemma spoke in her cold way. Cal turned to Mike.

Mike nodded. 'Of course ma'am he will have that opportunity in due course, in accordance with his rights. You are?'

'A lawyer, Gemma Smythsone.' The tone was ultra crisp and frosty.

'Mr Forsyth's brief?'

'No, of course not.'

Mike nodded to the group. 'Please accept our apologies for the interruption to your business. Inspector Martin.' He waved his hand at the door. They walked out and shut it silently behind them.

In the room, silence reigned as people took in the enormity of the moment.

'Meeting adjourned. Let's think things through and meet later at my club.'

'Thanks, Marcus.' Gemma rose and left in quick time.

Within a minute Maybelle was the only person left in the office. Her stomach churned. She sensed isolation. She wept.

* * *

Back in their car, moving in the traffic, Mike and Cal enjoyed their shared memories of the arrest. *They don't like it up 'em. Rattled their cages didn't we? They're shitting bricks. See their faces when the handcuffs came out ...*

'He'll walk.' Cal said.

'Course he will.'

'Yeah, you can't win all the battles, but that one was a beaut. One in the eye for the lah-de-dah fuckin' crooks.'

Mike cackled. 'Fuck 'em. Fancy a pint, big man?'

'Yeah. More than one. Some jambalaya too. Fancy a feed?'

'Too bloody right I do.'

'Young Fullerton did his walk-on part well.' Cal said.

'Yeah, he's a lovely kid. Has the makings of a good cop.'

'Playing favourites are we?' Cal gave the full 100-watt smile.

'Fuck off.' Mike grinned.

* * *

Next day the hangovers were almost enjoyable. Charlton expressed great satisfaction about the boat-rocking. By mid-afternoon, alcoholic haze drifting away, people were bright-eyed and charged up.

Charlton toured the office, enjoying the sense of motivation and high morale. He stopped and bantered with people in his dry, encouraging way.

In his room, alone, he subsided into the thoughtfulness of experience. Let them enjoy the fun.

154

EILIDH SEEMED CALMER and even smiled once or twice during the evening. They were all asleep by midnight, except for the watchers.

Sam, still awake, lay relaxed, naked and cuddled up to Karen. He smiled, remembering Cal's drunken call, and his rambling description of the arrest. Good on them.

A look of contentment eased on to his face, invisible in the darkness to all but God. He drifted into an easy dreamless sleep.

* * *

In London and beyond, business discussions raged as powerful greedy people experienced agonizing mental distress and anguish of a type they were more accustomed to inflicting … poor wee souls.

THE END

Have you read DICE?

DICE

A Dark Art

PREVIEW

second in the series …

1

COOL AS A frosty morning, the man ambled into the restaurant past a couple reading the street menu in its gold-crested mahogany case. He inhaled the pleasant humid aroma of fresh bread, garlic-infused sauces and grilling seafood, paused and gazed around. Diners' heads rocked back and forth as they ate and socialized. The clink of silverware and subdued buzz of chatting folk echoed, warm and convivial. Bursts of laughter sounded and faded like waves on a shore. *There he is.*

A waiter, busy taking orders at a crisp linen-clothed table, questioned him with his eyes. He smiled and inclined his head towards a group of people. A nod of understanding gave permission. He walked over.

Near the window, the man held court at a laden table, surrounded by glasses, bottles and plates of food. He had his back to an earthy Mediterranean yellow wall, inlaid with a scattering of blue and white ceramic tiles showing ancient ships and castles. Pieces of netting hung here and there with multi-coloured glass spheres, oars and gaff hooks supporting the fishing theme.

A happy, somewhat theatrical focus for adulation, the mark waved his fork like a conductor's baton. His two companions laughed on cue. *Grovelling bastards*. The stranger walked over stone-faced. This'll make your day. The pistol wasn't suppressed, the better to terrify the diners.

The thunderous flat bark of the first shot made ears ring, and silenced the talk. The bullet slammed into the diner's upper lip to the right of his nose. Front teeth blew out from a ruined mouth and across to nearby tables, where they tinkled amongst the glassware and utensils.

The exit wound sprayed a fantail of sticky red-orange up the wall. The victim bounced backwards, cheeks flapping. Two shots to the centre of the chest splashed gore on the food and tablecloth. The dying man lurched forward onto his meal. His last jerking sigh bubbled into a plate of linguini, adding a soupçon of bloody foam to a lustrous creamy sauce as his body juddered.

One of the guests leapt up. *No, you don't.* A bullet in the thigh slapped him down, face whitening with shock. A surround-sound of screams erupted. Cutlery clashed and glasses crashed to accompany the terror. Then silence. Nobody moved.

The killer turned for the door and, unimpeded, walked into a crowded Poplar High Street near Canary Wharf, London. In moments he vanished, dissolving into a bustling herd of humanity.

* * *

Two minutes after the murder the assassin entered a gent's toilet, removed his blond wig, spat out the mouth padding. He replaced his white shirt with a red t-shirt and pulled on a baggy, grey hooded training top sporting a Boston Red Sox logo. He threw his discarded clothes in a surveillance-free restaurant dumpster as he moved on.

A short time later, on the Tube, the killer continued his mission. He dropped his plastic gloves on the tracks when he changed for the Circle Line. Ghost-like hands, they puffed away up the tunnel as air blew in from an approaching train.

2

'EXTREME PREJUDICE is what Americans call it.' The fluent speech bore a slight accent.

Icy, upper-crust English frosted the air. 'We decided to let sleeping dogs lie.'

'We didn't agree, and we don't approve.'

Bloody foreigners. 'Ah, I see.' The chill deepened.

'We must eliminate the danger areas.'

Jumped up bureaucrat. 'We've agreed on—'

'There is no agreement. No ifs. No ands. No buts.' The inflection became more pronounced, forceful.

'Do you know who I am?' Brittle British blue-blooded anger crackled into the phone.

'Of course, you're a powerful and well-connected person.' The silent pause seemed, at first, to be respectful. 'Why don't you answer the door?'

'No one is there.' *Fool!* He allowed himself a tiny snicker. The bell rang.

'There's a present for you. Go and have a look.'

The knight of the realm and Privy Counsellor put his phone on a side-stand, rose slowly and walked from the lounge, into the hall. A small box, wrapped in shiny black paper, lay on the mat. He glanced about, fearful, and moved with some speed back to his seat. He sat with a bump.

'What is it?' He couldn't control a slight quiver in his voice.

'A little treat. Chocolates from Belgium. Trust me, that's all.'

'Chocolates?'

‘Chocolates from Bruges.’ The foreign laugh hinted at disdain.

‘Bruges.’ An aristocratic voice squeaked.

‘The bearer of gifts could still be in your apartment.’

‘*Now see here*.’ The fearful British indignation lacked conviction.

‘A gift of chocolates … to make a point.’

‘How did he get in?’

‘I have no idea. It’s what people like that do. The package is delivered and the messenger gone. The door is locked and the security chain in its place … no? You’re safe.’

‘This is outrageous. You’ve no right to—’

‘Listen to me.’ A tendril of fear stroked the aristocrat’s bladder. ‘Duncan will be dealt with. Forget kidnapping, gunfights and crazy chases.’

‘Unfortunate decisions.’

‘Most unfortunate.’ The foreigner slurped saliva. ‘Our organisation needs no publicity.’

‘It won’t happen again.’

‘No, it won’t. We’ve assigned the task.’

‘Assigned the task?’

‘Your new leader approves.’

‘New leader?’

‘New leader.’

‘But—’

‘No buts. No talk! I don’t want to supervise any more … ah … dismissals. Understand?’

‘Understood.’ The line clicked as the European disconnected. A shaking hand put the phone down. *Shtum*.

A chastened government minister called in a bad attack of flu, switched off his mobile and computer, and poured himself a large glass of Scotch.

3

'WHERE ARE YOU, Cal?' DCI Mike Swindon sounded tense. Leaning forward, General Ben Charlton, Head of Agency, listened by a speaker.

'Embankment Station,' Cal said.

'There's been a killing.' Mike said.

'Killing?' Cal Martin thought of Sam Duncan and stopped. A pedestrian crashed into him, bounced off his large frame and walked away muttering.

'One of the Bizz amigos, Devlin Forsyth.'

'He should've stayed in jail when we nicked him.' Cal said.

'Too right. The revelations at the meeting won't have helped the Chair.'

'So, they're in ruthless mode.'

'I'll text you an address and contact details for Maybelle Jones.'

'Thanks.'

'Are you armed?' Charlton said.

'Yes sir.

'Better get one up the spout.'

'Will do.'

'We need to protect Ms Jones. Fair chance she's on the list.' Charlton said.

Cal's mobile pinged as he received her work address, phone information and a picture. 'Beautiful big sista, isn't she? Do you think she fell in love with me when we arrested Forsyth?'

'Put your willie away, Inspector.' Charlton said.

'Sorry, sir. I'll be about ten minutes.'

'Fast as you can.'

'I'm rushing, willie and all,' Cal said. Mike choked off a snicker. 'You sure she's in?'

'Mike?' Charlton said.

'I've spoken to her secretary,' Mike said. 'Maybelle Jones is in the office and not available. Bloody power stuff, and we're trying to save her life.' Cal kept moving. 'Douglas Fullerton is two or three minutes ahead of you.'

'He's armed and needs backup, soon-as,' Charlton said. 'Mobile units are on the way. They should arrive when you do.'

'Okay, sir, I'm moving. I'll keep you posted.' Cal broke the connection and took the remaining stairs out of Embankment Station two at a time. He jogged along Embankment Place and out across Northumberland Avenue, head turning and body twisting as he searched for a taxi and avoided traffic. The first three in sight were taken.

For a big man in his early fifties, Cal loped along in an easy rhythm, handsome features, similar to a younger Muhammad Ali, unstressed. His broad shoulders, height and athleticism were impressive. The swaying sports jacket concealed his weapon as he jogged.

He trotted along for three more minutes, looking over his shoulder until, at last, a cab heading the other way did a fast U-turn and pulled over.

* * *

'DCI Swindon.'

'I'll be there in five minutes.' The click of a seatbelt engaging sounded through the phone. Cal sat back as pine air-freshener mixed with a scent of leather filled his nostrils. Quite pleasant.

'You're doing fine, mate. The line's still engaged at that fuckin' woman's office.' Mike's voice vibrated with frustration. 'We can't get someone to interrupt her. Still,' a long sigh caressed Cal's ear, 'Douglas is close.'

'He's a good lad,' Cal said. 'I'll arrive soon. Tell the boss I've one up both spouts.' Mike smiled. 'One for him and one for her.'

'Who's the *him*?' Mike said.

'The killer.'

'How do you know?'

'It's always a man. Don't you watch TV?'

'Our intel reports a male,' Mike said.

'See! She's a smart looking woman. I like big sistas. I'll save her, she'll be grateful and the passion will flow. You need to watch more TV, Mike.'

'Time you got your brain out of your trousers and on to the task in hand, Inspector,' Charlton said, unable to hide a twinkle in his dark eyes from Mike. He sat erect, lean left thigh resting on the side of his battered desk. The other leg, relaxed at the knee, dangled a trade-mark, gleaming, black brogue. His tanned bald head gleamed in its frame of short dark hair. The hawk-like nose and thin-lipped mouth gave him a desert warrior's profile.

'Want me to take myself in hand, sir?' Silence. 'Sorry sir. A bit adrenal.'

'Of course,' Charlton said, 'testosterone too, by the sound of things.' Mike coughed.

4

'IT'S A SHAME, but he really had to go.' Jim Thomas said, his Geordie accent sharp as a blade. 'Once he was arrested the dangers were too great to ignore.'

'It's a tragedy, we had such high hopes for him.' The Right Honourable Sir Marcus Attenwood-Leigh MP managed to sound mournful and appear comfortable at the same time.

Gemma Smythsone looked at Kenneth Chen, the banker and new member of the Bizz Board. 'An interesting time to join us, Ken.'

'I'm up to speed on the situation Gemma. Nightmare.' Chen nodded handsome, expressionless, Chinese features.

'Thanks for the use of the room, William.' Smythsone spoke to another new co-director of Bizz, and a Director in UK Counter Terrorism. They were in a secure meeting facility near Kings Cross which provided government quality safeguarding of their conversation, in much the same way their mobile and internet connections were insulated from prying.

'A sad pleasure, my dear.' Bizz director William Wardle's plummy English disclosed icy indifference.

A message pinged into Smythsone's mobile. Her face stiffened and reality frosted her eyes for a moment.

'One down.' Wardle's voice blurted from the speaker. 'I have business to attend to. Speak soon.'

'Coffee gentlemen?' Smythsone called the break as Chair. When they stood with their drinks, only Jim Thomas could hold his saucer without the cup rattling.

5

Sir Marcus checked his watch, nodded to his colleagues and moved to a corner of the meeting room to make the call.

'Maybelle, my dear, could you join me for a coffee?'

'Marcus, this is a pleasant surprise,' she said, voice gushing with an oily mixture of respect and smugness.

'Thank you. I'm out of the House, fresh from a meeting, and we must meet urgently.' The plummy tones were part of his persona. She'd never known him to laugh.

'Can you give me thirty minutes?'

'No, I need to see you straight away. You are the Chair after all.'

'Okay, I'm on my way.'

'I'll be in the coffee shop on the corner by the time you get there.'

She did a quick check and adjustment of her make-up, rose and left her office. Her gleaming black skin and bouffant medium length hair suited her high-cheeked, beautiful face. Her snub nose, full lips and dark almond eyes were arresting. 'I'm stepping out for half an hour, Liza.' She sprayed some Japanese Flower perfume below each ear and a dash on her wrists which she rubbed together.

'You smell wonderful.' Her assistant gave a cheeky smile. 'Anyone dishy?

'Only a knight of the realm.'

'Now there's posh for you.' They both chuckled. Maybelle went to the lifts, her heels clicking on the corridor floor as she stepped off the carpet on to the tiles. Her red jacket over a bright coloured summer dress was smart and gave her a solid business-like presence. A lift arrow lit with a ping as she entered the foyer.

A good omen, she thought. Head held high, the smile on her faced lasted well out into the street.

* * *

Sir Marcus returned to the table. 'She's on her way.' He checked his watch again. 'Timing is everything.'

6

'JUST ARRIVED, sir.' DC Douglas Fullerton spoke to Mike Swindon as he paid for his taxi. Forty yards away Maybelle Jones stepped on to the pavement outside her office. 'She's just come out.' He accelerated towards her, with a rugby player's athleticism. 'Oh shit! Back-up, sir. I need back-up!' …

ABOUT MAC

Hi, I'm Mac Logan. Thanks for reading my work.

Corruption, Crime and Establishment mischief

Short of spending a lifetime in jail, a vengeance trail of murder and mayhem has few acceptable alternatives. Writing is one of them.

Sad to say, the pursuit of evil people may end in tragedy for both sides of an investigation. Tears may trickle down my cheeks, as I write, because my world as a writer is real to me.

Crime fiction provides a means of pursuing nasty people with satisfying, imaginative robustness. My thrillers offer a sense of recourse against corrupt people and cadres who screw us and steal our money.

Pay back?

Even though such people hurt me in the past, I wish them no harm. In fact I'm grateful to such deceivers for providing, as they do, the basis of The Angels' Share series. It's good to have a solid foundation for fiction: rooted in grievance and amplified by a surging (if somewhat graphic) imagination.

Personal

I love family, cooking, good company, banter, sport, fun, and an occasional drop of 'The Cratur'. I live in the beautiful East Neuk of Fife, Scotland.

Prose, poetry and all that

Writing is part of me. It took me many years to admit I'm a poet. Could it be a man thing? My efforts started in childhood, ebbing and flowing until the present day.

It seems I'm approaching 150 blogs … can I be that old?

Articles and such

With many articles published, often on business, some commissioned and the human side of work, I changed direction a few years back. Tired of the dry-stuff, my muse hauled me into writing fiction, non-fiction and poetry.

As an author who aims to entertain, I'm eager for feedback. Your views on any aspect of my work are important to me. Please do get in touch.

Belonging

I'm a Member of the Society of Authors and the Crime Writers Association.

I am the founding Chair of Colinsburgh Galloway Library Trust in the East Neuk of Fife, Scotland.

ACKNOWLEDGEMENTS

The only thing I do on my own is writing. With the willing help and support of wonderful people, life gets easier.

Thanks to my dear wife **Meg** for her patience, cooking and support as I write and re-write.

THANKS TO:

Alastair Macfarlane for his early help with writing *The Angels' Share*.

Joe and **Ian Flynn** for early feedback.

Gale Winskill of Winskill Editorial for her forthright feedback and fast turn around. She's as professional as she is helpful.

Mariana Sing for permission to use her picture 'Keep Breathing' on an early cover.

Helen Lloyd, **James Warrior** and Choice Voices for their willingness to support the audiobook production. At 9.5 hours long, the diligence and commitment shows.

Andrew L Phillips for his interest in taking the project to the film and TV world … watch this space!

Hanne Partonen for her love of books, reading and feeding back with English as a second language, and forthright support of the marketing effort.

Maryann Ness for her diligence in reading and feeding back from an American perspective.

Steffan Gwynedd-Lewis for his practical help with video, editing and connections.

Michael Reynolds for his help and expertise in marketing.

Phil Wadsley (audiobook) for his encouragement and audio and visual technical expertise (one of the best in the business).

Polly St Aubyn and her eagle eye.

Thanks to everyone else: **family**, **friends** and **helpful strangers** who read parts or the whole manuscript and shared their thoughts.

CONNECT

Twitter:	@maclogan_writes
Blog:	jyngs.com
Website:	logan.co.uk
Angels Share:	facebook.com/angels.share.series/
Reborn Tree:	facebook.com/reborntree/

CPSIA information can be obtained
at www.ICGtesting.com
Printed in the USA
LVHW03s1711100618
580220LV00003B/595/P